ARCHES

Second Chance
AT L♥VE

CATHRYN LYONS

Cover art by Maria at SteamyDesigns.net

Image by Wander Aguiar photography

Model: Matheus R

Edited by Michelle Fewer

ISBN 9781969897016

ARCHES

Second Chance
AT L♥VE

Cathryn Lyons and team respect our readers and want you to be well-informed. If you would like to know if this book contains elements that may be of concern for you or triggering in a way that would prevent your enjoyment, please visit the Content Warnings section of www.CathrynLyonsAuthor.com.

Prologue

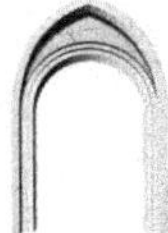

Ross

10 months ago

A soft tap signaled his arrival. Ross smoothed the neckline of her silk robe, the atypical flutter of her nerves pairing a symphony with the thrum of arousal that had been building since they'd shared a charged look across the room earlier that evening.

She opened the door and, with its reveal, sucked in her breath, her pulse racing, heart pounding in anticipation. *Damnation*, he was a Hottie McHot Pants.

Ross tugged him into her room, grinning over her shoulder as she guided them in further toward the bed. "Best man and maid of honor hookup after the rehearsal dinner? We are such a cliché, but...shall we?"

He laughed, a deep sexy sound that amped her desire higher. "I've never been one to appreciate a cliché before, but I believe I need to revise my opinion. A beautiful woman brings me to her bed and has her naughty way with me for hours on end? What's not to like?" He cocked a grin at Ross, endearing dimples appearing in his cheeks.

"'Hours on end,' you say?" Ross raised her eyebrows. As her heart kicked up another notch, she wondered if the heat she saw in his maple-syrup brown eyes mirrored her own.

"*Hours*, Maid of Honor," he whispered against her ear, causing a bloom of chills to cascade down her arms.

Somehow, she found her voice, raspy with anticipation. "In that case, Best Man," she murmured, touching her lips to his, "in for a cliché penny in for a cliché pound."

CHAPTER ONE

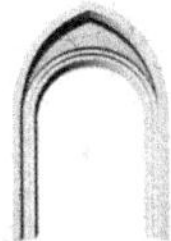

Ross

Traffic crawled along I-81. The winding four-lane highway through the Shenandoah Valley was a popular pass-through for eighteen-wheelers, which struggled up and down its hills. Right now, one semi was trying to pass another—sort of like the faster turtle passing the slower one—bogging down the rest of traffic.

Ross unleashed her impatience on her steering wheel with a resounding whack. "Move, you douche-nugget! Get over." She was in a bad mood and the traffic wasn't helping. She'd been dreading this drive since her grandmother talked her into it. Not the traffic so much. Rather, the destination. And what it held in store.

Although she'd been on this road as a passenger many times in her youth, Ross had only driven it once before. The summer she'd turned sixteen and was learning to drive, her intrepid dad had deemed her ready to try an interstate. And the scenic route to her grandmother's was his selection.

She tilted her head back and sighed. It was to be expected—these unbidden, unwanted, visceral forays down memory lane. She was almost thirty-five years old and returning to a place she hadn't visited in more than half her life. Ross had resolved never to go back to her grandparents' home...a place she, her older sister, and her parents had visited regularly until her sixteenth year.

Ross forced herself to stare down the memory of the drive that presaged the start of the most awful summer of her life. She didn't often allow herself to dwell on the specifics of that time, but the ache was always there—a faint pain her mind would seek out and linger on, just like a tongue repeatedly finds a rough spot to worry on a tooth.

Her phone buzzed and Ross turned down the alternative rock/new wave playlist she'd been listening to on the drive. A man she'd been seeing (a term she used loosely), had turned her on to the genre. Ross's favorite photo of her best friend, Tiercy, popped up on her iPhone. Ross grinned at the image of Tiercy wearing an elegant Carolyn Bessette Kennedy-style wedding dress, with her eyes crossed and an exaggerated pout...Ross photobombing in the background, holding two thumbs up.

She tapped the hands-free. "What's up, Hooker Hips?"

Tiercy's laughter filled the car, magically easing Ross's crotchety mood. "I'm just checking in. How's the drive?"

"I'm on eighty-one, behind a string of obnoxious tractor-trailers that won't move into the slow lane. I wish my car had a missile launcher on it. Or that I had an Inspector Gadget car with tires that extend out and up, and I could just go over these asshats. Also, I need to pee, and I really should get some gas, but I don't feel like stopping. And, of course, with every mile, I get closer to the inevitable."

"That good, huh?" Ross heard the smile in Tiercy's voice. Her best friend waited a beat, hesitated, and then jumped in, deploying her bestie mind-reading skills. She knew the emotional tightrope Ross began navigating when she stepped in her car and headed south. "I know this sucks, Ross. Want to talk about it?"

"No, I don't really want to talk about it." Ross didn't believe for a second her bestie would let her get away with that. She drove in silence for a few moments, accompanied only by the hum of her car's tires on the interstate and her friend's patient breathing through the Bluetooth speakers. Eventually she cleared her throat and voiced the thought that had been beating an incessant tattoo. "I'm dreading this, Tierce." *Seriously, fiercely dreading this.*

"I know, sweetie. I'm sorry."

"It feels so surreal to be doing this drive. I look back on that teenager driving my parents' car, and I know it was technically me, yet she and I have nothing in common. It's me but it's not me. Time is bizarrely elastic."

"Trust me, I remember that drive. I was praying with your mom in the backseat."

"Ha!" Despite herself, Ross chuckled at the memory. "Remember when I threatened to drive up the runaway truck ramp?"

"Your dad was so ticked off when you pretended to turn the wheel toward it," Tiercy reminisced.

"'Now, Adam. She's just kidding. Ross is a very responsible girl.'" Ross giggled as she parroted that long-ago conversation, ignoring the pang of loss that shot through her heart. She forced humor into her voice, wondering if Tiercy would see through it. "If she only knew how wild we were that summer!"

Tiercy laughed. "I remember your sister driving your mom nuts complaining about *everything*. She was so mad to be stuck in the back of the minivan with your mom and me."

"Gaby—whatever." Ice coated her response. "Didn't she want to bring her own car so she'd have it there for the summer, but Dad wouldn't let her? She was always wound up about something." Ross turned on her blinker to pass another slow truck.

"Sorry. I shouldn't have gone there." Tiercy quickly changed the subject. "What's your ETA?"

"If I don't stop to empty one receptacle and fill another, I guess about thirty minutes." Ross gnawed on her cuticle, a bad habit she'd broken in young adulthood. She looked down in horror. God...she *was* going back in time. She rubbed her hand over the dull ache in her chest and groaned. "Tiercy...I don't know if I can handle six weeks at Hon's."

Ross's grandmother had been born and raised in Baltimore. Her husband used to tease her with the popular local idiom, which was short for Honey. When Gaby, ten months Ross's elder, began talking, she called her grandmother "Hon" one day, having heard it thousands of times. From then on, Hon's plans to be called something glamorous and Continental, like Grand'Mere, were scuttled.

"I know, bestie. But you can call me whenever you need me."

"You know I will," Ross replied, brightening her voice even as she battled the soul-drenching darkness the drive evoked. "I'll FaceTime you and text you nonstop."

"You better," Tiercy warned. "I can't believe you're leaving me. My hubby told me to stop with the pity-party. He knows what you said about us being in touch nonstop isn't hyperbole—"

"Oooh! Good SAT word." Ross smiled as she thought about the ongoing competition the two friends had, dating all the way back to high school SAT prep, to drop big words into their everyday conversation.

"I know, right?" Tiercy laughed and then added on a whine, "But what will I do without you right here with me?"

"Have more fun than I will?" Ross complained.

"It'll be fine, Ross. The days will fly by. You'll help Hon pack the farmhouse and get settled in her condo, and then you can head home, finish packing your own place...and then head to your new gig in New York as the world's most amazing memoir editor."

"I can't believe I'm spending my time off between jobs doing this. I should be topless on a beach in Tahiti, drinking a cocktail from a coconut, a hot man by my side nibbling my toes *and* my ladybits. Instead, I'm about to spend six weeks in the Shenandoah Valley, that hotbed of glamor and sophistication. *And* I'll be living under Hon's roof. I probably won't get laid for almost two months. I'll be practically re-virginized when I get to Manhattan." She sighed, her mini-diatribe finished. "I hope Gideon's in town when I get there."

"Aw, poor you. You'll figure something out. Hey," she announced, "you can always sneak out of your bedroom window like the old days." Tiercy snickered at her own suggestion.

"Ha! Tempting. *Not.*"

"You just need to suck it up, buttercup," Tiercy cajoled. "Enjoy the downtime. Catch some rays by Hon's pool. Read for pleasure instead of work. Find a new cocktail to enjoy. I'll be down soon for your birthday and we'll relive the glory days."

"God help us!"

Much-needed laughter filled the car. As it faded, Tiercy asked the next hard question. They'd danced around it for weeks. Ever since Hon announced a condo had become available in an "active seniors" community and she was moving. And then requested Ross's help at the Virginia farmhouse her grandparents had bought and renovated in a labor of love over the years. "How do you feel about her selling it?"

"It's the right thing to do, Tierce." Ross knew Hon couldn't keep the big house up. Gaby had her own place. And God knew Ross herself would never want the farmhouse. She swallowed past unexpected dryness in her throat, taking a swig of water from her Yeti despite the protestations of her full bladder. "I'll do what needs to be done, get her moved into the new place, and that's that."

"So many good memories," Tiercy mused. "Best summers of my life."

"Yep," Ross agreed, equally wistful. "A lot. But some really crap memories too. I'm not thrilled at the idea of Gaby wallowing in all that and losing her shit again—especially so close to the anniversary of Mom and Dad's deaths. I can't deal with her theatrics. Maybe she and I can help at separate times."

"Come on, Ross. She's not that bad," Tiercy admonished. "She's a completely different person now."

"You think?" Ross heard the snark creep into her voice, a common occurrence when discussing her sister.

"I *know*," Tiercy rejoined. "People change, Ross. You just said you looked back at the teenager doing that drive all those years ago, and you know it's the same person, and yet you feel so different. Why can't it be that way for Gaby?"

"Bitch. I hate it when you're reasonable," Ross grumbled. "You're a good man, Charlie Brown. I don't know what I'd do without you." She heaved a sigh. "Almost there. I'm finally moving faster than a herd of turtles stampeding through peanut butter."

"See? Things are looking up."

"Oh yeah. Everything is hunky-damn-dory."

"Seriously, Ross Ellen Beaufort. You've got this. I know it's hard, but Hon needs you. And *you* need to do this. Ross...you have unfinished business there."

Ross was quiet, absorbing her friend's gentle reproach. Tiercy was right. And that was one important element of a true friend—to say the things that needed to be said.

"I guess sometimes you've just gotta chuck it in the 'Fuck-it Bucket,'" she muttered in resignation. "You're right. I know you are."

"Of course I am," Tiercy soothed, and Ross smiled at her friend's teasing lilt. "I'll see you soon in person and talk to you even sooner." Tiercy paused. "When I see you, I have something I want to talk to you about."

Ross's Spidey-senses alerted. "About...?"

"Never mind. It'll keep."

"You sure? I have a rock-star bladder. I can easily hold it at least another seven minutes before I need to pull over into a field and pee."

Tiercy laughed. "Classy. We'll talk when I see you in person. This will keep. Now, drive carefully, Speed Racer," she admonished. "And... hey, Ross? Take care of you."

"*Take care of you.*" The line from *Pretty Woman* was their standard closer before any big undertaking. Ross herself had said it to Tiercy just before she went out on her first date with Cole—the handsome, thoughtful man who'd healed her widowed friend's heart.

Ross disconnected the call, turned her music back on, and raised the volume as she lowered her windows, enjoying the rush of air.

"Let's do this, Beaufort."

The sooner Ross got there, the sooner this tour of duty in hell could begin. And then she could go home. Or, rather, go to New York and her new job. She was both nervous and excited about it. Tiercy had her new beginning. Now it was Ross's turn.

Over the car's speakers The Cure sang about how boys don't cry.

Neither do I, Ross thought as she sang along. *Neither do I.*

Chapter Two

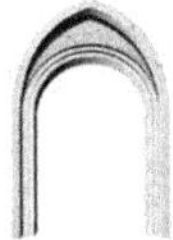

The sexy male Australian voice on Waze told her to turn left. Not that she needed GPS. The turn onto the long, one-lane road leading to the farmhouse was carved into her brain, a vivid memory of excitement at that first sight.

"Stay in the present, Beaufort."

She knew she'd be facing her past, and was prepared to do so on some level. But the next six weeks would be excruciating if she gave into memories every time they bubbled to the surface.

To distract herself, she indulged in her little fantasy about the man behind the GPS guidance. She envisioned herself on a busy Manhattan street. The unmistakable voice that had navigated her on many drives and facilitated speed trap avoidance (always helpful, given her lead foot) would carry over the crowd behind her. She would turn around to see a gorgeous man—tall, with surfer-tousled blond hair and maple-syrup brown eyes. Their eyes would meet. The chemistry palpable. Later, that seductive voice would whisper in her ear as they *navigated* their way around each other.

Ross smirked at her pun while she also squelched any

acknowledgement of her fantasy man's physical resemblance to her partner in that incredible one-night stand ten months ago.

As she eased down the road, the thicket of old elm trees opened up, revealing the farmhouse. She sighed, her favorite fantasy dissolving into unwanted reality. "Sexy bubble officially burst," Ross mused aloud. She slowed her car to a temporary stop well ahead of the driveway, turning off the GPS.

"Fuckety fuck fuck." Ross stared at the house. It had been close to two decades since she'd last seen this view. She remembered looking over her shoulder from the backseat of Tiercy's parents' car. One hard look, taking it all in. A silent, angry farewell punctuated by stabs of grief around her heart that she fought to ignore. Then she'd turned back around and stared straight ahead, stony and silent, for the rest of the drive to Baltimore.

"Fuuuuck," she breathed. Ross adored the f-bomb. She made her living editing and had a love of beautiful words. But there was something satisfying about the "f-word," as her mother used to call it. The functionality of it—adjective, noun, verb—delighted her. One of her favorite lines from *Bull Durham*, a movie she'd watched over and over with her dad, came to mind and she said it aloud. "Well, fuck this fucking game."

Except this wasn't a game. It was real. And any moment, Hon would see she'd arrived, thus officially launching what she was sure would be the worst summer of her life since...that summer.

Ross puffed out her cheeks as she exhaled in resignation, feeling more like a prisoner headed toward incarceration than a granddaughter coming to what was once a place of joy. She eased her car down the last bit of lane in silence, accompanied only by the sound of her breathing and the small branches crunching beneath her tires. There had been a big summer thunderstorm the night before, the trees sacrificing the most brittle of their arms.

As she pulled her car behind Hon's aging convertible and turned off the motor, the front door opened and Hon moved to the top step of the wraparound porch. Clearly, she had been watching for Ross.

Suddenly, her nerves kicked in. All the saliva dried up in her mouth and her lips were sticking to her teeth. She took a quick sip of water, swishing it around in what she knew was a vain attempt to hydrate her arid mouth, and slowly exited the car. Ross was an accomplished woman in her thirties, but in that moment, she may as well have been sixteen again.

A smile spread across Hon's face, instantly thawing the invisible ice that had formed around Ross, who offered a genuine smile in return. She adored her grandmother.

Hon opened her arms. "Welcome home, Ross Ellen."

Despite the words of greeting lodged in her throat, her grandmother's magnetic love propelled Ross forward, and in moments, she was safely enfolded in Hon's embrace. She still had the same homey powdery scent Ross remembered from growing up. She closed her eyes and softly inhaled, hugging Hon back.

They had once been the exact same height—five feet, seven inches. Ross remembered her excitement at age fourteen when she stood back-to-back with Hon and her mom announced it was even. Pulling back just a bit to smile into green eyes so like her own, Ross noticed Hon had lost at least an inch, maybe more.

Leah Waldheim turned eighty in August. Perhaps her great aunt Francesca, Hon's younger sister by two years, would throw a party at her Delaware beach house. Ross made a mental note to email her aunt, who was one of her favorite people in the world.

Hon may have been seventy-nine, but didn't seem it. Maybe she wasn't as tall, and her ivory skin was lined with age, but her pearlescent, stylish white bob shone in the June sunlight and there was a vigor about her that belied her age. Hon had been a beautiful young woman and was still handsome in her senior years.

Privately, Ross had often wondered if Hon had ever had a romantic relationship after Pop died fifteen years ago. Ross knew she walked several miles every day and had even attempted yoga before dismissing it because she couldn't stand to be silent that long. In truth, as she examined her active grandmother, Ross was stunned to realize there was a nascent frailty about Hon she'd never noticed before. *When had that happened?*

"How was your drive?" Hon asked in a gentle, age-softened voice, smoothing Ross's dark brown braid where it rested over her shoulder.

Ross reached up and gave Hon's hand a light squeeze. "Smooth sailing," she lied, the first of what she suspected would be many on this visit.

"You always were a terrible liar." Hon rolled her eyes. "Eighty-one sucked, right?" she called over her shoulder as she descended the wide stairs and headed to Ross's car.

Ross burst into laughter as she followed Hon to her trunk to retrieve her bags. "I always forget how well you can read me."

"It may be almost twenty years since you've been *here*, my love, but I do see my beautiful granddaughter a fair amount. You are a lot like me —I see it more and more. And like your mother." Hon's eyes saddened momentarily, and then she brought a smile back into them, something Ross recognized from her own repertoire of emotion-concealing behaviors.

Two could play that avoidance game. Ross cocked her head, her mouth dropping in mock indignation. "Hey, I remember when you used to tell Tiercy, Gaby, and me we weren't allowed to say 'sucked' because it's vulgar and there are a thousand better words to describe something. Do I detect some leniency in your old age?"

Hon winked at her. "'Sucked' *is* a tacky word. But in my seasoned maturity, I've decided it's the best word to describe that damn interstate when trucks won't move out of the way. Now, here"—she motioned to the bags—"hand me the smaller one with the strap and I'll carry that in for you."

"Hon, you really don't have to. I've got this." Ross reached for the bag.

"Nonsense. I'm old, not decrepit. I think I can carry the damn bag." Hon grabbed the bag, chin jutting, and headed back up the steps toward the house.

Ross laughed, her tense heart easing just a bit. She was indeed a lot like Hon—stubborn and single-minded.

Thankfully, Hon had always been very respectful of, if saddened by, Ross's refusal to visit her in Virginia. Instead, Hon went to Baltimore to see Ross at least once a month. At least, until her college graduation and her first job. Then, busy schedules made the visits a bit more sporadic. But they always celebrated holidays together. Just not in Virginia.

Ross's great aunt Francesca always hosted holidays at her beach house in Bethany Beach, Delaware—a tradition that began out of necessity when Ross refused to return to Virginia for that first holiday without her parents. Francesca had several children and grandchildren, so the large beach house became the natural hub of family traditions.

With a smirk and a head shake at her mulish grandmother's back, Ross hung her head in resigned acceptance. No use dallying. She bent into the trunk to get her suitcase and realized some contents of her smaller bag had fallen out. She'd had trouble zipping it and had propped it between the other two bags. It must've fallen over during the drive. "Damnation," she muttered, using Hon's favorite expletive, smiling to herself as she reached farther into the trunk for the hairspray bottle that had rolled to the back.

"Leah, just a second. Let me get that door for you. And the bag."

Head deep in the trunk, Ross heard a male voice carry across the front yard and the sound of feet running up the steps. Was that Moose, her sister's lunkhead of a husband? From the interior of the trunk, where Ross scavenged for pieces of her cosmetics that had fallen out, it didn't sound like him. She listened closer as Hon responded.

"I've got it. I was just telling Ross Ellen the same thing."

The disembodied deep male voice sounded familiar to Ross as he cajoled, "Come on, Leah. I am officially a Virginia gentleman now and you cannot deny me the opportunity to assist you." As Hon's laugh echoed, the voice continued with unmistakable curiosity as it moved toward her. "So Ross is here? I know you're happy about that. And I've been looking forward to seeing her. It's been since the wedding."

Ross's insides gave an involuntary little flip. She knew the body attached to the voice. Knew it, as in carnally.

She popped up...and smacked her head on the roof of her trunk. "Son of a—fuck! Ow!"

Backing away, she gingerly rubbed the top of her head. She blinked her eyes to clear her vision, and as her eyes refocused, they confirmed her accurate identification of the man.

"What in the ever-loving fuck are you doing here?" she blurted, bewildered and still smarting from the whack on her head.

Two dimples accompanied a familiar smile on the sexy face in front of her. "If I had a nickel for every time a beautiful woman said that to me..." Xander mused, winking at her with laughing eyes.

Ross was stunned speechless. Standing before her, at her grandmother's farmhouse, was Alexander Grace, the best man in Tiercy's wedding. The groom's best friend. And the man who—she remembered with a flush creeping up from her lady parts, which clearly recognized him, too—had kissed every inch of her naked body the night of the rehearsal dinner...and the following morning too.

"Ross Ellen Beaufort," Hon admonished. "Where are your manners? That is not how you greet someone."

"No worries, Leah. I have that effect on women." More dimples.

Holy sex-on-stick! What in the hell was he doing here? Ross tried—and failed—to reconcile this unexpected appearance of her partner in the hottest one-night stand she'd ever had with the expectations she'd had around her return to the farmhouse. One of Tiercy's favorite words came to mind. *Gobsmacked.* There was no other word to describe the punch of emotions rioting in her body.

Hon darted glances between her and Xander, one eyebrow slowly raising. "Ross Ellen, of course you remember Alexander from the wedding?"

"I—uh, yes." Ross gave a small shake of her head and tried again to form a coherent sentence. "Yes, Hon, I remember *Alexander*." Her disrupted molecules slowly arranged back to their normal state. Feeling slightly wicked with memories of their sexy night, she added, with what she hoped was a subtle enough nuance for only Xan to catch, "We had a good time hanging out after the rehearsal dinner."

She was immediately rewarded with a deepening of his dimples. "Yes, I did my best to keep up with your granddaughter. That was quite a...memorable...after-party, wasn't it, Ross?"

Ross and Xan had pulled toward each other, their eyes flirtatious and challenging, smiles broadening. Was Hon onto them? After all, she had raised a daughter and two granddaughters, and had taught young women on a college campus for decades. She absolutely had to know the smell of hopped up horny-pheromones firing.

Fuck it. If she figures it out, so be it, Ross thought, examining the gorgeous specimen standing tantalizingly close. *Jesus, he's hot.* Ross took in his height, easily a half foot taller than she was, broad shoulders, and long legs. His hair, dark blond, longer on top, and tousled, like he'd just run his hand through it. His tanned skin, and those eyes...they could melt her with their promised heat.

She realized they'd been standing there in silence while she ogled him. She wiped her sweaty palms on her shorts—*please let him not have noticed*—and reached for his hand to shake it. When he closed his much larger hand around hers, there was a zing of arousal from her arm to between her legs. *Damnation.*

Xander gave her a knowing grin. *Was her reaction that obvious? Or had he experienced the same response?*

She cleared her throat...and her head of dirty thoughts. It was self-preservation, or she'd climb him like a tree, despite Hon's presence. "And now I'll ask again, minus the impolite cursing." Ross aimed that last part in apologetic deference to Hon "What are you doing here?"

"Specifically, I'm here to ask Leah if she has a light bulb. The one over my sink burned out and I was trying to avoid a trip to the store—"

"I meant," Ross interrupted, "what are you doing *here*"—she motioned around the property—"at my grandmother's?"

"Oh that," Hon chimed in, waving a dismissive hand. "I was sure I'd mentioned it to you."

"Mentioned what?" Ross asked, still baffled by this unexpected visitor. If this trip wasn't bizarre enough, the sexy man behind her steamiest-ever one-night stand, who had lived rent-free in her memory and served as her favorite tub-rub material, emerging from the edge of Hon's property line was enough to fully fry her brain.

She hadn't seen or talked to Xander since their smoking-hot encounter followed by sexily charged social chit-chat at the wedding. Conflicted feelings warred in Ross—the expected angst of being at the farmhouse, shock at hearing Xander's sexy, deep voice, the mental dissonance of seeing him at Hon's house, and—she had to admit—the pleasure at seeing him. OK, truth to self: she was very turned on. In fact, pleasure was winning this war, full stop.

Forcing herself to focus, she tuned back in to Hon's explanation.

"Alexander and I were talking at Tiercy's wedding reception. He mentioned he'd signed a lease, sight unseen, on what he thought would be a lovely house near UVA, but that he hated it. Too loud. He didn't realize the neighborhood would be full of undergrad frat boys, and the partying was disturbing him and Petey."

"Petey? Who's Petey?" Ross hadn't even walked into Hon's house yet and this trip was already beyond surreal.

"His son. Precious little boy." Hon issued a grandmotherly beam toward Xander.

His son? Ross goggled at Xander. He'd told her he was unmarried.

"Yes, my *son*. Petey's six. His mother and I are divorced." Ross noticed the smile in his eyes fade, although the warmth in his voice when he spoke of his son was unmistakable.

"I don't recall you telling me about a son."

A small frown appeared between those beautiful eyes. "I guess the topic didn't come up." The frown disappeared, replaced by a roguish grin. "We didn't exactly get to...uh...talk much. There was a lot going on."

Ross shot a look at Hon, praying she wasn't putting two and two together. Hon might be able to smell pheromones, but she didn't need to know—or even suspect—about Ross's decadent dirty deeds with Xander at Tiercy and Cole's wedding.

Xander continued, "Petey was with my parents. They had planned a trip to St. John with him before the wedding date was set."

Hon continued the story with no apparent recognition of the byplay between the other two. "Alexander was sharing his frustration with the house. He had complained to the landlord, who was willing to let him out of the lease. I mentioned that we had a two-bedroom cottage on the property that we'd just started renovating, and that we are about twenty minutes from campus, and that was that."

"And that was that," Ross muttered. Then it hit her. "Pop's writing cottage?" Ross had never seen *The Twilight Zone*, but she was pretty sure she was in it. Her fingers itched to text Tiercy. "You're staying at my grandfather's cottage? Here?"

"Yep. I *do* remember telling you I took a job as an assistant professor of architecture. Anyway, the rental house was a failure. I should have checked it out in person first. Or asked other professors. Never trust online photos, by the way."

Ross flashed to the Manhattan apartment waiting for her. She, too, had only seen pictures. But Gideon, her no-strings-attached, whenever-she-was-in-Manhattan hookup, had been there often. It belonged to friends of his who were leaving for a two-year stint at the Germany office of the wife's company. Ross's stomach tightened. For some reason, her stomach did that whenever she thought of moving to New York. Ross chalked up her reaction to an unwelcome case of nerves.

"And then Leah came to the rescue with the cottage," Xander continued. "Petey and I love it here. And we love Leah. Best cookies in the world. Makes my belly very happy." He patted his slim stomach and Ross flashed to a particularly vivid memory of her mouth on those abs.

She realized she was standing with her mouth agape as she tried to process everything. Classy. And probably not very attractive. She snapped her mouth closed.

"Ross, honey? Are you OK? How's your head where you hit it?" Hon put a soft hand on Ross's arm.

Ross looked at the thinning skin and light beige spots of time dotting the back of her grandmother's pale, elegant hand. Once again she was struck with the signs of Hon's aging, and how fast life was flying by—including the ten months that had passed in the blink of an eye since her smeggsy times with Xander. And here he was. She mentally rubbed her hands with glee. Smeggsy Xan times part deux!

Ross shook herself mentally. She needed to get inside and call Tiercy. *Now.*

She gave what she hoped was a convincing smile and patted Hon's papery skin. "Yes, I'm fine, Hon. I just didn't realize the cottage was in that great a condition."

"It hadn't been." Hon nodded in the direction of the cottage nestled in their woods about one hundred yards from the house.

Ross's grandfather had been a history professor at University of Virginia, specializing in colonial Virginia. Hon had taught literature at nearby Mary Baldwin University. They met at a guest lecture at UVA and fell in love. In addition to teaching, Frederick had written historical biographies, which never achieved bestseller status, but were highly regarded among history buffs and helped ensure his tenure at the prestigious university. When he was deep in writing, he'd escape to the cottage.

"After Pop died, you know I couldn't go in there. It was probably just my imagination, but it still smelled of him—his cigars, his cologne. I had someone come and clean it every couple weeks all these years. Last year, when I started thinking about selling this farmhouse, Ted talked me into renovating the cottage. He's sure it will add to the value, and he's smart about these things."

Ted. Ross still thought of him as *Moose*, using his old nickname. Ted "Moose" Monroe had been her sister's high school boyfriend. He'd been a classic jock—played inside linebacker in high school and later at UVA. He hadn't been talented enough for the NFL, so after an athletically successful but academically unimpressive college career, Moose had switched gears and became a firefighter. He and some buddies also did home renovation projects on the side. He adored her sister. And he disliked Ross. The feeling was mutual.

"Moose renovated Pop's cottage? Why didn't I hear about this?"

"I guess it never came up at the holidays, what with all the hurly-burly at Frannie's. And, Ross dear, it's not like you're around Gaby and Ted to hear about it that way."

Ross winced at the gentle recrimination in her grandmother's voice. While Hon reluctantly supported Ross's avoidance of the farmhouse, she knew the more dismaying thing to Hon was the icy relationship between the two sisters who had once been close. After the accident, Ross and Gaby's deep sibling bond fractured, and it had never healed.

Ross caught Xander's eye, who was watching them with a small frown between his eyebrows, clearly uncomfortable at stumbling on a note of family drama. *Not to worry, Hottie. I'm an expert at drama avoidance. And you, Professor McHot Pants, are just what my lady parts ordered.* She gave him a small smile, insides heating at the memory of him, and at the potential of more. Oh, this was gonna be *good*.

CHAPTER THREE

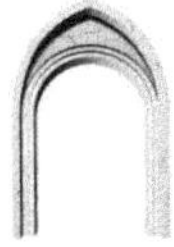

Well, damn. This wasn't exactly the scene he'd imagined—and he had, over and over—when he'd learned that Ross was staying at the farmhouse. Hearing the crunch of her tires on the gravel carry over the high oaks, he'd scurried across the property like a kid darting for the tree on Christmas morning.

Ross Beaufort. The witty, gorgeous, vibrant woman who had consumed his thoughts for months. And that was saying something, since his thoughts were often jam-packed with a million different things. Xander had a busy life. Raising a six-year-old solo, albeit with an amazing cobbled-together support system, wasn't easy. While he often felt like an intermittent monk—raising a son made hooking up difficult, and he'd sworn off serious relationships after having his heart stomped on by Petey's mom—his career was truly fulfilling.

He was reinventing himself professionally. After years of searching for where he "fit," from buying and rehabbing properties, to partnering with his best friend, Cole, on various construction projects, he was putting his master's in architecture to use by paying it forward with the next generation. When he'd gotten the call to take over a mentor's classes at UVA, he and Petey had just returned from several weeks in Europe. Xander was preparing to enroll him at an elementary school outside of Baltimore where Cole's step daughter attended.

Then the stars aligned.

As soon as he'd walked onto that campus, he'd had a sense of homecoming. He'd needed to move quickly, as his mentor had just suffered a debilitating stroke and they really needed a replacement immediately. So he'd moved him and Petey to the Shenandoah Valley and enrolled Petey in kindergarten there.

Xander had quickly realized the beautiful old home he'd rented was smack dab in the middle of other old Victorians that were carved into apartments for fraternities and other undergraduates. Not exactly family-friendly. Xander and Cole had lived in a similar place in college as carousing roommates, but it sure wasn't where he wanted his small son to live now.

In a double stroke of luck, he met Ross—and also Leah, who was as charming as her granddaughter—at the wedding in August. Within a few months, Leah came through with the renovated cottage, quickly evolving from landlady to grandmother figure for him and Petey.

But what Xander didn't count on was the constant reminders of Ross. Her pictures all over the farmhouse. Mentions of her by Leah at meals. He wasn't sure if it was the powerful memories of the absolute heat and magic of their evening together, or Leah's never-ending praise for her (she was quite the hype woman for her granddaughter), but for the past ten months, Ross was never far from his mind. Plus in addition to gleaning things about her from Cole, he managed to subtly—he hoped—do the same from Gaby and Ted, with whom he'd built strong friendships these last several months. Ross seemed to be omnipresent in his mind.

In fact, he had taken himself in hand far too many times to memories of their night, and morning, together. So when Leah had shared that Ross was staying for six weeks... Xander's surge of anticipation resulted in an aching need in his groin. One he'd needed to handle that night in the shower. Twice.

Still, with all the fantasies he'd conjured about their time together this summer, he never envisioned stumbling immediately into what he knew to be the family's third rail.

Thanks to his friendship with Ted and Gaby, he knew more than a torrid one-night stand partner ever would, or should, about why that pain clearly flickered then disappeared behind Ross's eyes when Leah gently admonished her lack of knowledge about the cottage renovation. The tug in his gut when Ross's gorgeous moss-colored eyes scanned the property, along with his need to ease her pain, was almost primal.

Casting what he hoped were inconspicuous glances between the two, he had the strangest sensation. Their postures were an echo of each other as they stared at each other with matching eyes. Perhaps it was a manifestation of silent dinners with his parents, who had more of a chilly partnership than a marriage, but Xander defaulted to peacemaker whenever possible. It was ingrained.

He was about to make a joke, his tried-and-true icebreaker, but then Ross turned her magnetic gaze to him, offering him a wry, sexy smile. Any trace of sadness or hurt had evaporated. In its place was a distinct note of promise in her eyes. And he found he didn't mind it. Not one bit.

"OK," he announced a bit too heartily, cringing at the volume of his voice. *Good lord, have zero chill, why don't you, Gracie?* "How about I help bring these bags to Ross's room and then grab that light bulb?"

"I'm perfectly capable of carrying my own suitcases," Ross responded, the corners of her eyes crinkling in amusement. To his regret, the hum of chemistry between them stilled as Ross turned her attention to the house in front of her. "Hon can get you the light bulb. I'm going to head to"—Ross quirked an inquiring look at Leah—"my room to unpack and settle in?"

Leah nodded in assent that Ross would be staying in her old bedroom and Ross bent to pick up the bags.

Xander was helpless to avoid checking out her luscious backside. Thank the tiny baby Jesus, Leah appeared focused on Ross, a thousand-yard gaze in her sad eyes, and didn't notice his inappropriate ogling. He tore his eyes away from Ross's tempting backside, watching as she straightened her back. Xander saw resolve anchor itself between her shoulder blades, and heard the small sigh escape her lips as she headed up the steps. *What a glorious and complex woman.* He forced himself not to follow her and press against her in a hug, offering solace he thought she likely needed—as well as indulging his own need to feel her warm body again.

Leah had clearly heard Ross's exhalation as well and dropped her head. Xander reached for her hand and gently squeezed, seeing her blink tears out of green eyes that were a rheumier version of Ross's. For as much as Ross had inhabited his thoughts, he also had a soft spot for Ross's grandmother. She was extraordinary, just like the granddaughter slowly moving into the house she hadn't entered in decades.

"Good to see you, Ross," Xander found himself calling out. He was rewarded with a turn of Ross's head and a knowing smile on her face.

"I look forward to seeing more of you during my visit," Ross replied, with a hint of sultriness. "We can relive some of the fun of the wedding." Ross winked at him as the screen door closed behind her.

Xander's cheeks reddened at the blatant double entendre. In horror, he realized that wasn't the only part of his body responding like a teenage boy. *Light bulbs. Think light bulbs,* he commanded himself, praying Leah wouldn't notice as he subtly adjusted himself.

He needn't have worried. Leah was already on her way in, looking over her shoulder with a wicked smile. "If you truly need a light bulb, feel free to follow me to the pantry. Otherwise, I'm sure Ross and I will see you later."

Xander offered a sheepish grin in confirmation that she'd seen through his ruse. As he ambled back to the cottage, he realized that as much as he physically yearned to see Ross later—all of her—he was also impatient to dig below that beautiful, cool, sarcastic surface. He'd caught a glimpse of a different Ross...and he was intrigued.

Chapter Four

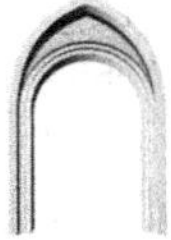

Ross

"I knew it!" Tiercy hollered into the phone. "I *knew* you and Xander Grace were bumping uglies the night before the wedding!"

Ross leaned back on the fluffy pillows that had been artfully arranged on the four-poster bed. *Fancy.*

"*Bumping uglies*?" She snorted, her goofy laugh resounding in the room. She heard Tiercy laughing in response. "Who writes your scripts?"

"The senior class of County High School," responded Tiercy dryly. "Welcome to the life of an English teacher at a school in the Baltimore suburbs. I heard it walking past the girls' locker room. I believe the exact line was, 'I'd kill to be bumping uglies with Chris Hemsworth.'"

"Hmmm...interesting. Thor is indeed a hottie. Maybe a bit old—not to mention illegal—for a high schooler, but he sure isn't too old for *me*. Damn Elsa Pataky for getting to curl up next to that gorgeous thing."

"Damn her," Tiercy sighed in affirmation.

"As for the phrase...," Ross trailed, "...bumping is right, at least somewhat. It was rather *rigorous* and repeated bumping." She snorted again. "And I am getting older by the second, but my memory assures me that Xander's uh... bumping thing... wasn't ugly. In fact, I wouldn't mind taking a gander at it again."

The friends dissolved into more laughter.

"Wait! Wait, wait, wait! You can't distract me, Ross Ellen," Tiercy reprimanded. "I freaking *knew* it. When I saw you at the salon and you looked exhausted and yet so... pleased with yourself... I should have figured it out. I expressly told you to behave. But you just couldn't help yourself. I can't believe I fell for your line that you were up half the night working on your maid of honor speech."

"It was a good speech," Ross teased.

"It was. But don't sidetrack me!" Tiercy laughed and lowered her voice to a conspiratorial whisper. "So... don't leave me hanging. What happened? And, more importantly, how was it?"

"What happened is that we had one of those moments at the rehearsal dinner where we had an entire conversation without talking."

"Bullshit. You eye fucked at my rehearsal dinner, didn't you?" Tiercy exclaimed. "How did I miss this?"

"Mmmhmm," sighed Ross. "In your defense, you were a bit distracted. That said, you, dearest, were kind enough to book us all at the same B&B. I casually mentioned the name of my room—McHenry, I believe it was—and then about twenty minutes after I safely tucked you into your virginal bed"—Tiercy interrupted her recollection with a snort—"I heard a little tapping on my door, which ended with some epic *bumping of uglies*. Honestly, Tierce, it was the best sex I've ever had. He was amazing. It went on all night. I lost count of my orgasms after five, but trust me when I tell you, there were many more after that."

"Staaahp," Tiercy moaned. "I seriously cannot believe you didn't tell me any of this before. It's been *ten months*. Plenty of time to spill the tea. Hang on just a sec. Cole just walked into the room. I'm asking him if he knew. I'm putting the phone on speaker."

Ross heard Cole's deep voice. Her sex clenched at the memory of Xan's even deeper voice. "Asking me if I knew what?"

"That my best friend and your best friend totally got it on all night after the rehearsal dinner—"

"And the morning of your wedding, too," Ross interjected, laughing.

"Of course I knew about Ross and Gracie," came Cole's response.

"Whaaat? What what? You knew and you didn't tell me?"

"I thought you knew…" Cole trailed off. Ross grinned at the laughter in his voice.

"I guess your best friend told you while my best friend kept shockingly mum?" Tiercy harrumphed.

Ross could hear Cole cleaning up the kitchen in the background and smiled, thinking of the newfound domestic bliss her friend had found. Running water. Dishwasher being loaded. The low hum of him talking to her five-year-old goddaughter, Jemma.

"Not really. I just figured it out. They both looked unusually tired and kept shooting each other loaded glances all day. It doesn't take a degree in rocket science to figure out when a guy's gotten laid. We're pretty obvious about these things."

"Aaagh! Not fair!" wailed Tiercy. "I feel like I was the only one not in on it. I'm officially peeved."

"Now, now, Tierce," cooed Ross. "I really was going to tell you all about my night with your sex god best man. But you were all wedding-day glowy and I didn't want to take away from your beautiful day. I wanted the day to be about you, not about me and the glorious pounding my vajayjay took courtesy of Xan."

"Glad to hear it was awesome, Princess Overshare," Cole drawled. "I did *not* need to hear that."

"Go away. You aren't needed here anymore. Shoo," Tiercy admonished her husband with obvious affection. Ross heard Cole kiss Tiercy as the speaker phone was turned off, replaced by low talking and some laughter.

Ross smiled reflexively. She loved that Tiercy was so happy. After the tragic death of her husband six years before, Tiercy was finally getting her happily ever after.

"Sorry about that." Tiercy returned to the call. "Cole is heading back over to a construction site to deal with some issue and I'm grading end of year papers. It's so blessedly humdrum. I love it." Tiercy's wistful tone turned bantering. "Besides, I may have been in the dark about you and Captain America—"

"Captain America?" Ross interrupted.

"Yes. He resembles Chris Evans, don't you think?"

Ross closed her eyes and summoned an image of Xan, an effort that was all too easy as he was quite at the top of her mind... and also parts lower. She became intensely aware of her growing arousal just thinking of their time together. Those honey brown eyes. That dark blond hair, longer on top, close cut around his ears and in the back. Tall. Not as tall as Cole, but maybe about six two. Slim hipped but nicely muscled. Sexy man legs with just the right amount of hair. Perfect teeth. (Ross was sure he flossed. She had a thing for good teeth. Nothing turned her off more than bad dental hygiene.) And those dimples. Ross sighed.

"Yep. You are absolutely right. Totally Chris Evans as Captain America, minus the shield and plus the dimples. Actually, I recall having that same thought the night before your wedding as we were—"

"Anyway," Tiercy cut in, "I did know he was at Hon's, now that you mention it."

"You *knew*?" Ross challenged. "Now who's holding things back? Why didn't you tell me?"

"I just remembered it when you brought it up! Cole mentioned it in passing. I honestly didn't think it really mattered to you," Tiercy defended. "I just forgot about it. I mean, I truly had no idea you'd slept with him, and you only met him that one time and never mentioned him again, so why would I think to tell you? Plus you've been so busy with lining up your new job. I just didn't think of it to tell you. If I'd known..." Tiercy teased. "You were never tempted to hook up again?"

"I might have if I'd seen him—he is quite yummy. We didn't exchange numbers. And he told me he was living near Charlottesville. I live south of Baltimore, so why bother? I wondered if maybe I'd run into him at something with you and Cole, but it didn't happen and it's not something I really thought about. He was just a one-night stand." *And possibly maybe the subject of all my sexual fantasies since,* Ross thought but refrained from saying aloud.

"And now he's staying a stone's throw from you? How fortuitous!

Just when you thought you'd have a six-week dry spell, Xander is on the scene to save you from Chastity Summer," Tiercy announced brightly.

"Fortuitous. Nice SAT word," Ross affirmed.

"Maybe this summer won't suck as much as you thought it would?"

"No, it's still going to suck," Ross answered, aiming for stoic. "But I'd be lying if I said at least one part of me doesn't see a bright spot."

"Your ugly wants to bump Xander's ugly," Tiercy stated, a laugh under her professorial pronouncement.

"For sure," confirmed Ross. "Maybe I *will* have to sneak out my window. I hope I still have those mad skills."

"Muscle memory. We did it so much back in the day, it'll come right back. It's just like riding a bike."

"Riding something," giggled Ross.

"Ok. But I'm still ticked at you for not telling me about this at some point in the last year, Ross."

Ross could hear the smile in Tiercy's voice, even as she wondered why she hadn't told her best friend about Xander. Maybe it was just a selfish desire to hoard that all to herself? Or perhaps she was a tiny bit afraid if she talked about it, some of the steamy magic of that night would be diminished. However, after seeing Xander today, it was clear their powerful chemistry hadn't faded.

"Just...an innocent omission." *Bullshit.*

"Hmmm...bullshit." Tiercy's unknowing echo of her thoughts elicited a bark of laughter from Ross. "As much as I want to see you dig yourself out of this hole, bestie, I really need to get back to reading these lovely essays on *My Antonia*. Poor Willa Cather would roll over if she could read some of this," Tiercy sighed. "Before I run, I have to ask—have you seen Gaby yet?"

"You think I wouldn't have led with that when I called you? No. Haven't seen her. It's only 5 p.m. now. Hon mentioned something to me about them coming over for dinner as I was heading upstairs. Maybe I can practice sneaking out sooner rather than later."

"You have to see her eventually, Ross. May as well get it over with."

Ross sighed. "I just can't deal with her. She sucks the joy out of a room like the energy vampire she is."

"Now who's being the drama queen?" Tiercy challenged. "You are both grown women. She's married with three kids. She has her own life and you have yours. Just deal with it, for Hon's sake. Fake it 'til you make it, as they say. And by 'they,' I mean Taylor Swift, of course."

"You're full of pithy phrases today."

"Nice SAT word, Ross."

"Thanks," Ross replied, smiling despite herself. The gift of a best friend is that much-needed smile when you feel like you want to cry. Except Ross never cried.

She sighed again.

"Hang in there, kiddo. I'll be down in a little more than three weeks for your birthday. We will ring in the holiday and celebrate a real-life cousin of my Uncle Sam..."

"...born on the fourth of July," Ross sang back.

"Love you, Ross Ellen Beaufort."

"Love you too, Mrs. Colburn."

Ross disconnected the call and tossed her phone on the bed. She lay back, hands behind her head, and examined the space that had been her childhood bedroom—the one she'd stayed in every summer and every holiday break until she was sixteen.

Hon had redecorated. The teenage hideaway of a young girl, including all her posters of *Sex and the City*, Paul Walker, Will Smith and Justin Timberlake (circa *NSYNC but still a hottie), was no more, transformed into a gorgeous guest room. A four-poster cherry wood bed was the centerpiece, covered with a soft white duvet with indigo edging. The walls were a soft gray-blue, with a toile accent wall. Sheer curtains draped the windows. Framed black and white scenes from the Virginia countryside adorned the walls. An indigo deep-cushioned chair-and-a-half with an ottoman sat in the corner, a simple glass table next to it. The adjoining Jack-and-Jill bathroom (Gaby's childhood room was on the other side) now featured a claw-foot tub, a double shower, and a gorgeous distressed white vanity.

Curious, Ross got up, passed through the bathroom, and opened the door to the other room. How many times had she done this in her youth?

Ross closed her eyes, a memory of an early Christmas coming to her. She had been about six. Gaby, her "Irish twin," was seven. They'd still believed in Santa. That evening, after the Christmas pageant (they both played "wise women"), they put out food for the reindeer and cookies for Santa. Ross hadn't been able to sleep. Eventually, in the early morning hours, prior to the light of dawn, she'd crept into her sister's room, the scarred hardwood floor creaking. Gaby was sound asleep.

Ross remembered their black lab, Shirley, padding in the room behind her. She always slept with Ross. She'd whispered her sister's name until Gaby eventually stirred, wordlessly pulling back the blankets in an unspoken invitation to snuggle. Ross had climbed in, with Shirley settling on the foot of the bed.

Ross had worn footie pajamas with reindeer on them. Gaby had on a long green flannel nightgown with snowflakes and ruffled sleeves. Her blonde hair, normally down to her waist, was up in curlers for the next day's festivities. Ross's own dark brown hair was in two braids. She had wanted it to look "crimped" with her new scrunchie on top. They had whispered in excited speculation about the presents they hoped were under the tree.

Go back to sleep, Skipper. The sooner you sleep, the sooner we get to open presents, Gaby had yawned, snuggling against her. She always called Ross "Skipper." Gaby was Barbie and Ross was her little sister, Skipper. They'd played with those dolls for hours, and the names carried over. Even Ross's dad sometimes called her that. It was a nickname that stuck in the family.

Until that horrible day.

Ross had banned her sister from ever using it again. Soon after, Ross had driven off in the car with Tiercy's family, never to return.

Until now.

Ross moved further into the room, the memory dissolving. Gaby's room, just a bit bigger than Ross's, had been turned into another guest bedroom. No sign of the explosion of teenage pink that had once been Gaby's domain. This room was decorated in hues of green, with a pale cream bedspread. A cozy chair-and-a-half was nestled in the corner. For a moment, Ross allowed herself to grieve—in the compartmentalized way she permitted herself—the loss of what once was, even if they were just childhood bedrooms. It was another symbol of how things had changed, and could never be again.

Resolute, Ross turned the original crystal handle (she'd always loved those), and moved soundlessly down the hall on her bare feet. One of the bedrooms down the hall had been converted into an office for Hon. Unlike Pop, who wrote novels, Hon was an inveterate researcher. She was a now-retired expert in Jane Austen and the Bronte sisters, and had given her only child "Jane" as a middle name in homage to the former. Retired for fifteen years, Hon still accepted the occasional guest lecture at the various universities near her Shenandoah Valley home. She was a force unto herself, even at nearly eighty, and Ross hoped she'd be even half as vital—and wickedly perceptive—in forty-five years. Not much got past Hon.

The office was very Hon. It was as if she were walking into Jane Austen's home. The room was simple, spare and elegant, with an antique writing desk and a thin laptop computer on its surface. It seemed so out of place in the quaint space. Hon had filled her bookshelves to the brim with 19th century British literature, and a small sofa and table offered a cozy place to read.

Next to one of the floor-to-ceiling windows was a high table with framed photos arranged amid simple silver candlesticks. The walls held more family photos. Ross looked at each one, starting with her favorite —Pop and Hon's black-and-white wedding picture. Ross examined it closely. Other than Hon's hair, which had been blonde like Gaby's, there was a definite resemblance between Ross and her grandmother.

Pop, twenty-three and handsome in a dark suit, stood proudly next to Hon. He wore his trademark mustache, which he'd patterned after Errol Flynn. Ross fondly remembered watching her Pop shave, and the care he took with his facial hair. She had been fascinated with his shaving cream as a little girl, and he would often put a dollop on her hand and let her play with it.

The next photo was a candid engagement photo of her parents. They were sitting on the front porch. Adam Lancaster Beaufort had his arms wrapped around Ivy Jane Waldheim as she rested against his legs, his chin resting atop her head of long dark hair. Adam's blond hair was long then too, hanging somewhat in his eyes. Both had clearly been laughing. Their hands were clasped, and her engagement ring was just visible.

Ross stared at the photo, taking in every detail. She had seen this image countless times, but it hit her in the gut this time. Her mother, just twenty years old. So much younger than Ross herself was now. Her whole life in front of her. The next year, right after graduation, she'd marry Adam. Both wanted to teach and got positions at the same private school in Baltimore. Within a year, they'd had Gaby, and ten months later, Ross completed the family. And everything had been so good.

Not for the first time, Ross wished she were able to cry. Could finally weep and let it out. But every time she tried, it felt forced and contrived. The tears she ached for just wouldn't come.

Ross put down the photo, but not before pressing a gentle kiss on her parents' frozen-in-time smiling faces.

She quickly scanned all the other photos. Pictures of her and Gaby over the years. Gaby's wedding picture. Gaby's kids. A picture of Ross at Tiercy's wedding, and then another of her standing with Tiercy, Cole, and Xander. Tiercy must have sent them to Hon. Ross leaned in to get a better look at her and Xander. They were flanking the newlyweds, all of them laughing into the camera in an informal candid between the formal shots. Xander had a charming cock to his head, and if she looked closely enough, Ross could see the hint of surprise in her own eyes.

Heart tripping, she remembered that exact moment. As they were posing with their arms wrapped around each other, Xander had reached over with his left arm and stroked his finger across her right hand, eliciting an unexpected jolt of electricity.

The back of her hand drifted to her mouth. It was as if she could still feel his unexpected but thrilling touch.

"Roooossss!" She startled from her reverie at the sound of Hon calling her from downstairs.

"Coming, Hon." Ross hurried out of the office. Heading downstairs, she saw Hon at the foot of the steps.

Hon smiled with sad eyes. "I never thought I'd see you walk down these steps again." She embraced her granddaughter. "Thank you for coming. I don't think I've said that to you yet. I know it's a sacrifice for you to be here, using your sabbatical between jobs to come to a place you never wanted to see again. I know this is hard for you. And I will do what I can to make this OK for you, Ross Ellen. I really need you here for this." Hon's voice broke a bit and Ross gathered her in tighter. When had Hon gotten so frail? Ross could feel her shoulder blades.

Hon stepped back, clapping her hands together. "Enough of that. Listen, would you mind popping over to Gaby and Ted's? I tried calling them and texting, but haven't heard back. I just want to get an ETA on their timing. Dinner is almost ready. I suspect they're just busy herding the cats—I mean *kids*." Leah winked at Ross. "You know where her place is, right?"

"Yes, ma'am." Ross was shocked by how quickly she'd slid back into her childhood manners. Sir and Ma'am were mandatory in the Waldheim household. It was all about the manners. And the grammar— the latter of which stood her in good stead in her role as an editor. Maybe the former did too, Ross mused, particularly when dealing with hubris-oozing celebrities amid writing their memoirs. Good manners diffused many a challenging interaction, she'd learned.

It was a shame her manners deserted her when she faced her sister— and vice versa, much to Hon's chagrin. Ross squared her shoulders and prepared to head over. *Be nice, be nice, be nice,* she chanted to herself in preparation.

CHAPTER FIVE

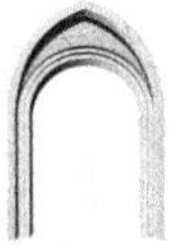

Ross

When Gaby and Ted "Moose" Monroe married, Leah gave them a wedding gift of five acres of property about one hundred yards away from the farmhouse in the opposite direction of Pop's cottage. Ted and his firefighter buddies built most of the house themselves, calling in expert help for the more difficult aspects.

Ross had seen photos on social media, and also shared on smartphones at various family gatherings, but she hadn't physically been to the Victorian-style house yet. Over the years, Ted had added on different features, which Gaby religiously chronicled on social media. Ross fought the urge to roll her eyes every time a post flashed by in her feed. Gaby and her perfect life, handsome husband, three children, and their beautiful home—she really seemed to be the Golden Child who had it all.

But Ross knew behind the Golden façade was the same self-centered drama queen who'd wreaked havoc that could never be undone. She could hear her father's voice. *You can't unring a bell.*

Ross's heart thudded, the throb of anger pulsing in her veins as her blood pressure rose. Every time she thought she was finally past all the resentment and hurt, just the briefest of reflections about the days after her parents' deaths would bring it all back. It was the chief reason she'd been dreading this trip. She had held on to so much anger for so long, she feared if she unleashed her barely held full fury, Hon would never forgive her.

And she would never hurt Hon.

Ross grabbed her battered Toms from the bottom of the staircase, then squared her shoulders and headed in the direction of Monroe Manor, as Ted jokingly referred to it. The house was hidden by a large copse of trees, affording both Leah and the Monroes important privacy. They lived close but not on top of each other, benefitting from proximity tempered by a feeling of seclusion.

When the white clapboard house came into view, Ross was grudgingly impressed. The house was two stories, with a large wrap-around porch. On the second floor, just above the front porch, was a second balcony, presumably off the primary bedroom. Black shutters framed elegant windows. Grassy property with simple landscaping framed the home. It was lovely. A large oak tree held a tire swing, similar to one Tiercy had at her house growing up. Gaby, Ross, and Tiercy had spent a lot of time on Tiercy's swing. Their families were next-door neighbors. Until...

The sound of crying interrupted the idyllic scene. Ross climbed the stairs and knocked on the wooden frame of the open front door, simultaneously calling through the screen. "Hello?" Her nine-year-old nephew, Nick, came to the door.

"Hey, Aunt Ross." Nick was the image of Moose. He could be somewhat taciturn in the way of his father as well. "Come on in. Tara is having a tantrum. Mom is trying to calm her, and Dad and Kingsley are out walking our new puppy. She's a golden retriever. And a total nut job. She's really cool." Ross was pretty sure that was the most she'd heard her quiet nephew say at once.

"Oh...gotcha. Hon sent me over to see if you all were almost ready for dinner."

"Well, we were. But then Tara flipped out because she wanted to bring the puppy and Mom wouldn't let us because she isn't house-broken yet. Dad decided that Kingsley should walk the dog, but she was scared to go alone. And I'm supposed to be in the kitchen making sure the pie doesn't burn. When the timer goes off, I hafta take it out of the oven."

Just then, a chime sounded in the kitchen. Ross heard her sister call down in an exasperated voice from some upstairs space where she was grappling with her youngest. "Nick? Was that the timer? Would you please get the pie out? I don't want it to burn. No—Tara. Stop that! I need to get a brush through your hair. If you don't calm down, you will lose your doll." The unmistakable tantrum hollering of her niece escalated.

Nick rolled his eyes. "She's so dramatic."

Ross bit back the comment on the tip of her tongue. *Like mother like daughter.*

Instead, she followed Nick into the homey pale-yellow kitchen. "Your mom is baking?" Ross asked, eyebrows raised. "I didn't realize she knew how."

"Nah, Dad made it. All the firefighters cook and bake. It's how they spend their downtime on shifts. Making food, eating it, cleaning it up, working out, and playing poker. That's what Mom says." Nick bent down and carefully removed the pie from the oven, placing it on a trivet on the large trestle table. Apple pie. Ross's mouth watered.

"Ah," Ross smiled. "That makes more sense. The last time I saw your mother bake she was about your age and almost burned down Hon's kitchen trying to make blueberry muffins. She turned the stovetop on by mistake and put a potholder on it, which promptly caught on fire. She was screaming bloody murder and yelling 'Fire' at the top of her lungs. Pop happened to be coming in to get a Coke and put the fire out pretty quickly. Then Hon came running and tried to comfort your mom while Tiercy and I about died laughing. We kept yelling, 'Stop, drop and roll!' We weren't laughing so much when we all got punished for it—your mom for using the kitchen without permission and Tiercy and me for making fun of her."

"I had no idea Mom did anything like that!" Nick marveled in the way of a child beginning to figure out that a parent is actually a person

—and a former child themselves, with all the attendant childhood foibles. Ross and Nick laughed companionably. She wasn't close to her nephew and nieces the way she was with her goddaughter Jemma, who was the niece of her heart. She didn't see them enough to develop that bond. But Nick was a pretty cool kid. They were still chuckling when the kitchen screen door opened.

"If it isn't the prodigal granddaughter. Shall we kill a fatted calf?"

Ted Monroe stood in the doorway, arms folded across his broad chest. Ross's laughter died on her lips. Ted was her brother-in-law, and she'd known him since high school, where he'd earned the nickname "Moose" for his large stature and fierce presence on the gridiron. But they'd never been close. He was Team Gaby all the way—as he should be, Ross conceded.

Initially, he was just a boring jock with a crush on Gaby. He'd linger around her at school and at practice, mooning over her with puppy dog eyes. Gaby, of course, was a varsity cheerleader. Later, after the accident, Gaby moved to Virginia to finish her senior year. Ted, back in Baltimore, was morose, until the following year, when he gained admittance to UVA, where Gaby also had been accepted.

Moose, as she still thought of him, was nice enough. He seemed to love her sister. He just was kind of a meathead in some ways. Ross really didn't have anything in common with the guy. As it was, they barely tolerated each other.

She smiled with barely veiled snark at her brother-in-law. Leave it to Moose to launch the opening salvo. Still, Ross gave as good as she got. Ted had just been out in the swampish Virginia early June heat. Stifling an evil grin, she sniffed and wrinkled her nose. "Still the problem with body odor, Moose?"

He narrowed his eyes. Once, in college, he'd eaten an excessive amount of garlic and then practiced with his football team in the hot August sun. When he came to a family function at the beach house after a long drive to Delaware, he positively reeked, despite clear attempts at scrubbing himself clean and much cologne. Ross had never let him forget it.

Ted squeezed his arms a little tighter against his body, barely hiding the sweat rings under his arms.

OK, she was acting incredibly immature. But it sure was fun that she could push his buttons after all these years. She may be almost thirty-five, but a bratty little sister was still in there somewhere. Ross grinned at him.

Just then they heard a bellow from upstairs. "Lady Tara still having a fit?" he asked, turning his attention to his son.

"Yep. Mom's really mad. She said that everyone had to behave because she didn't want to be embarrassed in front of Ro—" Nick halted, remembering who else was in the room with him and his dad. "Well, you know..." he recovered, shrugging his shoulders and darting a glance at Ross.

"Yes, I know, Nick." Ted sighed. "Thanks for taking the pie out. Kingsley, put the puppy in her crate. I need to help your mom." He shot a look at Ross. "And freshen up. I suppose Hon sent you?"

"Affirmative. She just wanted a sense of when you'd be over. Apparently, she'd timed dinner for five thirty." Ross looked at her watch. It was now five forty.

Ted winced. "It's been a bit of a day. We don't normally run late like this," he justified. "Just some stuff came up. Tell Hon we'll be over in fifteen minutes."

"Aye-aye, Moose." Ross gave a sharp salute and Ted rolled his eyes. *Jaysus*, Ross thought. *I've been here all of two hours and I'm already reverting to my bratty teenage self.*

Her brother-in-law left the room and Ross bent down to pet the furry gold puffball wriggling at her feet. Her heart melted. "Well, hello! You must be the new puppy. Aren't you yummy!" She sat on the floor and the puppy curled into her lap, apparently exhausted from her walk.

Kingsley came over with a shy smile. "Hi, Aunt Ross."

Her niece was a sweet, bookish girl. She'd inherited her mom's blonde hair, but didn't appear to have inherited her mother's classic features, although that might change as she got older. Instead, she favored Ted in looks, which, Ross grudgingly admitted, wasn't a bad thing either. Kingsley was also missing at least three teeth. She was cute. She was a high introvert, nothing like Ross's own extraversion. But there was something about her that reminded Ross of herself at the same age. That, along with her love of books, was probably why Ross felt closest to this child of her sister's. Ross stifled a familiar pang for the children she'd never have. Smiling, she held her arms open and Kingsley gave her a bashful hug.

"Mommy said she'd bet Daddy a thousand dollars you'd never show up at Hon's." Kingsley bit her lip, her small brow furrowing. "I-I don't think I was supposed to say that."

Ross let out her trademark goofy snort-laugh, so incongruous with the rest of her. It was a cleansing, true laugh and eased the chill that had formed around her heart at the sound of her sister's voice.

"No worries, Kingsley. I won't say a word," Ross whispered with a wink, still smiling. "Come on. Where's the puppy's crate? I'll help you."

The two held hands and moved toward the living room. The golden retriever puppy was soon in place and already curling up to sleep in an adorable furball.

"OK. I'm heading back to Hon's. See you in a few." Ross smiled at Kingsley and skipped down the stairs.

Encounter one was in the books. Check. Now to face her sister.

Chapter Six

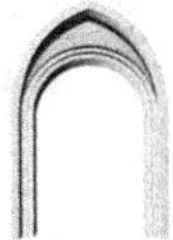

Xander glared at the clock in the cottage. Leah had texted him and invited him to dinner, suggesting an arrival by five thirty. Surely some internal malfunction was causing it to creep like molasses. He glanced at his watch and sighed. Nope. Clock was working, time was just creeping by this evening.

He drummed his fingers on the end table. After months of fantasizing about Ross, then weeks of waiting to see her once Leah shared the news of her granddaughter's upcoming arrival, followed by that short, awkward, but tantalizing glimpse of her earlier, it had come down to these last fifteen minutes. Soon he'd have an opportunity to be with Ross for one of Hon's cozy, but infamously lengthy dinners.

The few minutes he'd spent with Ross earlier had been just enough of a tease to whet his appetite for more. *Much more.* He hoped they'd be able to pick up where they'd left off after the rehearsal dinner.

Xander pressed the palm of his hand over his hardening cock, attempting to focus on something other than the steamy memories that had filled his thoughts—and shaped some spectacularly erotic dreams— for close to a year. Sporting wood at the farmhouse would not be a good look. Leah had embraced him and Petey as family, but she definitely wouldn't appreciate this particular show of appreciation for her granddaughter.

He'd even taken care of himself in the shower earlier, hoping to avoid this. *Down boy.* He glared at his stubborn cock. Clearly the Ross Effect was in action—and it was potent. Xander smiled ruefully and glanced at the clock again. *Jesus.* He wished Petey were here instead of at a sleepover. He could use the distraction his son's energy typically provided.

He examined the cottage in contented contemplation. Xan and Petey were happy there. For the first time in his adult life, Xan knew he was where he was meant to be. A dad. Teaching at the university. And this place...it was glorious. Sure, he could afford more—and he had a long-term plan in mind—but for now, what more did they need than the two bedrooms, a shared bathroom, and the great room/kitchen this place offered? Plus, there was something inviting and cozy about living in proximity to Leah, as well as Ted, Gaby, and the kids.

It was...peaceful, and filled a part of him he hadn't realized was empty. In fact, he had spoken to his financial advisor to free up some funds. He hadn't told Leah yet, but he had every intention of making her a sweet deal on the farmhouse, cottage, and the land she owned. He could picture him and Petey living there for a long time.

He thought of Ross's face when she learned about Petey. It wasn't his intention to keep it from Ross that he had a son. Given that her best friend was married to his best friend, he'd assumed on some level she already knew. Xander hadn't been joking when he told Leah there hadn't been much talking when they were together. No...only the most amazing, explosive sex he'd ever had.

Ross was sexy, uninhibited, fun, and had been as insatiable as he was that night. Nope, not a lot of talking. Unless you counted a lot of *God, you feel good...yes...more...harder...just like that...*as talking.

Xander groaned. He had to stop thinking of that night. There wasn't time to rub another one out before dinner. And even if there were, he knew it would never be as satisfying as the real thing with Ross.

His iPhone chimed an alert for an incoming call. *Saved by the bell.* It was Cole. Good, he could distract Xander for a few minutes until it was time to head to the farmhouse.

"What's up, brother?"

"Are your ears burning, man?" The laughter in Cole's voice was evident.

"Why? What happened?"

"Only that my wife and her best friend blew up the phone lines talking about the night you spent with Ross after the rehearsal."

Xan closed his eyes, not sure if that news made him happy...or nervous. "Ross and Tiercy were talking about that? When? Today?"

"Just a bit ago. Tiercy had no idea what happened between you both, so she was naturally flipping out. And then she pulled me into the conversation—on speaker, fuck you very much—and I had to hear about what a...pardon while I gag...sex god you are, brother. I may never be the same. I think I need to bleach my ears—"

"Dude, I thought you knew?"

"I strongly suspected, but that's not the point," Cole huffed. "The point is that my wife and her best friend were going on nonstop about you, so I figured I'd call. See what gives. And now I'm curious. What's the scoop? You going to hook up with her again?"

Xander exhaled. "Before I answer, I have to ask—you gonna tell all this to your wifey?"

"Of course. To an extent. You know what they say, 'happy wife, happy life.' I know it's just a matter of time before she starts harassing me to ask you about Ross. Consider this a preemptive measure as I prepare a deposit in the bank of marital goodwill."

"I see," Xander laughed. "You're using me to get in your wife's good graces."

"Yep," Cole admitted, matter-of-factly. "And you would, too, if you got the kind of loving I do from my sexy woman."

"Keep your woman's loving to yourself. My short foray into threesomes is over, no matter how much you ask, Colburn," Xander teased, his mind briefly wandering to a hot night in college with two sorority sisters.

"Ha," Cole responded. "You know what I meant. And you know I don't share. OK, enough deflection. Ross is there for six weeks. What are you thinking?"

Xander heaved a sigh. "I'm thinking I'd like nothing more than a reprise of our evening together. In fact, I've been *thinking* of nothing else... for almost a year."

Cole whistled. "Someone's got the hots for Ross."

"Yeah buddy." Xander couldn't even deny it. It was pointless—Cole would see through him anyway.

"You know, Gracie..." Cole hesitated. "I'd never tell you not to go for it, if it's something you want. But, as your best friend, I've gotta tell you, Ross isn't the...easiest...person."

"What's that supposed to mean?" Xander surprised himself, hearing the sharp edge of defensiveness in his response on behalf of a woman he barely knew.

"Easy, Gracie," Cole soothed. "I adore Ross. She's fun, hilarious, loves sports.

She's like a second mom to Jemma. She's been Tiercy's rock, and she's a fierce, loyal friend. Hell, it's because of her meddling that Tiercy and I even got together. You know that story from my wedding speech."

"But..."

"But, she isn't relationship material. Not my words. Her words, many times, to me and to Tiercy. She's sort of a 'fuck 'em and leave 'em' type. Tiercy says Ross is tough as nails on the exterior, but deeply wounded on the inside—though I've never gotten all the details behind that. My wife has a theory that Ross won't let herself love because she's afraid of losing more people she cares about."

"You mean because she lost her parents."

"Precisely. So, you know about that?"

"Yeah. From hanging out with Gaby and Ted. Leah's mentioned her daughter and son-in-law before, too. I also found their graves early on after I moved here. I was out for a run and came across it. So fucking sad." Xander raked his hand through his hair, pain slicing through his heart for that entire family.

"Definitely tragic. And Ross has some thick scars." Cole paused. "Look, man. I know how much Aubrey fucked you up. I just don't want to see you get hurt again. Ross is charismatic. But she leaves a trail of lovelorn men behind her. I don't want you to fall into that trap."

"Lovelorn?" Xander cracked an incredulous laugh.

"Tiercy's SAT influence. But I'm serious. You'd be a fool to pursue her. She could chew you up and spit you out."

Xander sucked in a breath. "That's harsh, man. I'm not sure that's a fair statement. To Ross or to me. I think most of us have chewed up and spat out some people."

"Yes, but you have a tendency to fall hard when you fall. What Aubrey did to you—"

"I'm pretty sure I can take care of myself in this situation, brother," Xander drawled. "Cole, man, I appreciate you. I really do. But let's not mention the A-word. She's the past." Xander fought to suppress the old hurt. Best to let some people remain in the rearview mirror.

He continued, voice quiet yet firm. "And I'm not interested in falling in love. Ross is a sexy woman, and I'd be lying if I said I didn't want to get her into bed. Or pretty much on any surface." He paused, taking in Cole's quiet laugh. "Petey is my life. We already got screwed over by one woman. I can't let that happen again. I don't want or need a relationship. I just want to have a good time. Ross is a gorgeous, smart, sexy woman. I'd be foolish not to enjoy that while she's here. And then when she leaves, that'll be it."

"OK. Look, I get it. And I'm sorry for the A-word. I just worry about you, Gracie."

"You don't need to worry, brother."

"I know. And, for the record, Ross truly is awesome. I've always thought one day a guy would crack that surface, and she'd rock his world."

"Dude, if you are referring to me, I think married life has turned you into mush and you're taking this too far. I'm just looking to hook up for a little while with my hot temporary neighbor." Xander knew Cole couldn't see his eye roll, but he was sure his friend heard it in his tone.

"Got it, brother. I understand. Listen, I'm at work dealing with some contract and vendor issues. I just wanted to give you a quick call."

"Yeah, you wanted to gossip and maybe get some pointers from a— what was it? A sex god?" Xander teased.

"Brother, it's you who needs pointers from me. My lady is well and thoroughly, *multiply* cared for—"

"Okay, okay. I get it," Xander laughed, glancing at his watch. *Finally.* "Gotta go, Cole. Dinner at Leah's in a couple."

Xander smirked at the classic sign off from their twenties. They'd probably be saying it in their eighties as they swallowed the little blue pills.

"Always am, brother. Now *be* gone." Xander hung up, chuckling and shaking his head.

He studied the cottage, peace in his heart, and another *be-* word popped into his head. *Belonging.* He and Cole had been best friends since college. Many years later, they could still say what they needed to each other. Cole was a brother in every way but blood. And while the call with Cole had passed the time, it also planted a seed of...what... caution? Or was it curiosity? Ross Beaufort appealed to him on every level, and with each interaction, she intrigued him more. This was going to be a good summer.

He smoothed his slacks and popped into the bedroom to run the brush through his hair—and spray a bit of cologne. He remembered Ross commenting how much she liked his scent as she'd nuzzled his neck... and worked her way lower.

"Enough, Gracie," he reprimanded aloud. "Get going." And think of something else, or he would definitely embarrass himself.

Chapter Seven

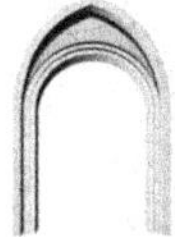

Ross

Ross came through the front door humming, kicking off her shoes and putting them in the designated "shoe spot" by the staircase just as she had thousands of times in her youth, amazed at how quickly something long lost could become familiar again.

"Hon? I'm back. The Monroes will be here soon," she called toward the kitchen, heading in that direction and loving the feel of the weathered hardwoods on her bare feet. It was the feeling of summer and her youth. "Want help?"

Hon was standing over a beautiful roast, surrounded by veggies. "No, dear. Thank you. Do you mind just finishing the table? I was going to get the kids to do it." Hon smiled at Ross with the affection of a beloved grandmother.

Ross leaned in and kissed her. "It smells wonderful. I'll take care of the table and then come back and help you bring this in." *God, it was amazing to be back in Hon's kitchen.*

She went through the pocket door into the dining room and

stopped short. Standing in the middle of the room, pouring from a bottle of red wine, was Xander Grace.

"I know. I keep turning up like a bad penny." He put the wine down and moved toward her, shrugging with a bashful smile. "I feel like I didn't properly say hello earlier. I'm sorry." He held out his hand and Ross placed hers in his. He leaned in for a chaste kiss on her cheek, easing her toward him with the gentlest of tugs on her hand. "It is good to see you, Ross."

"Thank you. I should apologize too for the way I greeted you. It was just...surprising...to see you. I sort of forgot myself." A blush crept up her neck.

"No problem. We're officially old friends now. We can be real with each other." Xander smiled at her, dimples deepening. Without thinking, Ross put her forefinger in one dimple and traced from there to his mouth. The expression on Xander's face transformed, his eyes darkening. Ross remembered that look, and a shiver of anticipation slid down her spine.

"I'd like to kiss you, Ross. May I?"

Ross's insides liquified with need at the low, gruff request. She wondered if she could come from his deep voice alone. "Yes," she whispered, not sure if it was to prevent Hon from hearing or because she couldn't seem to effectively manage her vocal cords when Xander was near. "Please..."

Those soulful eyes lowered to her mouth as he pulled her close. He pressed his lips against hers—just the gentlest of caresses. The barest touches...slow, yet decadent. His tongue teased the seam of her lips and Ross opened to him. As their breaths mingled, Ross gave in to the intoxicating feel of his tongue against her and moaned. Xander growled, deepening their kiss and pulling her gloriously, impossibly closer to him. She pressed against the hard ridge of his arousal, creating a reciprocal ache of longing between her legs. Ross's heart quickened and she swore she could feel the thud of his heart against her own chest.

A small crash from the kitchen startled them and they jumped apart, breaking off the kiss, both slightly panting.

"Everything OK, Hon?" Ross called, hoping the waver in her voice wasn't apparent to her grandmother, or the gorgeous man who'd nearly kissed her breathless. She held the back of her hand to her lips, as if to hold in the warmth of his lips.

"All good," Hon called from the kitchen. "Dropped a pan. Go about your business."

Not for the first time, Ross wondered if Hon had some form of ESP.

Xander leaned down and dropped a quick kiss on her lips, grinning as he looked over his shoulder toward the kitchen to ensure they hadn't been busted in the act.

"I wondered, Best Man..." Ross paused, somewhat nervous, and then—*fuck it*—decided to admit the truth. She toyed with the buttons on his shirt. "I've thought about you and that night so many times over the last ten months. I wondered if it would feel the same way if I saw you again."

"What's your verdict, Maid of Honor?" He stepped back a bit, a teasing, tempting sparkle in his warm brown eyes mirroring the tease and temptation of that endearing dimpled smile.

"Even better than I remember."

"I have to admit, I've been looking forward to this in a very similar fashion. However, if I don't behave, Leah will kill me. And I'm terrified of her." Xander gave a slightly breathless laugh. "Even more than death, I'm afraid of missing her delicious meal." They smiled at each other. "I best pour the wine. And think of dead slugs crushed on a muddy path. I need something to distract myself from the siren granddaughter of my landlady."

Ross pressed her kiss-swollen lips together, amused. "That was oddly specific."

"Indeed. I've had to come up with a multitude of these since meeting you."

The look he gave Ross could only be described as a smolder. She read about smolders all the time in romance novels, but experiencing it directed at her? Lord, he was a Hottie McHot Pants. Her undies were practically removing themselves. *Here,* she imagined they said, *we're out of the way. Dive on in. Mouth, fingers, or that glorious cock. You pick. All good.*

Swallowing a smile, she turned to the chest of drawers that

contained Hon's good silver. Striving for safe conversation for both of their sakes, she ventured the question that had been on her mind. "Where's your son? Pete, right?"

Xander's huge smile reflected in the mirror above the sideboard. It was obvious how much he loved his son. "Right. Petey. Currently, he's at a sleepover at his friend's house. It's his first one. I've texted the mom like ten times. I'm a total wreck. He, unlike his old man, is doing awesome. Last time I checked, they were watching *Star Wars* cartoons and eating pizza and corn on the cob. I'll go pick him up tomorrow morning. Assuming, that is, we make it through the night."

"You think he won't?" Ross placed Hon's silver with care, just as she'd been taught decades ago, adjusting the glasses Xander had filled along the way. "How old is he again?"

"He's six. And *he'll* be fine. I worry I'm the one who won't last the night. I don't know why I'm so nervous about this for him. He goes on trips with my parents, he stays at their home in Kiawah. He's even going to a two-week sleepaway camp after school lets out next week. This is just his first friend sleepover. It feels like a big deal."

Xander shot her a self-conscious glance. "Wow. Sorry about that. I guess I needed to talk. How about I change the subject. Do you want red wine?"

Ross nodded and slowly cataloged him as he poured. He was darling, and crazy sexy in his black slacks and pale pink button down, the sleeves rolled up to reveal his muscular forearms. Sweet Jesus...his arm porn was epic. She remembered those forearms bracketing her, and the way she'd traced her fingers along the veins as he leaned over her, riding her to an intense explosion.

Tearing her eyes away, lest she forget herself and just climb him like her own personal jungle gym in Hon's dining room, Ross changed the subject. "I just realized that you're dressed for dinner and I am not. Hon isn't very formal, but with dinners like these, she always liked us to spiff up a bit. I told Hon I'd help bring in the food. Do you mind giving her a hand while I run up and change?"

"Not at all. It would be my pleasure. I've got your six." He winked at her.

Freaking hell. Throwing in the military lingo, like all her SEAL Team book boyfriends. She was absofuckinglutely sneaking out the window tonight.

Ross darted up the wide hall steps, skidding into her room. Reaching into her suitcase since she hadn't yet had an opportunity to unpack, she pulled out a fitted ivory maxi-dress with spaghetti straps. She'd seen it on a clearance rack and grabbed it, always annoyed to find summer clothes on clearance and fall clothes on display in June.

She swiped her underarms with deodorant, pulled out her braid and ran a brush through her hair, which crackled with electricity. Sliding on her favorite wedge sandals, she spritzed a tiny bit of perfume and gave a quick pat of her foundation powder and a slick of tinted lip gloss. That was about as good as it could get.

Ross caught herself in the realization that her primping was entirely for Alexander Grace. Damn. She decided to put on a fresh—and sexy— pair of underwear. Especially since her current pair was a bit damp from their dining room interlude. She reached for a lacy, cream La Perla thong and smiled as she fingered the material. She might have to spend time with her sister (her good mood dimmed a bit at the thought) but at least Xander would be there... along with the promise of later.

As Ross descended the stairs, the front door opened with the commotion of five tardy people spilling into the house. Ross froze. And so did her sister. As the kids ran ahead, calling for their great-grandmother, Ted waved the pie and offered a weak excuse as he disappeared into the dining room. *Chickenshit*, Ross thought.

The sisters stood and looked at each other. Gaby bit her lip and twisted the modest but elegant solitaire engagement ring on her finger. Ross pushed her hair behind her ear, just as uncomfortable as her sister clearly was. How had two sisters become such awkward strangers? Then a flash of memories of the aftermath of the accident pelted Ross, accompanied by a fresh wave of anger toward her sister. Just as the long-lost house had become quickly familiar again, so too were her feelings of resentment.

Ross fought to suppress the old ire and be polite. "Hi, Gaby. Nice to see you. You look pretty."

Gaby, too, had spiffed up, wearing a turquoise sundress, her thick, wheat-colored hair pulled into a low ponytail. Ross knew that she herself was attractive. But her sister was stunning. High cheekbones. Perfect nose. Full lips. Blue-green eyes. Fair skin with nary a freckle. Wavy hair that annoyingly never seemed to frizz. Shorter than Ross at five-foot-five, Gaby had fuller curves that had driven the boys crazy. Ross's more beanpole build (inherited from her dad), had thankfully finally filled out on top a bit in adulthood.

Ross noticed her sister looked pale and tired. Even so, Gaby was still Golden. And suddenly Ross was the geeky, gawky younger sister all over again.

"Hello, Ross. You look nice too. I like your dress."

Strangers, offering inane pleasantries. This was beyond surreal for Ross. Likely feeling the same way, Gaby began to walk toward the dining room, and Ross moved in step beside her.

"Ted told me you stopped by. Sorry to miss you. Tara was having a moment." Gaby offered a small but genuine smile. "Apparently she's in the midst of her frightful fours. I thought the twos were bad, and three-nager was just as trying, but this sucks." She put her hand over her mouth. "Oops. Forgot I'm not supposed to say that here."

Despite herself, Ross laughed. "No worries. Hon used it herself earlier."

"Seriously?" Gaby's eyes widened in surprise.

"Seriously."

The sisters looked at each other again, this time with a hint of long-lost warmth. They had achieved an initial thaw.

Success. For now. Ross, ever a realist, knew there was too much frozen tundra to give much credit to this surface thaw.

"Mooommy. Aunt Rooooooss. Diiiiiinner," Tara bellowed from the other room.

"We have been officially summoned."

"By a four-year-old tyrant," Gaby replied, clearly still irked at her daughter's earlier antics.

Ross stepped back and let Gaby go before her.

First time with Gaby in the farmhouse. Check. No verbal fisticuffs. Double-check. But, Ross thought, bracing herself, exactly how long could that truly be avoided?

CHAPTER EIGHT

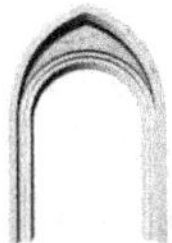

Ross

Dinner passed in a polite, if restrained manner. Hon presided over the table, keeping the dialogue to safe topics. Ross and Gaby did their parts to engage in benign, superficial conversation. They were practiced hands at this, having to navigate the same decades-long minefield on various holidays over the years. Every now and then, the adults in the group would lapse into awkward silence, with just the clinking of the silverware on the plates as the soundtrack to dinner.

The children, however, created good cover, as they captured everyone's attention. Nick didn't say much, but Kingsley was surprisingly talkative (and articulate), and Tara was a silly chatterbox. Remembering that Kingsley and Jemma were close in age and had hit it off at Tiercy's wedding, Ross said something about Jemma, which got Kingsley going again.

A furtive eye roll from her sister to Ted caught Ross's eye. What was that about? Ross sensed it was about her and bit down on her annoyance. *Breathe, Ross. Breathe.*

Xander seemed to sense her disquiet. "Hon, this meal is delicious.

I'd ask for your pot roast recipe, but we both know I'm a menace in the kitchen." From his seat across the table he picked up the wine bottle with a little wink. "A little more red, Ross?" Grateful for his presence as a buffer, and unexpectedly touched by his solicitous gesture, Ross gave a small smile and nodded.

Within minutes of Ted's apple pie being fully devoured (Ross had conceded it was off-the-charts delicious, earning a miniscule but sincere smile of thanks from her brother-in-law), the kids asked to be excused, haphazardly clearing their own plates and then tearing outside. They'd successfully lobbied to get the puppy and bring her back to the house, agreeing to keep her on the porch. Hon had offered to go along, just to referee if needed, but Ross suspected her grandmother was trying to orchestrate "normal" time between the sisters. Ross scoffed in her head —*as if.* Too much water under that bridge.

As soon as they were gone, Ted chuckled, shaking his head. "Well, that was a full-court press from all three mini-Monroes. Gabs, babe, we are toast. You know that, right?" He reached across the table for her hand.

Gaby smiled and placed her hand in his. "Completely. They can be very tenacious when they work together. Like a pack of wolves."

"That's how we ended up with a puppy," Ted added. "One minute everything was normal—well, as normal as we get—the next, Nick's friend came over and announced their Golden had had puppies. The kids dragged us over, and before we knew what was happening, we had Laverne the puppy."

Gaby laughed. "It was masterful, really. Kingsley led the charge. She is going to argue before the Supreme Court one day, I swear. She could talk a polar bear out of its ice."

Ross froze as she stood to begin the clean-up, reprocessing part of that information. "*Laverne?*" she asked, her blood pressure ticking up once more.

Gaby met her look and nodded, a defensive set to her chin. "She's my first dog since Shirley." She stood as well, and then looked askance at Ted, who was still comfortably ensconced in his chair. Chagrined, he hopped up and started clearing.

"Laverne," Ross said again, hitting both syllables hard.

"Yes," Gaby responded, hitting that solo syllable just as hard.

Ross was quite certain her face held a matching glower to the one Gaby was aiming her way.

"Seriously, Gaby?"

Anyone watching the tableau unfold would get the distinct sense of two generals gearing up across the battlefield.

Ross was stunned. She'd named their rescued black lab Shirley all those years ago, and it was no secret she'd wanted to get a Golden and name her Laverne when she grew up. Ross bit the inside of her lip against a wave of hurt that she couldn't tamp down. Ever since their parents' accident, everything—truly everything—had been about fragile, emotional, wounded Gaby. Her sister had taken so many deeply meaningful things from Ross—their grandparents' devoted attention, Ross's ability to return to the farmhouse, and now even a damn dog's name. Granted, her lifestyle didn't allow a dog. But, still...Gaby could have at least checked with her.

Xander broke the tense silence. "Um, something the matter with Laverne?"

Ross's voice was sarcasm frozen in ice. "Only that my sister appropriated the dog name I said I always wanted."

Gaby threw down her napkin she'd balled in her fist, launching to her feet. "*Twenty-five years* ago! Are you honestly mad that we named our dog Laverne?"

Ross stalked around the table to grab a serving dish by Xander—probably with more force than Hon would have liked with her wedding china. "Irked and, to be frank, unsurprised. It's just another example of how you only think about yourself. You know, the world doesn't revolve around you anymore, Gaby."

"Hey now—" Ted shifted toward Gaby, ready to defend his wife.

"It's not as if we talk, Ross." Gaby rolled her eyes, a staying hand on her husband, fully prepared to defend herself. "And, really? You aren't married. You don't even own a home. You're getting ready to move to an apartment—that you are leasing—in Manhattan. I don't think a dog is on the horizon for you. It honestly never occurred to me that you'd still want that name. I always thought of it as 'our' name."

"I called dibs and you stole it," Ross said through clenched teeth.

She knew she sounded juvenile. *Dibs? Ugh. Regressing again.* But, still, it was the larger point. Gaby being selfish and self-absorbed. Barely three hours back home, and she was already dealing with yet another example of Gaby appropriating what she wanted and making it about her.

Ross closed her eyes and took a deep breath into her strained lungs. *Just let it fucking go. Six weeks. Six weeks and you're out of here.* She exhaled her ire, the fight going out of her. If she spent the next month-and-a-half digging in against Gaby, she'd be exhausted heading into her new job. Embracing her new life, as refreshed as this draining sojourn made possible, had to be her priority.

"Whatever. Fuck it. Not worth the energy." She shook her head, weary already of the drama.

She moved to Xander's side to remove the meat platter, enjoying the warmth of his body near hers and the faintest whiff of his intoxicating, spicy cologne. He stood, easing the platter from her hand and shrugging with a sheepish grin as he drew everyone's attention—especially hers. "I didn't want to be the only one not standing."

He pressed gentle fingers against the small of her back. A tiny beat of support. He smiled at her, and in that moment, they were the only people in the room. Those eyes held kindness, an unspoken acknowledgment of her frustration. Together with the warmth of his hand at her back...the heat of promise suffused her. *Later,* his eyes said. *It's going to be OK.* He certainly was a handsome distraction, and some of her sister-induced tension diffused under his attention.

Another tacit truce. This one courtesy of Xander, who motioned between Ross and her sister. "So, uh, at the risk of asking the obvious... your dogs have been named Laverne and Shirley?" Xander looked amused as he sprung to work alongside Ted, who had continued expertly gathering plates. "Feeling kinda bad for Lenny and Squiggy. They don't rate?"

Feeling lighter inside—*Xander is magic*—Ross burst out laughing. "When Gaby and I were little, we found an abandoned black lab on the property here. She was young, less than one. Sort of gangly and wild. All long legs and floppy ears. We *had* to have her. It was during the summer, and we were here with Hon and Pop while our parents had gone away for a long weekend for their anniversary." The sisters shared a reluctant smile at the memory. "We convinced Hon and Pop to let us keep her until we could find her a good home."

Gaby added, "By the time our parents got back, Shirley was a member of the family. That dog wasn't going anywhere. Even if she was a wild goof."

"She was sweet," Ross insisted. "Just lots of energy in that lab way."

"But why Shirley?" Xander asked. "That's an interesting choice. It wasn't really a show that was popular when we were kids. I only know it because of a pop culture class I took in college."

"We'd been watching reruns of *Laverne and Shirley* that summer. Pop would only spring for basic cable. And he only let us watch 'wholesome' shows. We were sort of obsessed with the show. Shirley had dark hair..." Ross trailed off. "It just made sense." She looked at Gaby. "And Laverne, being a Golden, is blond like Laverne DeFazio. The name suits your puppy," she conceded.

Ted wrapped his arms around Gaby from behind and kissed her neck. "My wife loves that dog. You think Kingsley is a tough negotiator? I think this one put her up to it, even if she won't admit it."

"I'll never tell."

Her sister and brother-in-law gazed at each other with palpable fondness. Ross had never wanted a relationship, but seeing Gaby and Ted in action triggered a surprising twinge of jealousy. She knew that type of two-ness would never be in the cards for her. But that recognition didn't prevent a quick pang of regret when she was smacked in the face with such a clear example of love.

"Ted, bro, you two need to get a room. Seriously."

The voice that was becoming her favorite aphrodisiac pulled Ross from her reverie.

Xander shook his head in mock consternation. "Need I remind you that all this flirty-flirty business is what led to the humpety-humpety business that got you that gaggle of kids in the first place."

If Ross had blinked, she would have missed it. Just a quick look between Gaby and Ted—an unreadable, fleeting moment.

Ted gave a loud laugh and Gaby joined in gamely. "Just can't keep my hands off her. My lady is hot."

"And clearly has terrible taste. I can't figure out how you landed her." Xander grinned at the other man.

"Mad wizard skills. I spellbound her, married her, and now she's stuck with me."

"You wooed me and won me, is more like it," Gaby corrected. "Or maybe I had my eye on you all along and you fell into my wily trap."

Ross cocked her head at Xander. "You two seem all buddy-buddy." She motioned between him and Ted.

"You mean Ted and me? Hell, yeah. You try being brand new to an area with a young son. My life was teaching, grading, helping Petey with whatever he needed for school, then rinse and repeat. When I wasn't calling the police on reckless drunken undergrads, that is. It blew. Then when I moved in here, Petey changed schools. Leah had already introduced me to Ted and Gaby back in the fall, thank God. But once I was here, I'd run into them at the school, and of course over here. Petey has a huge crush on Ms. Gaby, and I have a crush on Ted's meatball subs."

"Ted's meatball—I swear this day keeps getting stranger and stranger." Ross didn't know how she missed it at first, but there was a clear friendship among Ted, Gaby and Xander. She swallowed hard against another small frisson of jealousy. Xander was *hers*. Well, maybe not technically. But the notion that the object of her infatuated fantasies was friends with her sister...hurt.

Ross couldn't help but wonder if Xander would be absorbed into GabyLand, leaving her out in the cold. Again. With her realist's logic, Ross knew whatever she was feeling for Xander was just intense desire, but it still rankled. As only things connected to Gaby could. *Sigh*.

"Please explain..." She strove for an even tone, hoping that no one—especially Xander—could sense her conflicted emotions.

"No. There is too much. Let me sum up." Ted cracked up, impersonating Inigo Montoya from *The Princess Bride*, as Xander and Gaby laughed.

Ross winced. She knew that was one of Gaby's favorite movies, so as a rule, she had avoided it at all costs—post-accident.

Ted continued, "Last fall, Xander was being all pathetic one night at dinner over here. I had pity on him and invited him to join my weekly poker game, at which I serve the finest meatball subs and the not-finest scotch."

"And I proceeded to eat his food, drink his crappy liquor...and take his money," Xander continued, a gleam in his eye. "Ted even invited me back after that."

"You're purty to look at." Ted waggled his eyes at Xander.

"And I bring the good scotch," Xan retorted with a laugh.

"OK, men-children." Gaby's 'mom voice' rose above their banter. "Enough now. I'm exhausted. It's been a long day. Let's clean up and head home. We need to rescue Hon and then put those kids in bed." Gaby reached up and tousled Ted's hair. Leaning in, she whispered into his ear in a voice loud enough to be heard. "Take me to bed or lose me forever."

"Show me the way home, honey."

"Isn't his nickname *Moose*, not Goose? OG *Top Gun* flirting. How very cliché of you both," Xander teased.

Ross's head shot up and she pinned Xander with her green eyes. "I don't know," she said coolly. "I personally like a good cliché."

She reveled in a surge of victory as she saw his Adam's apple bob in response.

Oh yeah, she thought. *Game on.*

CHAPTER NINE

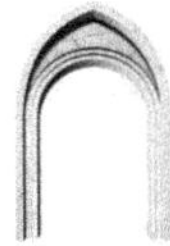

Ross

Once dinner had been cleaned up, the Monroes headed back to their place on what Ross was now calling the family "compound."

"It's very Kennedyesque of us," she'd insisted to Hon, gradually becoming more and more comfortable at the farmhouse.

It was just past nine o'clock and she was exhausted. Hon had returned and said her goodnights, and as Xander had hugged Leah goodbye, he made eye contact with Ross over her shoulder and raised his eyebrows in silent invitation.

Yes. Oh yes. Ross offered a small, subtle nod in reply. She watched his long muscular legs carry him out the door into the night toward the cottage, gaze trailing to that tight ass she'd grabbed over and over in passion, her only goal to pull him inside of her as deep as she could. *Damnation.* Now began the countdown to Operation Sneak the Hell Out and Get Laid. She giggled. Good thing she wasn't in charge of naming military operations.

One of the renovations Hon and Pop had made to the house was moving the owner's suite to an addition off the main level. Ross loved their "quarters." It was a beautiful space with a bedroom, a small adjoining sitting room, and a sumptuous bathroom. The downside was its proximity to the front door, limiting a teenager's ability to sneak out. And possibly an adult's.

The Beauforts had spent every summer at the farmhouse. When Ross and Tiercy were eleven, they'd invited Tiercy to come along. It was easier than listening to Ross whine about missing her friend, and far better than the high phone bills as the friends talked long distance for hours on end.

By the time they were teenagers, Ross and Tiercy had figured out how to climb out Ross's bedroom window, shimmy two feet across the latticework along the side of the house, grab onto a thick tree branch, and climb the rest of the way down. Shirley—an elegant, calm dog by then—would lift her head and watch them go, and they'd find her waiting by the window when they crept back in after their adventures.

For the most part, it was tame, given the farmhouse was pretty far removed from the action. When they were younger, they'd just roam the Waldheim property, having the deep, philosophical conversations of youth. As they progressed into teenagerhood, they'd ride their bikes and then catch a prearranged ride into town with high school boys they'd met at the movies or the mall. By that last summer, there was some drinking, and a little pot (which Ross didn't care for, but Tiercy enjoyed, being the child of hippie-ish parents), and mild flirtations. Lots of French kissing. Some tentative explorations, which always stopped at the waist. And then they'd sneak back home. Altogether, it was a glorious time.

"Halcyon days," Ross said aloud as she watched her reflection in the window. "Good SAT word," she complimented herself. She looked at the clock for the fiftieth time in thirty minutes. Nine thirty p.m. Hon had gone to bed a half hour earlier. And Ross waited impatiently, just like twenty years ago, to be sure her grandmother was sleeping.

She was half-tempted to attempt a window departure, just for old time's sake, and then thought better of it. It would be just her luck to fall out of the tree and break something. Could you break a vagina? Certainly Xander had come close to that feat during their steamy, sex-fueled night. Lord, she'd been saddle sore. Enough that she'd worried she wouldn't be able to walk down the aisle without limping. Ah...good times.

Instead of the window, Ross crept down the stairs, anticipation humming throughout her body. She forgot how much the damn floors creaked. Easing the front door open, she scampered down the front steps, holding her sandals so as not to make any noise.

Ross released a quiet laugh into the Virginia summer night, feeling deliciously free. She knew there were hard times ahead as she helped Hon pack, and she was sure there would be more unavoidable confrontations with her sister. Their eventual truce this evening was fine, but it couldn't last. There was too much under it. For now, however, Ross was unconstrained and on her way to see her very sexy new neighbor. And, unlike twenty years ago, his explorations better not stop at her waist.

Chapter Ten

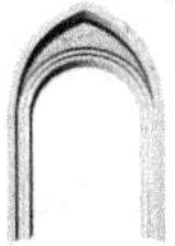

XANDER

Xander's ears were tuned to the night's sounds, like those of a wolf waiting for prey. He heard the light slap of sandals against the flagstone path, and his groin tightened. Until that moment, he hadn't been one hundred percent certain he'd read her correctly earlier. But his Spidey-senses had proved accurate. *Fuck yes.* This was happening.

Mirroring the start of their interlude last August at the B&B, Ross tapped on Xander's door. He opened it and caught his breath. She was stunning. Her cheeks were glowing and her chest was rising and falling faster than normal. Was that exertion, or anticipation? Or both?

Wordlessly, she stepped in the cottage and then froze.

"What is it?" he whispered, cupping her face as he eased the door closed.

"Just trying not to picture Pop frowning in consternation from his perch in heaven while his granddaughter defiles his writing cottage." She smiled. "Kinda dampens the ardor. I haven't been in here in a very long time. It's trippy. It's the same, but different."

"Want me to help take your mind off it?" Xander could feel his cock pulsing with need—the intense pressure of aching to be buried inside of her.

"So, we're doing this, Alexander Grace?" He was in a pair of athletic shorts, no shirt, and her gaze roamed over his body, stopping at the tent in his shorts with a knowing smirk.

"Indeed. May I?" He reached toward her, watching her nipples pebble under the thin dress. *Fuck.* He needed to taste her.

"Indeed," she echoed, and Xander's barely leashed control snapped at her assent.

Pulling her toward him, he crushed his mouth to hers, eliciting a moan from both of them. As he teased his hands down her sides, Xander tugged her flush against him, ensuring she could feel the hard length of him against the softness of her. Desire pooled low in his balls and he sighed against her soft, full lips. Deepening his kisses, he lost himself in the glorious taste of her. Her skilled hands were everywhere all at once—his hair, his back, his ass...his cock. *Christ.* He had to slow this down and take control, or this would be over before it started.

Reluctantly, he stilled her roving hands, placing them on his chest and caging them with his own larger hands. "When I got my thank-you note from Cole and Tiercy in the mail, I wanted to send them one back for contributing to the hottest, most memorable night of my life."

Ross laughed. "That would have been hilarious, given that Tiercy had no idea what happened between us until recently. How she missed it, I can't fathom, given that I showed up at the wedding with dark gray bags under my eyes and you looked like the cat that ate the canary—"

"I ate something else, more precisely." Xander grinned, releasing her hands to tug her close again.

"I was sure she'd know I shtupped the best man. And she'd expressly told me to behave." Ross reached up and twined her fingers in his hair.

"Shtupped?" He smiled at the term, now tracing lazy circles on Ross's back. "Is that Yiddish?"

"I learned it from a book I edited. These terms come in handy." Ross's breath caught as Xander moved his hand lower and traced the seam of her delicious ass through the thin material of her dress.

"Why did Tiercy warn you to behave?"

Ross gently tugged his hair as she ran her foot along his calf. "I like the bedsport," she admitted with a matter-of-fact nonchalance that both fascinated him and had him wanting to pummel her other bedsport-mates.

A shocking snake of jealousy coiled in Xander's gut. The thought of Ross with other men filled him with a primal sense of 'Don't touch. She's mine.'

What the hell? Where had that come from?

The gentle scrape of Ross's fingernails along the back of his neck raised the hairs on his arms and brought him out of his possessive reverie. *Chalk that one up to the blood rushing down from one head to the other, Gracie.* He dragged his nose against her elegant jawline and nibbled along the base of her throat, where her pulse fluttered under his lips. "Shtup. And now bedsport. You have an interesting vocabulary."

"I also have an interesting idea of something we could do." Ross moved against him, wrapping her left leg around him. "Hottest and most memorable, huh? That's a high bar."

He ran a fingertip over her cheekbone and then across her upper lip. "Only one way to see if it was just an aberration. More bedsport?"

"Indeed."

Xander skimmed kisses along her neck, causing chills to rise along her satiny skin. "My God, you are just glorious." He leaned back and took in every inch of her. "I had so much trouble focusing on the dinner conversation tonight. I was worried everyone could see what I was thinking."

"And what was that?" Ross asked, her voice low.

As she peeled the spaghetti straps off her shoulders, both he and his cock observed with gratitude that she'd had the foresight to remove her bra before she left the house. And when she let the dress drop around her waist, his breath caught in his throat.

"I was thinking of all the ways I want to touch you tonight," Xander rasped. "Ross. Beautiful Ross. You have no idea…"

Xander dropped to his knees, pressed his lips against her stomach and reached up to tease her erect, rosy nipples with the tips of his fingers until she began to moan. He worked his way back up, trailing kisses along her supple skin and burying his face in her long, dark brown tresses. He wrapped the length around his wrist, tugging her head back.

"I want to devour you."

"Bon appetit," she replied, pressing against him.

Maybe it was all the blood rushing out of his brain and into his hard-as-iron cock, but somehow the wrong thing came out next. "I gotta tell you...when you and your sister began that silly fight, I was worried you wouldn't be in the mood to do this—"

Ross pushed him back. "Silly?" Suddenly her eyes were no longer a verdant spring field. They were glacial.

"I just meant, I—" Xander dragged his hand through his hair, flummoxed, as he watched her ardor dissipate. *Fuck.* "I know there is some...stuff...between you and Gaby, but I didn't expect to hear an argument about twenty-five-year-old dibs."

Yanking her straps back up, Ross shoved past him, moving further into the cottage.

Xander took a deep breath. Why the hell had he brought that up? What sort of idiotic, cock-blocking stupidity possessed him to say that? Xander took some consolation that she stormed further *into* the cottage, rather than out, leading him to hope all wasn't totally lost. Thank God. He just needed to turn this around.

While he struggled to recover from his unfortunate blurt, Ross scanned the space. "It's so weird to be here. Not just here in my Pop's writing cottage. At the farmhouse. Just"—she motioned around—"*here*. All of it. I hate it here, Xander. I don't know what all you know, but there isn't just 'stuff' between Gaby and me. And the spat tonight about Laverne's name was representative of a much bigger issue with my sister."

Xander walked over and rested his hands on her shoulders, stroking with the tips of his fingers. This was no longer a seduction. He'd blown it, and now he needed to help soothe what he'd agitated. *Stupid fool.*

"Ross, I'm sorry. I realize we barely know each other. Sometimes I forget that. It feels like I've known you for years, instead of just having one incredible night together. There's this connection we have. And I know you feel it too."

He gently turned her to face him, tracing the line of her jaw as more chills rose on her skin, kissed a pale golden by the soft amber light of the cottage. Ross's mesmerizing, leafy eyes searched his face, intimate as a touch.

He continued his gentle caress, mapping the silky outline of her shoulder. "And that feeling of *knowing* you makes me unable to keep my hands off of you. And also apparently cuts off the blood flow to my brain, causing ridiculous things to slip out of my mouth."

Ross tilted her head down, but not before he caught an amused smile on her lips.

"Forgiven, but only because I'm also completely knocked off balance by whatever this magnetism is between us." Ross reached for his hand and squeezed it.

She does feel it. Xander's heart—and his eager cock—skipped a small celebratory beat.

"Honestly, I'm just knocked off balance in general. Being around my sister makes me not my best self." Xander watched as she sought the right words. "For two decades, Xander, I've had these... feelings... about my sister anchored in my gut," she began. "I know, in my rational brain, that my reaction to Gaby can be immature at times. But it's how it is with me. I'm not going into all the details, but just know that my sister has been... difficult... in my life, and she hurt me. Deeply.

"In the days and months following my parents' death, Gaby was impossible to deal with. She thoughtlessly demanded so much of my grandparents at a time when they needed compassion." She paused, then added in a whisper, "And I needed them, too. But they couldn't be there for me or heal themselves. Because of her. It was... infuriating." She sighed. "Suffice it to say, in my world, you are either Team Ross or Team Gaby. There really isn't any middle ground."

"Sort of like Team Jen or Team Angelina?" Xander flashed a grin, trying to lighten the moment but also hoping she could feel his sympathy. Cole was right—she was strong, but wounded by everything that happened around the death of her parents. Now it wasn't his dick aching for her, it was his heart.

"OK...early aughts pop culture reference. I don't know whether to be impressed by this, or scared."

"Same pop culture class as *Laverne & Shirley*," he admitted with a head tilt. "What can I say? I'm a veritable font of pop culture trivia."

Ross dropped her head on a soft snicker, and Xander could almost see her anger deflate. "Once again, just like at dinner, you've managed to diffuse a situation. Quite a skill you have there, Alexander Grace. Oh, and P.S., I was always Team Jen, and I remain salty at Brad and Angie. I'm convinced Jen and Brad still love each other after all these years."

"Hope springs eternal." He grazed her cheek with the tip of his index finger. "I'm sorry I called your argument silly. I shouldn't presume. I've never been a big one for picking sides, especially when I don't have the full picture. It's difficult for me because your sister and Ted have been good to Petey and me and I've gotten close to them. However, you and I do have"— he motioned between them—"this, as you say, magnetic connection. So how about for now, we just say your team is clearly special and really compelling to me. I want to get to know it better. Although I am with you on Team Jen."

Ross bumped his raised fist in solidarity, and he leaned in and rested his forehead against hers, bewitched. Xander dropped a conciliatory kiss on the upturned tip of her enchanting nose. He'd wanted to kiss it from the first moment he'd met her. "And I'm sorry I ruined our mood."

Xander bent his head toward her neck, inhaling her glorious scent. Looking up, he saw the heat returning to her eyes. And something else returned, too.

"I don't know, Xander," Ross winked, motioning toward the front of his shorts, which was visibly tented. "It seems *your* mood is doing just fine. What shall we do about that?"

"It does seem a shame to waste this nice time together." Xander eased up against her, peeling down the top of her dress and rubbing his knuckle against her nipple. A bloom of passion rose across her chest.

"Shall we pick up where we left off?"

Ross gasped as he eased his other hand under her dress, finding the slick vee between her legs. "Mmmm. Sounds good," he murmured, swallowing Ross's moan as he slid a finger under her thong and inside her. "God, Ross. You are so wet. Is that for me, beautiful?"

She arched her hips as he kissed her neck. "I'm taking that as a yes." He chuckled as she moaned some sort of unintelligible assent. "Ross, tell me what you want, sweetheart." He worked his finger in and out, his own blood heating with the evidence of her arousal. "Do you want another finger?"

He registered her nod, losing himself as he ran his finger along her seam, spreading her slickness. Then he plunged two fingers in, working her. She ground against them, the glorious tension in her body rising.

"That's right, gorgeous. Take them, take what you want." Xander worked open-mouth kisses down her neck, relishing the decadent feel of her shiver against his lips, fresh chills visible across her body. "My girl likes her neck kissed," he murmured.

My girl?

Xander froze for a moment at the slip, but Ross seemed caught up in what he was doing with his fingers, pressing her hips hard against his hand and offering low, panting moans. He knew from their last time together that when she did that, she was getting close.

He took one rosy, peaked nipple in his mouth, flicking it between his teeth and sucking as he filled her with a third finger. Ross released another deep moan and Xan pressed on her clit with his thumb, moving it in tight circles.

She tensed and then exploded, the pressure of her walls against his fingers deliriously tight. He couldn't wait for it to be his cock. Ross continued to cry out in ecstasy, reaching down to press Xander's hand harder into her wet warmth as she rode out the wave of her orgasm, eyes closed in pleasure.

He could feel pre-cum leaking from his tip. *Soon. Soon*, he promised, resting his head against her as he held her up, her legs having somewhat given out. He closed his eyes and lost himself to the sound of her breathing returning to normal.

Xander wasn't sure if it was seconds or minutes later, but he opened his eyes to see Ross watching him with intensity. He realized his fingers were still inside her.

"Holy. Shit," she whispered.

He slid his fingers from her channel, relishing her aftershocks as he took the opportunity to rub against the spot he knew drove her wild.

She arched her hips into him. "Mmmmm..." she moaned.

He knew he was igniting her desire for more. Easing his fingers from her again, and momentarily ignoring her whimper of protest, he slowly licked them clean, never breaking eye contact with her. "Holy shit is right, Ross. You taste delicious."

With his other hand, he stroked her hair, which splayed down her lithe back. He'd fantasized about wrapping that thick mane around his fist as he took her from behind. "You know what the French call the interval right after an intense orgasm?"

"Mmmm?" Ross said again, sagging against him in that glorious, somnolent state that follows a very satisfying sexual encounter.

"La petite mort. The little death."

He could feel the soft rumble of Ross's laughter and smiled.

"Then I'm pretty sure I just died."

Xander kissed her, taking his time exploring her gorgeous mouth. "Don't die," he whispered against her lips. "It's only ten thirty, and I'm hoping the girl next door doesn't have an early curfew."

Ross huffed a soft chuckle, an echo of her charming, incongruous laugh. She reached down to palm his erection and Xander hissed, his cock jumping with the attention.

"Now... I do believe turnabout is fair play, Professor Grace," she purred, lavishing Xander's neck and nipples with the same attention he'd just offered her. "Given that I seem to be on memory lane tonight, and I just had a wicked finger fuck by a hot guy, I think it's only right that I return the favor with a proper hand job."

"Jesus, Ross," Xander laughed, his voice strained with arousal. "I'm so hard and I want you so bad, I'll probably go off like a fifteen-year-old. This could be a bad look for me."

"Good thing I have prior experience with you and know better."

With that, Ross reached into Xander's shorts, reminding him of why hand jobs by hot women were highly underrated.

Chapter Eleven

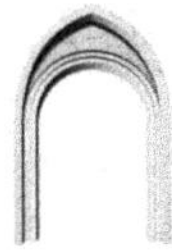

Ross

"Dawn's early light," Ross whispered as she crept in the front door of the farmhouse. Crossing to the stairs, the floor creaked and groaned in the otherwise silent space. "Fuckety fuck," she hissed. She tiptoed up the stairs, taking pains not to make a sound. She wasn't sure what time Hon usually woke, but she hoped it wasn't earlier than five thirty a.m.

Ross resisted the urge to giggle. Here she was, just a few weeks from her thirty-fifth birthday, sneaking back into Hon's house after getting thoroughly, deliciously finger fucked and then giving a masterful hand job (if she did say so herself) that left Xander shaking and sweating and calling out to Jesus.

They'd talked into the wee hours, about anything and everything, before he finally fucked her—repeatedly—the way she'd been fantasizing about for months. She would definitely have to call Tiercy later.

Safely ensconced in her room, Ross peeled off her dress and climbed into bed. She could still smell Xander on her. Smiling, she drifted off to sleep. No Chastity Summer for her!

She awoke to the smell of bacon wafting into the room. Her stomach growled, and she inhaled, filling her lungs with the inviting scents of breakfast. And coffee. Ross didn't normally eat breakfast, but the idea of bacon and coffee effectively lured her out of bed and into the shower. She stood under the hot spray, reveling in the feel of it on her tender skin. The stall was big enough for two, and she indulged herself in a fantasy of fucking Xander there. Maybe when Hon was at her church meeting.

Lord, she was insatiable. She'd spent the better part of the night exchanging orgasms with Alexander Grace, and yet she couldn't wait to touch him again.

She stepped out of the shower, dried off, and smeared the steam off the mirror, gasping as she caught a glimpse of herself. In addition to stubble burns all over her face and chest that were reminiscent of their first night together, she had what was clearly a hickey on her neck.

"A hickey? I really am back in high school." Ross sighed and tried to remember all her hickey-covering tricks.

Her hair pulled around her neck, makeup somewhat camouflaging the mark, Ross slipped into the kitchen. Hon was standing at the sink, gazing out the window. When Ross came up behind her and wrapped her arms around her grandmother, Hon startled and then beamed at her.

"Ross! You shouldn't sneak up on old ladies! You scared me," Hon laughed, hand to her chest. She turned and gave Ross a brief once-over. Ross wasn't sure, but she thought she saw Hon's eyes stop a fraction of a second longer on her neck. "You look lovely today, albeit a bit tired. Have a seat. I'll get you some coffee and breakfast. I hope you slept well."

"I had a great night," Ross replied, smiling inside. She stilled her grandmother's hand. "Hey, I can fix my own coffee, Hon." Ross reached for a cabinet, opened it and smiled. "You still keep your mugs in the same place."

Hand shaking, she reached for the mug that had been her father's. It was an Orioles mug from 1983—the last time the team had won the World Series. Hon had offered it to Ross in the days after her parents' deaths, but she'd refused. It was his mug, and it was too raw a symbol that her dad was gone forever.

"Have a seat, Ross Ellen. This is your first morning back and I get to spoil you a little. Pretend this is the Waldheim B&B." Hon stroked Ross's hair. "Sit," she commanded.

Ross obeyed, by habit, taking her childhood seat at the battered oak table that had hosted countless meals, snacks, and late-night conversations. Hon placed the O's mug in front of her, steaming with fragrant coffee, and the perfect amount of cream. Ross held the mug between her hands with reverence and lifted it to her mouth. "Oh, sweet nectar of the Gods. Thank you," she breathed.

Hon laughed, turning her back to scoop bacon and eggs onto a plate for Ross. "I don't normally eat like this, but with it being your first breakfast here in a long time, I thought I'd splurge. Just don't tell Doc Welsh. He'll read me the riot act about heart health."

Ross sat in contented silence, enjoying the sounds of Hon bustling around her kitchen. An unexpected sadness settled around her heart as she thought of the house going on the market, and with it, the hub of her best memories of her parents. And the worst ones too, for that matter. But, in this moment, it was the joy of her youthful summers and holidays that echoed in the chambers of her memory.

Hon placed a plate in front of her and the two ate in companionable quiet. Eventually, Hon cleared her throat. "Ross Ellen, as you can see, I really haven't started packing. I've done some things in my bedroom and a bit in the office, but I just haven't been able to face it. I really wanted you here. We have our work cut out for us. Gaby will be by to help, too, but she has a couple new clients and her schedule is a bit variable. And she has to work around Ted's shifts at the fire station."

Swallowing a bite of perfectly scrambled, fluffy eggs, Ross tried to respond sans sarcasm, which was her default tone for all things involving her sister. "Sounds like her interior design business is really taking off. I was thinking this was just another thing to dabble in, like being a Yoga instructor and then that jewelry she was hawking." Oops. A touch of snark slipped in there at the end.

Hon aimed a warning look her way. "Ross, she is very talented. She made 'that jewelry she was hawking.' She is so artistic. This seems like a natural outlet for her gifts. She did your room and my office, you know."

"It does look amazing," Ross conceded in genuine admiration. "Her own place looks good too. Simple. Homey."

"You should give your sister the benefit of the doubt. Maybe try getting to know her a bit better on this trip."

Ross put down her fork. "Hon, I know in your heart of hearts you have grand aspirations for a reconciliation, but it's not going to happen. I just got here. Can we maybe go easy on the Hon-full-court-press?" Ross winked at her grandmother to ease the words, but she hoped the message got through.

Once more, they turned to their breakfasts. Still, Ross got the sense Hon was working herself up to something else. Sure enough, within a couple minutes, Hon cleared her throat again. "Ross, I thought we'd start with the basement and go through the things you left. I moved everything from your room there, as well as the things fr-from Ivy and Adam's house in Baltimore." Hon's voice broke as she clearly struggled to contain the vein of sadness she'd tapped.

Ross pressed a hand to her knee, hoping to stop her leg's light bouncing, a common stress response for her. "Hon, I know we need to get all this done. And we will, I promise. But, do you think we can start with something a little less, um, charged? Maybe pack your good china and silver? Or kitchen stuff you don't use much? I need a little bit of time to psych myself up for the rest, truth be told."

Hon breathed a sigh, one that sounded suspiciously of a reprieve granted. "Yes. Yes, that will be fine. Let's start with all the knickknacks. And we'll begin in the dining room and the formal living room. How does that sound?"

"Perfect." Ross nodded, relieved. She ran a hand through her hair and caught Hon's eyes fixed again on her neck. Ross looked down quickly, pretending to be absorbed in the last of her eggs.

"Right." Hon rose, bustling to the sink with the plates. "These dishes won't clean themselves up. Why don't you pop into the basement? I have a bunch of boxes, tape rolls, and newsprint. You can get that set up in the dining room and I'll finish all this."

"Sure thing, Hon," Ross answered, eager to get out from under her grandmother's practiced eagle eye and touch up her neck makeup.

Damn Xander. She tried to be angry at him for the juvenile act, but found herself swallowing a smile as she plotted her revenge.

Hon called over her shoulder as Ross pushed her chair out and headed toward the door to the basement. "Those hardwoods near the bottom of the stairs creak just as much as when you were in high school, don't they?"

Ross froze, unsure what to say.

Hon continued, an undercurrent of amusement beneath her innocuous tone, "If you see Xander again tonight, do give him my best. Oh, and you could take that light bulb to him."

Ross stared at Hon, whose back was turned as she scrubbed a frying pan. She opened her mouth to say something, thought better of it (what can you say when your seventy-nine-year-old grandmother busts you for sneaking out?), and headed down the stairs. As she turned the corner in the drafty old basement, Ross was pretty sure she heard Hon chuckling.

Chapter Twelve

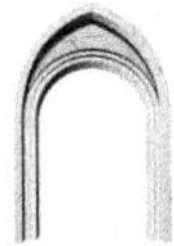

Ross

All things considered, it wasn't as terrible as Ross had imagined. She and Hon worked in easygoing efficiency as they packed the contents of the china cabinet and antique sideboard that had been Hon's own grandmother's. Those two pieces of furniture would come with her to her new apartment in the "active seniors community." *Active* senior, thought Ross, amused. They wouldn't know what hit them. Ross was quite sure Hon would take charge of everything within three months, similar to how she led the vestry of her Episocpal church as a senior warden.

As the morning moved on, Ross and Hon sang along to a variety of music. Ross had been shocked to discover Hon had an Echo, and they took turns asking Alexa to play different genres of music. By 1 p.m., they were almost finished with the dining room.

As Hon stood and stretched, Ross did the same, feeling little pops in her neck. "Hon, I'm going to take a quick break and check my email. I may also take a little nap."

"That sounds good, dear. I have dinner plans tonight that I need to confirm, and I'm going to grab a quick bite to eat before we tackle the formal living room." Hon headed to the kitchen. "You want anything? I have curry chicken salad in the fridge."

"Mmm...sounds delicious but I'm still satisfied from breakfast. You enjoy and I'll be back in a bit." Ross smiled at Hon. "I'm home one day and you're already dumping me for some other dinner plans?"

Hon frowned. "I'm sorry, Ross. It's a church vestry thing and I need to be there."

Ross swallowed a private giggle. Yep, Hon would be running her retirement home in no time. "Hon, I'm just teasing. Really, I'm good." She dropped a kiss on Hon's cheek. "I may stay here. I may go into town. I'm fine with not having specific plans." *Maybe I'll swing by and see my favorite architecture professor...*

"OK. I won't be too late."

"I hope not. Unless maybe this is just a cover for a hot date for you?" Ross teased.

Hon laughed and then gave a small private smile. "No hot dates for me. At least not tonight," she clarified.

"What?" Ross was shocked.

"Kidding. Or am I?" Hon winked, squeezing Ross into a hug. "I love you. Thanks for your help this morning. Meet up again at two?"

Ross hugged her back, savoring the warmth of her grandmother, and that special smell of her perfume (worn even when doing mundane tasks like packing) and the laundry detergent she had always used. "See you at *three*," she replied, voice firm. Both she and Hon needed the rest.

She took the stairs two at a time and flopped on her bed, anticipation thrumming. A certain professor had been on her mind all morning. Grabbing her phone from her charger in her room, she sent a text to Xander.

ROSS

> Booty call tonight at 6? Your place? Or even mine? Hon will be away until at least 8:30.

She tapped her nails on the phone screen, waiting for his reply. She was already plotting a revenge hickey when her phone rang.

"Hey, got your text. Thought it would be easier to talk."

Ross loved the rumble of Xander's voice. This was the first time she'd heard it on the phone. Deep. Sexy. Warm. Sort of gravely. A little like Johnny Cash, whom she'd listened to with her grandfather. A lyric popped into her head. *Bound by wild desire, I fell into a ring of fire...* She fell into a fiery surge of wild desire for sure. *I get it, Johnny. I totally get it.*

"Talk is fine, but I have other things in mind. Oh...but first I need to yell at you for that ridiculous hickey. I can't believe you did that."

Xander laughed. "You did say you felt like you were back in high school with all this, so I thought I'd add that element of authenticity. We architects are known for our attention to detail."

"I'll *detail* you, Alexander Grace," Ross threatened. "Hon saw it."

"Ruh-roh," laughed Xander again. "I'll be in trouble with Leah. She'll know what a lecher I am. Soon she'll figure out we're cliché-ing."

"Oh, I think she knows that. She completely busted me this morning."

"She *what*?"

"Yep," Ross confirmed, firing up her laptop to scan for emails from her new employer. "Her hearing is as sharp at seventy-nine as it was when I was a teenager. She made some comment about creaking floorboards and then said to give you my best if I see you *again* tonight."

Xander let out a low whistle and chuckled again, this time with admiration. "I love that lady. She is something else. Nothing like my grandmother was, that's for sure."

"What was she like?" Ross was curious. Thus far, in her very few interactions with Xander, she hadn't really connected him with a family. She knew about Petey now, of course, and that Xander's parents lived on tiny Kiawah Island in South Carolina. Ross was beginning to glean some family texture around Xander. Her M.O. was to dodge that type of sharing, since those were trappings of a relationship. And Ross avoided those like the plague. But something about Xander Grace piqued her curiosity.

"Oh, I'll bore you with those details some other time. Suffice it to say, she was the anti-Hon."

"Interesting. I'll hold you to that," Ross said, and was shocked to realize she meant it. "So, shall I pass along Hon's best to you tonight in person, and also share some of my own—how should I put it—*best regards?*"

Xander's low growl rolled through the phone lines and straight to her ladybits. "If what I've experienced thus far hasn't been your *best regards,* I may die in bed at the tender age of thirty-six. But it would be a happy death."

"Or just la petite mort," Ross offered.

"You paid attention. Good student."

"I'm hot for the professor. What can I say?"

Ross found herself grinning like a fool into the phone. *What in the hell is happening to me?*

Stifling that uncomfortable thought, she asked again, "So...dinner together and then you can have me for dessert?"

Xander hesitated. "Ross, I wish I could. But...remember I have a son?"

Petey. Damn. She hadn't even considered that when she suggested getting together.

He continued, a strange tone in his voice, "It's OK. I'm thinking this is where you walk away. Guy with a son, even if the guy is good in bed and teaches you apropos French phrases, is not what you want. I get it."

"What is that supposed to mean?" A bolt of ire replaced her brief disappointment at not being able to have her desired dinner-tryst.

Xander was quiet a moment. "It means I know you don't do relationships or anything that involves emotional complications. And, therefore, by extension, you definitely wouldn't be interested in men with children."

"And how exactly did you come about this knowledge?" Ross was accelerating into full-fledged pissed off. Never mind that part of what he said was mostly true. She loved kids. She just didn't want anything close to a relationship. Hearing it from him, though, somehow offended her. As for kids, she'd never slept with anyone who had children, but she didn't think it would be a deal-breaker. Just possibly logistically challenging—as their earlier conversation had proved.

"Ross, I didn't mean to upset you," Xander tried to explain, but he'd stepped in it once again with her. And, just like last night, he should have shut the hell up. But, to her chagrin, he continued, "I just have heard about you a bit and I know things."

"You've heard about me a bit and you *know things*," Ross repeated, her calm voice not betraying her pounding heart. "Such as..."

"Such as you've never had a serious boyfriend. You refuse to own a place, even though you are perfectly able, because you don't want to be tied down. You love your goddaughter, but don't want kids of your own—"

"Wow," Ross interrupted, her voice steel. "You've just got me all figured out. From where did you garner this information? My dear sister?" Ross had been somewhat sleepy and looking forward to a nap, but now adrenaline coursed through her. "I can't believe you've been discussing me with other people."

"It's not like that. I just—I was curious. I am *intrigued* by you, Ross. I have been since the wedding last August. I've been to a good number of dinners with Leah, as well as Gaby and Ted. They don't talk about you much, but sometimes things come up."

"Things come up." Ross was beginning to sound like a parrot, but she was mortified...and livid. "I don't like being the topic of others' conversation. Especially people like Gaby and Moose, who do *not* know me at all."

"And Cole," he admitted.

"You and *Cole* were talking about me?" Ross hissed.

"Not like that, Ross," Xander soothed. "It was after you got here. He said you and Tiercy had been talking about the night we spent together. Girl talk, huh?"

He was clearly trying to defuse with a joke again, but Ross met it with stony silence. Quietly, he continued. She could hear his remorse, but also—she thought—a tone of defiant justification.

"When people start talking about you...I listen. After that night we had, I will admit to being so fucking fascinated by you, I wanted to know more about you. You're captivating. Most women would at least exchange cell phone numbers. Have some...I don't know...*expectations*. But you're different."

"I don't give a flying fuck what my sister and Moose say, but what did Cole say?"

"He said you're awesome. That you are Tiercy's rock and you got her through the worst time of her life. That you were gorgeous but had never been serious with a man, at least that he'd seen. That you are amazing with Jemma, and she sees you as a second mother. That you love sports. And that there's a sadness to you that you work hard to hide, and that Tiercy won't discuss, citing your privacy."

"Is that it?" Sarcasm dripped from her lips as Ross's fingernails dug half-moons in her palms.

"No. He also said I should be careful, because according to Tiercy, you just aren't interested in long-term romantic relationships. Not that I am either, for the record. He said I'd be a fool to pursue you. But don't be mad at him for that, Ross. He meant well. He was just looking out for me—" he paused for a beat "—because of some stuff that happened to me years ago."

Ross was silent, hurt by Cole's bold assessment and her best friend's discussion of her with Cole. Tiercy wasn't actually far off. However, Ross's aversion to relationships wasn't something she cogitated on with any frequency. Or really at all. She was too busy enjoying herself. *Right? She was, wasn't she?* With practiced, almost unknowing skill, Ross ignored the small conflicting voice in her head.

The bottom line was that none of this was Cole's business, or even Xander's. And definitely not her sister's. Her mind whirled as she tried to process all Xander revealed.

Before she could even begin to formulate a reply, Xander continued, his voice gentle. "Leah only raves about you. What an accomplished and respected editor you are. How amazing you've been with her younger sister—Francesca?—as she's faced some health challenges. That you stayed with Francesca's children at the hospital when she had surgery for hip replacement. And that you were a tomboy growing up. And the editor of your high school paper as a sophomore—something that had never happened before in your high school. And that you were the most stubborn child she'd ever met."

Ross couldn't help herself. "And my sister? What does she say about me?"

"Not a lot," Xander answered quietly. "That there is a lot of hurt between you both. That a long time ago you were close, but you haven't been since your parents died. That she only sees you a couple times a year. You send cards and presents to her kids, without fail, on their birthdays, but you aren't really a part of their lives." Xan halted, and then proceeded. "And Ted, well, he has a lot of anger at you. At how you've treated Gaby—"

"How *I've* treated *Gaby*?" Ross was incredulous. "First of all, he doesn't fucking get to have an opinion about me. He's—he's nothing. And he knows zilch about me. He's just a meathead who married my high-maintenance sister. And as for Gaby, let's just say there are two perspectives to this. Gaby has a gift for making everything about her—everything."

Ross raked her hand through her hair and let out a shaky laugh. "Wow. OK, then. This is not how I was imagining this conversation would go." Frost infused her voice as she recognized territory she could manage, a well-trodden pathway of dismissal. "But that's for the best, I think. One aspect of your assessment of me is accurate. I don't do relationships. And it's for exactly this reason—I detest drama. I've had more than my fill courtesy of my sister. After one day here I've already been a party to more than I care to experience."

She sucked in a calming breath. *My God this conversation went sideways.* "Listen, I'm only here for a month and a half. I have no desire to get involved with anyone or do anything other than help Hon pack, then move and settle in, and then get the hell out of here. I have a life waiting for me. This is just—a thing I have to do. So while it would have been nice bumping uglies with you, Alexander Grace, this thing between us just isn't gonna happen. I suspect we'll run into each other—sort of hard to avoid it with you living on the *family compound*," Ross drawled. "But we can call this part of it done and dusted."

"Ross—please wait. I'm sorry. I don't know what possesses me to obliterate what is normally a highly functioning filter when I'm talking with you. This is the third time I've said the wrong thing, and the only thing I can say in my defense is that you have me all twisted up. You are the most incredible, singular woman I've ever known. And somehow with you, I keep managing to say all the wrong things. Look, I know I've royally fucked up again—"

"Yes. Yes, you have. And this time there was no blood flow to your loins to blame."

Acid burned in her throat, alongside an unwelcome note of regret. She really liked him, and had hoped he would be the antivenom to the deadly sting of this summer. Now, it was a premature fun-times death knell.

She inhaled a calming breath. "Next time you want to learn about a person, try asking her yourself instead of talking about her behind her back. Especially to people who know fucking nothing. And then mansplaining to her about herself as if you are some sort of expert in her psyche."

Ross's tone shifted to the brisk, no-nonsense one she used with writers who were behind on their revisions. "But honestly, Xander, it's for the best. I really don't need any complications. You are clearly a good guy, the last ten minutes notwithstanding, and a great fuck." She cringed at her cold assessment of their encounters. "But this ends here. Now, if you'll excuse me, this conversation is over. I've had a busy morning and still have a full afternoon ahead."

"Listen, Ross, for what it's worth—I really am sorry. I totally butted in where I didn't belong and then I just kept running on at the mouth. *Again*. I didn't mean to hurt or offend you. I understand why you're upset. Jesus. I wish I could have a do-over for this conversation. I feel like an ass."

"I accept your apology." Her affect was cold, but her heart beat against an unfamiliar ache around it.

Fuck him. Fuck this place. *Six weeks. Six weeks.* She repeated her mantra. Anyone could do anything for a short period of time, no matter how hard. She would stay here until Hon's move-in date. And then she was out of here. For good. It would be the last time she saw the farmhouse in her rearview mirror.

"Goodbye, Xander."

A loaded pause stretched across their phone connection.

"Goodbye, Ross."

As she disconnected the call, she could hear the regret in his voice. But the only thing she could feel was her heart hardening.

Ross snapped her laptop closed, not in the mood to think about Manhattan, and tried to force a nap. But the only thing she could hear was Xander's words echoing in her head. *I'd be a fool to pursue you…You don't do serious relationships…I wish I could have a do-over.*

Chapter Thirteen

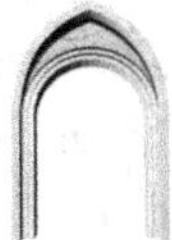

Ross

As they made headway in the formal living room, Ross sensed Hon casting not-so-subtle glances at her. She knew waves of anger and sadness were emanating off her, and she was powerless to stop it...even under the watchful gaze of her concerned grandmother. Ross was gentle with the packing, but every now and then she'd get lost in a thousand-yard stare, or give an angry sigh, and then resume packing with unnecessary fervor.

Hon and Ross were close, but there was an awkwardness to their relationship in Virginia. For two decades, their time together was based at Ross's rented condo in the suburbs between Baltimore and DC, Aunt Francesca's beach house in Delaware, and occasionally in New York, where Hon would sometimes visit Ross when she was there for work. She'd take Hon to Broadway shows during her brief, but regular stays at a corporate apartment owned by the publishing company that employed her. Or *had* employed her, until two weeks ago, when Ross officially left on a personal sabbatical that would fill her time until she began her new job.

Ross's sudden stillness captured Hon's eye, causing her to look up from her own packing. She could see Hon's wheels spinning, surely working up to addressing the elephant in the room.

Damnation, Ross thought. *I hope she doesn't ask...but I know she will.*

She tried to stall the inevitable by avoiding Hon's searching eyes, slipping into her own thoughts amidst the mind-numbing repetition of bubble wrapping and taping. Ross didn't show her emotions often. She wasn't one to lose her temper. It was a long fuse that, once lit, could smolder for a long time...until it ignited. Then the explosion was powerful. After, Ross would recede, emotions under tight control again, striving to convey a remote courtesy that ended any further argument.

Except for where Gaby was concerned, Ross conceded to herself. In her case, Ross was an ever-simmering tinder box and it didn't take much to set her off.

That seemed to be carrying over into her interactions with Xander. Only a few days here and she was already tangled in emotional complications, her final circle of hell.

A deep sigh from Hon brought Ross out of her musings. She looked up, catching a glimpse of them in the mirror. What a picture they made. Grandmother and granddaughter, motionless copies of each other, each lost in thought.

Hon squeezed her eyes closed for a moment, uttering her favorite expletive under her breath. "Damnation."

Ross knew time was up. *Here we go.*

"I'm sorry I made you come here." Like her granddaughter, Hon wasn't one to mince words.

Two sets of green eyes found each other and held. The only sound was the ticking of the grandfather clock. Hon's eyes filled with tears, a skill her own didn't possess.

"You don't owe me any apologies, Hon. I came of my own volition."

"You wouldn't have come if I hadn't applied a fair amount of Grandmother Guilt."

Ross's heart fractured at the rueful smile from Hon. She returned a brighter smile, eager to wipe the sadness off her grandmother's face.

"Hon, I love you. But even your special brand of coercion wouldn't have been necessary in this case. I'm honored to help you." She walked over and kissed a fragrant, wrinkled cheek, and then laughed. "You know what we used to call you when we were teenagers and you got all bossy with us?"

Hon quirked an inquiring eyebrow.

"Attila the Hon." Ross snorted, her signature goofy laugh bubbling up. "Get it? Hun-Hon?" She cracked up, snorting, with Hon joining in...sans snort.

"Oh, that awful laugh. So unladylike. I love that you still laugh that way." Hon wiped her eyes. "I didn't know you called me that! How did you keep that from me?"

"Oh, Hon. Come on. Give us a little credit! Besides, half the fun of getting older is telling your elders all the bad stuff you did when you were younger and a reprobate."

"Nice SAT word, Ross Ellen. Tiercy'd be proud. For the record, I don't know how proud I am to hear that my granddaughter was a reprobate," Hon scolded in mock recrimination. Soothed by the balm of shared amusement, they continued their work, the pensive mood broken.

This time it was Ross's turn to dive in. "But you knew about the creaking floorboards..." she led.

"Absolutely," Hon confirmed. "Now you give *me* a little credit. Your —what did you call us? *Elders*?—knew more than you give us credit for."

Now Ross was intrigued and relishing the banter with Hon. "For example?"

"For example, both Pop and I knew your preferred nocturnal escape route was your bedroom window to the latticework to the tree."

Ross burst into a startled laugh. "Really? You knew?"

"Mmhmm. So did your parents."

"My parents knew? Why didn't you all say anything? And you just let us get away with it?"

"Well, Adam and your Pop wanted to tan your hides. But your mom was more pacific and philosophical about it."

"Pacific. Nice SAT word, Hon," Ross murmured. She could have been knocked over by a feather. "Go on..." she urged.

"Your dad was the disciplinarian, as you know. But your mom wanted you to have wings. She believed you needed to have a certain amount of benign exploration. As a teacher, she saw kids—especially young ladies—whose parents were excessively strict. It was those girls who always went wild—got a taste of freedom and went too far."

"True," mused Ross, shocked. It wasn't often they spoke of Ivy and Adam, except with some of the favorite old stories that were safe and didn't evoke sadness or, God forbid, a quarrel between Gaby and Ross. Ross was ravenous for more. "Why have I never heard this? Tell me more," she encouraged.

"Ivy convinced your dad that watchful monitoring would be better. One memorable instance comes to mind. You were thirteen at the time. You and Tiercy went into town to see a movie. Your mom had told you no because it was PG-13, and she wanted to learn more about it first. But you kept insisting it was PG-13, and you were thirteen, and therefore you could see it."

Ross threw her head back and laughed. "I had no idea! I remember that movie. It's when I had my first kiss."

"I know," Hon revealed with a soft chuckle.

"You know?" Ross screeched. "How? Did Tiercy tell you? Or Gaby?" Ross struggled to say her sister's name without venom. She was still salty about Gaby talking about her to Xander.

"Your parents bought tickets and sat in the very back of the theater. I'm told you sat alone with a handsome young man. Your sister and Tiercy sat together on the other side of the theater."

"Tom," Ross offered, closing her eyes and smiling at the lost memory. "Tom... Oh crud, I can't remember his last name—Wait! They *saw* me with him?"

Hon nodded, a twinkle in her eye.

Ross put her head in her hands. "Oh my God. This is mortifying. My parents saw my first kiss? Noooo," Ross moaned with the melodrama of her past teen self.

"It's not just young people who enjoy revealing fun secrets from days gone by." Hon reached over and patted Ross's hand.

"I feel so *violated*. How is it possible to be dying of embarrassment so many years after something happened? Wilson! That's it. Tom

Wilson. He played hockey. He was a sophomore at the high school where Gaby ended up going for senior year."

Ross struggled to finish her sentence with a normal tone, thrusting away the memory of Gaby's school switch and the reason behind it. She narrowed her eyes. "What else did you know?" she accused.

"That you and Tiercy would sneak out a fair amount. That it was, by and large, innocuous. That as you got a little older, every now and then you'd experiment with beer, or even pot." Ross's eyes were so wide, she was sure they'd pop out of her head.

"Your dad didn't know all of that at first. But your mom did. And she told me. We'd discuss it, and she'd ask my advice about when she should intervene. She didn't want to tell your dad, because she was worried he'd go ballistic and ground you for the rest of your life. And then be mad at her for keeping it from him."

"What did you tell her?" Ross prodded, utterly fascinated. Here was another insight Ross had never imagined—her mother as a daughter, seeking advice from her own mother. Ross swallowed hard, thinking of all the times she'd wished for her own mother to confide in, to share a secret with, to just... have nearby.

"I told her to keep a close eye on you. Your mom would wait up. When she heard you come in, she'd sneak in. Make sure you were OK. She could tell you weren't drunk because you still managed to be relatively quiet—something you wouldn't have been able to do if you'd had too much to drink...or smoke."

Hon looked off in the distance. "That last summer was the first time she smelled pot on you. Your mom was cagey about these things. You and Tiercy were getting older. The nights out later. The hickeys visible." Her smiling eyes flicked to Ross's neck.

Damnation. Ross had forgotten about Xander's hickey. She flashed to their fight, and then shook it away. Later she'd process it all, probably with Tiercy.

"She'd decided to call Tiercy's parents. After all, Tiercy was her responsibility that summer. Your mom fessed up and told your dad, who was, as predicted, livid. And she called Tiercy's folks, who were concerned, but not as livid. Cathleen and Neal Flynn were such good friends to Ivy and Adam. The four of them talked on the phone and decided they'd conduct a sting."

"A sting?" Ross parroted, horrified. "What do you mean 'a sting'? Was snooping on my first kiss not enough?" Ross wasn't sure whether to laugh or be mad.

"Do you remember when your dad handed you, Gaby, and Tiercy each a bell at dinner that one night?"

"I do. It's a vivid memory. Pop was in his writing cottage. It was just us at dinner. I remember being all confused about why we each had a school bell in front of us."

"He told each of you to ring the bell, right?"

"And then he told each of us to unring it." Ross smiled at the memory of their confusion. Them all looking at each other, pretty sure her dad had lost it.

"And then he proceeded to tell you that you can never unring a bell. And some rung bells have serious consequences."

"I remember. So, the bell was the sting?"

"No. That was just a life message. That night, they followed you again. This time you went to a house—"

"I remember it. It belonged to a girl we'd met at the mall. We rode our bikes over to her house and just hung out. Her parents were away for the night. But she was kind of a goodie-goodie and only wanted to talk about Jesus and being saved." Ross rolled her eyes. "Tiercy faked being sick so we could leave. She even made up a sickness—we called it gastritis ignitis." Ross laughed at the memory. "That fake malady, as stupid as it sounded, saved Tiercy and me, even Gaby, from so many things we didn't want to do with other people. I can't believe anyone ever fell for it."

She swallowed, throat tightening at the fond memory of their long-ago hijinks. "OK...go on..." she urged, eager to move away from the direction her thoughts turned.

Hon smiled with knowing eyes and continued the story. "Your parents chalked that up to a close call. After that, they instituted the policy that you and Gaby could call them, anytime, if you'd been drinking or your driver had been drinking." Hon halted. They both knew this was moving into dangerous territory.

"I thought they were so dramatic about it. It was, as my sweet Jemma would say, 'cringe.'"

"So now you know." Hon pinned her with a classic grandmother look. "And some other time you can tell me all the other Big Reveals from your teen years." Hon turned back to her packing. "Attila the Hon," she muttered under her breath, laughing.

CHAPTER FOURTEEN

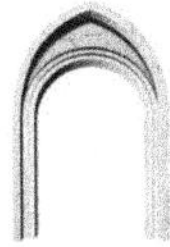

Ross

"I cannot believe your parents sneaked into the movie theater and saw you kiss Tom Wilson!" cackled Tiercy with unfettered glee.

"You are enjoying this way too much," Ross grumbled. "It's awful. I feel like my memory of kissing my very first Hottie McHot Pants has now been sullied." Hon had left for her church meeting and Ross was alone, soaking in the huge clawfoot tub, an exceptionally large glass of red wine nestled in her hand.

Tiercy snickered again and then sighed. "I don't even want to be anywhere near Jemma as a teen. She's already a handful. Good lord..."

"But we would be the best partners in a sting to catch her..."

"The *best*," Tiercy laughed. "Hey, if Hon is out for several hours, why are you calling me from a tub alone at the farmhouse? I figured you and Xander would be all in for some 'Netflix and chill.'"

Ross slugged a fortifying gulp of her wine. "First of all, you really need to stop picking up these euphemisms for hooking up from your students. Second, I didn't realize anyone used that terminology anymore, so be careful you don't quote a kid who isn't up to date on the lingo. Third, I regret to inform you that Professor Alexander Hottie

McHot Pants Grace is no longer in the picture. It's back to Chastity Summer for this girl."

"Not in the picture? What happened? Does he not floss? Bad vocabulary?"

"Hardee-har-har, Tierce. You are just a laugh riot." She slid further into the tub, lacy bubbles tickling her chin. "Worse, I haven't even come up with a good summer drink. I had to snag a bottle of red from Hon's wine rack."

"Seriously. What happened?"

"What happened is that nosy Xander got all up in my business. Apparently, he's been asking about me—to Cole, Hon, even my sister and Moose."

"Asking about you? That's so sweet. He digs you, Ross. And I mean, I hate to admit it, but I have been harboring a not-small hope that maybe you would become a couple. I know, I know," she hurried on, "you don't want any attachments. And Cole said Xander was still stinging from his divorce. But, c'mon. Just the idea of you two together appeals to my overdeveloped sense of romanticism."

Stinging from his divorce. Ross tucked that nugget away into her Xander File, all the while convincing herself it didn't matter because things were over...before they had barely begun. She forced herself back into the conversation. "Trust me, bestie. From the moment I arrived, I could see your wheels spinning all the way down here. You're all awash in marital bliss, and I figured you were hoping that Xander and I would get together as a couple. And then we'd be all cute with you and Cole, your bestie dating his bestie." Ross fake vomited, and smiled when she heard Tiercy's laughter in response.

"Guilty as charged," she admitted. "And I'm not sorry. Come on, Ross. What's not to like? He's hot, he's good in bed, he's funny, he's kind, he's an amazing dad, and he's loaded to the gills."

"He is?"

"Duh, Rocket Scientist. How can someone so smart be so oblivious? He bought a huge piece of property in Baltimore horse country and renovated it just as a side gig. He's a silent partner in the restaurant on site."

"That's right," breathed Ross, hitting her head with her hand. "The

Manchester Inn," Ross snickered. "The scene of the crime. Where Tiercy and Cole met and experienced simultaneous sexual combustion. And it also begs the question, if he is a Hottie Deep Pockets, why is he teaching, which you know better than I can be exhausting. I'd be relaxing and counting my investment dividends."

"No you wouldn't," Tiercy retorted playfully. "You'd want to keep busy, and I suspect Xander is the same. Now," she chastised in her don't-mess-with me teacher's voice, "stop trying to distract me. Finish telling me what happened already."

Ross sighed. "It's a long story, but it started with a booty call text for tonight—"

"Now who's using teenager slang," interjected Tiercy.

"That is *so* not teenager slang. It's a ubiquitous term for a very important type of assignation," Ross responded haughtily. "By the way, outstanding SAT word times two, me."

"Enough. Keep going. Spit it out."

"Instead of texting me back, he called me. And reminded me that he's a father of a young child—whom I've yet to meet by the way. He may be apocryphal for all I know. A cover story."

"Now *that's* a nice SAT word. But I can assure you that Petey is real. I've met him."

"You have? Tell me more."

"No. First you finish."

"Bitch."

"Strumpet."

"Hussy."

"Trollop."

"I love you," Ross sighed. "So, anyway, he told me he couldn't indulge my booty call because his son is there. Sidebar, I do feel like a fool that I forgot that rather major detail about him. And then he went on to preempt any dumping of him that I might do, saying that he knows I don't do relationships."

"Oooh..." breathed Tiercy. "And..."

"And then in an epic episode of verbal diarrhea, he proceeded to share everything he'd ever been told about me. Good, bad, and ugly."

"I knew it."

"You knew what?"

Ross shifted in the tub. She was getting overheated. Perhaps a sultry June night was not the best choice for a hot bath. She stood up, catching a glimpse of herself in the mirror, flushed from the heat, and huffed out a frustrated breath. She'd be the only one seeing her nakedness tonight.

"You knew what, Miss Know-it-All?" she asked again, reaching for her robe.

"That's *Mrs.* Know-it-All these days, please," Tiercy snickered. "I knew he has the hots for you. He never asked me about you when he came up during spring break, but I did catch him spending a rather long time looking at the group wedding photo. Now it's coming together. OK, girlie, what's the big deal? Is it that he has a son?"

"No!" Ross downed the last of her wine, clanking her stemless glass on the porcelain sink. "It's that—it's that he *assumed*. He made this assumption about me and he doesn't even know me. I just wanted to have some fun and he blew it!"

"Why are you so mad?"

"*Because*," Ross wailed. "Because he basically dumped me. And for no good reason. First, he made a point of telling me when I got here that he's not interested in anything serious. Which is a *good* thing. But then he just *expected* I would be turned off by the fact that he has a son. He went on to tell me all kinds of things he thinks he knows about me. And it was like he was all resigned to commitment-phobic Ross being shallow. It was just off-base and it was...not how I expected our conversation to go." Ross's rant lost its steam. "It hurt, Tierce. And I got mad."

Ross could hear Tiercy breathing quietly, doing her mom thing when she was collecting her thoughts.

"Hey, Ross, we both know you aren't shallow. I can see why what he said would hurt, because *I know you*. But, and don't kill me here, could you be overreacting just a touch? Xander *doesn't* know you. Yes, he was wrong because he made an assumption—that you don't hook up with guys who have kids. But, he did sincerely apologize. Right?"

Ross examined her empty glass, contemplating a generous refill. "Shit. I don't even know why I'm so pissed. Being here has me all messed up in my head. I'm not myself."

"It's not that, Rossie Ross." Tiercy gave a knowing laugh. "It's because it's a rare occurrence for Ross Ellen Beaufort to find herself made atwitter by a man."

"I'm hardly 'atwitter,' Tiercy."

"You're pissed. You said it yourself. And you haven't stopped talking about him. Here you are back in the farmhouse and facing a ton of memories, and all you really want to talk about... is Xander."

Tiercy was right, as usual. Ross was a ball of atypical feelings. But in this case, it was less about being at the farmhouse and around her sister than Xander hearing anything about her that might be damning. She knew she overreacted—which was embarrassing—and she didn't want him thinking poorly of her. But Ross certainly didn't trust Gaby and Moose—who were apparently his BFFs down here—to paint a flattering picture. She and Xander weren't really anything to each other, except spicy bedmates. Still, his opinion of her mattered to her, more than she really wanted to admit. Yep, she was definitely atwitter over Xander.

Ross let out a long sigh of capitulation. "You're a pain in the ass."

"Or maybe I'm the only person who will stand up to you and tell you what you don't want to hear."

"And what is that, Oracle of My Life?"

"You wish I were," Tiercy teased. "But look, instead of being all mad, just prove him wrong. You said you don't want a relationship, but that you were enjoying being with him. So do that. Show him that he was wrong about you. Show him that you respect his relationship with his son. And that you can give him the space to be a great dad and still rock his world in bed. And, voilà, you don't have to suffer through Chastity Summer." Tiercy delivered this last part like the pièce de résistance.

Ross absorbed and then conceded her friend's good point. "When did you get so freaking wise?"

"Since I've been an old married lady. I now have the super-secret decoder ring for relationship wisdom," Tiercy intoned.

"I don't want to be in a *relationship* with Xander. And he doesn't want one either."

"I stand corrected. You are merely extending the rehearsal dinner cliché for six more weeks."

"Precisely. But I'm still pissed."

"Get over it."

"I will. But only because he's spectacular in bed and I'm counting on that to counterbalance the hell of my sister. And I'm not calling him tonight. That feels pathetic."

"Then what will you do tonight?"

"Probably finish this bottle of wine. Binge something on Netflix. And then go to bed. I was up *veeery* late last night," she goaded.

"Goodnight, hussy. Love you."

"Goodnight, hooker hips. Love you too. Thanks for talking me off the ledge."

"Anytime."

Chapter Fifteen

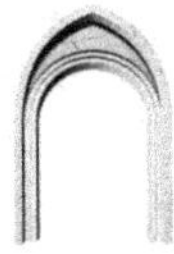

Xander

"Daddy, did I have a lot of corn last night?" Petey Grace called from the bathroom. "There's a bunch in my poo."

"Peter Anthony Grace, that's revolting," responded Xander, shaking his head and trying not to laugh. "First of all, why would you announce that? Secondly, how would I know? You were at your friend's house."

"Nick Monroe says that when you have corn, your body can't agest it and so you poop it out," Petey declared as he exited the bathroom.

"One, wash your hands. Two 'digest' not 'agest.' And three, close the door. Those are some noxious fumes."

"Yessir." Petey headed back into the bathroom, cackling with the glee of a young boy around potty humor. In addition to little factoids about corn, at least his son was picking up some decent manners from the Monroe kids. He heard the water run and then shut off.

Petey scurried back into the room buoyed by the boundless energy of a six-year-old. Xander caught a whiff of Petey's children's shampoo from his shower and inhaled deeply. He regarded his son, who was yanking at the Power Rangers pajama shorts that had twisted around his waist, and gently adjusted the pants for him, a powerful love coursing through him.

He never imagined fatherhood this way, single parenting in a rented cottage. Xan had many regrets in his life, but Petey was not one of them.

He sat and patted the cushion next to him and Petey climbed on, snuggling against his dad. "What're we watching?"

"A little baseball."

"Excellent," Petey intoned and Xander had to smile at the inflection. He was becoming a mini-Nick.

Xander swigged his beer and tried to concentrate on the game. Hard to believe it was a little less than twenty-four hours since he had his fingers inside Ross. They twitched on his bottle at the memory. Now that had all been put on ice. Thanks to him opening his big mouth. A-fucking-gain.

"You and I both had late nights last night, buddy. We'll watch a bit and then hit the hay."

Petey cocked his blond head, the towheaded hue an exact replica of Xan at the same age. In fact, his mother often commented that Petey was a clone of him. Same hair. Same brown-sugar eyes, as his mother would say in a show of rare affection. Same build as when he himself was a kid. Xander frowned.

There was very little of Aubrey in him, thank God. Sometimes he'd see it in the set of Petey's chin, or in the mutinous look Petey would deliver if Xander issued some directive that didn't sit well with him. Aubrey hated to be challenged. And she'd hated being a mom. At least that's what she said in her note four years ago. *I'm just not cut out for this, Alexander. I never wanted this.*

Xander shook his head. How could a mother leave her child? Especially Petey, who at this moment was studying his father, with the sweet tilt to his head that usually signaled an onslaught of questions from his curious boy.

"What did you do last night, Daddy? Hang out with Mr. Ted and play cards?"

Probably best not to lie. Ted would cover for him, but he wasn't sure he wanted to tell his friend that he messed around with his wife's sister, even if he did suspect after the post-dinner flirting. Especially given the estrangement between the sisters. "Just hung out with a new friend I made. We had a good time." Understatement of the century.

"Someone from your job? I thought you said you weren't teaching this summer, Daddy?"

"I'm not, buddy. I have the summer off. No, it was Hon's granddaughter."

"Ms. Gaby?" Pete perked up. He had a serious little kid crush on Gaby Monroe.

"No, not Ms. Gaby. Her sister."

"She has a sister? Why haven't I met her?"

"Ross doesn't live around here. She actually lives near Uncle Cole."

"Why does she have a boy's name?" Petey scrunched up his nose, an endearing habit that melted Xander's heart. No one prepared him for the fierce love for his son that brimmed far past the mortal confines of his heart, and it made Aubrey's desertion even more inexplicable to him.

"You know what? I've never actually thought about that. But names are names. They don't have genders."

Petey nodded, even if the topic of androgynous naming likely went over his head. "You should ask her. Is she your girlfriend?" Petey's brown eyes were trained on him. The problem with an only child raised by his father, with his childhood largely spent around other adults, is that they became preternaturally aware of things. "Do you like her?"

"Peter! That isn't any of your business. And, no, she isn't my girlfriend. She's just...someone I met once. At Aunt Tiercy and Uncle Cole's wedding. She's Jemma's godmother."

At Jemma's name, his son beamed. Gaby wasn't the only one Petey seemed to have a crush on. During their spring break visit to the Colburns, Petey and Jemma had hit it off. At one point, Xander joked about a dowry to Cole and Tiercy. Cole had shot him a quelling look and, in true girl-dad fashion, joked with Xander that if the apple fell anywhere near the tree, he would never allow his daughter to date Xander's son. Xander pretended to be shocked. But what he most remembered about that was how heartwarmed he was when Cole referred to Jemma as his daughter.

Jemma was the biological daughter of Tiercy's first husband, Luke, who had died of a thoracic aneurysm years before. It wasn't until after

Luke's death that Tiercy had learned she was pregnant. She'd raised Jemma alone, with abundant, loving help from her parents. And from Ross. Tiercy and Cole met and fell in love. And the rest was history. Xander had never seen his friend so happy.

"When will we see Jemma again, Daddy?"

Petey's question nudged Xander from his ruminations. "Soon buddy. Maybe we'll go up and visit later this summer. I'll talk to Uncle Cole."

"Is she pretty? Is she nice?"

"Who, Jemma? You know she's very nice and, yes, pretty."

"No, Daddy," Petey sighed, clearly impatient with his father's cluelessness. "I know *Jemma's* nice. Ross. Is she pretty...and nice?" There was a tiny frown between his little winged eyebrows.

Xander opened his mouth, pondered a moment, and decided on the truth. "She's very nice, and gorgeous. Honestly, she's the most gorgeous woman I've ever seen—inside and out. She has a really big heart."

"You've seen her insides and her heart?" Petey looked aghast, and somewhat grossed out, clearly not comprehending what Xander was saying.

He coughed to cover his laugh. "Not technically. It just means she's a really good person. Loving. She takes care of the people she loves, and she feels things deeply. And...she's beautiful too."

Xander slumped back against the couch, shocked all that had come out of his mouth, especially in front of his impressionable son. He was even more shocked to realize he truly meant it. Ross was knock-your-socks-off stunning. That long dark hair with streaks of gold. Those green eyes. Sexy, lithe body with a juicy little ass he longed to bury his dick in.

But there was something warm and fabulous about her, too. Her goofy, uninhibited laugh. Her genuine smile. The way she was with her grandmother at dinner, teasing and tender at the same time. Her obvious affection for her nieces and nephew—which surprised him based on what he'd been told.

In frustratingly clear hindsight, he clearly should have stopped listening to others and let Ross, who was more than capable, speak for herself. *Fucking hell.* Because what he did know by his own observation was that she was a fierce protector of those she loved. Christ. It wasn't just Petey who was crushing on a Beaufort sister. And reflecting on all this made him feel even lower for what he said and assumed.

"Does she like kids?" Petey's eyes were wide.

Xander paused, regret coursing through him for his wrong assumptions. "Yes, I think she does. She adores Jemma, and she's really good with Nick, Kingsley, and Tara."

"Wow," Petey responded, clearly impressed, the little wrinkle between his brow now gone. "So you do liiike her, don't you?" he sing-songed with a goading, gap-toothed grin.

Good God, the smack talk starts young. "Peter Anthony, I am not going to answer your question. That's personal." Then, falling back on the time-honored parental exit clause, he announced, "Now, it's late. Time for bed."

He ushered his son into the second bedroom. When the cottage was built, they had put in two rooms, a bedroom and a second smaller room for writing. It was the latter room that was now Petey's, furnished with a twin bed, a bookshelf, a nightstand with a Star Wars lamp, and a pile of sports gear. The bathroom was situated between Petey's room and Xander's, which was larger, big enough for the king-size bed he'd bought, with room left over for his own chest of drawers and an overstuffed chair and ottoman. The rest of the place was just as cozy. A great room with a stone fireplace encompassed the living room, dining room, and kitchen. It wasn't much, but Xander loved the lines of it.

Moonlight filtered in through the window as Xander leaned down and brushed a kiss on his son's forehead, smoothing back the mop-top light blond hair. He'd need a haircut soon, Xander mused. His heart expanded with love. It wasn't a perfect life, but it was a good life. And he loved his son. "Goodnight, moon."

"Goodnight cow jumping over the moon," Petey yawned as he responded in their bedtime routine.

"Hey, Daddy?" Petey whispered as Xander was closing the door. "You like her, right?"

Xander broke into a dimpled grin at his son's unexpected, audacious question. Once again, he decided on the truth. "Yes, buddy. Yes, I do."

After closing the door, he flopped on the couch. A burst of

adrenaline, and shame at his fight with Ross, had him reaching for the phone. He needed advice on Ross, and texted the person he knew would guide him like the True North she was.

XANDER

Sorry to text after 8:30, but I'm pretty sure you DND your cell at night since I'm the one who taught you how to do it. Can we talk tomorrow? I need your sage counsel.

Xander hit send and put his phone down, rubbing his hand down his face in exhaustion.

CHAPTER SIXTEEN

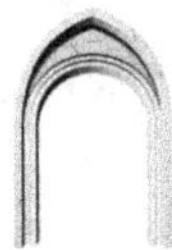

XANDER

Xander was surprised when his phone buzzed almost immediately with an incoming call.

"Hi. Sorry for the late text." He kept his voice low. Even though Petey usually slept like a rock, he didn't want to risk disturbing him... or having Petey overhear this conversation.

"It's no problem," Leah replied, her voice much more energetic than his. Clearly he hadn't woken her. "I did some more packing tonight. Got on a roll. And I had some church work to do. I was just winding down when your text came through."

Leah paused, and Xander figured Leah—with her uncanny prescience—likely knew why he was calling. Maybe not all of it, but certainly the subject.

"Let me guess," she continued. "Does this call have something to do with the reason my granddaughter spent the day morose, cranky, and at times bitchy?"

Xander couldn't contain his bark of laughter. He glanced at Petey's door. Still quiet. "You are amazing, Leah." Xan shook his head. "Does anything get past you?"

"At the age of seventy-nine, and having seen a lot in my time... not often, no," Leah confirmed. "But even though I don't get to see her as much as I'd like, I'm something of an expert in Ross. You see"—Leah's voice turned sad—"she is so much like her mother. Sometimes I feel as though I get a tiny bit of Ivy back every time I'm with Ross."

"Oh, Leah. I'm so sorry."

"I am as well. But that's not why you called." Leah had harnessed the sadness in her voice and was back to business. Xander had so much respect and affection for her. In many ways, she'd become a grandmother to him as well.

"No. I called because—and it's entirely my fault, let me say that upfront—Ross is mad at me for some things I said on the phone this morning."

"What sort of things?"

Xander sighed. "Look, without oversharing that's uncomfortable for both of us—"

"Thank you for that," Hon interrupted with a chuckle.

"You're welcome." Xan smiled, feeling a bit better. Leah had that effect on a person. "Let's just say that I really like Ross, and I've been looking forward to spending time with her this summer."

"You don't say," Hon muttered.

Xander chose to ignore that and continued, "I was under the misconception that Ross wouldn't be interested in hanging out, since I have"—he again checked the bedroom door—"Petey. It's a lot to ask someone."

"Oh, Alexander," Leah chided. "Now it makes sense. Ross loves kids."

"I know that," he replied miserably. *How had he been such an off-base ass?*

"But I'm thinking there's more to this than that."

"There is. I've been... ugh... sort of hanging on to every snippet that I've managed to learn about Ross. I... oh, hell. I'm just saying it. I have a crush on your granddaughter, and have for a while. So it's made me a bit... hungry, you could say... for any little morsel about her that people share."

"Xander, there isn't anything wrong with that."

"There is when you pretty much spew out everything you've ever learned about someone—on top of that other wrong-headed notion—and basically alienate the girl you've been thinking about nonstop for almost a year." Xander's eyes widened. He hadn't expected to admit quite that much.

"Oh, dear. Well, as they say, the course of true love never did run smooth. You can get past this."

Xander choked on his saliva. "I didn't—we don't—this isn't a love situation, Leah."

She snorted, and he chose to ignore that, too.

"It's that I like her a lot and I'm not sure how to fix this. I've been a miserable jerk all day. I almost went over there so many times to apologize in person, but I wasn't sure if she was ready to hear it. Or if she'd even believe me. She's amazing, Leah. And I want her to know I feel that way. That I respect and admire her."

"Well, my goodness. I think you do know her pretty well. She doesn't have much of a temper, but when it blows, it's best to give her time to get back into her wise mind. But she'll get there. Especially if she feels about you the way I think she does."

Xander was intrigued, and hungry for more of Leah's insight. But he left that statement alone. He wasn't ready to take all that in.

"There's more. I think she's upset that I'm friends with Ted and Gaby. It really bothers her. But I can't give up my friendships, even though it may be loaded for Ross." He dropped his head into one hand. "This is probably pointless."

Hon tutted. "No, Alexander. It's not pointless or hopeless. Ross Ellen has a tremendous capacity for forgiveness, she just hasn't tapped it yet. But I know her like I know my own heart, and when she loves, she loves big. That means that when she hurts, she also hurts big. But I see the forgiveness in her. She wants to let it out. She's just... stuck." Leah sucked in a breath. "Oh... I am sorry. I may have turned this conversation away from your tiff and made it about—"

"Ross and Gaby."

"Yes," Leah admitted. "I feel so selfish bringing Ross home to the farmhouse. But, damnation, it's just so good to have her here. In some ways, it's jarring to see her here at this age. She's just a handful of years younger than Ivy was when I had to do the most horrible thing a parent ever has to face—burying your child. Ross's resemblance to her mother always takes me by surprise. I wonder if Ross even realizes how much she favors her mother. She lost her so young."

Xander heard Leah's quiet sob and gave her grief space. After a moment, when her sniffles ceased, he took a deep breath and crossed the bridge he'd never broached before. "Leah," he began, "I, uh, I know about the night Ivy and Adam died." He paused. "All of it."

Leah gasped. "How? When?"

"A little bit of Ted. A lot of Gaby."

He waited. Leah was silent for long moments on the other end. He tried to imagine those green eyes, staring into the painful memory from long ago.

Eventually, he heard her shuffle around. From the sounds, she was taking a sip of something. Then she cleared her throat. And then again. God, how much pain was he going to cause in one day?

"Leah... I'm sorry. I shouldn't have brought it up. Here I was calling you for advice, and now I've upset you—"

"No, Alexander. You haven't upset me at all. All my emotions are right under the surface these days. Between the move, and saying goodbye to my home—even though I know it's time—and having Ross back here, it's just...a lot. But, honestly, I'm glad you said something. I'm glad you know. Even my sister, Frannie, doesn't know everything, so there really isn't anyone I've been able to talk with. Well, except for a therapist many years ago, and my priest. You know, it speaks volumes of your character that Gaby confided in you."

"I'm honored that she trusted me enough to share. And I'll protect that. Even—"

"Even at the expense of Ross? Keeping her in the dark?"

Xander was stunned into silence.

Leah gave a rueful chuckle. "And now you get it...the rock and hard place I've lived between for two decades."

"Jesus, Leah. What a burden."

"Oh, don't feel too sorry for me," Leah replied. "Some of this—a good bit of it—is my fault. I can't tell you how many times I've berated myself for letting this estrangement between Ross and Gaby fester for so long. The truth of that night years ago is the root of the deep hurt suffered by both those girls. And I mishandled it."

"Leah, you need to give yourself some grace... no pun intended."

Leah laughed. "You are too kind...and funny. I can see why Ross is drawn to you."

She was quiet again for a moment, her muffled sobs breaking his heart over the phone. If Petey weren't in bed, he'd run over to the house so he could hold her. Instead, he tried to hug her with his words, his support.

"Tell me, Leah. Tell me about it. Your perspective. And maybe I can help?"

Leah heaved a deep breath, her lips motoring from the air. Xander wasn't sure if she would share, but then she began in a voice so low he had to strain to hear her.

"I was devastated. I'd just buried my only child and her husband, who was like a son to me. The whole thing was just...an emotional maelstrom. I couldn't see my way through it. At first Ross was so raw. She had disappeared inside of herself, doing the thing where she goes into her protective shell. I couldn't blame her for that, but I also didn't know how to reach her. She was a lost soul, and the only way her grief would emerge was in ferocious anger directed toward her sister.

"And Gaby...oh, she was a wreck. I was truly fearful of losing her altogether. She was one breakdown away from complete collapse—the one-two punch of that night too much for her, or really anyone, to bear. For quite some time, I truly feared the eviscerating edge of Ross's wrath would be the knock-out blow for Gaby. Frederick pleaded with me to just *tell* Ross everything, but I was so afraid Ross would blame Gaby and hate her forever...Except it happened anyway," she added on a whisper.

"Oh, Leah."

"Burying my daughter is the chief sorrow of my life, even more so than losing Frederick. But this...antipathy...between the girls is my chief regret. Because it's my fault."

"It's not—"

"Over the years, I tried to find a time...a way...to talk to them," she continued, as if he hadn't spoken. Xander wondered if she was so lost in her sorrow that she didn't even hear him. "But I was a coward."

"Even the most courageous heart falters at inflicting soul-wrenching pain."

"I'm not courageous. I have failed my daughter. And now I don't know how to fix this rift. Or if it even can be fixed at this point."

"Leah, you said yourself that Ross has a tremendous capacity for forgiveness. She has a huge heart. It's just a bit battle-scarred. And she's stubborn to boot. But I believe in all three of you. You need to tell Ross the whole story."

"I know you're right. But not yet. I think she's still reeling from her re-entry into Waldheim orbit. But soon, Alexander. Soon. This has gone on too long."

"How can I help?"

"You just did, dear boy. And, now, I'm going to return the favor and help you."

Xander smiled. His respect for Leah, already manyfold, grew even more in that conversation. "What do you have in mind?"

"Well, if you'll indulge an old woman who just wants her girls to be happy, truly happy—"

"I don't know any old women. Just a sassy, spectacular, amazing lady."

"Gah... enough with that. Save your flirting for Ross. You're going to need it. Now, to fix this little pickle," she announced, all brisk business, "how do you feel about pizza tomorrow?"

Xander grinned as he listened to Leah's plan.

CHAPTER SEVENTEEN

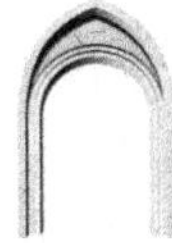

Ross

The next morning, Ross shuffled into the kitchen, feeling like a grouchy bear awakened too soon from hibernation. Hon, observing her disquiet, kept a safe distance, particularly when she shared that Gaby would be joining them around nine thirty. Together, they would identify the non-sentimental items in the basement that could go to Goodwill.

Ross, still cranky from her unsatisfying interaction with Xander the day before, the thwarted booty call, and a thudding red wine hangover, tried to mumble something vaguely intelligible into her Orioles coffee cup, which was full to the brim out of necessity.

Hon fixed perceptive green eyes on her granddaughter, fetched something from a cabinet, and placed three ibuprofen in front of her along with a tall glass of ice water.

Said granddaughter rewarded her with a small smile summoned from the last dregs of her absent manners.

"That's better. A tiny sign of humanity from my precious granddaughter."

Hon dropped a kiss on Ross's hair, which she knew was snarled and going every which way. It just seemed like too much trouble to fix it this crappy morning. She sighed at the soothing sensation of Hon smoothing it between gnarled fingers.

"I saw the empty bottle in the recycling. Did you kill that alone?"

"It seemed like a good idea at the time." Ross shrugged, trying to shake off her mood. "Once the coffee and ibuprofen kick in, I'll be good as new."

"Good. Because I'd like to put a serious dent in that basement today."

"Aye-aye, Atilla." Ross offered a half-hearted salute. "Let me go upstairs and scrape myself together. I'll be back down soon."

After a shower, which marginally helped her mood, Ross glared with resignation into the bathroom mirror, girding herself for the day ahead. "Check yourself before you wreck yourself, Beaufort. It's gonna be a long six weeks if you don't get your shit together."

Ross sighed. A day of packing with her sister. *Wonderful.*

She stared again in the mirror, reminded of the story 'Bloody Mary,' which used to freak her and Tiercy out when they were young. (OK, Ross had to admit, it still sort of freaked her out.) To summon the evil otherworldly entity, you stare in the mirror and repeat the name five times.

Ross narrowed her eyes. "Gaby. Gaby. Gaby. Gaby. Gaby."

The doorbell rang, and moments later, she heard her sister greet Hon.

"Damnation. It worked. I've summoned the demon. Now I'll never be rid of her."

All things considered, a morning with the summoned demon wasn't horrible. The three women moved with efficiency through decades of items, generally agreeing on what needed to go. Occasionally, Gaby would request something for herself, a gesture Ross avoided. When this was over, she was walking (well, driving) away, and she didn't need items from the past dragging her down.

It was tedious work, but productive. Ross had pulled her hair into a ponytail and stripped down to her sports bra. Gaby and Hon both had on sleeveless shirts and shorts. By rare stalwart granddaughter agreement, Hon's work was accomplished seated, though she complained about not being decrepit, a mutinous set to her jaw. Still, all were sweaty and moving quickly toward needing a break.

Her stomach growling loudly, Ross glanced at her watch—1 p.m.—and, as her stomach emitted another loud grumble, announced "I'm hungry. Verging on hangry."

"Me too." Gaby rolled her head, small little pops sounding. "We've kicked butt down here. I'm glad Theresa offered to watch the kids. I can't imagine trying to get anything done with hell's angels underfoot."

"She's a good friend to you." Hon came up behind Gaby and rubbed her neck.

Ross watched and tried to ignore a twinge of jealousy. As nice as things had been in the forty-eight hours she'd spent with Hon, there was just an easy way between Hon and Gaby that was the byproduct of sharing more of their daily existence.

Her stomach growled again. "OK. I'm going to need to feed the beast. Please tell me you have more of that curry chicken salad, Hon."

"Actually, lunch should be here any minute. Your timing is perfect. Let's head up."

"You ordered something?" Ross was pretty sure she hadn't seen or heard Hon on the phone.

"Pre-arranged. I offered food for service."

Ross and Gaby exchanged perplexed looks.

Ten minutes later they heard a banging at the kitchen door. Ross smelled the pizza before she saw the delivery guy. "Hallelujah and praise the sweet baby Jesus! Greasy, cheesy, wonderful food." She opened the door and was rewarded with a view of pizza boxes, framed below a gorgeous set of dimples in a handsome face.

"Did someone here order some pizza?"

Ross wasn't sure if she was happier to see Xander or the pizza. Currently the pizza was winning.

"What are you doing here?"

"You keep asking me that. At least this time you didn't say 'what the ever-loving fuck' am I doing here." Xander placed the pizza boxes on the table. "Progress." He waggled his brows, dimples firing, which always caused a fluttering in her lady garden.

"Alexander. Language," Hon reprimanded.

"Yes, ma'am. Sorry." Xander lowered his head penitently and took that opportunity to toss Ross a quick wink. "I brought you your pizza as requested, and I offer you my manly muscles for as long as you need them this afternoon."

Ross recovered her equilibrium as the four of them settled around the table. "So, side job as a pizza guy? Professor work not as lucrative as you thought?"

"Summer break," Xander noted. "Today, I like to think of myself as the Uber Eats of the Waldheim Estates."

Ross folded a slice in half and devoured it. "God this is amazing," she moaned, mouth full. "I'm so esurient I could eat this entire box of pizza."

Xander raised his eyebrows. "I'd give you a hard time, except I have no idea what that word means."

"Hungry," Gaby clarified, with a pronounced roll of her eyes. "She can't just use normal-people words."

Xander mouthed the word.

Ross grinned, dabbing her lips before reaching for a second slice. Her hand bumped Xander's in the box, and a charge zapped through her as their gazes collided. He pulled his hand away, motioning for her to take the slice, and she tuned in to Hon, who apparently was mid-explanation.

"...and Alexander was kind enough to offer to help bring up some of the furniture we're donating. He's going to take it to the donation center for me. I can't lift it, and Gaby certainly can't, so Ross, I'm hoping you and Alexander can do it."

Gaby paused, a pizza slice partway to her mouth. "Bad back," she said, not meeting Ross's eyes. Gaby and Xander made brief eye contact and she flushed a bit, offering a wan smile.

What's all this? Ross's antenna went up. She'd bet her favorite

Manolos that Gaby didn't have a bad back. She'd get it out of Xan later. She smiled privately. The idea of *Xander* and *later* held a lot of appeal for her. Except...damn. They'd ended it. *She'd* ended it. Fuck. Time to listen to Tiercy and fix it.

"No problem," Xander jumped in. "Xan Xan the Macho Man has it covered, along with my able-bodied assistant, Ross."

Ross turned toward him, incredulous. *"Xan Xan the Macho Man?* You can't be serious."

"No? Not feeling it?" He sighed. "That was going to be my Marvel name."

"Mmmm...no. Captain America." It was out of her mouth before Ross even realized she said it.

Everyone looked at her.

"I mean, speaking of Marvel. Captain America. Chris Evans. He's my favorite," she explained. Hurrying on to cover her slip, she added, "I mean, if he were here, I'd have to excuse myself...and him. To, you know, do Avenger things." Ross shoved another bite of pizza in her mouth before she could insert her foot any further.

"Mee-ow," purred Gaby in appreciative agreement of Evans' physical attributes and Ross acknowledged an unexpected, long lost note of warmth for her sister. "Sometimes Ted and I watch Marvel movies as foreplay, and my little eggies explode like popcorn kernels at those scrumptious men." Gaby grinned wickedly as Ross busted out laughing.

Hon choked on her drink. "Oh, dear God," she gasped, when she could catch her breath. "I'm never getting popcorn at the movies again."

"Too much, Hon?" Gaby laughed.

"Definitely. File that under things a grandmother does not need to know."

Still laughing, Ross shifted her attention and narrowed her gaze at a red-eared Xander, who was pretending to be absorbed in his slice of pizza. "And for the record, Alexander Grace, you can be *my* assistant, not the other way."

Xander's eyes swung up to her and she refused to look away. Ross was acutely aware of the pull of his sexy presence right across from her, his cheeks and ear tips still adorably flushed with embarrassment from the conversation detour. She was also acutely aware that she had spent the morning sweating in Hon's basement. She wondered if she could subtly sniff her armpits to ensure she wasn't offensively odiferous.

"Anything you say, ma'am." He winked, and...speaking of popping ova...it was like Orville Redenbachers in her lower belly. Now it was Ross's turn to become fascinated by pizza.

Following Gaby's hilarious overshare, the four engaged in casual chatter as they finished lunch. Eventually, Gaby excused herself, stepping out on the back porch to call her best friend and check on the kids.

She popped in a few moments later. "They're doing great. Xan, Petey is with them now, too. Your nanny brought him to Theresa's. Hon, I need to go over to the house and let Laverne out and put something in the crockpot for dinner. I'll be a little bit."

"I'll come help you. I could use a stretch of the legs."

Ross caught a quick look between Hon and Xan. And possibly a wink...from Hon this time.

"You sure? I just need to throw in some meat and veggies."

"We'll be back in a bit." Hon kissed Ross's head and followed Gaby out the door.

CHAPTER EIGHTEEN

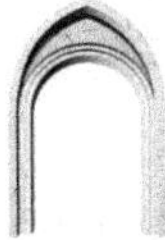

Ross

Xander looked across the table and made meaningful eye contact with Ross, who jumped up like a skittish foal. She scurried to the door, calling out, "Just going to run upstairs for a minute. Be right back."

Chickenshit, she reprimanded herself.

Hurrying into her bathroom, she examined herself in the mirror. *Ack*. She was sweaty, and her hair was coming out of its ponytail in several places. Lovely.

She turned on the shower and returned to the bedroom, stripping out of her clothes. As she struggled with her perspiration-saturated sports bra, she heard a knock on her door. "These are fucking torture devices," she muttered to herself, contorting to get it over her head. Thinking it was Gaby needing something, she grabbed her nearby robe. "Come in."

"I remember that robe."

Ross gasped and backed up as Xander came into the room and closed the door, his gaze roaming over her.

"What the—"

"Ever-loving fuck am I doing here?" Xander finished. "At the moment, I'm watching a gorgeous woman who can drive me to distraction, even eating pizza. But very soon, I'm going to be touching her." He stalked toward her like a blond panther, eyes intent.

"You—you can't be here. Gaby and Hon will be right back. They'll wonder where you went."

Xander responded in a deep, husky rasp. "I think we have a little time."

Ross cocked her head at him, wondering how he could be so sure. But then he was leaning in, doing that thing with his lips along her neck that heated up her insides.

What were we talking about anyway?

"I don't want to disrespect Hon, or you. But you went upstairs, and the next thing I knew...I was outside your door." He reached down and trailed his fingers along the tie of her robe. "Do you want me to leave?"

"No." Her response came out hoarse, and without hesitation, and she cleared her throat.

"Then we'll have to be expeditious...and quiet." He grazed kisses toward her mouth.

Ross put her hand out, whether to stop him or balance herself, she wasn't quite sure. "Wait just a second. I'm still mad at you."

"No, you aren't." Xander shifted closer, and Ross backed away until she was up against the bed. "You were mad, but you're over it."

"How do you know?" Ross was annoyed to find that her voice shook a bit, both with nerves and with something more primal. Wanting.

"Because if you were still mad, you wouldn't have been making goo-goo eyes at me at lunch."

"Goo-goo—! I was doing no such thing," Ross sputtered.

"Sssh. Yes, you were," Xander confirmed, leaning in to run his lips across the other side of her neck. "Mmmm...salty."

"Just a second." Ross pulled herself together. "One, I was not making goo-goo eyes. Two, Xan? You called yourself Xan earlier, and so did my sister. Do you prefer Xander or Xan? Three, I'm down for a quickie. But I need to make something clear."

"One, I maintain my goo-goo eyes stance." He sucked a bared

nipple and she gasped in pleasure as want surged between her legs. "Two, I go by Xander and Xan. Some of my friends shorten it to Xan. Plus, Xander Xander the Macho Mander would have sounded stupid." Xander smiled at the low husk of her laugh. "Three, Ross, I'm going to be honest. You can call me anything you want right now, as long as we hurry this conversation." Xan stroked his fingers where she hoped his cock meant to head shortly. "And four, clarity is always good. But please...hurry." He pressed up against her, letting her feel his urgency.

"I don't care if you have a son." Ross stopped, breathless and rendered somewhat senseless at his ministrations, and shook her head to clear it. "That came out wrong. What I mean is, it's fine that you have a son. And I don't mind working around that. I'm not interested in anything serious. I like being with you Xan-Xander, and your son is not an obstacle to that. So, you can officially un-dump me as your cliché buddy." She said the last with a sultry smile as she reached for the part of him that was straining toward her, and pushed down his shorts. "God, I love your treasure trail."

Xander sucked air between his teeth as her hand drifted down said trail, and then encircled him with a tight hold. She'd learned quickly how he liked his cock worked.

Xander managed to respond. "I didn't dump you. I was just letting you know I understood if you did mind. I *would* have been disappointed...because I dig getting naked with you, Ross. And for the record, once again, I'm not interested in anything serious either. Thus, we're good."

His hands were roaming all over her, pushing down her robe. Suddenly, he swept down and lifted Ross into his arms, placing her on the bed and easing on top of her. She wrapped her legs around his hips and tilted up as his glorious cock—long, thick, and very hard—bounced temptingly against her lower belly.

Holding his gaze with her own, she reached between them and worked his length, twisting her wrist at the very end of each tug. "Thus...we are indeed."

"Are you sure?" Xander whispered, his voice clogged.

"Absofuckinglutely," Ross murmured against his lips as she pressed against him, feeling the power of his arousal between the vee of her legs. "Wait...I stink. I need a shower."

He ran his nose along her neck. "You smell like fucking heaven to me, and in a bit, you're going to smell like sex."

"Fuck," Ross breathed. "I need you inside me. Now." She arched against him, the head of him nudging at her aching pussy.

Xander growled. In one fluid motion, he was sheathed in protection he'd grabbed from his pocket and then, at last, sheathed so deep in her that she gasped.

"You feel so incredible, Xan." Ross lifted her hips, urging him on with her own frenetic pace. Again and again, he slammed into her, an inexorable slapping of tender, aroused flesh. He was so deep inside her, and the sensation of building quickly toward a powerful explosion had her breathless and tightening all her muscles, fully focused on that one glorious knife's edge. Together they rose higher, harder, faster, until she clenched around him in deep spasms, followed by a gush of her arousal.

"Fucking hell, Ross. That's. So. Fucking. Hot." His words were punctuated by each powerful thrust. "You. Fucking. Squirted. On. My. Cock." He gave into his own climax with a deep growl, rearing back and pounding so hard she saw spots of glorious agony, before he collapsed to her side and pulled her onto his chest.

She could hear his heart racing. Xander began tracing lazy circles around the breast near his free hand. He nudged her onto her back and leaned over, sucking her nipple and causing a new wave of arousal. She couldn't stop smiling, twisting his hair in her fingers, just as she'd done at the cottage.

Xander rolled off and leaned on his elbow, still playing with her erect nipple. "What's that smile for?" he asked.

Ross let out a low laugh and shrugged, arching a bit as he played with her, teasing her and turning up her arousal again. "We were bumping uglies."

He barked a laugh, drawing circles on her stomach. "You used that term on the phone yesterday. Do I even want to know where you learned that...interesting...phrase?"

"It—it's something I picked up from a high school locker room."

Ross sucked in her breath as Xander slid his hand lower, a slick finger now inside of her happily sore entrance.

He leaned over her. "I seem to remember from the other night that you enjoy an interesting turn of sex phrase. I recall...*shtupped*, was it?" He moved his finger over the excruciatingly sensitive nub between her legs and Ross's breath caught. "And *bedsport*."

Xander circled his finger on the perfect spot, causing Ross's breathing to come in staccato bursts. He sped up the movement, pressing her onward and up the crest of her release until Ross exploded silently, except for the gasp of air as she hit her climax.

"Hey, Ross?" whispered Xander, his eyes drooping closed as he pulled her to him.

"Mmm?"

"I like bumping uglies with you."

Ross laughed against his chest. "I cannot believe you came up here."

"That's the problem, Ross. I want to come everywhere with you. After our call yesterday, it was all I could do not to sneak in your bedroom window. I couldn't wait to see you. When Leah suggested I help this afternoon, there was no way I could say no. To her and to you."

She wriggled out from under him. "Now we have to sneak you out of here."

"Really?" Xander scrutinized her, amused.

"Really. Out the window. Across the lattice. Down the tree. Back in the front door."

"You've got to be kidding."

"Nope. No way am I getting caught having some 'afternoon delight' with you when we're supposed to be moving furniture."

"You really are serious."

"Yep."

"Damn." Xander ran a hand through his hair as Ross reached down and threw his clothes to him. He motioned to the used condom. "Guess I'm taking this and hiding it in a trash can outside." He winked. "This really is so high school."

Good God, Ross loved a good Xander wink. Only the knowledge that time was running out before Hon's return kept her from jumping him again. Instead, she needed these last couple of minutes to clean herself up. The shower was still running, and as she headed into the bathroom, she whisper-yelled, "Don't fall!"

"Helpful. Very helpful," she heard him grumbling. Moments later, she was pretty sure she heard the window open.

Ross took the quickest shower in the history of showers—a nod to both her guilt at all the water she'd wasted (in the heat of passion, she'd forgotten all about the running shower) and the knowledge that Hon would be back any time now. She threw on fresh clothes, taking care to fix her ponytail.

Bursting with curiosity, she looked out the window in time to see Xander crossing the yard. Like he sensed her eyes on him, he looked back, blew her a kiss and saluted.

Grinning, she returned the salute. Xander was wrong. This was way more fun than high school.

Chapter Nineteen

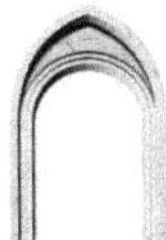

Ross

Xander returned through the front door as Ross descended the wide stairway and Hon and Gaby came out of the kitchen, all converging just by the door to the basement. Gaby was chattering away, giving an update on her kids and Petey. They were all miniature golfing in town, to be followed by a trip to the movies.

"Where were you?" Hon asked Xander, one eyebrow raised. "Did you pop over to the cottage?" She darted amused looks back and forth between him and Ross, who studiously avoided looking at each other.

"I left my phone at the cottage. I wanted to run and get it," he lied. Ross was pretty sure his voice alone gave them away. It was...almost smug. And sated. Ross bit her lip to contain her smile.

"You must have run, because you are very flushed," Hon replied. "And did you shower, Ross?" At her granddaughter's quick nod, Hon cocked her head. "Just going to get sweaty again, but if that's your story..." she finished in a leading voice, then clapped her hands. "OK, break's over. Let's get this part of the basement finished." As Hon chivvied them along to the basement, Gaby stopped in her tracks, leaning in to take a closer look at Xander.

With a wicked grin, she declared, just a degree louder than sotto voice and clearly with the intention of being heard by all, "Xander, I think you have something on your neck. I hope you didn't get bitten." Gaby skipped down the steps after Hon, obviously proud of herself for stirring the pot.

Xander's eyes darted to the hall mirror and then he shot a look at Ross, who broke into an impish smile.

She grazed against him as she passed on the way to the basement. He grabbed her arm gently, tugging her to him. "I've been bitten all right. By a vixen," he whispered.

Ross laughed. "Consider us even."

Today was turning into a good day.

Ross and Xander spent the afternoon hauling pieces of furniture out of the basement and into the bed of his truck. More than once, Ross found herself distracted by the play of muscles across his body. The flex of biceps. The definition in his calves. *The expression of a well-made man*, Ross mused, recalling the sexy Walt Whitman homage to the physical beauty of a man.

Ross was also distracted by her sister, but in a much less pleasant way. Both Hon and Xander seemed solicitous of her. With practiced ease, Ross's blood pressure rose at the sight of those two pandering around Gaby. It was par for the course with her sister. There was something going on with Drama Gaby, and now Xander was falling for her damsel-in-distress routine. All her old insecurities and her frustrations roiled at a slow simmer each time she saw Xander jump to grab something from her. *Nothing ever changed.*

Rolling her eyes, she grabbed her end of a scarred mahogany table with a rickety leg, which she remembered used to be in the upstairs hallway. She could feel Xander's eyes on her as they eased up the old wooden steps, down the hall, and out of the house, but she refused to meet his gaze. She acknowledged she was jealous of the attention Xander was paying to Gaby, bringing her water and refusing to let her carry even the lightest pieces of furniture up the stairs. Granted, he also brought Hon and Ross water, but there was something so... typical... about the Gaby interactions. Everyone always seemed to swirl around delicate, fragile Gaby. It may have been twenty years since Gaby's peak dramatic performances, but clearly she had honed her skill in being cosseted. As they hoisted the table onto the truck, Ross let out a grunt and a sigh that was more an expression of her frustration with the situation than the weight of the table.

Xander tightened the rope he'd affixed around the table to hold it in place for transport, and then came around to Ross's side. He reached a hand toward her and then let it drop.

"What's up, frowny-pants?" he asked. "You were fine before and now you're... not."

Ross bristled and then decided to be frank with Xander, surprising herself. For some reason, she wanted to tell him what was bugging her. This was out of the norm for her. But then, everything about this trip— and Xander—was out of the norm for her.

"You know the phrase 'same shit, different day'?"

Xander nodded, face quizzical.

"That's the way this trip is. Same shit. Two decades later. 'Plus ça change, plus c'est la même chose.'"

"The more things change, the more they stay the same."

"You speak French?"

"Enough. Mother insisted. Seven years of it, in fact, at my prep school."

"Ooo la la...prep school. Very fancy," Ross teased.

But something in Xander's face changed. "There's a lot you don't know about me, Ross. And a lot I don't know about you." He sighed. "You know I have some idea of the strain in your relationship with Gaby. And I recognize I don't have the benefit of your point of view," he hastened to add.

Ross ground down on her back teeth, remembering their argument and not wishing to touch that third rail again.

"But could you possibly be painting your sister with an old brush, and maybe not an accurate one anymore? It's like selective perception. We see things the way we want to see them."

Ross narrowed her eyes and shook her head, a small smirk playing on her lips. Another person Gaby had wrapped around her finger. "I didn't realize you're a psychology professor in addition to being an architecture professor."

"Don't be bitchy, Ross," Xander retorted, frustrated. "You're better than that. It doesn't suit you."

"It suits me fine when people I barely know start telling me what I see and don't see, especially where my sister is concerned."

Ross's heart thudded with anger and disappointment. She stared at the ground, trying to inhale a deep, calming breath. Why did he insist on pressing Gaby's point of view? Why couldn't they just enjoy things as they were, without the specter of her sister looming over them in every fucking conversation?

Xan moved in close to her and tipped her chin up, forcing her to make eye contact. "The thing is—" he held her gaze "—while I may not know a lot *about* you, I feel like I do know you. I know not in terms of length of time. But sometimes I think you can meet someone and just *know* them on a very fundamental level. I'm not sure how it happens, but it does."

Before Ross could form a response, he leaned down and brushed a soft kiss to her lips. Tucking a lock of hair that had escaped the ponytail behind her ear, he whispered, "Enough about your sister. I know you have good reasons for how you feel."

"You don't know the half of it."

"I wish you'd tell me." He wrapped his strong arms around her, and Ross sunk into the glorious sensation of just... being held.

"Maybe one day. But not now." She nuzzled into his muscular chest.

"This could get interesting," he murmured against the top of her head.

Ross closed her eyes for the briefest moment, whether in acknowledgement or denial she wasn't sure. "Interesting is fine, but nothing more than that. We have fun, and then I go to New York."

There was that damn feeling in the pit of her stomach again, the one that happened every time she thought of her upcoming move.

She resolved to ignore it, as per usual, and focused on Xander. "There really isn't any point."

"No point?" Xan raised an eyebrow that was a shade darker than his blond hair. "To what? To this?" He motioned between the two of them. "Or no point to relationships at all?"

"I guess I'm OK with getting to know each other better. But what I meant was, for me, there is no point in pursuing a relationship. It's not how I'm hardwired." Ross looked at her watch. Hon would wonder where they'd disappeared to. "Look, as you've been accurately informed"— she held up her hand in silent warning not to interrupt — "I don't do boyfriends and I don't do relationships. But I do like to enjoy men and hang out in a casual way."

Xander broke into a huge grin, flashing those alluring dimples. "Let me get this straight. You don't do relationships. You don't have boyfriends. You 'hang out,'" he emphasized, using air quotations.

"Yes," responded Ross, an unwelcome defensive tug deep in her belly.

"Ross, my beautiful vixen, it's just semantics. You can call it what you want, but it sounds to me like you absolutely do 'do relationships.'"

"I don't!" she proclaimed, feeling her cheeks burn. "And it's not semantics. A relationship, and definitely a boyfriend, connotes a level of emotional commitment. I like to hang out, but I have no desire to commit. Because as soon as you get into a 'relationship'"—now it was Ross's turn to use the air quotes—"suddenly there's this anchor, this binding thing. And when it comes time to unbind, it gets ugly. That is not appealing to me at all. When you're just hanging out enjoying each other, it's easy and fun. Then when it runs its natural course, as all things do, you just...walk away. No drama."

"No drama," repeated Xander. "You really don't like drama, do you?"

"Loathe it," confirmed Ross. "Despise. And I seem to have it in spades here in Virginia, unfortunately."

Xander let out a low whistle and then scratched his chin in a mock-professorial way. "I'm one hundred percent with you on the commitment aversion. Thus, I'll make you a deal, Ross Ellen Beaufort. You 'hang out' with me for the next six weeks, no strings. No 'relationship.' No drama. The point will be just to have a good time together."

"No drama, no strings, no clings?" Ross hated clingy guys. Even as she said it, however, she knew Xander wasn't the clingy type.

"No drama, no strings, no clings," he confirmed with a resolute nod, the dimple in his cheek giving away his amusement.

"I'm serious," she warned.

"Me too." Xander nodded. "Although I will admit that I like the way you were clinging to me earlier after lunch," he added with the smile that made Ross's insides go flippity-flop.

Ross paused before continuing. "There is one thing. I'm not a prude, as I think you've figured out, but I don't sleep around. If I'm... intimate...with a guy regularly, I don't have sex with other guys. And I expect the same."

Xander's eyes softened. "You fascinate me." He reached for a piece of her hair that had loosened from its ponytail and gently tucked it behind her ear. "OK. Here are the terms for your consideration, Ms. Beaufort. Six weeks. No commitment. No boyfriend-girlfriend thing. Nothing but good times and hot sex. Just 'hanging out.' And within that, we both are monogamous. Further, for this time period, I am staunchly Team Ross. And when it, how did you say it, 'runs its natural course,' we walk away. No drama." Xander held out his hand with a satisfied smile, penetrating brown eyes trained on her. "Deal?"

Ross returned the smile, reaching out her hand to complete the shake and seal the deal. Xander's hand closed over hers and he pulled her close. "Just two things to add. One, thanks for the hickey payback. How about we call it even and leave those back in high school where they belong?" Ross threw her head back and laughed. "And two, no falling in love with each other despite our best intentions. I'm over the whole falling in love thing. It doesn't end well."

He was teasing, but Ross glimpsed a flash of unguarded sadness in Xander's eyes and an unexpected tenderness rose in her.

"No hickeys. No drama. Definitely no falling in love. Just hot sex. Deal."

"Shall we seal it with a kiss?" Xander offered.

"Seems kind of cliché," Ross mused, "which is par for the course with us." Then she reached around his neck, twining her fingers into the damp strands of golden hair as she pulled him down to her mouth for a deep kiss, feeling the press of his rising arousal against her.

The kiss continued for some time, until she broke it off and laughed breathlessly. "Now, back to work before Attila the Hon comes after us."

"Yes, ma'am." Xander saluted.

Ross motioned to the other part of him saluting. "Um, you may want to wait a bit before going back inside."

Xander laughed. "Your fault, you saucy wench."

"Saucy wench? I like that." As she headed back up the steps of the farmhouse, she smiled at him standing in the bright afternoon sun. God, he was delicious. This might not be such a horrible summer after all.

Chapter Twenty

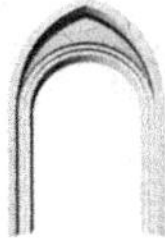

Xander

The crunch of tires on gravel heralded their arrival at the bar. It had become a routine for Xander and Ted to work out at the gym and then go out for drinks a couple nights a week. The evenings varied depending on Ted's schedule at the firehouse, but for Xander, it—along with the occasional poker night—had become a saving sense of community in what would have otherwise been a lonely adult existence. He loved Petey more than his own life, but he did need adult conversation.

Today he and Ted had taken multiple trips to Goodwill with furniture from Leah Waldheim's basement. They'd skipped the gym, figuring all the hauling counted as their exercise, and decided they'd earned their drinks.

"Good lord, I am ripe. I feel like even those swipes of deodorant and a shirt change didn't help."

"That you are, Professor. But in good news, no one here cares." Ted held the door for him and motioned toward two seats at the bar. "Besides, word on the street is half the single ladies here and some of the married ones have been scheming to get you in bed for ages. They'd put up with your foul stench. Though God knows why."

Xander cocked a brow, as he nodded to the bartender in wordless assent for the on-tap Stella he always ordered. "'Word on the street'? Is that a euphemism for...?"

"My wife? Yep." Ted grinned. "Gaby knows everyone, and when she's in their houses decorating, they tell her all kinds of shit. Plus, the Mom Underground is hard core. She knows all. It's impressive and fucked up at the same time." Ted took a healthy sip of his own recently poured beer. "Firefighters are gossipy too, bro. We're all talking about you." Ted smirked.

"Nice," Xander replied, his dry tone not hiding his amusement. "Always good to have your potential sex life the topic of the 'Mom Underground' and the fire station."

He paused to order some wings and debated broaching what was on his mind. He was tempted to talk about Ross...and then he remembered their fight and swallowed his words, along with his beer, instead.

"You know what else Gaby says? She thinks you and Ross are having sex. And I think she's right."

And there it is. So much for not talking about her.

"What makes you guys say that?" Xander hedged.

"Well, you two were flirting wildly at dinner the other night. And Gaby said you both were behaving suspiciously after lunch. That—her words, not mine—her sister had that 'just fucked' look about her. And —" he fixed Xander with an evil grin "—you have a hickey on your neck, brother, that wasn't there yesterday. Now I know you and I aren't joined at the hip, but Gaby says that little hickey wasn't there before lunch, either, but magically appeared after. *That* is what makes us guys say that." Ted folded his arms in triumph, a prosecutor successfully closing his case.

"Damn." Xander shook his head, smiling. "I guess we haven't been too subtle, have we?"

"Nope. I'd say at this point even Laverne is on to you."

Xander rolled his eyes. "It's not serious. We're just having fun."

"I would hope so." Ted's voice was filled with disdain.

"Why would you say it like that?" Xander heard the challenge in his tone, bracing for what he suspected would be an attack on his girl. His girl for only the next six weeks, he carefully amended.

"Ross is...well...I know she's my sister-in-law, but she's not the type of woman you marry."

"Marry?" Xander spluttered. "Who said anything about that? Did I not just say we're only having fun?"

"Chill, Xan. I'm just making a point about her. Ross is perfect fuck-fling material. She'll admit it herself. That's what she does. And that's exactly what you need, even if I'm not the hugest fan of her as a person."

Xander ground his jaw, hating that vulgar description of Ross, and wanting to defend her. And yet he heard her own words in his head.

"Ted, I know you're Team Gaby—"

The other man cut him off with a laugh. "Christ, now you sound like her! That's exactly how Ross talks."

"—because Gaby is your wife. And she's amazing. But I like Ross. She's..." Xander searched for the right words to capture her. "She's smart, and funny, and sophisticated, and she's unbelievable in bed. And for the next six weeks, we're going to hang out. So be careful how you talk about her."

Ted cocked his head and let out a soft whistle. "Professor Grace, if I didn't know better, I'd say you have a crush on Ross Beaufort."

"We're just having fun, but I want to speak of her with respect. Let's be classy."

Ted nodded. "Damn, brother. OK. Just...be careful. Ross is a broken woman down deep. Not that she'd ever admit that. She's the kind of person who could really hurt you." Ted turned serious eyes on him as Xander heard the déjà vu from his conversation with Cole. "I've known her a long time. You've been through enough, what with Aubrey—"

"Hey man," Xander cut him off before they could go down that fucking rabbit hole. "You sound like Cole. And as I told him, I've been burned before by a complex woman. And now I have Petey to consider and protect. I won't let that happen again. To him or to me. But this thing with Ross— It's just for fun while she's here. It's not serious now and it's not going to get serious. No one will get hurt. No one will catch feelings. We're going to enjoy each other and then say our goodbyes. She'll head to Manhattan, and that will be that."

"Sounds like you got it all figured out."

"Yep." He did. Xander cleared his throat. "There's, uh...there's another thing."

Ted turned and faced him slowly, hearing the warning tone in Xander's voice.

"I told Leah I know all about the night of the accident. She was helping me navigate something, and it...just came out. We ended up having a long talk."

His friend sighed. "So now that's out in the open."

"Except it isn't. And you know that. So much of the bad blood between Ross and Gaby stems from Ross only having part of the picture."

Ted got defensive. "That's because the truth could make her hurt Gaby even more than she already was."

"No, man. I disagree. I get that it's what you've all thought all these years. And maybe it was partly true all those years ago. Who's to say? But that's not fair to the woman Ross is today. Leah, Gaby, even you have to give Ross some credit for growing up and being able to handle the full story."

Ted shook his head. "I don't know, Xan—"

"*I* do," he emphasized. "And more to the point, so does Leah."

"What's that supposed to mean?"

"It means that Leah is finally ready to shine a light on all that darkness. To debride a festering, toxic wound and then trust her granddaughters to finally heal."

Ted was quiet, nursing his beer and watching the TV. Xander would bet his entire bank account his friend couldn't have told him what he was actually watching.

"When?" he finally asked.

"I don't know. But I'm sure it'll be before the move."

"Fuck. I need to prepare Gaby."

"That's why I told you."

"I can't bear to see her hurt again, Brother."

"I know. But she's a strong woman. And Ross will rise to this. I know it."

They finished their beers, the chatter of the bar around them filling their silence, both weighed down by the pain of the Beaufort sisters.

CHAPTER TWENTY-ONE

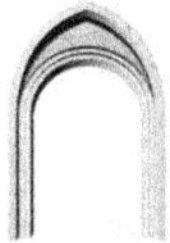

Ross

Ross awoke to the hum of the summer locusts in the trees. Nestled in the cotton sheets, the duvet rumpled around her, she sank further into her pillow, luxuriating in the softness. As she closed her eyes and listened to the rising and falling waves of the insects' chatter, Ross stretched in bed, feeling the rewarding pull of sore muscles.

They'd made an impressive amount of progress, identifying three truckloads for the donation center. The fireflies were coming out when they'd finally finished the last load. Xander had offered to pick up all the kids from Theresa's and drive them home. By mutual agreement, the packing crew disbanded and headed to their respective homesteads.

When Ted and Xander had said something about still having their Bro Date Night, Ross just shook her head. She was still uncomfortable with that particular friendship, since she wasn't really in the Moose fan club. She'd have to work through that, she guessed.

With everyone gone, Hon and Ross had decided to eat leftover pizza for dinner, and both crashed early, exhausted from the day's work.

Hon had announced she was sleeping in, followed by a church volunteer event and then an early dinner with friends, which left Ross with an entire day to herself. Hon had instructed her to enjoy the day, and forbade her from doing any packing.

An entire day stretched before her, with no work, no obligations. Just whatever she wanted to do to fill it.

The thought immediately came to her. The pool. Growing up, she, Gaby, and Tiercy spent hundreds of hours splashing around the pool, "laying out" to get tans, and sharing summer reads.

Perfect, thought Ross, rising and opening a dresser drawer to grab a bathing suit. She dropped into a small drawstring bag with some sunscreen and her Kindle loaded with recommendations from her bestie. Tiercy may have been a high school English teacher with an affinity for the classics, but she also loved a good beach read—particularly the panty-soaking kind. It had been ages since Ross read a book for fun.

Within thirty minutes, Ross was ensconced in a lounge chair, protected from the sun by copious amounts of sunscreen and a large umbrella. Her days of deep summer tans were long over. She took a sip of iced coffee, which was next to a large thermos of cold water, and opened her Kindle. Such a joy to read for pleasure and not as an editor.

The rest of the morning passed in sun-drenched bliss. Ross alternated among reading, swimming in the pool when she needed to cool off, and napping. Hon and Pop had installed the pool when Ross and Gaby were little. There was a big pond on the property, framed with beautiful weeping willows, but Hon and her mother hadn't liked the idea of the girls swimming in there after they'd found too many snakes for their comfort. Pop was reluctant, stating accurately that they were just harmless water snakes, but capitulated under the unrelenting pressure of his wife and daughter. In the years since Ross had been there, Hon had added a little cabana and an outside sound system, from which Jack Johnson was now singing about banana pancakes.

Ross was stretched out on her stomach, dozing in contentment, the back of her string bikini top untied, when the feel of something ice cold on her back startled her awake. She jumped, clutching the front of her suit. "What the—!"

Standing by the side of the chair was Xander, who was holding a beverage container and laughing. "I'm sorry-not-sorry," he said, holding one hand up, trying to contain his mirth. "I came by to see you, and bring you this drink." He motioned to the Yeti tumbler in his hand. "And there you were all deliciously stretched out, with your top undone, and something high-schoolish just came over me." Xander's eyes darkened as they raked over her. "I couldn't resist putting this on your back." He bit his lip, still shaking with laughter, as he proffered the tumbler.

Ross's heart was settling back to a normal cadence and she found herself giggling along with his contagious laughter. "You scared the shit out of me, you prick." She swatted at him with her free hand.

"My intentions were good," he laughed.

"My father would have said, 'The road to hell is paved with good intentions,'" Ross retorted.

"Maybe," Xander grinned. "You're saying you don't want this?" Again, he held up the tumbler and gave it a little shake.

"What is it?" Ross eyed the container.

"Whiskey sour, lots of ice."

"Sounds nasty." She crinkled her nose.

Xander feigned offense. "Certainly not. This, mademoiselle, was the cocktail of choice for my parents for many years when I was growing up. They would drink them at our club after playing tennis. I thought since our summer deal theme seems to be high school"—he touched the still-vibrant hickey with an ironic lift of his eyebrow—"I would bring you the drink I associate with my high school days."

"*Your* high school days? You mean what your parents drank while you were in high school?"

"Yep, and what I also drank. At home, sometimes they'd ask me to mix them a drink, and I'd make a little extra for myself." He winked and Ross's stomach did that little flip again.

"Juvenile delinquent."

"Totally. I own it. Oh, and I also brought you some lunch." He pointed to a small nylon cooler by his feet. "Would you like to try your cocktail?"

Ross reached for it with her free hand, still holding her bikini against her with the other.

"You seem to be having some trouble with your top. May I assist you?" Xander asked, roaming, hungry eyes betraying the desire behind his courtly speech.

Ross tilted her head. "Where's Petey?"

"Who?" Ross's seeming non sequitur appeared to confuse Xander.

"Petey. Your son." Now Ross was laughing again.

"I didn't mean to say who. I meant, why?"

"Just answer the question."

"We spent the morning at his end of school field day and picnic, and I just dropped him off at an afternoon party with friends."

"So, he's not around?"

"No? Why?"

Now it was Ross's turn to drag a slow gaze down Xander's body, her gaze lingering around his swim trunks.

"I can manage my own top." With her free hand, Ross reached up and fully untied the top of her bikini, letting it drop to the ground. Without breaking eye contact, she took a deep swallow of the cocktail and then licked her lips. "Delicious. Would you like to taste some?"

Xander nodded, and then his jaw dropped as Ross poured a bit of the drink on her chest, dribbling the delicious cold libation across her nipples, which were now hardened pink buds due to both the icy drink and her desire. "Have a taste," she offered.

"With pleasure," Xander replied, his voice low and husky as he bent his head and complied.

Xander ran his hand along her spine, bringing it to rest on Ross's naked bottom. They were resting on the lounge chair, Ross lying on top of him, their legs entwined. The sun had shifted, and it was beginning to beat down on them, heating their bodies externally, while their insides still simmered from their recent combustion. "That was the best whiskey sour I've ever had."

Ross laughed against his shoulder. There was something decadent about having sex in the broad daylight, by the pool in which she'd swum thousands of times. She almost wished she could go back in time and whisper in her own adolescent ear, "You think you're having fun at the pool now? Just you wait."

"Thank you for the drink. I think it may be my new cocktail of choice. I go through phases with drinks. Most recently it was a vodka gimlet, but I've been looking for a summer drink."

"Glad to be of assistance."

Xander was scratching her back with his fingertips, sending chills everywhere. After a moment, his hand stilled.

"Ross, not to break the moment but—" he hesitated. "I—we didn't use any protection. I actually have something in the cooler." Ross lifted her head and raised her eyebrows. "I had a plan. Liquor you up a bit and have my way with you. You can't blame a guy for that..." he teased and then focused serious eyes on her. "I truly am sorry. I know better. I just...got carried away in the moment. I've never done that before. I promise. I—do we need to be concerned? I mean, you don't. About me, that is. I haven't been with anyone, bare, since my ex-wife. Are you on any birth control?"

Ross lifted herself off him and wrapped a towel around herself.

"I'm sorry. I didn't mean to offend you. I took you by surprise so it was my responsibility and I should have—"

"Relax, Xander," Ross cut him off. "You didn't offend me. It's OK. And it's my responsibility too. I got caught up as well. I certainly don't have any sexually transmitted diseases and I can't get pregnant."

Xander exhaled a bit. "Me too."

"You can't get pregnant either?" Ross teased, trying to lighten things, and was rewarded with deep laughter from the gorgeous naked man on the lounge chair. God—she'd never look at that chair the same way again.

"Ha. I mean I've also tested negative. God. This can be so awkward. Anyway, so you're on birth control and now we've established the other part is good—"

"I never said that."

"What?" Xander startled, pulling a second towel across him.

"I never said I was on birth control," Ross clarified. "However, I am on the pill. What I said was, 'I can't get pregnant.'"

Xander's eyes were questioning, and Ross continued with reluctance. This wasn't a topic she'd ever discussed with a partner before. "I can't get pregnant. I've been told by my doctor. It's a female thing. *God... this is the least sexy post-coital conversation ever.*"

Ross shook her head with a small, uncomfortable laugh. When it was clear Xander was waiting for more of an explanation, she resumed. "I have endometriosis and fibroids. I take birth control to help regulate my cycle and control symptoms. The birth control part of it is unnecessary, given my condition. It's pretty bad, and all of it prevents me from being able to get pregnant. Or so I've been told. Many times. It runs in my family. On both sides, in fact."

"But, Gaby..."

"Yes, well, the Golden Girl seems to have escaped it, as is fitting. My dad was an only child. His mother almost died in childbirth. She hemorrhaged. Hon only had my mother. It took her a long time to get pregnant, and then she was never able to get pregnant again. My mom had Gaby and me, but then she had an ectopic pregnancy. It was awful, and she had fibroids too. They ended up having to do an emergency hysterectomy. Only Gaby and my Great Aunt Francesca, Hon's sister, have the fertile genes."

Xander had moved to her side on the lounge chair. He stroked her hand. "I'm sorry."

"Why would you be sorry?" Ross knew her voice was sharp but she was powerless to control it. "*I'm* not sorry. It is what it is, as they say."

"Do you want kids?"

"Kind of a moot point, Xan." She cringed at her caustic tone and laid a conciliatory hand on his leg. "It's...it's not that I *don't* want them. I *can't* want them. No sense in wanting what you can't have."

Ross rolled her lips between her teeth, swallowing the old pain. She summoned a smile, and not all of it was fake.

"Besides, it's good news for you vis a vis our summer deal. You don't have to worry about accidentally knocking me up."

"I just meant—never mind. I thought you seemed sad when you told me you couldn't have kids. I must have misread."

"You did misread," she lied. "I'm not sad. It's a relief. I've never had to deal with a 'whoops.' Never had to worry about protection, beyond STI prevention. Never had to stress about waiting for my period to come, and then peeing on a stick, praying you don't see two lines."

"And you really don't want kids, even via adoption?"

"I don't even do relationships, Xan. Why would I want a child? My life is full," Ross responded.

"I guess I thought maybe you didn't want any of that now, but you seem like the kind of person who likes to keep her options open."

"True," Ross conceded, uncomfortable that they'd gone from fun, fabulous sun-sex to a strained conversation about a heavy topic. "I do like to keep my options open. And that includes the freedom that comes from no commitments, be they boyfriends or children. I've designed my life this way for a reason. And I like it."

Xander was quiet, obviously processing all of it. After a moment, he shifted and captured her head between his hands, lacing his fingers in her hair, gently tugging.

"And I like *you*, Ross Beaufort." He leaned in, kissing her deeply, and she relished a corresponding zing of arousal between her legs.

Ross let go, getting lost in the feel of his soft mouth against hers, and in the smell of suntan lotion, whiskey, and the scent of their earlier encounter.

An ill-timed growling interrupted them.

He smiled against her lips. "Hungry?"

"Famished."

"Good thing I came prepared." He reached into the cooler and grabbed two sandwiches and two bottles of water. His eyes landed on the condoms he'd brought and he smiled, dimples popping. "Guess we don't need those bad boys anymore. Remind me to throw them out later so Petey doesn't go into the cooler looking for a juice box and find them." Xander widened his eyes comically.

Ross burst into laughter, relieved that they'd moved away from uncomfortable topics. "Whiskey sours, hot poolside sex, and PB&Js. I think I like this summer deal we made."

"I know I do."

They spent a lazy afternoon at the pool, swimming, reading, and further discovering each other's bodies under the guise of checking for sunburn. When Xander left to pick up Petey, Ross—pink in some interesting places—practically skipped to the farmhouse.

It had been a glorious day.

Chapter Twenty-Two

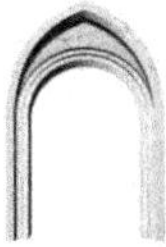

Ross

The next four days flew by. Ross, Hon, and Gaby were caught up in a whirl of move prep. Sorting and packing an entire lifetime's possessions was not a task for the faint-hearted, Ross had decided. They still hadn't tackled the belongings from Ross's room that had been moved to the basement, or her parents' personal items, but they'd made major progress elsewhere. One week in, and they were about one-quarter finished.

Hon was moving on July fifteenth. Ross had hoped not to be anywhere near the farmhouse on July sixteenth—the anniversary of her parents' death—but she would need to stay a couple of days past the move to help Hon unpack in her new place, and then do some last-minute cleanup of the farmhouse. They'd hired a staging company to prep it for show, and Ross agreed to facilitate.

Then she needed to pack her apartment in Maryland, something that would happen quickly, as she didn't have much in the way of personal possessions. By July twenty-fifth, she'd be in New York, ready to start her new job. Moving away from Tiercy and Jemma would shred her, but they had Cole now.

A pang of grief hit her hard. Ross knew in her heart that she and Tiercy would always be there for each other. Always need each other. That kind of timeless friendship goes to the core. But Tiercy was married. Unlike her surprise pregnancy with Jemma, during which she'd relied on Ross, Tiercy had a husband now by her side—one who cherished her and adored her. It was a fresh start for her beautiful friend.

And now it was time for Ross to have a fresh start, too.

Given all the packing activity, Ross had barely seen Xander in four days. They'd had one afternoon quickie during a packing break that coincided with a birthday party for a friend of Petey's. The following night, Xander had arranged a blanket under the moonlight behind the cottage. When Petey fell asleep, he'd called Ross. They spent several hours together under the moonlight, with Xander periodically checking on his son.

Ross still hadn't met Petey Grace. She got the sense that while Xander wasn't preventing them from meeting, he wasn't trying to make it happen either. Ross was ambivalent. On one hand, she was curious to meet Petey. On the other, something deep inside her recognized that meeting Xander's son would signal a verboten shift in their summer deal.

She was nine days into her stay at the farmhouse when their unexpected meeting happened.

Hon was at lunch and a movie with friends, and Ross decided to sleep in and then spend some time at the pool. She donned her favorite red bikini, snagged her Kindle, and headed out the kitchen door. In the distance, but coming closer, she heard shrieking laughter.

"Laverne, no!" High peals of laughter. Two voices. A girl and a boy. "Laverne, come!" Through the trees came the gold furball, running on puppy legs that had grown longer just in the last week, a stick between her teeth. Behind the puppy were her niece Kingsley and a young towheaded boy. They were sprinting after the dog, laughing.

"Catch her, Aunt Ross!" called Kingsley, breathless both with exertion and merriment at the dog's hijinks. "She got out of the house!"

Acting on instinct, Ross dropped her pool gear and lunged for the puppy, who was barreling toward her. "Here, puppy! Here, Laverne!" She kneeled and clapped her hands, making kissing sounds. The puppy ran toward her, pell-mell. She swept her up, loving the feel of wriggling puppy in her arms.

"You got him! Nice job!" Kingsley ran to her aunt, beaming. "We came in to get a snack and Laverne escaped out the door. We've been running after her." She bent over, catching her breath. "That was a close call!"

Kingsley and the boy, who'd caught up, high-fived. In one glance, Ross knew exactly who he was—the dimples were a dead giveaway. She kissed Laverne, now worn out in her arms after her adventure, and handed the puppy to Kingsley with a warm smile.

Turning to the boy, she said, "And you must be Petey. I'm Kingsley's Aunt Ross." She held out her hand, which was absurd, but this awkwardness around her lover's young son was mortifying and completely out of character for her. She liked to think she had some level of comportment. But in this case, it had utterly deserted her.

But Petey, displaying a countenance so like his father's, took it in stride. He placed his hand in hers and responded with the serious manners of a child well-schooled in appropriate adult introductions. "Nice to meet you too, Aunt Ross."

Ross choked back a small laugh. "How about you just call me Ross? That's what all my friends call me."

"You're my dad's friend, too, right?" Petey asked.

Somewhat taken aback, Ross stammered a yes and cocked her head, examining Xander's son. Except for his nose and the set of his chin, he looked just like Xan. The hair was much lighter, but so similar. "Has your dad told you about me?"

"Only that you're Ms. Gaby's sister and you're nice, and beautiful inside and out," he responded with sweet sincerity. "He likes you."

Kingsley, who had affixed Laverne's leash to her collar, clapped her free hand over her mouth, eyes wide, a scandalized giggle sneaking out.

Ross's jaw dropped. Unaccustomed to being at a loss for words, she cast around for something to say.

But Petey continued smoothly, just like a mini-Xan, she thought with a small inward smile. "It's OK. I made him tell me. He wasn't gonna."

A flush crept up her skin, and realized she'd barely said a word. She'd been utterly flummoxed by the mini-Marvel.

"Well..." Ross cleared her throat and tried for adult composure. "Um, thank you for the lovely compliment." She fought to regain some semblance of internal balance. Even the son seemed to have an innate capacity to knock her off keel. It must be genetic. "And I'm glad Laverne ran this way and I could help. It's nice to finally meet you, Petey. Your dad has told me all about you."

Ross wondered if she sounded like a weird grown-up to him, trying too hard. She thought about how easy Cole had been with Jemma. He had taken to his new girlfriend's daughter immediately, a reciprocal feeling. Not that Xander was her boyfriend, Ross corrected in her head. *Ugh.*

"Is your dad around, Petey?" Why did her voice sound so high and squeaky?

"No, ma'am. He had to take his truck in for an oil change and Ms. Gaby is watching me until he gets back."

"Are you going swimming, Aunt Ross?" Kingsley peered at her.

Ross folded her arms over her chest, now self-conscious in her red string bikini and sarong. "I-uh, yes. I thought I'd spend some time at the pool."

"I love Hon's pool," Petey interjected. "But Dad says we can't just go over now that you're here because you might want privately."

"Privacy," Ross automatically corrected, and then cringed. "Is that what he said? Do you normally swim in Hon's pool?"

"Yeah—I mean, yes ma'am. The Monroes have a pool too, but Hon's is bigger and I like to jump off the dive. The Monroes don't have a diving board."

Kingsley cast a mutinous look at her friend. "Then you don't have to swim there."

Petey turned to her. "Fine."

"Fine."

Ross watched the children bicker for a few moments and then decided to intercede, recognizing the defiant set of Kingsley's jaw from her own sister. Whenever Gaby got that look, a battle was soon to follow. Ross knew only too well.

"OK. I'm sure both pools are awesome in their own way."

"We have a *beach entry*," announced Kingsley, clearly still smarting from what she seemed to perceive as an insult from her friend.

"That sounds very cool. I'll come check it out sometime. But, Peter, you need to do me a favor—"

"Just Grandmother calls me Peter, and only when I'm in trouble. And my dad when he's mad."

"I'm sorry. *Petey*," she emphasized, a smile in her voice, "I want you to know that you are always welcome to swim in Hon's pool, as long as there's an adult around. You don't need to stay away because of me. There's plenty of room. And I'm good at sharing."

Petey broke into a big smile. "Cool. Thanks, Ross."

Ross could hear the distinct sound of her sister whistling for the kids. It was a sound so reminiscent of her own childhood, when she and Gaby would wander around the property, and then return at the sound of their mother's sharp whistle over the trees. She remembered practicing with her sister and Tiercy until they got the hang of it.

"You better run. That's your mom. You don't want to get in trouble." Ross reached out and gave Laverne one last scratch, then, impulsively, hugged her niece and ruffled Petey's hair. Kingsley leaned into the hug, still holding the puppy.

"I love you, Aunt Ross."

She had never heard that from Kingsley before. After the barest moment of shocked hesitation, Ross responded, "I love you too, sweetie." She sighed at the primal tug inside as she realized she truly meant it. "See you both soon!"

Settling into the lounge chair—and feeling a thrill at the memory of her interlude with Xander on said chair—Ross couldn't help but feel a sense of something shifting. Maybe it was a product of more than a week at the farmhouse, coupled with her niece's growing familiarity with her and Ross's own increasing comfort in her environment, but

Ross recognized what was going on inside her. It was the feeling of being Home. And it felt undeniably good.

A couple hours later, Ross's phone buzzed. Xander. She broke into a smile as she took the call. "Hey you."

"Hey you. I heard you met someone today."

Ross sat up, grinning. Despite the molten noon sun, a chill went down her back at the sound of Xander's deep voice over the phone. God, he was so fucking sexy. She wanted to lick every inch of him. "Yep. I have finally made the acquaintance of one Peter Grace."

"Oh, don't call him Peter. That's reserved for when he's in trouble. Or with my mother."

"As I've already been told. Duly noted." She shifted in the chair, reaching for her water thermos. "He's cute. He looks like you."

"As I've been told," Xan bantered. "He told me you were very nice."

Despite herself, Ross was beaming. "And what did you say?"

"I said, 'Told ya so.'"

Another little shiver danced down her spine at Xander's deep, warm laugh. She paused, enjoying the feeling. And then frowned, remembering a snippet of the conversation with his son. "Listen, Xan. Petey also told me you didn't want him hanging out at the pool while I was here. Did you not want me to meet him?"

Xander exhaled a quick breath. "No! That's not it at all. I told him that before you even got here. I'd only met you the one time, and I just —well, from what I'd heard, I thought you wouldn't want a kid around." He rushed on, "And now I know that's not true." Xander's voice turned soft and apologetic. "I'm sorry, Ross. Truly. Again, I didn't even really know you. I assumed and I shouldn't have. From now on, if I want to know something, I will ask you."

"Thank you." Ross's voice shook just a bit, shocking her. "I appreciate being given the benefit of the doubt."

"In that spirit, would it be OK with you if Petey and I came over for a swim in a bit?"

"Really?"

"Really. As soon as I got back to the cottage, my son began begging me to come to the pool. He is obsessed with the diving board and the little waterfall. Now that he has your permission..."

"Of course you can come over." Ross hoped she didn't sound too eager. *This will be interesting.* If she was being honest with herself, she was dying to see Xander, and also beyond curious to observe him with his son. What kind of a dad would he be? Not that it mattered, she reminded herself.

"You sure?"

"Absolutely. I wouldn't mind seeing Petey's dad..." she trailed off.

"Petey said you had on a red bikini." Xander's deep voice curled around her, soft and husky. "True?"

"True."

"Is it one of those tiny string ones like you wore the other day?"

"Tinier." Ross giggled into the phone as Xander gave a low growl. "No hanky-panky in front of your kid, mister."

"Not even just a little hanky?"

"No, nor any panky."

"Damn."

CHAPTER TWENTY-THREE

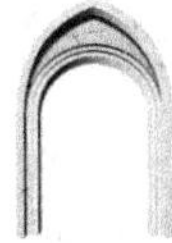

Ross

Thirty minutes later, Ross grinned as she heard the Graces coming across the property toward the pool. She couldn't make out what they were saying, but heard Petey's high child's voice, followed by Xander's deep tenor. She sat up higher in the chaise lounge and smoothed her hair. *Why in the hell are you nervous, Beaufort?*

Xander came through the glen, holding Petey's hand, towels under his other arm, pool bag hooked over his shoulder. He broke into a dimpled smile at the sight of her. Within moments, they'd crossed the distance and he dropped the towels onto a chair next to Ross.

"Hello, Ross Beaufort."

"Hello, Xander Grace. And Petey Grace."

"Hey, Ross! Dad—can I show Ross my cannonball? Ross, do you want to see my cannonball? I can make a huge splash."

Ross laughed, the knot of nerves in her belly unraveling as the whirlwind six-year-old hopped up and down in front of her.

"Take it easy, bud. We just got here. We have all afternoon." Xander winked at Ross as he settled into the chair next to her. Ross watched his eyes move behind his sunglasses as he scanned her in the bikini.

"I would love to see your cannonball, Petey." Ross pictured the fun adults at the outdoor pool connected to her fitness center back home. "In fact, I'm going to sit by the side of the pool and I bet you can't get me wet."

"I bet I can!" Petey announced, challenge accepted, and skipped to the diving board in his Black Panther bathing trunks.

Ross rose from the chaise, leaning forward in front of Xan to give him full view of her cleavage. "I bet I can make you wet too," he muttered under his breath, giving her a dangerous, sexy look.

"Now, now, Alexander," Ross teased, prim and proper. "Remember, no hanky-panky."

She may have been teasing on the surface, but her insides heated up, and she sashayed to the side of the pool, feeling his eyes on her every step.

"Three. Two. One. Launch cannonball!"

With a squeal, Petey leapt off the board, his body crunched into a tight ball. As he went under, generating a small splash, Ross quickly dripped water all over her legs. He came up sputtering for air, triumphant.

"You did it!" Ross called out. "Look at my legs! You got me!"

Petey cackled with glee.

"My turn!" came a deep voice from the back of the diving board.

Xander had peeled off his T-shirt and was wearing a pair of navy board shorts with a subtle hibiscus print. Ross sucked in her breath at the sight of his bare muscular chest with that sexy trail of hair leading into his trunks, her memory again flickering to the last time they were poolside.

Moments later, he was down the board, leaping into the air and then crashing into the pool in a semi-supine position, one knee tucked into his chest. In an echo of his son, Xander's head popped out of the water, grinning at the sight of Ross drenched from the splash and laughing.

"That was *epic*, Daddy!"

"And that, my friends, is known as the Xan-Bam, which I

perfected... in high school." He aimed a playful smirk at Ross, heating her insides and melting her with his reference to their summer theme.

"I wanna try it." Petey was already climbing the ladder.

Xander swam three smooth strokes to where Ross's legs were dangling in the water. He wrapped his arms around them and pulled himself closer, looking up to her, a wicked smile playing on his face. "I told you I could make you wet this afternoon," he whispered.

Ross's breath caught with desire. She bent and brushed a quick kiss on his lips. "Game on," she whispered back.

Xander and Petey took turns doing crazy jumps off the diving board, with Ross rating them on a scale of one to ten as assessed from the safety of her chaise. She invariably gave Petey the higher score, causing Xander to fake pout and generating jubilant laughter from Petey.

After a bit, Xander professed the need for a break and flopped into the adjacent chair, droplets of water drying on his chest. Petey was occupied in the shallow end with a pool noodle, a Barbie he'd swiped from Kingsley, and a foam nerf football. Good lord, kids were random and hilarious, Ross mused.

She stood, a flash of inspiration guiding her steps. She sauntered to the diving board, making sure she undulated her hips. Standing on the end of the board, Ross stretched, bounced once, then again higher, and executed a perfect swan dive. She glided under the water, coming to the surface at the ladder, her hair splayed down to the middle of her back. She climbed the ladder one slow step at a time, pinning Xander with her best come-hither look.

Checking to be sure Petey wasn't watching, Ross turned her back to where he was playing and pulled the triangles of her bikini top to the sides, exposing her breasts to Xan as she traced her nipples. Covering herself again, she gave him a wicked smile of her own, said, "Now it's your turn to rise to the occasion," and looked meaningfully at the growing bulge in his bathing suit.

"In the name of pop culture...Holy Phoebe Cates in *Fast Times*," breathed Xander, whuffling a soft laugh. "I capitulate. You win. We need to stop now or..."

"Or...?" led Ross, just as turned on.

"Or I'm going to die on the spot and then your summer deal will go to hell in a handbasket," Xander recovered, holding up his hands in a gesture of mercy. "I give in."

Ross gave a satisfied smile. "I like winning."

"I can tell. You don't exactly play fair." Xander turned and checked on his son, and then looked back at Ross. "Listen—and you can say no —but how would you like to join me and Petey for dinner tonight. And then maybe you and I can play another round after he goes to bed?"

Xander's tone was light, but Ross could see hesitation in his eyes. Was he nervous? Worried?

"We'd have to be quiet, but I've been dreaming of having you in my bed. Once Petey goes to sleep, he's out like a light. Would you like to join me this evening?"

Ross examined him as he made the offer. His blond hair was damp, the shadows of tree leaves dappling across his strong chest in the hot afternoon sun. The tip of his nose was getting pink and Ross resisted the urge to kiss it. She watched his hand tattoo a nervous cadence on his thigh as he awaited her response, and her heart gave an unfamiliar tug.

"You want to get it on with me with your son in the next room?"

Xander shrugged his shoulders, a gleam in his eye. "Why not? Parents all over the world do it all the time. Why shouldn't we?" He swallowed and hurried on, "I mean, not that we're his parents. I mean, I am, of course. And if you want to skip the dinner part, I could just call you later to come over—"

"Xan," she interrupted. "Will you give me a second to answer? I'd love to have dinner with you and Petey. Especially if you're cooking, because I hate to cook. Bake, yes. Cook, no. And, yes, I'd like to stay for round two tonight—or perhaps we should just consider it the culmination of round one from this afternoon?"

He broke into an easy smile. "OK. How's six o'clock?"

"Perfect." Looking again at Petey, absorbed in dunking himself and resurfacing, she remembered her goddaughter's favorite pool game, her nerves easing a tick more. *Thank you, Jemma.* "Now, let's have a noodle war with Petey."

Dinner was relaxed and comfortable, grilled chicken and summer squash, served at a reclaimed wood table in the great room. They toasted—Petey with his milk, Ross and Xan with a crisp Sancerre.

After dinner, Ross grabbed the reusable grocery bag she'd brought. "You made dinner, so Petey and I are going to make dessert."

In a flash of what she'd hoped was inspiration earlier, Ross had found a way to forge a connection with Petey and get past her own small awkwardness with her lover's son. This afternoon was a success, but Ross was not a practiced hand with kids.

Petey's eyes widened. "We are?"

"Yep. Homemade fudge brownies. Maybe your dad will clean up dinner while we delve into chocolate decadence."

"Whass decdence?"

"Decadence. It means 'yummy goodness.'"

For the next half hour, Ross and Petey worked on the brownies. She showed him how to whisk butter and sugar, and then beat the eggs, folding in flour and cocoa. "Now we bake these for exactly twenty-one minutes."

Ross turned to find Xander watching her with a look of pure happiness on his face. Her breath caught in her throat. He was spectacular. This...was special. A small smile spread on her face, matching the one on his.

Chapter Twenty-Four

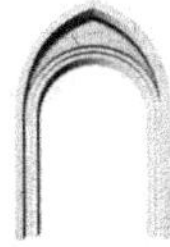

Xander

Xander had long since finished cleaning up the dinner dishes and was leaning against the table, wine glass in hand, watching his son with Ross. She was wearing a navy halter top and white shorts, which skimmed the tops of her tanned thighs. Her low, wavy ponytail would occasionally drift over her shoulder. Without thinking, he moved toward her and dropped a quick kiss on her shoulder. Ross's lips parted in surprise, and then she gave him a soft smile.

Damn. If he let himself, he could be in danger of breaking one of the rules of their summer deal. He watched Ross laughing and teasing with his son, and his heart skipped a beat—and not in a good way. He could very easily fall in love with her. And it scared the hell out of him. His heart still hadn't healed from the damage Aubrey had caused.

No commitments. Ross's rule was a good one, for him and for Petey.

"So, *exactly* twenty-one minutes?" Xan quirked an eyebrow. "Why not twenty minutes thirty seconds. Or twenty-two minutes?"

"Because," Ross turned to him, pointing a wooden spoon, "I've perfected a method to achieve the perfect fudgy goodness and still get that wonderful crackly top."

"Dad, she knows what she's doing." Petey looked at Ross and rolled his eyes at his father. In that moment, he looked just like Aubrey.

Xan fought a lump in his throat. *How could she have left him? Left us?*

Then he looked at Ross and recognized something unique and powerful building in his chest. He checked himself. She was a beautiful woman, and—like Aubrey—fiercely independent. More than anything, it was probably his own physical desire for Ross he was misinterpreting.

The room had gone quiet.

"Daddy? I asked if you trusted us to make the perfect brownies." Petey looked at Ross and rolled his eyes again in comically adult fashion, as if to say, "Ugh. This guy. Whaddya gonna do?"

Thankfully, Ross covered his awkward silence. "If he won't trust us, then he doesn't get any brownies..."

Xander shook himself, locking on Ross's clear green eyes like a lifeline. He recovered, putting on a large smile and ruffling his son's mop-top hair. "Wait! OK! I defer to your expertise and to my own desire for these brownies, which are making my mouth water!"

"Should we let him have some?" Ross asked, rubbing her chin with her thumb and forefinger in theatrical deference to Petey.

Petey giggled and tried to swallow a smile as he scratched his own chin. "Possibly. He did make good barbecue chicken for dinner." Petey tried to make his voice sound deep, mimicking Ross's ponderous tone.

"You make a good point, Petey. I guess we should let him have one."

"Two!" called Xander.

"Two?" Ross raised her eyebrows before throwing a conspiratorial glance Petey's way. "Thoughts on that?"

"He did play a lot with me in the pool today."

"Yes, that was very fun of him. I supposed he earned it," she nodded, gracious as a queen, toward Xan.

Later, they sat at the table, played *Sorry!,* and ate the brownies, Xander moaning in delight with each bite, and Petey parroting his father. Ross won the spirited game, and the adults cleaned it up while Petey took his shower.

Xander couldn't stop brushing against her, trailing his fingers across her bare back, his meaning clear. *Soon.*

By eight thirty, Petey was sound asleep. Xander checked on him several times, until he was satisfied with the outcome.

"He's in the land of Nod. Thank you for a great evening with him. You were awesome."

"Petey's cool. He's like a mini-Xan. I like *you*, so it stands to reason that I like *him*."

"I like you, too, Ross." Xander held out his hand to her. "Come to bed."

"I shouldn't be here when he wakes."

"I understand. But you're here now. Let's take advantage of it."

He wrapped his hand around hers, and as he led her to his bedroom, he marveled at how such a relatively chaste touch could ignite such a storm of desire and need.

Sated from the orgasms he gave her, Ross lay curled against him. The summer moon rose in the sky, bright and full, and Xander watched the play of moonlight across her back. In that moment, a deep contentment suffused within him—even more so than in the best of times with Aubrey. Relaxed from his own releases, he stroked Ross's soft, dark hair, shining in the moonlight. Their first time that night was so intense it was all he could do to suppress the sounds of his climax to not wake Petey. The second time was tender and, if he was being honest with himself, as close to making love as he'd experienced in years.

"Tell me about your name."

Ross turned her face up toward him, resting her chin on his chest. "Hmm?"

He dropped a lingering kiss on her upper lip, which was just slightly fuller than the lower. "Your name. In the spirit of 'If there is something I want to know about you, I should ask you,' I'd like to know why your parents named you Ross."

She smiled against him, rubbing her lips against his pecs. "OK. I have questions for you too. One for you, one for me, back and forth."

"Deal."

She sat up and they shook, and he kissed the back of her hand, tugging her back to his chest, where she fit so perfectly. She was simply... irresistible. In that moment, he understood Cole's early obsession with Tiercy. Not that this was in any way the same thing. Those two had hurtled full-speed into a relationship, despite Tiercy's reservations and a lasting broken heart over her late husband.

No, this was different. Yep. Totally different.

"You know my sister and I are what they call 'Irish twins'?" Xander nodded, still stroking her silken hair, occasionally rubbing it between his fingers. "My dad named Gaby. He had read this biography on an Edwardian actress named Gabrielle Ray, who was considered the most beautiful actress of her time. He liked the name, and so did my mom."

"I didn't ask about your sister's name. What about *your* name?"

"Patience, grasshopper. I'm getting there. I was a surprise. My mom had a lot of trouble in her pregnancy with Gaby, and the doctor told her she'd likely never get pregnant again. Imagine her shock when she found out she was expecting just nine weeks after Gaby was born.

"She immediately announced that it was her turn to name the baby. She carried me very differently than she carried Gaby, so she was sure I was a boy. M-mom—" his heart ached as Ross's throat caught on the word "—loved watching the soap opera *The Guiding Light*. One of her favorite characters was Ross, and she liked his name. She started calling unborn me 'Ross', and everyone went with it.

"She'd had the required anatomical ultrasound, but didn't want to know the results since she was sure I was a boy. There was never any doubt in my mom's mind, or anyone's for that matter, what she was having." Ross grinned. "And then out I came. Hon says my mother kept asking, 'Are you sure?' when they told her I was a girl. By then, they were so used to calling me Ross, they decided to keep it. Mom told me I was meant to be a Ross."

Her voice was soft and wistful as she recounted those conversations with her mom about her naming. "They gave me 'Ellen' as a middle name, after my dad's mom. She died before I was born. My mom always called me Ross, but my dad called me Ross Ellen, just like Hon does."

"So, you're named after a soap opera character? Cool story. I love your name. It suits you." Xander turned her face up and touched his lips to hers. "Ross..." He whispered her name, drawing out the last sound, and kissed her again. "Your name sounds like a kiss. Ross."

Ross sighed and nestled her head into Xander's shoulder.

"And your sister is named after an old-time actress?"

She snorted in response. "Yep. Famous and gorgeous, as befits our Gaby. Of course, *that* Gabrielle ended up having a mental breakdown, so it's indeed a fitting name for the drama queen."

Xander gave a low whistle. "You really don't hold your sister in high regard, do you? Will you share what happened with you two?"

"Nope. Negative, Ghostrider. That's another question and it's my turn. I get to ask about you." She propped herself up on his chest. "What do you teach at UVA?"

He smiled. "I actually got pretty lucky, considering I'm low professor in the pecking order. I've taken on the course work of a former professional colleague who had a debilitating stroke last summer. I've taught his classes the last two semesters."

"Which are?"

"Architectural Techniques, for the undergrads—two sessions of that. And I teach Modern Building Design to graduate students, as well as a 3D modeling course, which is co-taught with a computer science professor. And I'm really excited about a new cross-disciplinary class I'm teaching with a professor of African-American Studies about the role enslaved persons and forced labor played in the construction of some of this country's most famous buildings. Marquis and I will be exploring both the architecture and the specific stories of those who were enslaved. We're even planning a field trip to Monticello. It's gratifying for me, after many years of searching for my place."

"Permission for a related follow-up question?"

"Granted," he inclined his head, "even though you didn't allow me the follow-up."

"You are clearly a better person than I am," Ross deflected, with a smile. "Why architecture? And why teaching?"

"Because it was different. It was unexpected. And it appealed to me. I think you'll have gathered that my family has a certain amount of wealth. We traveled a lot when I was growing up. As an only child, my parents basically took me everywhere they went. In Europe, I fell in love with architecture. Soaring cathedrals, labyrinthine castles, airy Mediterranean villas. I was fascinated. I went against the family grain of Harvard and enrolled at Duke, just to be difficult. That's where I met Cole. We were both engineering majors. And then I went on to Harvard for my master's, making my parents very happy."

"That explains architecture. But why teaching?"

"That's another question."

"Which you didn't answer before."

He laughed, pressing a kiss to her lips.

"You are persistent." He rubbed his hand down his face, resigned to revealing a personal fact that often made him uncomfortable. And, yet, he didn't feel that with Ross. Somehow, he knew she'd understand him and accept that what appeared to be an asset in his life had oftentimes been a burden. "You could call me a trust fund brat, and that would be true. I'm sorry if that makes me sound cocky. It's just the reality of my world. Both my parents made their money the old-fashioned way—they inherited it. And through shrewd investments, it grows. My dad is a smart businessman. The money, it—frees you, but it also untethers you in a way that for me has been…unsettling.

"My entire adult life, I've tried to find the professional anchor that fulfills me. It's always been connected to architecture. I got close when I invested in the property in Maryland and rehabbed it and built the restaurant on the grounds. But something's always been missing. When Jack—my former colleague at the firm—got sick and they offered me his teaching post as a trial, it spoke to me. I had guest-lectured for him and left energized every time. At the same time, I needed to put down roots for Petey, and for me too. He was heading into kindergarten. It was good timing."

"And you love it?"

"I do, from the moment I started. It's been a huge learning curve for me. But I love the pulse of the campus. I love how it renews itself each semester. I enjoy my colleagues. I like using my brain. I get a thrill sharing something I care about with people who share that passion." He paused and laughed. "Sorry. I got a little carried away."

"Don't apologize. I asked."

"OK. My turn. Since I know you aren't going to tell me what's up with you and your sister—" Ross's eyes narrowed so he hurried on "— tell me about this big career change."

Her frown turned to a smile. "It's in Manhattan, the epicenter of publishing. You know I edit books? Early on, I took on anything. But then I got lucky. I read a memoir that had been pitched at a writer's conference. All these big-name agents and editors turned it down. She couldn't get representation, but she cornered me and begged me to read it. I was young and hungry. So was the author. Her story captivated me and I lobbied hard for it. My boss agreed, we backed the book, and it hit big. *New York Times* bestseller. From then on, I was niched in memoirs for the most part, but I love it. My specialty is celebrity autobiographies, but I edit all types. This position is with a rising publishing house. It's a big job—a chance to guide the direction of my own division."

"Permission to follow up?"

"Granted." They laughed quietly at the parallel request.

"How did you get into your field?"

"You know from Hon that I wrote for and edited the school paper. That continued in college. Tiercy and I both went to University of Maryland. An alum who worked in publishing spoke at an event, and I covered it for the paper. By the end of the interview, I had a plum summer internship in New York City. I guess I comported myself well, and they invited me back each summer. When I graduated, they offered me a position.

"I lived there for a while, but I didn't like Manhattan that much. Big cities aren't my jam. Just before Tiercy's husband, Luke, died, I had moved back to Maryland. I'd established myself in my profession by that point, so they let me commute up several times a month. I can do most of my job from my computer, FaceTime, Zoom, and by text. I don't really need to be there."

"Why are you moving up there, then?"

"For the record, that is a second follow-up, Professor Grace, but I shall deign to answer it."

Xander laughed and pulled her in for a searing kiss, murmuring her name as he bent his head, leaving them both slightly breathless.

"Go on. Why the move?"

"Even though I know my new boss, and he knows my work, it's a new company for me. I need to see and be seen. I have a team working for me. And I already have a place to live. A friend of mine arranged it. He has friends who are moving to Europe for a couple years, so they're subletting their apartment to me. Upper West Side."

"Swanky."

"Indeed."

"You don't seem particularly thrilled."

Ross gave a small smile. "I am... about the job. The moving—I'm not so sure. Like I said, I'm not really a big-city girl. I like my space. The idea of being jammed in with 1.65 million of my closest friends on a tiny island does not particularly appeal to me. That, and leaving Tiercy."

"Your friendship with her is rare and special."

"It is. My turn again?"

"Go for it."

"That look on your face earlier after dinner. That was about her, wasn't it? Tell me about Petey's mom."

"That's not one question. That's a story."

"Then tell me a story."

Xander inhaled a fortifying breath.

Chapter Twenty-Five

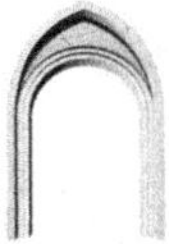

Ross

Xander sighed deeply, and looked up at the ceiling. From the look on his face, she almost regretted asking. Almost. The need to know more about him was just too strong.

"Aubrey is her name. My ex-wife. Our families are good friends, so we grew up in the same social orbit. I think there was always some kind of hope we'd get together, but we never did until our mid-twenties. I was working for an architecture firm in D.C. and she had a job as a Congressional aide. Her family connections got her the job, but she is whip smart. She has a law degree from Yale. Tall, blonde, pedigreed. I'm sure you know the type. We ran into each other at a function and started dating.

"As you can imagine, our families were thrilled and encouraged the match. It was only the second time I've ever seen my mother look truly pleased with me—the first being when I graduated from Harvard.

"I fell in love with Aubrey. She was quite charismatic. People were just... drawn to her. Including me. It wasn't long before I proposed with the requisite Cabot family diamond, which her father bestowed upon me when I came to ask for her hand. He was thrilled. The Grace and

Cabot names, coming together. We married at twenty-seven, which seems so young now. We had fun, we worked hard, we played hard. I was beyond infatuated. We were happy and in love."

"*Were* happy…" Ross swallowed against a frisson of jealousy at the notion of Xander in love with another woman.

Xander ran his hand through his hair, and then rested it on her hip. Ross fixed her eyes on his long, tapered fingers, which had known her so intimately physically, and realized she had never known a man emotionally. And yet here was Xan, revealing what was most definitely his deepest hurt. It scared her, and yet the need to know more was as compelling as her physical need for their climax.

"*Were* happy. And then I pushed her to be something she wasn't. Aubrey and I were nearing the end of a long vacation in Australia and Tahiti when she started throwing up. It didn't take a rocket scientist to figure out she was pregnant. She'd missed her Depo shot and thought she'd be fine to get it upon our return. She must have gotten pregnant early in the trip."

Ross tried to ignore another small, unwanted tug of jealousy at the thought of Xander making love to his then-wife. "And then?"

"She wasn't sure she was ready to be a mom. Her career was taking off and she didn't want to be saddled with a baby. But I was totally ready to be a dad. As an only child, I always wanted a big family and I told her she'd be amazing. She wasn't convinced. She-uh…well, she also struggled with depression. Sometimes, it got really rough for her, although when she took her meds, her moods dramatically improved. She said she was worried about the impact of the medications on her pregnancy. I think she was more worried about her career than the medications. But, either way, she talked about ending the pregnancy, which I just couldn't fathom.

"In my hubris and my myopia," Xander continued, his voice tinged with both sadness and self-recrimination, "I just knew we could protect her career and her health. We had huge arguments. She called her mother for advice, who proceeded to tell everyone Aubrey was expecting, and then the horse was out of the barn.

"Our families went nuts. It was hard not to get caught up in it, and she was glowing. The morning sickness passed quickly. We came home from the trip. She was back at work and digging into a new project. It was the best time of our marriage. I felt truly happy, and I believed she was too. We were both excited about the baby."

Xander was quiet for a long time. For a moment, she thought he wouldn't continue. Then he began again, in a pained whisper.

"After Petey was born, she changed. She was a mess. Emotional. Volatile. Remote. She'd go long periods not holding the baby. She'd rally and do better, but then it would start all over again. She quit her job, which was so unlike her. I dragged her to the doctor, who diagnosed postpartum depression and anxiety. After that, it was a roller coaster of medications. I could feel everything fraying. I tried everything I could to help her. Doctors. Therapists. A wellness retreat in California. You name it. But she was gone. The Aubrey I knew had disappeared.

"One day when Petey was about two, I came home from work early. I just had this... feeling. Petey was at Kindermusik with the nanny. While they were out, Aubrey had packed her bags and left a note. *I'm just not cut out for this, Alexander. I never wanted this. I'm sorry.*

"She was gone.

"My mother-in-law eventually contacted me. They'd taken her to a depression rehab resort in Sedona. About six months later, I got served divorce papers. Our lawyers went back and forth for a while, but I was never permitted to speak to her."

"That sounds awful." Ross gently reached out and laid her hand on Xander's. He flinched, and then turned his hand over, lacing his fingers in hers.

"It was. The saddest day of my life was the day I signed divorce papers ending a marriage to a woman I still loved. I haven't seen her since that last morning. She'd seemed better. It turns out, she'd just made up her mind to leave. I mistook her relief at leaving for healing."

"And you haven't seen her? Has she seen Petey?"

He shook his head and blinked back tears. "Every now and then I think I see her. In a crowd. At a restaurant. But it's never her. She sends presents to Petey via her parents, who live not far from Cole's family. But she's had no contact with him. She relinquished her parental rights to me, which just blows my mind. How can you walk away from him?

He's just...such a gift. But I can't help thinking it's all my fault. If I could've helped her through, Petey would have his mom."

"You're a great dad to Petey, Xan. He's lucky to have you. That's more than some kids ever get."

Xander stared up at the ceiling. After a minute, he turned and gave Ross a wry smile. "Aren't you glad you asked?"

"I *am* glad. I am so sorry, Xan. So...you still love her." It wasn't a question.

"Yes. No. I don't know." Xander sighed. "I love what I thought we had, who I thought she was. I loved the idea of us. And, yes, on some level I guess I still love her. But it's over. She's gone, and I have a good life with Petey. The rest is ancient history. But now you know."

"It doesn't seem so ancient. At least, not based on the look on your face."

"It is ancient. Except for the fact that she's the reason I'm not interested in a relationship. I will never go through that again." He blew out a huge sigh and then smiled. "And now you know why I love it here."

Ross looked at him quizzically.

"This cottage, Hon, Gaby, Ted, and the kids... this is the closest I've ever come to feeling like I'm part of a family. Cole is my best friend, but we didn't hang out growing up the way you and Tiercy did. I lived in that hell-house near UVA for months with Petey, loving teaching, knowing right away that this area was home. I could've moved out sooner into a different and better place, but once Hon showed me the cottage in the fall I knew no place else would measure up. I just fell in love with this property.

"I knew I'd have to wait for the renovations, but in the meantime, I bonded with Ted over poker night. Gaby helped me find an awesome nanny to help with Petey during the school year. And I just adore Leah. I've only been in the cottage for a few months, but in that time, I feel like I've made my first real home."

Ross pressed a kiss to his chest and grinned at him.

"You think I'm corny, don't you, Ross Beaufort."

"Nope. I think you've been Waldheimed."

"Wald—what's that mean?"

"Call Tiercy and ask her. It happens here. It's a thing."

Xander cupped her face. "Can you talk to me about what happened to your parents, Ross?"

She turned away from him, and she knew he had to register the tension in her body. "It's not something I ever talk about."

"Would you trust me? Please give me the gift of your trust, like I did with you when I told you about Aubrey."

Ross was still. For a long time, the only sound was their breathing. Finally, she nodded, surprised at the small comfort of her cheek resting on his chest.

"They were killed in a car accident, by a drunk driver." Her voice sounded flat and toneless in her ears against the quiet of the night. "Gaby was out with a girl who lived in the area. My parents had been on a date night. It was a late dinner and I remember they were excited because there was a jazz band playing in the bar. My parents loved jazz. Hon and Pop were at the farmhouse, and so were Tiercy and I. We watched a movie on DVD. Pop had finally gotten a player and it was a big deal. I kissed my parents goodbye. Then Tiercy and I watched the movie and went to bed. The next morning, I woke to Hon telling me they were gone. They'd been killed."

"My God, Ross. I'm sorry." He stroked small circles on her back. "What an awful thing to go through. How old were you?"

"It was right after my sixteenth birthday. I left here after their funerals and I never came back. Until now." Ross shifted up on her elbows, facing Xan again. "Can we talk about lighter things now? My God this got heavy fast."

Xander pulled her fully on top of him. "How about we don't talk at all anymore."

"Deal." Ross brushed his hair back from his forehead, leaning in for a deep kiss. Some minutes later she came up for air, slightly breathless. "Is it tacky if I tell you I'm horny again?"

Xander shook his head, smiling, as he took her face between her hands. "Stop talking," he whispered and proceeded to do things to her that ensured no coherent thought.

CHAPTER TWENTY-SIX

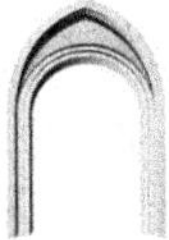

Ross

At 4 a.m., Ross crept back into the house, wincing at the damn creaking hardwoods. She was too old for this charade. Even though she was sure Hon already knew, she'd officially come clean to her later. But, first, she desperately needed sleep.

Ross climbed into the four-poster bed, quite sure she'd fall into a deep, dreamless sleep. Instead, she tossed and turned as snippets of her pillow talk with Xander darted around her brain. She was intensely curious about Aubrey and fought the urge to Google her. Xander clearly still had strong feelings for his ex-wife, and yet Ross was impressed that he shared as much as he did.

"So...you still love her." Ross's heart had skipped a beat as she made the statement earlier. Why? It was just a summer deal between her and Xan. She was moving to New York in a little more than a month. She had Gideon in Manhattan—who, if she were being honest, was becoming rather unsatisfying in comparison with Xan. And since when was she this deep soul-searcher?

Maybe since she saw Tiercy settled with Cole? Since being home in Virginia? And there it was again... thinking of Virginia as *home*.

Ross flipped over to her other side, trying to get comfortable, frustrated that sleep was eluding her. She'd lived in Maryland her entire life. *That* was home. Should be home. And yet… just a short time back here…and it was quickly beginning to feel like home. It didn't make sense.

She punched at her pillow to plump it.

A short time with Xan, too…and he was…what? Just a summer deal? Summer deals didn't unveil the deep and hurting crevices of a heart. Yet that was exactly what Xander had done this evening. She'd even told him about her parents.

On the other hand, she had resisted talking about Gaby and allowed him to change the subject.

Ross sighed and flipped to her other side, pulling the soft cotton duvet over her head. She was exhausted, but couldn't turn off her brain.

She could hear Xander's voice. *You really don't hold your sister in high regard, do you? What happened with you two?*

Ross squeezed her eyes shut tighter. Go to sleep, she commanded herself.

What happened?

What happened, indeed.

Ross had replayed that time period after her parents' deaths an exhausting myriad of times. Each time, her anger surged, fresh as new. Hon, forced to push aside her own grief to cater to Gaby's drama. Gaby's inability to calm herself. Her self-centered, histrionic grieving meant no one else could grieve her parents because Gaby sucked up all the energy and attention. Not Ross, and not her grandparents—who had lost their own child after all! And then that September, when Hon couldn't make Ross's first field hockey game of the season, when she was named captain as a junior, because Gaby had had another breakdown. Or that winter, when only Hon had attended her induction into the National Honor Society because she and Pop couldn't both leave *fragile Gaby.*

Even Ross's high school graduation had been an ordeal. Tiercy's family hosted the after-party. Ross hadn't wanted her sister there, but Hon had put her foot down. Gaby was there, a blonde, suffering specter, with guests swirling around her asking *how she was doing,* the older folks clucking their tongues in commiseration at how hard *the poor girl* was taking the loss of her parents. Ross deeply resented that her entire graduation party was about Gaby—at least from her perspective.

More than once that day, Tiercy had talked Ross off the ledge. Without trying, Ross could come up with a dozen more examples—all of which made her blood hum with two decades of accumulated resentment, all aimed at her sister.

It had been ugly then, and even now it didn't take much to tap the deep font of anger Ross had stored.

Still, even with all that, there were times she grappled with guilt, remembering how close she'd once been to her sister. On a certain level, she missed her sister. The way they used to be. *Before.* There were moments this last week when she felt that old iciness around her heart thaw. When she wondered if they could begin again.

And then she remembered. Remembered her grandparents coaxing an overwrought Gaby out of bed the morning of the funeral. The incessant weeping and wailing. Hon and Pop unable to properly grieve because they had to attend to Gaby. It had been unbearable. Ross had wanted to weep, but found herself inhibited. Stifled. Unable to feel anything but anger at her sister.

Ross flopped on her back and stared up at the ceiling.

She should just confront her sister, once and for all. Say what needed to be said. What she should have said all those years ago. Slay the dragon of anger eating her up, and then move on with her Gaby-less life.

What would Xan think of that? She knew he considered Gaby a good friend.

"You can't be Team Ross and Team Gaby. You have to choose," she announced to the room, knowing it was immature, and yet at the same time, unable to feel otherwise. Some rifts ran too deep to mend.

Ross closed her eyes and willed herself to stop thinking about her sister, eventually succumbing to exhaustion and falling into a fitful sleep.

She woke shortly before eleven, shocked at the time, and hopped into the shower. They were supposed to pack all but the essentials in Hon's room today. "Fuck," she muttered, throwing on clothes and hurrying down the stairs.

"We're in here," came Hon's voice from the primary bedroom. "Grab some coffee and come join us."

Us. Hon and Gaby. When all three of them were together, it was hard not to feel like a third wheel. Ross sighed and headed into the sunny kitchen, inhaling deeply as she poured the fragrant brew. Slowly she headed to Hon's room.

"I always think the smell of coffee is almost as revitalizing as the caffeine itself," Hon remarked, as Ross settled on the end of the bed, legs crossed, Orioles mug nestled in her hands.

For about the billionth time in her life, Ross was sure Hon had ESP —or at least hidden cameras. Ross lifted the mug in a toast of agreement, sharing a smile with Hon, two sets of green eyes holding in deepest affection.

"We weren't sure if you'd ever emerge, Sleeping Beauty," added Gaby, with a caustic edge.

Ross bit back an unkind retort. Gaby looked terrible. She had dark circles under her eyes and her beautiful face was waxen and lined with exhaustion. This was not Gaby-drama; it was the real deal. "You look like shit. Maybe you're the one who should have slept in?"

"Tara has a bad summer cold and was up all night coughing and congested. Ted is on a shift, so I think I slept about two total hours."

"I told you to go home," Hon chided, stroking the side of Gaby's cheek. Ross stifled an unwanted burn of jealousy at the tender display. "You need your rest," Hon admonished.

Something was definitely up with Gaby. Was she sick? Both Hon and Xan had helicoptered around her the other day, and the concern on Hon's face this morning was about more than just Gaby's need for sleep.

Gaby offered a tired but affectionate smile at Hon. "I'll take a catnap this afternoon. Promise. But let's get this finished." Turning to Ross, she raised a sardonic eyebrow. "And you may need one as well. Hon tells me you got in after 4 a.m."

Ross's mouth dropped open, her gaze moving between Gaby and Hon, who was shaking her head in consternation at Gaby.

"Are you serious? You were talking about me?" Ross was vacillating between irked and horrified.

Hon put down the figurine she'd been rolling in bubble wrap and wrapped her arms around Ross. "Oh, sweetie. I'm sorry. We weren't talking in a mean way. I just mentioned to Gaby that you and Xander seem to have really hit it off, and it was a late night last night."

"Actually an early morning," chimed Gaby.

Ross shot her a hot look at the same time Hon delivered her own quelling glance at Gaby.

"The floors do creak, dear. There is nothing wrong with you coming in late after a date. You're a grown woman. And we weren't talking about you, per se. I was just asking Gaby more about Alexander, as she and Ted know him well and you seem taken with him."

Ross opened her mouth to respond, shook her head, and rolled her eyes closed. "Unbelievable," she muttered. "Not that I owe anyone an explanation, but I'm not *dating* Xander. We're just...hanging out. He's fun."

"Apparently," drawled Gaby. "There's nothing like 4 a.m. fun..."

"Gaby," Hon warned in a tone reminiscent of their youth.

Ross ignored her sister and turned to Hon, who'd resumed her wrapping. "Listen, I was going to tell you anyway. Again, while I'm not *dating* Xan," she emphasized the key word, "I am spending time with him, and that may include some late nights." Ross was appalled to feel her cheeks flaming. "I'm tired of feeling like a sneaky teenager. I just wanted you to know I'll have some late nights, and...uh...possibly some overnights." The tips of Ross's ears now joined in on the embarrassed burn. "I didn't want you to worry, or wonder."

Hon stroked a small sculpture of a mother holding a baby. "I always loved this. Frederick gave it to me after I had your mother." She placed it with care on a sheet of bubble wrap. "Ross, you are a grown woman. You don't owe me any explanations. But I do appreciate you letting me know. You may be in your thirties—" Ross groaned in mock protest at her age "—but you are still my baby granddaughter under my roof, and I will always worry about you, and your sister as well." She rested the wrapped sculpture in the plastic bin of treasures to be installed in her new home. "I want you to have fun this summer, Ross Ellen. Alexander is a good man."

"He's the best." Gaby was studying her younger sister, eyes narrowed. "Does Petey know his dad is dating you?"

Ross took a deep sip of her coffee and returned her sister's gaze. "Once again, for the slower folks in the room, we are *not* dating. And, not that it's any of your business, but Petey does know that Xander and I are friends."

"It is my business because Xander is *my* friend," retorted Gaby. "He's a good man, and he's been very hurt. He doesn't need you flitting in, seducing him, and then chewing him up and spitting him out on your way to your fancy Manhattan job."

"Flitting in—?" Ross was incredulous.

Actually, she was furious.

She vaulted off the bed and slammed her mug on the bedside table, splashing coffee on it. "How dare you talk to me that way! You don't even know me. Who do you think you are, inserting yourself into something that is none of your business?" She glared at her sister, who returned the look, equally incensed.

"As I already said, for the slower folks in the room," Gaby mimicked, "he is my friend, so it *is* my business. Xander deserves more than how you usually treat men. And I won't have you hurting him. Or Petey. They've been through enough." Gaby reached over and used a cloth to clean Ross's spill, rolling her eyes and shaking her head.

"Ha!" Ross hollered, reaching for the mug and intentionally spilling a bit more in the process, smirking as she drew a low growl from Gaby. "That's rich. Overreacting as usual." Her eyes traveled over Gaby's face. "What is it? Oooh, I get it. You have a thing for Alexander Grace, don't you?" As she pronounced it, old, unwanted insecurity stabbed at her gut. "Old Moose pales in comparison. Does our little hausfrau have the hots for the sexy single dad next door?" Ross's hands shook as she mocked her sister. Even as she said it, she knew she'd crossed a line.

"Bitch!"

"Girls!" snapped Hon, standing between them, easing the mug out of Ross's shaking hands.

"No! I won't listen to her hurl nasty accusations." Gaby's voice shook with anger. "I love my husband very much. Xander is a *friend*. And you"—she pointed her finger at Ross—"are a cold, unfeeling woman. If Xan knows what's good for him, he'll drop you before you can shred him."

"You. Don't. Know. Me." Ross hit every word.

"I know you've never been in love. I know you close yourself off from everyone except Tiercy and your precious Jemma. I know you prefer your friend's daughter over your own nieces and nephew. I know you don't cry. You never even cried for Mom and Dad. You are *cold*."

"That's ironic, coming from you, Gaby. Did it ever cross your self-absorbed mind that with your never-ending drama and tears, you single-handedly ensured there was no room in this family for my feelings—or Hon's or Pop's for that matter."

"Enough!" Hon's single word sliced through the sisters' hostility like ice. "Enough," she repeated, closing her eyes.

"It is enough. I'm finished talking to her." Ross glowered at her sister, who returned the look with equal force. "She isn't worth my breath."

"Enough," Hon whispered, holding up a trembling hand.

Ross fought a pang of remorse at the tears in her grandmother's eyes. In that moment, Hon looked every bit of her seventy-nine years.

"I'm sorry, Hon." A strange mixture of anger, regret, sorrow, and self-loathing churned in Ross.

"Me, too," added Gaby, although to Ross's ear it didn't sound fully sincere.

Ross turned her back to Hon and rolled her eyes. "Let's get back to work."

The women worked in relative silence, with both Ross and Gaby directing most of their sparse conversation to Hon. Periodically, Hon would leave to grab more items, with the ensuing oppressive quiet punctuated by brief, stilted comments only as necessary between the sisters.

It was exactly the type of interlude Ross had dreaded when Hon asked her to come to the farmhouse. She wanted to text Tiercy, but she'd left her phone charging in her room. Paranoia, likely unreasonable, kept her from leaving Hon and Gaby alone in the room, as Ross sensed the fight would become a topic of conversation that Gaby would twist to her advantage. *Not a chance, sister.*

They ate sandwiches in the bedroom as they packed, and Hon played music to fill the silence. By 2 p.m., the room was packed, with a pile of items for donation in the back of Ross's car.

"How about we call it a day?" Hon looked as anxious to end the misery as Ross.

"Sounds good to me," Gaby answered.

Don't let the door hit you on your way out, thought Ross.

"Don't forget, no packing for the next few days. I've got the first of my two summer trips tomorrow. I'm sorry about that. I paid the trip deposits long before I learned the condo was going to be available."

"Gotcha, Hon. No worries." Ross knew how much Hon was looking forward to these vacations. Going to Myrtle Beach with her Bunco ladies then Cumberland Island a few weeks later to visit with Francesca would be wonderful distractions for her grandmother. She suspected the stress of moving, and likely the tension between Ross and her sister, made them even more appealing.

"Ted and I are taking Nick and Kingsley to camp in West Virginia, and then we're going to spend a couple days there with Tara. We'll be back on Tuesday."

Ross knew Gaby's reminder was for Hon, but succumbed to mental pettiness. *Like. I. Care.* Oh, to say that out loud! Then it hit her. *House to myself!*

Ross's mood lifted. She had three days all to herself, without the specter of her sister, without packing, without any responsibilities. Ross contemplated driving up to see Tiercy, but then Xander's face flashed in her mind. She was shocked to find herself torn between her bestie and her summer deal.

Hon cleared her throat once, and then cleared it again. She looked sadly at her granddaughters. "There is a lot that clearly needs to be said between the two of you—and among the three of us—and when I get back from my trip with Frannie, I will make that happen. But, for now, I think everyone needs a break. Gabrielle, you head home and get some rest. Ross Ellen, you, too."

"Love you, Hon." Ross gently squeezed Hon, doing her best to infuse an apology into her hug. She stepped away, already missing the timeless comfort of her grandmother's arms around her.

"I love you. I'm sorry." Gaby dropped a kiss on Hon's powder-soft cheek.

"I love both you girls. Now skedaddle. I need a nap myself."

Ross fled from the room. She craved exercise, and she missed her Peloton. As she'd been doing periodically since her arrival, she pulled on a sports bra, running shorts, and her sneakers and headed outside. She needed air.

Desperate to put distance between herself and her sister, she sprinted toward the end of the long lane leading to the house, and then circled around the property—avoiding the part Gaby now owned—running toward the main road. Five sweaty miles later, she made it back to the lane leading to the farmhouse, where she slumped against a tree, head on her knees, as she fought to catch her breath.

As her heart rate calmed, utter exhaustion settled into her bones. Ross looked back down the lane and realized she did not have the energy, or the heart, for the half-mile walk back to the house. A bumblebee buzzed a summer afternoon lullaby as Ross stretched out on the thick, verdant grass and closed her eyes.

CHAPTER TWENTY-SEVEN

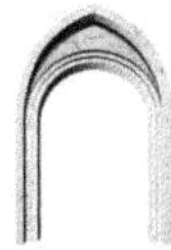

Ross

Ross awoke, groggy, curled in a fetal position and shaded by the leaves of the oak tree. She could see the sun had dropped a bit. She remembered enough from learning in Girl Scouts how to tell time by the sun position to know it was late afternoon. Something tickled her forearm. Focusing her gaze on the culprit, Ross gently removed a ladybug trekking across the terrain of her arm. She sat up, resting her head back against the trunk of the tree.

"Fuck," she breathed, the fight with Gaby flooding back to her.

That was a shitshow. An image of Hon's tear-filled eyes came unbidden. Ross's chest was heavy with guilt. She had behaved like an immature brat and hurt Hon in the process. With fewer than five weeks remaining here, she was determined to make the best of it, for her grandmother's sake. Ross would ask for forgiveness. But first, she had a stop to make.

Ross knocked on the front door of her sister's house, but no one answered. Where were the kids? She walked around to the side and peeked into the screened in porch. Gaby was sound asleep, Laverne curled against her. The puppy saw Ross and emitted a high yip of excitement, startling her sister awake.

Ross froze in her tracks as her sister slowly sat up and deposited the wriggling puppy on the floor. The sisters locked gazes for a long moment.

"May I come in?"

Gaby hesitated and then nodded.

Ross opened the screen door, careful not to let Laverne out. She reached down and picked up the puppy, smiling as the golden squirmed and licked her. "Good girl. No kisses." She nuzzled the soft fur for a moment, enjoying the puppy breath. "She's a cutie."

"You didn't come here to say that."

"No, I didn't." Ross's ire had calmed, but it was just under the surface, threatening to emerge. She was trying to be the bigger person, but somehow her sister always reduced her to feeling like an awkward teenager. "I came to apologize for insulting your marriage. That was out of line."

Gaby stared at her in silence, a small frown between her eyes. Even newly awakened from a nap, her hair mussed, Gaby was still remarkably beautiful. Ross swallowed the bitter old jealousy.

When Gaby finally spoke, her voice was soft, but not unkind. "I accept your apology. And you *were* out of line. I love my husband very much. He is a good man. My feelings for Xander are those of friendship and nothing more. He's also a good man, and his heart's been broken once before."

Now it was Ross's turn for a frown. "I know that. He told me about Aubrey."

"He did?" Gaby sounded surprised.

"Yes, he did," Ross confirmed with a certain amount of vindication —proof that Xander at least didn't find her to be "cold and unfeeling."

"Then you'll understand why I feel protective of him. Under that Captain America yumminess is a lot of hurt."

For some reason, Ross found herself bristling at the notion that

Gaby believed she knew Xander better than she herself did. She swallowed her resentment and continued. "I didn't come here to talk about Xander or get advice from you." She sighed. Why was everything so hard with Gaby? "I came to offer a truce. A détente."

"Nice SAT word." Gaby's eyes crinkled in a small smile. "Do you and Tiercy still do that?"

"Yes, we do. It was all I could do not to pepper my maid of honor toast with big words." The corner of Ross's mouth turned up in a smile, a forced effort, but hopefully a small sign of easing into rapprochement.

"I wondered," Gaby mused, a faraway look in her eyes. "I always envied you that friendship. Tiercy's awesome."

"Yes, she is."

"Tell me about this détente."

Ross sighed and rubbed the top of Laverne's head. "Gaby, I'm sure you realize I didn't want to come to Virginia. But I'm here because Hon asked me, and I love her. I only have five more weeks. For Hon's sake, can we try to get along? We touched a third rail today, and we both got zapped. But worse, we hurt Hon.

"I keep seeing her face as we were fighting. I don't want to be the cause of any more hurt for her.

"Listen, we both said a lot of things, and there's a lot more that we didn't say. Can we just table it? Try to get along, just to get through the packing and the moving? As Tiercy and Taylor Swift would say, fake it 'til we make it? Then I'll be leaving and we'll be out of each other's hair."

"Just like old times." Gaby almost sounded dejected, but that couldn't be. "My sister, the stranger," she continued. "You know, I—uh, I had hoped that maybe with this visit, you and I could—never mind."

"You and I could fix things?" Ross finished for her. She blew the air out of her lungs. "Honestly? I don't think that's possible. Twenty years and a lot of hurt. Too much water under the bridge, you know? Some things run too deep."

Gaby nodded, her eyes sad. "I, um...I owe you an apology too. For calling you cold and unfeeling. And I'm sorry I called you a bitch. I don't think I've called you that since your freshman year of high school when you put a hole in my favorite Tommy Hilfiger sweater."

Ross released an unexpected laugh, despite herself. "I'll never live that down."

"Nope," Gaby chuckled. "I really am sorry. And what you do with Xander is your own business. Just—just, be kind?"

"I accept your apology. As for Xan, we have an agreement. So, no worries. It's all good."

Gaby arched an eyebrow. "An agreement?"

"Let's just say we have a 'summer deal' with conditions and ground rules, and leave it at that."

"A summer deal?" Now Gaby really laughed. "You are a piece of work, Ross. Oh, to live your life for a day."

"The glamour is positively exhausting," Ross teased. "Trust me. You wouldn't want to."

"I don't know about that." Gaby held out her hand. "Détente."

Ross shifted the puppy and placed her hand in her sister's. "Détente."

Heading back to the farmhouse, Ross found Hon and apologized. To her surprise, Hon was brisk. Clearly, she was still smarting from the fight. Once again, Ross was struck by how frail her grandmother now seemed—frail, but still a force of nature and not one to brook any nonsense from her granddaughters, no matter that they were both grown women themselves.

Hon pierced Ross with a frank, green gaze. "Ross, my love, you may be an adult, but you still have a lot of growing up to do. You and your sister both. When I return, you are going to have to deal with your feelings for each other...in a kind and reasonable way." She held up a staying hand, fingers arched with arthritis, as Ross began to speak. "No. I think you've said enough. I get the final words on this unfortunate topic for the day. I love you and your sister very much. It's time you two realized that underneath all the hurt is a hell of a lot of love that you both need. Now, let's have some dinner and then I need to get my things ready for the trip."

From her bedroom that evening, Ross called Tiercy, who picked up on the second ring. "Oh, thank God. I was just having a pity party. I had a fight with Cole."

"Oh, honey. A bad one?" Ross could hear the sorrow in Tiercy's voice and a tremor of fear slid down her spine. Tiercy was the most important person in Ross's world and she couldn't bear the thought of her vibrant friend suffering.

"No. I wasn't feeling well, and he was trying to take care of me, and I barked at him, and then he yapped at me, and we went a couple rounds. He just stormed out. I've been staring out the window watching for his car." Tiercy's voice was sad. "The worst thing is it was a fight about nothing."

"Oh, Tierce. I'm sorry. Why didn't you call me?"

"I guess I didn't want to be disloyal to Cole. I'm mad at him. But I'm madder at myself. He was just trying to take care of me and I bit his head off."

A painful thought came unbidden to her mind. It was out of her mouth before she could stop it. "I feel like you don't need me anymore now that you have Cole. You have a whole life with him, and your friend —who doesn't have a clue about relationships—would be the last person you'd call when you fought with your husband."

"No! Oh, Ross. No! No way. I'll always need you. Please don't think that. I didn't call because it wasn't a *fight* fight. It was just a spat. You know if something were really wrong, you'd be my first call. And, Ross, I always need you. Cole is my husband and I love him. But you are my *bestie.* The Meredith to my Cristina. The Monica to my Rachel. The Ethel to my Lucy—"

"Why do I have to be Ethel? I feel like I'm more Lucy-like. You can be Ethel."

Tiercy burst out laughing. "Ross, you are the best of the besties. And you can bet your sausage toes I'll be there soon and we can properly hang out."

"You had to bring up the toes…"

"How you ended up with those on the base of your gorgeous, jealousy-inducing, willowy body, I'll never know. I feel like it was God's way of making you a bit more like the rest of us. You needed one imperfection, otherwise we'd hate you."

"Ha. According to my sister, I have many imperfections. And I'm 'cold and unfeeling.'"

"She actually said that?"

"Yep. We had a big ol' fight, right in front of Hon. And she chewed me out for seeing Xander, got all territorial about him, and called me cold and unfeeling."

"Bitch."

"She called me that too."

"Shut up! She did not. In front of Hon?"

"Yep."

"Damn." Tiercy gave a low whistle. "I can't believe Gaby said those things."

"Why? I can. She's a shrew."

"She's not."

"I don't know why you defend her."

"Because she's a good person. You two just have a lot of *stuff*."

"Now *that* is the understatement of all time." Ross was quiet. "Tiercy, you don't think I'm cold and unfeeling, do you?"

"Oh, Ross Beaufort. You have the biggest, warmest heart of anyone I know. You changed your whole life around to take care of me, and Jemma, when Luke died. You were the one who nudged me, not so gently, toward Cole. You dropped everything to help Hon. You are the best godmother in the world to Jemma—"

"Oh, Maleficent is mad about that too. She says I prefer Jemma to her kids. Which is true, I guess."

"Only because you see Jemma all the time and you only see her kids at holidays. It's not quite fair."

"Tell her that."

"Ross, I'm going to give you some tough love here. You are amazing, and warm, and funny, and kind. But you are also stubborn and you hold a grudge better than anyone I know."

"Thank you." Ross giggled and then snorted.

"That was *not* a compliment." Tiercy tried to sound stern but she gave in to Ross's infectious laugh. "What am I going to do with you?"

"Put up with me until we're wild old ladies?"

"Deal. Even after then. Someone has to rule the nursing home."

"She did apologize. And I think she meant it. Maybe."

"She meant it, Ross. Now, enough about your sister. Tell me about Xan."

"He's good. Great actually. Petey's cool, too, once I got past my own weird awkwardness with him. And Xan, well...he's just easy to be around. We laugh a lot, we have a ton of amazing sex, and he just rocks. I like him."

"But you're not *dating*..." Tiercy teased.

"Nope." Ross's tone was jovial and yet matter of fact. "Dating implies a level of commitment. We don't have that. We're having a good time, and then we both walk away. Besides, he's hung up on his ex. *Aubrey*." Ross said her name like it was toxic. "I get the sense that if she walked back into his life tomorrow, he'd drop me like a hot, sausage-toed potato."

"Somehow I doubt that..." Tiercy mused.

"I know it," Ross confirmed. "You should hear him talk about her. And he still has a photo of the three of them. It's in Petey's room."

"Well, that only makes sense. She's his mother after all."

"You don't see his face when he looks at it."

"If you say so."

"I say so."

"Okaaay. What fun packing is on the docket for tomorrow?"

"No packing. Hon is going on her Myrtle Beach vacation, and my sister and her family are dropping Nick and Kingsley at camp and then taking a little family trip. And I have the entire Waldheim compound gloriously, blessedly to myself."

"What about Xan?"

"Hmmm...I guess he'll be around, so I won't be completely alone. But I don't mind *his* company at all. It comes with hot sex."

"You are such a wanton."

"Triple bonus points for an SAT word in your pathetic, woeful state."

"Thank you," Tiercy laughed. "Thank you for calling, you warm, feeling, sausage-toed wanton. I love you."

"Love you, too, sad friend. Cole will be back soon, and, in good news, you get to have make-up sex."

"Ooh...good point. Trust you to find the silver sex lining. And, hey, Ross? I get to be Lucy. My hair is redder." Tiercy disconnected the call, giggling.

S till smiling, Ross texted Xan.

ROSS

Too late for a booty call? I can be over in 10 mins

He immediately replied.

XANDER

I wish I could, but I have to be up at 5 a.m. to take Petey to camp. He's going to the same one as Nick this year, and he'll be gone for two weeks. It's ridiculous.

ROSS

Two weeks? That's a long time. Will he be OK?

XANDER

The better question is... will I?

ROSS

Why so long?

XANDER

He insisted. That's how long Nick goes, and
he wants to do any and all things Nick does

ROSS

Intense

XANDER

Big time

ROSS

I'd be happy to offer you some distraction to
help you pass the time…

XANDER

Now you're talking

ROSS

While Petey is at camp, we can have
sexapalooza

XANDER

Keep going. I like where this is headed…

ROSS

You, me, naked… poolside, inside, outside,
anywhere…

XANDER

Does this count as sexting?

ROSS

Hardly.

XANDER

Damn. I thought I was getting indoctrinated
into the club

ROSS

Wait—you've never sexted?

XANDER

Now I feel like a loser

> ROSS
>
> Hang on a sec

Ross slid out of her nightie and arranged herself on the bed, legs artfully open, finger strategically placed. She snapped a photo and hit send.

XANDER

Holy shit, Ross

> ROSS
>
> You like?

XANDER

I love. You're killing me

> ROSS
>
> Welcome to the club

XANDER

I like your club

> ROSS
>
> Not too late for me to come by

XANDER

Get your sexy ass over here

Ross grinned, slid on her nightie and a robe, and scurried down the stairs, ignoring the creaking. She was out of the Xan Closet now, and she ran into the warm night, toward him.

CHAPTER TWENTY-EIGHT

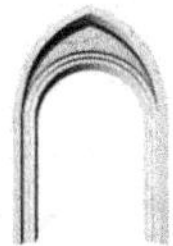

Ross

"Does our summer deal allow for going on a date as long as we're not dating?"

"Hmm...date?" Ross roused herself from sleep, pushing her tousled hair from her forehead.

Xander was up on his elbow, in her four-poster bed, grinning at her. Hon had left the day before, and Ross and he hadn't wasted any time sampling each other in the various rooms of the farmhouse. Every room, that is, except Hon's. That was a line they'd never cross. Exhausted, they'd fallen into bed and slept.

Never a morning person, Ross was not at her best. She cracked an eyelid. "No talkie 'til coffee," she mumbled and burrowed back under the covers.

Ross felt more than heard the deep rumble of Xander's laugh as the bed shifted. "Be right back, Principessa." He leaned in and kissed the exposed top of her forehead.

Some time later, she woke to the sounds of opera from the kitchen, and Xander's own tenor singing along. She snuggled into the bed, smiling at the sound. Fuck...was there anything wrong with this guy?

Did he not floss? Forget to flush the toilet? Leave the seat up? Drink Bud Light? *Anything?*

Ross slid out of bed and went into the bathroom. With Xander's stubble burns on her neck and torso, and her rumpled hair, she had the look of a woman well-bedded. *Indeed.* She rinsed her mouth with wash and pulled on her silk robe, then crept down the creaky stairs, not wanting to interrupt the performance.

"*Nessun dorma. Nessun dorma. Tu pure, o Principessa...Nella tua fredda stanza. Guardi le stelle che tremano...*"

Xander stood at the stove in nothing but a pair of boxer briefs, singing the aria as he scrambled eggs. The sight of him propelled her into the kitchen almost as much as the tantalizing aroma of coffee. "Buongiorno, Principessa," Xan greeted her, turning around with a smile, arms out.

She padded across the kitchen to him, enjoying the feeling of him pulling her to his chest. As she rested her head, he resumed singing. Slowly, as in a dance, he turned sideways with her so he could stir the eggs while holding her against him with his other arm. As he sang "*Vincero!*" at the aria culmination, he swung the spatula, making Ross laugh.

"Your breakfast, Principessa. But first, before we talkie...coffee." With a flourish, he poured the coffee into her father's Orioles mug, handing it to her with a deep bow.

Forgetting she wasn't a morning person, Ross curtsied. "*Grazie mille.*"

As they sat to eat, Ross couldn't help but indulge her curiosity. "I didn't know you could sing like that. Or that you liked opera."

"Hmm..." Xander looked at her with a raised eyebrow "Not a surprise, considering our...shall we say...carnal knowledge...of each other far surpasses other anecdotal tidbits we might know."

"Point well taken," Ross conceded.

"However, I propose to amend that. Just because we have a summer deal, involving exquisite carnal knowledge—" Ross gave a satisfied hum "—doesn't mean we shouldn't share pressure-free little morsels as the mood arises."

"I concur with this amendment to the summer deal."

"Excellent. Then I shall tell you about my love of opera. Victoria and Charles—my parents—"

"How very Brahmin." Ross used her best Katharine Hepburn accent, earning her an approving nod from Xander.

"Mmm, yes, quite. They endeavored to raise their only child to be quite cultured. They forced me to go to ballet and the symphony, things like that. To gain *an appreciation*. In high school, they took me to the opera. Now, you must understand that Victoria and Charles don't actually like the opera. But they attend because it's 'what one does.'"

"Do you really call your parents Victoria and Charles?" Ross held on to her father's mug, a tangible reminder of the loving relationship she'd had with the man she'd called "Daddy," or "Papa Bear" if she was feeling silly.

"Only behind their backs." Xan smiled. "The thing is...it backfired on them. We saw Puccini's *Turandot* at the Met in New York, and I was captivated. Shortly after, they left for a trip, and I bought the CD. I would warble *Nessun Dorma*, which is what you heard me singing earlier, around our home. Our housekeeper, Ines, encouraged me. She loved it when I sang."

"Warble? Hardly. You have an amazing voice. You could be on stage."

Xan laughed. "No. I have a decent voice. But when you listen to the real deal, the range is astounding. It gives me chills."

Ross swirled her coffee, fascinated. "What does it mean?"

"The song? Well, first you need to know the story. Calaf, who is an unknown prince, falls in love with the princess, Turandot, who is beautiful but aloof. No one can marry her, however, unless they answer three riddles. If the suitor fails, he is killed. Calaf succeeds, but she won't marry him because he is a stranger. He makes a deal with her. If she can figure out his name before dawn, he will die. If she doesn't, he will marry her."

"I think the summer deal is better."

"Quiet and let me finish."

Ross giggled into her coffee.

"Turandot says that no one shall sleep until she learns the suitor's name. And Calaf sings '*Nessun Dorma*—Nobody Shall Sleep.' It has such beautiful words from Puccini. 'Watch the stars that tremble with love and hope' and 'My secret is hidden within me...on your mouth I will tell it when the light shines...my kiss will dissolve the silence that makes you mine...at dawn I win!'"

"And? What happens?"

"I'm not going to tell you." Xander zipped his lips.

"What?" Ross shrieked. "How can you do that to me?" She came out of her chair and swatted at him. Xan grabbed her hand and tugged her into his lap.

"Oh, Principessa. I wouldn't do you any favors if I told you about it. Maybe one day I'll come to see you in New York, and we'll see *Turandot* together."

Ross snuggled a bit further down, her head rested on his shoulder so he couldn't see her face. She tried to make her voice sound noncommittal while a thousand pounds of emotional lead weighed on her chest. "Yes, Xan. That'd be awesome. Hey, I'm going to hop in the shower. Thank you for breakfast and Puccini." She left the kitchen before he could say more.

"What was that about?"

The door to the double shower slid open, revealing Xander wearing nothing more than a frown.

"What was what?" Ross kept her voice light. "You want to hop in here with me? Plenty of room."

Still frowning, Xander stepped in, closing the door. "Christ, Ross. It's June in Virginia and you're having a piping hot shower?"

"A little morsel about moi. I like very hot showers. Even in the humid summer."

"Duly noted. If I pass out, at least I know you give amazing mouth-to-mouth."

"Here"—Ross handed him a sponge—"get busy."

As Xan lathered her back, he picked back up where he'd left off. "Are you going to tell me why you left so abruptly earlier? You seemed almost sad and then you just scurried out." He kept up the massaging motion with the sponge.

Ross worried that, like a skittish colt, she'd be tempted to bolt again. But this time she didn't. She just sighed.

"I just was—I was having a really nice morning with you. And then when you mentioned Manhattan, it startled me back to reality. That's all."

Xan took her by the shoulders and turned her, bringing her face to face with those maple-syrup eyes. "Ross, why did you take that job? It sounds to me like you're really dreading living in Manhattan. Couldn't you have negotiated staying in Baltimore?"

"Turn around. My turn to get your back." She soaped his broad shoulders, enjoying the feel of the suds across his skin. "Here's the thing. I really am excited about the job. It's just the move I'm not thrilled about, which really was unavoidable. It comes with the gig." She watched the soap rivulets run down the line of his back. He was a glorious specimen. She couldn't seem to get enough of Xander Grace.

Ross sighed, fighting the growing sense of longing and emerging discontent with her life, and continued, "It all just feels like everything is changing. The place I lease in Baltimore is largely packed up. It wasn't much to pack anyway because I really don't have a lot of stuff. And I sent most of my non-day-to-day up to New York already. Plus, I feel like Tiercy and Cole are all settled. She doesn't need me much anymore. She has her new life. So now I need to build mine. In New York."

"Principessa, the way you say New York makes it sound like Gitmo," Xan laughed, turning to face her. "Manhattan is a great city. You're staying in a swank apartment with a rocking new job."

"An apartment that belongs to friends of a man named Gideon I see whenever I'm in New York," Ross added quietly.

"I see." He let out a slow whoosh of air, the smile falling off his face. "I see."

"What do you see?"

"This is someone you've 'hung out with'?" Ross couldn't miss the edge in his voice.

"Yes. And I think I've been pretty upfront about my life, Xander." Ross didn't try to keep the ice out of hers.

"And you'll hang out with him again, when you move there."

Ross paused, debating. She'd planned to be with Gideon, but now that looked less and less appealing. This man in her shower, in her bed, her life, fulfilling her physically and making her laugh, was becoming a compelling presence for her. Still, to answer in negative would mean acknowledging she wanted their summer deal to evolve into something more. And that was something she couldn't allow and he didn't want.

Ross swallowed past an uncomfortable lump in her throat. Forcing herself to look Xander in those deep brown eyes, she heard herself respond, "Maybe. Probably," and wondered why she lied to him. And herself.

"I'm overheating. I need to get out of this shower."

"Sounds good. I need to finish up," she managed to croak out.

Xan brushed past her, closing the door a bit too hard. Ross pressed her head against the cold marble wall. "Damnation," she whispered.

A little later, as she was drying her hair at the vanity table in the bedroom, she saw Xander come into the bedroom in the mirror's reflection. He dropped onto the bed behind her and watched her dry her hair, an unreadable expression on his face. When she turned off the dryer, he cleared his throat.

"I owe you an apology." His gentle eyes met hers in the mirror, holding them. "You are an incredible woman, Ross Beaufort. And you've been completely honest with me from the start about how you want to live your life. We shook hands on a summer deal. And here we are, two weeks into it, and I went and got a little—well, I got a little jealous about this Gideon guy. But I don't need to be jealous. You're my summer deal right now. And I'm cool with that, Principessa."

Xander ran a hand down his face, one of his tells that she now recognized as resignation, frustration...or acceptance. He'd done the same when sharing about his childhood. A secret part of her thrilled that she'd recognized it.

"Would you please forgive me for getting a little green-eyed about a beautiful green-eyed woman?"

"You do apologize prettily."

"Yes. I've had some practice."

Ross raised her eyebrows.

"Guys are stupid. We have to atone on the regular."

"We shall move on, Calaf."

"Well played. Now, moving on. Do you recall from your early morning pre-coffee stupor that I asked if the summer deal included going on dates—as long as we don't classify it as dating?"

Ross squinted at him. "Vaguely. Not much sinks in before java."

"Thoughts on taking a drive with me today?"

"A drive?"

"I need to head to the Paramount Theater in Charlottesville. It's only about a forty-five minute drive from here."

"Why in the ever-loving fuck do you need to go to a theater?"

"Language, dear."

Ross narrowed her eyes at him, fighting a smile.

"Might I remind you I am an esteemed architecture professor. All right, maybe not esteemed yet, but if I aim to get there, I do need to do some research for a possible spring class for next year. I thought you might like to go with me. I have a scheduled window to meet with the historian, but if we hustle, I can do my theater tour, treat you to a late lunch. Maybe drive you around to show you a few of my favorite Shenandoah views nearby? We can be back well before dinner."

"The idea of seeing you all professorial is turning me on. Will you use sexy architecture terms while we're there?"

"Hmmm. Like this?" Xander stalked toward her, murmuring words. "Diagrid. Gambrel. Gable." As he came to her, he knelt down, widening her legs with his shoulders, breathing the words against her skin, stroking her most tender places with his mouth and tongue.

He lifted her and carried her to the bed. "Joists...purlins...Palladian... crenellation." And then, as they joined together in their most intimate places, "Sheathing...bonds...pinnacle." Until he could speak no more.

CHAPTER TWENTY-NINE

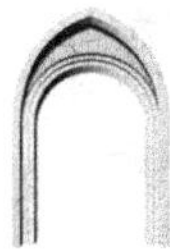

A couple hours later they pulled up in front of the theater. Xander hopped out and opened Ross's door, then guided her to the building's façade, his hand at her lower back. He marveled at how good it felt to touch her in this gentle, but proprietary way. If he was being honest with himself, he'd never before experienced the subtle joy of this touch. It had always been just habit. But this, with Ross—it was different.

Ross leaned in, a bewitching smile on her face. "OK, Professor. Time to profess. Wow me."

He laughed and winked at her. "As you wish."

Lowering his voice to the pedagogic tones of a stereotypical professor, he lectured, "This theater opened in 1931. At the time, America was besieged with the Great Depression. Movies were an indulgence. And this was designed to be a grand spectacle. The Paramount captures the golden age of cinema. It was designed by Rapp and Rapp architects, which boasted seven notable architects across two generations." Xander smiled at Ross, realizing he'd dropped his act and was whispering in churchlike awe.

"I take it this is not your first time here?"

"Oh, actually it is. I've done a lot of research online. But I'm hoping to do a class on Greek-Revival design for our graduate students. The theater is an amazing example."

"And this can fill a semester."

"Absolutely, Principessa." He kissed her cute nose. "There is plenty written about this design, if you know where to look. And pictures, paintings, written descriptions—a veritable treasure trove. But nothing matches seeing it with your own eye. The design is just gorgeous. Beautiful bones."

"You really are an architecture nerd."

Xander laughed. "Guilty as charged."

"What is your favorite feature in architecture?"

"My favorite feature?

"Yes. Is that an odd question?"

"Not at all. But no one's ever asked me that before." He paused, not to ponder her question, but only to catch his breath from his shock that she'd inadvertently asked a question that spoke so deeply to his soul. "The arch," he shared.

"The arch? Which arch? The Marble Arch? Arc de Triomphe?"

"Any arch. A structural arch in and of itself is a thing of beauty. And it's a metaphor for something truly exquisite." Xander stroked the building's edifice with reverence. "DaVinci said that an arch consists of two weaknesses which, leaning on each other, become a strength."

Ross lightly squeezed his hand, which he returned. In the theater-shadowed sunlight, the shade of her eyes was like freshly cut summer grass. He gazed into them, pulled to her in a way that felt shockingly... right.

Just as things were beginning to feel overwhelming and intense, inside him and between them, Xander broke the spell. "Come on, Principessa. Let's go in so I can nerd out."

Ross blinked a few times, and then grinned up at him.

"Nerd away."

They laughed and strolled into the building hand-in-hand to meet the historian. For a long time, they proceeded in companionable silence. Xander focused on his explorations, periodically releasing her hand to take a photo with his iPhone or jot a note. But he'd always take her hand, with a gentle squeeze, when he finished.

In the distance, an older couple was on a guided tour, and while Xander perused the painted tapestries, exquisite plaster moldings, and stunning chandeliers in the octagonal auditorium chamber, he caught snippets of their conversation. The husband would point something out to his wife, the excitement on his face genuine, as was the indulgent smile on her age-softened skin.

Xander, looking over at Ross, had a distinct sense of...well, whatever the hell the opposite of deja vu was. Of seeing a glimpse of a possible future, only he and Ross were in the role of the elderly couple. He'd gaze into mossy green eyes, the corners wrinkled with time and laughter, and bring her hand up to his lips, thumb lingering just a moment on her wedding ring. In a trance, he watched the couple, but saw himself and Ross.

I want that. I want her. He closed his eyes, just for a moment, long enough for the image to be branded onto his heart. Then he opened his eyes, reluctant to leave the fantasy, and found Ross watching him with warm eyes and an indulgent smile. *I'm so gone for her.*

CHAPTER THIRTY

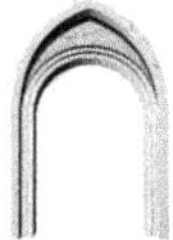

Ross

After a bit, Xan seemed to come out of his architectural trance and Ross found her voice. "That was beautiful."

"The theater?"

"What you said—about DaVinci and arches. How two weaknesses become a strength. It was lovely."

"Yeah, I thought it might make a nice element of my best man toast for Tiercy and Cole, but I was afraid it'd get misconstrued that they were both weak, so I ditched it."

Ross did a double take and then snorted a laugh, doubling over. "Oh my gosh, Xan... I didn't even think of that—" Her laughter echoed through the theater as she wiped her eyes, and Xan joined in, his arm hooked around her waist.

"Thankfully, I did think of that. Tiercy's parents might not have been happy with me."

"As it was, your speech was masterful."

"I think you were just lust-crazed. I'd had my way with you, and you weren't thinking straight."

"Is that so? You have a mighty fine opinion of yourself, Professor Grace."

"Yep, and my speechwriting too. And, as I recall, your maid of honor speech was mighty dang fine too."

"It was, if I do say so myself."

"Truthfully...I don't really remember any of it," he admitted with a shrug. "I just remember thinking, 'This hot woman was foolish enough to let me in her bed not twelve hours ago,' and then my mind wandered to twelve hours ago."

"Professor Grace!" Ross punched at Xan.

He gently caught her hand and kissed it, the unexpected romantic gesture causing a blush on her cheeks, and the brush of his lips a jolt to the apex of Ross's legs.

"I'm sure it was fabulous. We can always watch their wedding DVD if you want an honest assessment. But, my mind may still wander..."

"Classy."

"Just being honest."

Ross wrapped her arms around Xander's neck and touched her lips to his. "Thanks for your honesty, Professor. You licentious wretch."

Just then, the couple and the tour guide came upon them, smiling with knowing eyes. The elderly gentleman fixed a winking nod on Xander. "Ah, good man. It's nice to see a young couple in love. You both remind me of Mrs. Fitzer and me when we were young in love. There's nothing like that feeling. Honeymooners, are you? Gotta be something like that. You have the blush of new love. I'd know it anywhere." At his wife's gentle tugging on his arm, he turned away, but not before adding over his shoulder, "Hold onto her, lad. I can see this one's a keeper."

Xander gamely chuckled and lifted Ross's hand to his mouth again, this time kissing her palm. "A keeper indeed! Thank you, sir."

But the man's comment had made things awkward. There was an unusual tension between them. For the second time that day, Ross and Xander found themselves walking in silence, this time back to his truck.

Usually not at a loss for words, Ross struggled for something to break the awkward moment that seemed to worsen as it stretched on.

Xander let her into the truck, gently brushing her thigh with his index finger as he closed her door. Ross watched him walk around the front of the truck, the small frown she'd seen this morning back between his brows. However, as he climbed in on his side, he managed to clear, or at least cover whatever he'd been thinking. The frown was gone and Xander faced her with an amused cock to his head.

"Ross, thank you for making that so special. I think it's fair to say you and I have gotten a bit more than we bargained for with this summer deal. But I want you to know—I'm still good with the terms if you are." He leaned in and kissed her gently.

As she returned the kiss, their foreheads resting for a moment together, Ross couldn't decide if she was relieved or not.

What she did know was this was getting very deep, very fast. Perhaps it was just all the memories of the farmhouse, plus her impending move, weakening her defenses. And it didn't help that Xander was the ultimate Hottie McHot Pants. But she needed to set some emotional boundaries quickly.

Shifting away, she clicked her seatbelt into place with perhaps more force than necessary.

"Me too. Summer deal terms firmly in place," she said, her voice sounding much cooler and calmer than her roiling insides conveyed. "Clock's ticking, you know? Hey, can I pick the music?"

As she fiddled with the satellite radio controls, chatting lightly about finding a station with Depeche Mode and The Cure, she willfully ignored the frown that was back on Xander's brow.

Chapter Thirty-One

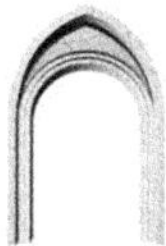

Ross

The next couple weeks were filled with a flurry of sorting, donating, saving, and packing a lifetime of a home. It was at times tender, exhausting, infuriating, and funny. And finally, it was mostly complete. One major task remained for Ross—the boxes in the basement that were her own from her childhood bedroom at the farmhouse, plus the boxes belonging to her parents that Hon had earmarked for her. Never a procrastinator by nature, Ross had decided to tackle those solo, when Hon left for her weeklong Cumberland Island trip on July 5.

With the major packing finished, Ross struggled with the eerie emptiness of the house. The rooms echoed.

So, with Petey still at camp with Nick and Kingsley Monroe until the first of July, Xander and Ross had moved their forays to Xan's cottage.

It was a good move. Even Ross's bedroom was boxed up, with only the items she'd need for the rest of the stay still out. She fought against a tug of melancholy, the feeling only growing when the real estate agent, a petite attractive redhead named Genevieve, came to the house to meet with Hon, Ross, and Gaby.

Xander joined as well. Hon insisted she'd invited him because she valued his input as an architect and someone who had rehabbed several buildings. However, Ross suspected that was a superficial excuse and Hon had other, deeper reasons—namely the moral support he could provide all of them. Especially Ross.

Genevieve ambled through the house, making the appropriate declarations of winning features, noting some things to address, taking notes in a padfolio, and snapping pictures. It didn't escape Ross's notice that Genevieve found every excuse to brush up against Xander, to laugh at his jokes, to effuse at his insights, and just to generally, well, be a pain in the ass.

Not that Ross cared.

Eventually, they ended up in the kitchen. "Mrs. Waldheim, this place is just amazing," Genevieve cooed from her seat, where she'd perched herself next to Xander on the far side of the table. Hon was at "her" seat at the head of the table, and Ross and Gaby had, out of some version of muscle memory, sorted themselves into the two seats of their childhood on the opposite side of the old farm table.

Ross watched Xander abstractedly trace a long divot in the wood with his index finger. A vivid memory of when that divot was made came unbidden to her mind. She was twelve, hormonal and angry at the world—for whatever pointless reason preteen girls are—and taking geometry. They had come down for the weekend, and Ross had an assignment to finish before returning to school the following week. Mad at her father for not giving her the answer and making her work through it herself, she'd gripped her compass with building frustration and dug it into the wood, leaving an angry line scoring deep into the table. By then, the table had seen better days. It was an antique find, so Ross thought no one would notice. But they did. She couldn't remember the punishment exactly, but it had been swift and severe.

Continuing to watch Xander's movements, she remembered that same index finger and what it had done to her—and specifically the forbidden pucker between her legs—in the shower at the cottage that very morning. Ross flushed, banishing that thought before she was tempted to grab Xander and drag him away for a quickie.

Her thoughts instead turned to what she had come to think of as the Puccini and Breakfast morning. Xan had sat in that same chair. When she'd come around, he'd pulled her into his lap, and held her...

"...and I think some sort of flooring allowance, right, Ross?" Genevieve's tone was much less sycophantic with her than with Xander.

Ross snapped out of her triplicate reverie, realizing four sets of eyes were on her. "Wha-oh, yes. Flooring. Important. Do that." She had no idea what she'd just agreed to on Hon's behalf. Damn. *Focus, Beaufort.*

Xander reached over, tapping the back of her hand with *that finger,* a private, knowing look in his eyes.

Damn. Could he read her mind? She realized she, too, knew what he was thinking. *Later,* she telegraphed.

Despite the unspoken hum of foreplay, Xander possessed the admirable skill of being able to participate in the conversation at hand. "I love these old hardwoods," he offered. "I think instead of a flooring allowance, it may be worth investing in refinishing it yourself, Leah. Well, hiring someone to ensure it's done properly, actually."

"Oh, *yes,* Alexander, good point," breathed Genevieve, smiling at him with what had to be cosmetically whitened teeth.

Ross cocked her head and examined the agent. Good for her on the shiny teeth. They looked great, and she clearly flossed. Ross would also bet her extensive shoe closet those were mink eyelash extensions the agent was batting at Xander. And, damn, they looked good, too. Ross touched her own bare lashes self-consciously.

"Bedrooms and bathrooms are perfect. You've done an amazing job, Mrs. Monroe, on the redesign and decorating. We need to keep some of this unpacked for the staging. As for the kitchen, I love how homey it is. I think just some paint."

"Really?" Again, Xander interjected. "I love the way the morning sun floods in. What I'd do is bump out these walls and make a much bigger chef's kitchen, put in top-grade appliances, huge windows to let that sun in, and maybe a big French door, leading to a new sun porch. You can extend that front porch to the side and have an amazing wraparound. And then with that, you can bump the top bedrooms, the one Ross is in and also maybe the one that was Gaby's, and have two small balconies. We'd have to work on the other side so it's not lopsided, so maybe an enclosed side room, with a small bedroom on top of that, maybe for an office?"

Xander had stood at this point, and was pointing around the room, describing everything with such animation and excitement that Hon's jaw had dropped. When he finished, everyone was silent.

Hon spoke first. "My, Alexander, that is incredible, indeed. You've really thought about this."

Xander regained his composure and sat down, an embarrassed flush creeping up his cheeks. "Hon, I am so sorry. Clearly, you aren't going to do all that to sell. I just got a little carried away. Occupational hazard." He shrugged his shoulders and dropped his head a bit.

"Wow," whispered Genevieve. "You are an *artisan*." She looked at him with such doe eyes that Ross was only saved from puking on the table by a stifled hiccup next to her. She turned to see Gaby reaching to get her water.

"Hiccups—" she tried to say as she brought the glass to her mouth. From Genevieve's angle, it seemed true, but sitting next to Gaby, Ross could see that her sister was fighting the giggles. Truly about to lose it.

"Oh no, really, Gabs? Hiccups? Again?" Ross knew this game. It had been years, but they quickly sorted into their roles. She put a look of what she hoped was deep concern on her face. "Come with me."

Genevieve's alarmed glance bounced between the sisters. "What is it? She has the hiccups? Is that *bad*?" And as she breathed the word bad, she drew it out and placed a French-manicured hand on Xander's arm, which only got Gaby going more.

"Yes." Ross stood and grabbed her sister. "I need to get her outside. She needs air." Ross grabbed the water too, pulling her sister out of the kitchen. "If she hiccups too much, she throws up nonstop for two hours, and then she needs IV fluids. It's a terrible—" she searched her memory for their made-up term "—gastritis ignitis disorder. We'll be back soon. I hope," she called over her shoulder.

Once the sisters composed themselves enough to return to finish the meeting and Genevieve had left, Hon seized the moment. Nick, Kingsley, and Petey would be returning from camp on the bus the next day, so Hon offered to take Tara and let her sleep at the farmhouse that night. Then she suggested the four adults enjoy some sort of adult game night at the Monroes' house before it was once again overrun by children.

Ross rolled her eyes and began to make an excuse to avoid the quality sister time Hon was devising. Despite the flashback of their close sisterhood, she wasn't sure she was ready for full-on Gaby time. Xander, however, was already in motion. Ted was coming off a shift in the afternoon, and Xan texted him, avoiding Ross's glare.

Later, still smarting a bit from the unrepelled fawning of Genevieve, but not willing to acknowledge it, Ross grumbled to Xan, "Is that really how you want to spend our final night alone? With my sister and Moose?"

But Xander was unrepentant, even a bit eager. "Come on, Ross. Ted's a fun guy. We'll have a few drinks. Maybe play a game or two. And then we'll head to my place and play spin the bottle, just the two of us." Xan quirked his dimpled smile, drawing his fingers down the sides of Ross's bare arms, giving her chills.

"Don't try to charm me, Xan. I'm still annoyed with you. Besides, spin the bottle seems a bit anticlimactic with only two people."

"Oh no, Principessa. I can think of lots of ways to make it *very* climactic for you." And he proceeded to whisper some of those dirty ideas into her ear.

Chapter Thirty-Two

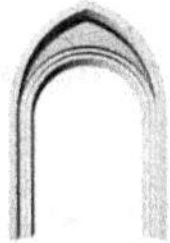

Ross

By the time they got to the Monroes' that evening, Ross was feeling more than a little turned on in anticipation of Part Two of the evening. If she had to suck it up and deal with her sister and brother-in-law, so be it.

Xander and Ted helped ease any potential tension by making very generous cocktails—whiskey sours of course—for Ross, Xander, and Ted.

"No drink for you, Gaby?" Ross noticed that Gaby was drinking a grapefruit-flavored sparkling water.

"No, unfortunately. I wish. I have a terrible UTI—"

"TMI!" hollered Xan, laughing and covering his ears.

"—and I'm on a mega-antibiotic. The doctor told me no alcohol whatsoever or it'll tear up my liver. So, I get the fun of watching you all get drunk while I enjoy sparkling water. Yay!" Gaby scowled at her drink.

"Sucks to be you," said Ross, and downed her drink, trying but failing to ignore Xander's frown at her.

Ross rolled her eyes, ignoring her own discomfort. She hated when

Xan looked disappointed at her like that—especially when she knew she was in the wrong.

She tried again, this time with a lighter, teasing tone. "That UTI comes from too much sex. Maybe you kids should ease off a bit, you know? Aren't you an old married couple? The well should be drying up soon."

"Oh, hell no," drawled Ted. "The day that well dries up is the day I'm on the wrong side of dirt." He leaned down and bestowed a sexy, deep kiss on his wife.

"Gross!" teased Ross. "That's the start of how babies are made. Don't I have enough of your kids to buy for at the holidays?"

The other three adults in the room all laughed gamely, but Ross had the distinct feeling she'd said something wrong. It reminded her of the time in college when she thought she was alone in the student lounge and she'd passed gas (after a bean burrito lunch), only to find that one of the hottest guys in the dorm had entered the room just before and heard —and smelled—it. Yeah, like that.

In a snap, though, the moment passed. Had Ross imagined it?

Gaby's eyes lit up and she started giggling, turning to look directly at Ross. "We *have* to tell Ted. I can't believe we've gone this long..."

"**G**astritis ignitis??" Ted had not stopped laughing since Ross and Gaby began telling the afternoon's story, in great theatrical—and embellished—detail. "Are you serious?"

"Hey...it worked. That excuse is tried and true!" The back of Ross's nose burned as she snorted with glee...and almost snorted out her whiskey sour. "Your wife was about to bust a gut at the table."

"Oh, my lord, Ted." Gaby was on the floor, resting against her husband's legs as he lounged on the family room love seat. She scratched Laverne behind the ears as she picked up the tale. "That woman, *Genevieve,*" Gaby said, breathing her name in an almost-perfect imitation and bursting into cackles again, "spent the entire walkthrough in heat for Alexander. I'm pretty sure she ovulated every time he opened his mouth. When she called him an artisan, I couldn't take it anymore."

At this, Ross, Gaby, and Ted erupted into howls of laughter, causing Laverne—who was learning to bark—to yip along in fellowship, making them laugh even harder.

Wiping her eyes, Ross looked over at Xander, who wore the countenance of a man resigned to suffering teasing abuse. But she could see the glimmer of amusement in his eyes.

"Hardee-har-har, guys. What can I say? I'm a stud. The ladies loooove me. And if that's what it takes to make you laugh, I'm glad I can be of service in your sad, pathetic lives."

"Ye-yep, you artisan of luuuuv," Gaby quipped and held her sides laughing.

"Wow, Alexander," breathed Ross to Gaby, "Gooood point. You are soooo smart. May I touch you again?" She batted her eyes.

"Why, yes, Genevieve," Gaby said, making her voice very deep, imitating Xan, "I like it when you rub against me every single chance you get. I have a plethora of ideas guaranteed to make you horny."

"Ok, alright, I capitulate." Xan held up his hands in surrender. "She really was a hot mess—although I do know she comes highly recommended as a real estate agent. But what I haven't done is share the pièce de résistance." With commensurate flourish, Xander produced a handwritten note from his pocket. "From Genevieve's padfolio, inviting me to discuss real estate...or anything else...with her anytime."

Gaby leapt up with surprising speed and snatched it out of his hand. "Oh my God! Oh, sweet William Shatner—it actually says all that! And, even better, she dotted the i of her name with a heart!"

"Sweet William Shat—never mind. Let me see that." Ross grabbed the paper and scanned it, then sniffed it dramatically. "Ha! You can practically smell the pheromones on this thing." She looked at it one more time and then sensed Xander's eyes on her. She waggled her brows. "So, what say you, Alexander the Artisan. Up for a real estate discussion?"

Xan tilted his head, as if pondering the offer, and then strolled over to Ross and held out his hand for the note. She placed it in his palm. In silence, he read it. Then, he looked up, pinned Ross with the most intense stare—causing her belly to flutter with something unnamable—and tore the note in half, half again, and then again, never breaking their eye contact. With a small frown on his face, he put the pieces in the large jar candle on the Monroes' table, where it whooshed up in a quick flame and then died.

As the flame settled, he strode back to Ross, bent her backward, and crushed his mouth to hers in the sexiest kiss she'd ever received. Their tongues tangled and their lips fused to the accompaniment of a low wolf whistle from Ted.

Just as Ross was about to wrap her legs around him—sibling and brother-in-law audience be damned—Xander broke the kiss with a soft smile, righted her, and announced, "I know enough about real estate, thank you. I'm good."

Ross was stunned. She stood speechless, knowing this had been more than a kiss. It was a display of something powerful from Xander. Of possession. *What the everloving fuck was going on?*

Gaby reached over and tapped her arm, nudging her back into functionality. "As much as I enjoy watching my sister and my friend suck face—NOT—are we doing Game Night or what?" Gaby's well-honed maternal voice of command snapped everyone to attention.

Ross tipped her chin at Gaby. She recognized the moment for what it was—a shifting of things toward rightness with her sister. Perhaps it started with Gaby grabbing her by the arm in shared hilarity during the fake rescue. Maybe it was the memory of long-lost sibling mischief. For sure it was her sister's astute intervention, sparing her from her own confused feelings. But something had definitely changed. "I'm in," she called.

"Me too," intoned Ted, lifting his scotch glass.

Xander turned to Ross, a smile spreading across his face. "Prepare to lose, weaklings. I call Ted on my team. Boys against girls."

Several hours later, they'd played multiple games, mixing up teams, the common denominator being that Ross's team won most games. Soon there was a spirited battle to "call" Ross on a team. As they were getting ready to start a trivia game, Xander challenged, "The one who kisses Ross the best gets her on their team."

Ted glared at his friend. "You're going to hell, man. That's cheating."

"All's fair on drunken game night." Xan grinned, and proceeded to plant a claiming kiss on Ross. "OK. Principessa is on my team!"

Two rounds later, even though Gaby—both smart in her own right and the only sober one—kept things quite close, Ross and Xan were victorious.

"Xan, brother, you are useless," Ted razzed Xander. "Your woman carried you in this last game. I think you're drunk."

"Well, brother," Xander rejoined with a laugh, "as the late, great Dean Martin said, 'You're not drunk if you can lie on the floor without holding on.' Pop culture class for the win!"

Xander threw an adorable wink at Ross, who was so hung up on Ted referring to her as *Xander's woman* she couldn't even fully appreciate the appearance of Xan's dimples.

As Ted and Xander cracked up, Gaby rolled her eyes and motioned toward the kitchen. "I'm going to grab a couple of these glasses, and then I have to pee."

"I'll help you in a minute, babe. Leave that for me. I want to show Xander the new telescope I set up for Nick in the yard real quick."

"Don't trip and break your neck going down the stairs." Gaby cast a fond smile at her husband.

"No way, Gabs. Besides, you and I have a date upstairs when these two yahoos leave. A broken neck could put a damper on that."

"Again with the TMI from the Monroes." Xander shook his head, laughing, as he walked companionably with Ted outside.

"I'll help you Gaby," Ross offered.

"Great. Let me pee first."

"Yeah, UTIs are the worst," Ross said, with very little conviction. She'd bet her bank account Gaby didn't have a UTI.

Gaby went into the powder room off the living room. A few

seconds later Ross heard Gaby cursing. "Damnation, house of kids! And Moose! Am I the only one who knows how to change a toilet paper roll? It doesn't cause brain damage. Ross? Ross! You out there?"

Ross came to the door. "Yep. You need toilet paper? You must be mad if you called Ted 'Moose.'"

"Only when he acts like one of the children. I know he was the last one in here, so I charge him as the culprit. Can you grab a couple rolls? Upstairs hall closet. Thanks."

Ross ran and grabbed two rolls, and then tore off a piece. Opening the door, she passed in the rolls, and then a bit more toilet paper. "Here you go. Torn off and pre-wadded for your convenience."

"Thanks!" As Ross turned away, she heard her sister's laughter fade. "Shit."

"Gaby, what is it?"

"Nothing. Hey, um. Do you think you can get Ted for me?" Gaby's voice sounded strangled and shaky.

"Gaby, you're freaking me out. Are you ok? Can I come in?"

"No! Ross, just get Ted."

Ross ran out of the house. At the look on her face, Ted sprinted up the steps in two long strides. Xander was right behind him, and Ross grabbed his arm as they got to the porch, stopping him.

"Xander, what the hell is going on?" Ross looked toward the house. As the door to the bathroom opened, and she watched Ted lifting Gaby out, Ross's heart raced. "Xander!" Ross's voice shook in fear.

Xander tore his eyes from the scene and reached for Ross's shaking hand. "It's not for me to tell."

"The hell it isn't. Tell me now, Alexander Grace, or I'll fucking rip your limbs off and beat it out of you with your own arms. What is going on with my sister?"

He gave a gentle squeeze to her hand. "Ease that grip, Killer." He sighed in clear assent. "OK, Principessa. You're right. You should know at this point. She's pregnant, Ross. There must be something going on with the baby."

"I knew something was up," Ross said. She looked up, realization dawning. "Oh no. Is she having a miscarriage? Should we call 9-1-1?"

"Ted's an EMT. He'll know what to do. Let's just—let's just stay out of the way a minute. He'll tell us if he needs us."

"How—how far along is she?"

"I'm not really an expert in this. I think like almost three months or something."

Ross shook her head to clear it. "And *why* do you even know? How do you know? Did she tell you?"

"No, she didn't. Ted did. The baby was a whoops. She was on birth control, but..." Xander shrugged. "I think they were both freaked and he just needed to talk. I was a friendly ear."

Ross's jaw dropped. "And he *told* you all this?"

Xander inclined his head in assent, his ear still cocked toward the house, on alert. "Yes, just recently."

"And Hon knows too."

"Yes, Hon knows."

"That's why you've all been so solicitous of her with the packing, not letting her carry anything or lift anything." Ross puffed out a deep breath of air. "Shit. Wow."

"When she found out I knew, she made me promise not to say anything. She actually gave me one of those friction burns—literally twisted my arm and burned my skin—and told me she'd do worse to my...you know—" he pointed down "—if I breathed a word." Xan aimed a small, guilty smile at Ross.

"She didn't!" Despite the seriousness of the situation, Ross coughed a small laugh at the idea of her sister literally twisting Xan's arm, or his willy, into silence. "She's a piece of work. I promise I'll protect my favorite appendage from any harm."

He rested his forehead against hers. "My appendage and I sincerely thank you for your protection." He dropped a small kiss on her nose and brushed one of those glorious, strong hands along her shoulder, sighing, the enormity of the situation settling in around them. "Here, let's sit. This might be a while."

Ross sat next to him, her legs rubbery with shock and fear for her sister and the baby.

About a half hour later, Ted came outside to get them. Ross rose from her perch on the step next to Xander.

"She's upstairs in bed resting. The bleeding stopped. We called the doctor. She said to keep an eye on things and go to the ER if it starts again or if she's in any pain." Ted scanned Ross, eyebrows knitted. "I take it you know?"

Ross nodded.

"Yeah, I figured you either put two and two together, or Gracie here told you."

"A little of both," Ross croaked. She was shocked to find herself shaking a bit. Xander noticed and put his hand at the small of her back, easing her toward him. She leaned into the solid warmth of him.

"She wants to see you for a minute."

"Is she-is she OK? The baby's OK, right?"

Ted's shoulders slumped a bit, whether in relief or exhaustion, Ross couldn't be sure. "She was bleeding pretty heavily. She's about ten weeks pregnant, so spotting is somewhat normal. She's had some light bleeding at points, but this was much heavier. They've been talking about bedrest if this keeps up. Her OB just said to get her in bed tonight. At this point, there isn't much we can do. I'll take her for an ultrasound tomorrow and they'll check for a heartbeat."

Ross put her hand to her mouth. "I'm sorry, Ted. I'm sure everything is going to be fine, with Gaby and this baby. You have three healthy children. This baby will be fine too."

"She's had two miscarriages, so this is really hard on her."

Ross was stunned speechless.

"I know you didn't know."

"Why didn't anyone say anything to me? I would have—"

"You would have what, Ross?" Ted bit out. "You would have done nothing. You didn't know because you haven't been a part of her life—our lives. Gaby didn't think you'd really care, and she wouldn't let Hon tell you."

"Didn't think I'd *care*?" Ross was stunned by the acid in his response. In a flash, the hurt, the anger, boiled to the surface—commingled with new feelings of guilt.

Ted wasn't totally off. While she would have wanted to know about the pregnancy—a new niece or nephew would be great—it was true she hadn't been a part of their lives. Not really. But only because once her parents died, she didn't seem to fit anymore. There was only space for Gaby.

"Oh, right, Ted. Of course," she whispered, choking down her sorrow. "Because Ross is 'cold and unfeeling.' Those were your wife's words. And let's not forget 'Ross doesn't cry because Ross doesn't care.'"

A bitter laugh pushed past her tight throat and she struggled to calm herself. This wasn't about her. Gaby was the self-centered sister, not her.

"Go take care of your wife. She needs you. Tell her I'll come see her tomorrow if she wants, and that I know everything will be fine with the baby."

Ross tried to say the last part with kindness, holding on to the final edge of her composure. Then, turning on her heel, she ran down the stairs and through the night. Away from Gaby. Away from Xander and the cottage. Back to the farmhouse for now.

Until she could put that place to rest too, and finally move on with her life. For good.

CHAPTER THIRTY-THREE

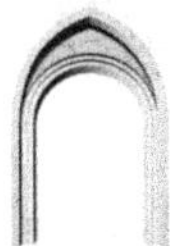

Xander watched Ross run away into the night, grappling with whether to high-tail it after her to comfort her, or give her space. He was also struggling not to give Ted a small piece of his mind in defense of Ross.

Xander chose giving her space—for now—because a wounded Ross was not one to welcome comfort. Instead, he heaved a sigh and went back into the house after Ted, who was doing a terrible job at starting to clean up, picking things up and putting them down in random places.

"Here. Let me. Just sit for a minute." He reached for the game board dangling from Ted's hands.

Ted startled. "Sorry man. Lost in thought there." He handed Xan the board and slumped onto the couch. "Thanks, brother."

"No problem." He cleaned up in silence for a few moments. Then, catching Ted's eye, he paused.

"What is it, Gracie?" Ted seemed to know the answer, but was going to make Xan say it. "Spit it out."

Xan debated for a moment, ultimately saying what he needed to. "I just think..." he hesitated. "You were just a bit harsh with her, weren't you?" Xander tempered his tone, and kept his voice low so as not to disturb Gaby, but he couldn't quite contain the ire that seeped in.

Ted pursed his lips, a frown wrinkling his brow. "Look, Xan," he replied, also sotto-voice, "I've potentially just witnessed the loss of my baby. My wife is wrecked. I knew you were going to say something in her defense, but right now I can't deal with a lecture from you on how I talk to my sister-in-law."

Xander raised his hands in surrender, swallowing the primal instinct to lash back. "Not trying to lecture. Just trying to look out for everyone. It's a scary situation. And I'm sorry. But no one's a villain here. I know you're freaked. But maybe don't take it out on Ross?"

Ted glared at him and then closed his eyes, shaking his head.

Xander reached out and put a calming hand on his shoulder. "What can I do for you, brother?"

Ted listed into the couch, arms resting on his legs, head hanging in defeat. "I don't know, man. Not much to do but wait."

"Want to go back up to her? I'll clean everything up." Xander's heart broke for his friend.

"I'll go back up in a bit. I just need a few more minutes for the adrenaline rush to subside."

Xander sat next to Ted in quiet solidarity. His own adrenaline had spiked as well, keeping company with a riot of emotions. Worry for Gaby and her pregnancy. Frustration with Ted, as well as aching sympathy. Deep concern for Ross. His own disappointment in how the evening ended. And the ever-growing gut punch that his summer deal with Ross had far surpassed either of their original intentions. What— as Ross would say—the ever-loving fuck was he going to do about that?

After several long moments, Ted rubbed his hand down his face, scraping it against his evening whiskers. "Fuck," he exhaled. "I'm sorry. You're right. I was rough on Ross. I mean, not everything I said was wrong, but what I said was mean. I'm better than that."

"You were revved on adrenaline and fear and she was a convenient target," Xander offered. "But I hope you can see she's not the person you've always painted her to be. You were one thousand percent wrong when you said she wouldn't have cared—about the miscarriages or this pregnancy. That shit hurts, man.

"I know she comes across as tough, but she gets wounded just like the rest of us. I think she just hides it better. You have one perspective of Ross, but she's much more than one-dimensional. And maybe she's also grown. Matured. Haven't you? Haven't we all?"

Ted closed his eyes, tipping his head back and exhaling through his nose. "I owe her an apology for jumping down her throat. For what I said."

"You do."

Ted started to stand, but Xander put a staying hand on his arm. "Not now, brother. Let her cool down. If you go over now, she's liable to rip your throat out." They shared a small smile. "And Gaby needs you alive and well."

Ted blinked back tears, wiping his eyes. "You think our baby is ok?"

Xander said a brief internal prayer for their unborn child. "I think... we'll all say some prayers—for you, Gaby, for the baby. And we've got each other's backs no matter what. But what I do think is that your wife needs you to go back upstairs and hold her. Good news or bad, you both have a special love, and you need to hold onto that and each other right now."

Ted stood, knees popping against the strain of the night, and leaned against the couch, eyes flitting across Xan's face in examination.

Xander squirmed under his close scrutiny.

"You have feelings for her, don't you?"

"Gaby? Absolutely. She's a true friend." Xander's intentional misunderstanding didn't stop Ted.

"Not Gaby, you ass. Ross. This isn't just a fling. You're falling for her."

Xander's heart thumped hard. His throat dried up and he couldn't seem to manage words.

Ted let out a low hum, and Xander braced for the inevitable lecture about how Ross was toxic, would hurt him, blah blah blah.

Instead, he was stunned when Ted broke into a huge grin. "She's going to give you a run for your money." He laughed. "I can't wait to watch this one unfold."

Xander chuckled, ignoring the shocked rat-a-tat of his heart. Feelings shmeelings. It was just a crush. A big one. "I've got it under control, brother." He stood, and began cleaning up.

"Sure you do, man. That's what we all say."

Chapter Thirty-Four

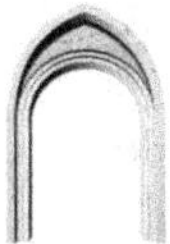

Ross

Ross was awakened the next morning by a missed call alert and then a text. And then another one. And another. She pulled her pillow over her head and tried to ignore the alerts. Why hadn't she DND'd her phone past her usual 7 a.m. turnoff?

Two more alerts came through. She needed coffee. What the ever-loving fuck time was it even?

She looked at her phone. Eight thirty a.m. A call from Tiercy. And six texts. Four from Tiercy. Two from Xander. Which to read first? The early atypical call from Tiercy alarmed her. She shifted up against her pillow and opened the texts from her best friend.

-Good morning, hussy! I tried to call you. I'm busting to tell you this. Call me.

OK. Based on the tone, it wasn't an emergency. And after last night, she was out of capacity for drama. Ross breathed a sigh of relief and continued reading the string of texts.

-Because you are not answering me (perhaps busy with your summer deal, which I do NOT need to hear the details about!) I will have to tell you in a text. Call me though. I'd rather tell you not in text.

- Patience is not my strong suit. Don't be mad. Maybe get some coffee first. And make sure you aren't holding any sharp objects. I'm glad I'm sort of far away. Here goes. Back when we started planning your bday bash, I went through your phone contacts to invite people. Since you were moving to the Big Apple, I thought it would be nice to invite your side piece. (Yes, I learned that from eavesdropping on my students too). And...he accepted. Late last night. Gideon is coming to your party on Saturday.

Ross nearly dropped the phone. *Gideon* was coming? Fuckety fuck! She kept reading.

-I am really sorry. I should have checked with you, but at the time you were digging the bedsport with him. I thought you'd be in the midst of Chastity Summer and you'd appreciate a little giddy-up with Gid. No? Too soon? I can't uninvite him. I feel like that would be tacky. Do you hate me? Call me when you get this. God I hope Xander isn't with you and reading your texts over your shoulder.

Oh shit. Xander.

Ross quickly opened his texts.

-Buongiorno, Principessa. You disappeared on me last night. I considered coming after you, but then I thought you might need some space. I'm so sorry you had to hear about Gaby's pregnancy like that. And the miscarriages. But what Ted said...Ross, he was off-base. For what it's worth, I told him that before and I told him last night...nicely. He agreed he was out of line. He was just hurting and scared and he lashed out at you. Call me. I need to pick up Petey and Nick from the camp bus at 9, but I want to see you.

She stared at the text for a moment and then read the next, which had arrived about two minutes after the first.

-And another thing. You owe me a game of 1:1 spin the bottle. Don't think I've forgotten. Graces (at least this one) have long, lust-filled memories.

Ross laughed. Leave it to Xander to lighten her mood.

Gaby, pregnant. Past hidden miscarriages. And what the hell was she going to do about Gideon coming to the party? What a steaming hot bag of mess. She needed to call Tiercy. But first, she needed coffee.

Grabbing her robe, she eased down the stairs, a whiskey headache pulsing behind her eyes. The owner's suite bedroom door was open and silent. Hon must have taken Tara somewhere.

Spying the full coffee pot, Ross breathed a sigh of deep thanksgiving. "Java..." She poured a mug and hit Tiercy's name at the top of her favorites.

"Please don't kill me."

"Good morning to you too, Hooker Hips. Thanks for the nice pre-java jolt this morning. That was quite the wake-up call."

"I am so sorry, Ross," Tiercy sighed into the phone. "No good deed goes unpunished."

"Honestly, if it weren't such a cluster, it'd be pretty hilarious."

"So, you don't hate me? You can't murder me. I have your precious goddaughter to raise."

"Don't you even try to play that card with me, Tiercy Colburn. You are way too sassy for that. Speaking of Jemma...who's watching her this weekend?"

"Jemma is staying with my folks. We're going to drive down Friday, help with the final set up for your birthday party, spend the night, party with you on Saturday, and then drive home Sunday. It's still OK with Hon if we sleep in her guest room?"

"Yep. We left enough of the room intact and unpacked. It's a bit spartan right now, but you'll be comfortable. Tiercy, I can't wait to see you. And I have to tell you about last night. It was a shitshow."

Thirty minutes and two cups of coffee later, Ross had regaled her best friend with the gist of the entire day, from Genevieve and the fake hiccups to game night, leading to Gaby's spotting and the big reveal of the pregnancy and the past miscarriages.

"Santa on a cracker, Ross. What a day. For a girl who hates drama, you sure are having to deal with your fair share."

"*Santa* on a cracker? Isn't it *Christ* on a cracker?"

"Yes, but I've had to clean up my mouth. Jemma's been repeating everything I say."

Ross burst into laughter. "Oh, Tiercy. I love you. I can't wait to see you!"

"Ditto, kiddo. And Cole is pumped to see Xan. It'll be a love fest. What will you do about Gideon?"

"I can call and tell him there'll be no humpety-hump on this visit—manage his expectations. He doesn't need to know about Xander. Gid and I are friends. There's no reason I shouldn't have my friends at my party. Buuut...I was hoping you could text him a couple nearby hotels? Tell him my grandmother is kind of prudish and wouldn't like him spending the night."

"I'd be happy to. I got you into this. I can at least help mitigate it. Is it going to be weird with Xan and Gideon there together?"

"Completely. Although it shouldn't be. Considering neither Xan nor I are interested in a relationship, I guess it's really just two guys I happen to have slept with, not at the same time. Both of whom are my friends. One I happen to be currently seeing."

"And one you may see again in the future?"

Ross tried to picture herself with Gideon—older, athletic, charming, urbane, with gorgeous skin that was the blend of his Ethiopian mother and Irish father—but whenever she did, Xander's face would appear.

"I don't know," she hedged. "I'll be really busy with work. And he travels so much. We'll see."

"Hmm."

"What's that mean?"

"What's what mean?"

"*Hmm.* What's 'hmm' mean?"

"It means nothing. I just made a vocalization. It's a nothing sound. Innocuous."

"Tiercy?"

"Yeah?"

"Shut the fuck up. You suck at lying."

"I love you too, Ross," Tiercy laughed into the phone. "See you Friday, birthday girl."

"See you Friday. Love you."

Ross gazed in adoration at the coffee pot. "I love you, too. Come to mama."

Chapter Thirty-Five

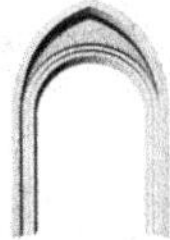

Ross

Ross had shaken off the hurt of the game night. She was adept at compartmentalizing painful, unwanted emotions and removing them from her daily existence. Fortified by coffee, and a dose of best friend strength, she'd called Xander. She wasn't sure what he was expecting, but it probably wasn't the blithe, cheerful woman on the other end. Ross had brushed off the previous evening's dissension, expressing sincere concern for her sister and the baby, and then changing the subject to the safe and happy topic of Petey.

She called her sister later in the day. When Ted picked up, she pretended like they'd never exchanged a cross word in their lives. She was polite and solicitous, ignoring the hesitant tone in Ted's voice, and then grateful when he seemed to go along with her ruse of normalcy. In somewhat shaky tones, she asked if they'd had the ultrasound. When Ted confirmed that they'd just returned and there was a heartbeat, Ross's own skipped a beat in relief. He'd started to say more, but she heard her sister in the background asking to speak to her.

As soon as her sister got on the phone, Ross sincerely congratulated her on the baby, and apologized for not coming up to see her, explaining that she didn't want to intrude on something serious and private between Gaby and Ted. Gaby sounded tired and relieved, but then thanked her for her help getting Ted. The call was quick and somewhat awkward, but in Ross's mind, that was to be expected.

And with that, Ross considered the situation handled and she moved on.

The next few days were filled with fun and frolicking with Xan and Petey. At first, Ross wanted to stay away and give the father and son time to bond after a two-week separation. But both Graces insisted on inviting her over for dinner and on joining her at the pool. Later, after Petey would fall asleep, Ross and Xander would slip into Xan's bedroom and have sex.

On Thursday afternoon, Xander had to run to campus.

"Why are you acting so squirmy, Professor?" Ross asked as she nestled on his couch, watching him pack his work satchel. She loved watching him in professor mode. It was crazy sexy. If Petey wasn't in the next room, she'd be tempted to jump Xander and have her way with him. As it was, they could do a lot in the sixty minutes before he had to leave. A shame...

"I have a favor to ask, and you can say no."

"Thank you for telling me what I can say," she teased, giving into temptation and wrapping her arms around him for a deep kiss.

After they tasted each other, lamenting the lack of privacy and whispering promises for later, Ross prompted Xander. "You were saying something about a favor?"

"I was wondering if you'd be willing to stay with Petey for a couple hours when I go to campus. Normally I'd take him, but I have to speak with the dean, and it wouldn't be right to have Petey there. I had the nanny lined up to do it, but she texted fifteen minutes ago canceling. I've been working up the nerve to ask you. I'm sorry if it's an imposition. I know we don't have that kind of relationship, but I'm sort of stuck and I'd really appreciate it," he rushed out.

"Xander," Ross laughed, putting her fingers over those beautiful lips. "Relax. No nerve-working-up needed. I'd be happy to help. I can't believe you were worried. We're *friends*, and friends help each other.

Plus, Petey's the hot-diggity-bomb. I'll just have him sign an NDA and all will be well." She grinned at him.

"Ross, thank you! You're a lifesaver. God, I love you." Xander blanched. "I mean—that is—"

Ross recovered first, and rescued them both with a playful whack on his chest. "Got it. Chill, Xander. We're good. No summer deal rules have been broken here. Move along, sir." She peeked over his shoulder, ensuring Petey was still in his room, and kissed him again, fucking him with her tongue the way she looked forward to him fucking her later.

"Christ, woman. If you don't stop, I'll be meeting the dean with a very visible problem."

Ross giggled against his lips. "Can't have that, Professor. That's one architectural formation you should keep to yourself."

Ross and Petey strolled hand-in-hand across the parking lot, the heat coming off the asphalt in powerful waves. Ross loved summer, and the sensation of intense humidity followed by an arctic wave of air conditioning. When she offered to watch Petey, she hadn't reckoned on the fact that it would be over lunch. Hon was out, and Ross was not much on fixing food. She was perfectly capable of making PB&J, but somehow this time with Petey seemed to merit more. Thankfully, she kept a booster seat in her trunk for Jemma, so when she suggested lunch in town, Petey was thrilled, and away they went.

She hadn't been inside Moby Dick's in years, but was delighted to see it hadn't changed at all. Wooden booths, a giant fiberglass whale hanging from the ceiling, fish nets—it was hokey and fabulous. One of Pop's colleagues had opened it in the late seventies, and Ross and her father loved the whaling kitsch and the menu. It had been tradition to eat there whenever they were in town, just the two of them.

"Petey, this used to be my favorite place to eat with my dad."

"Really?" Brown eyes, so much like Xander's, studied her. His tow head tilted in inquisition. "Where is your dad now?"

Ross steeled against a familiar wave of sadness, but somehow sharing this place with Petey brought a ray of sunshine into the sorrow. "My daddy is in heaven. But I swear this place hasn't changed a bit. Like I could blink and my dad would walk around the corner and say, 'Skipper, do you want a fish sammie and fries?'"

Petey giggled. "Skipper?"

"Yep. That was my nickname. Do you have one?"

Petey scrunched his nose, and Ross's heart melted. God, he was sweet. "Um, my dad calls me champ sometimes. And squirt." He paused, and Ross watched him puff his chest a little. "At camp, they called me Slugger because I hit the most home runs for my team."

Ross held out her fist for the requisite celebratory bump. "Slugger—that's awesome! Congrats! Camp's a big deal. Did you love it?"

"Yep. I wanna go *three* weeks next summer."

"Three? Wow. Your dad will really miss you."

"Nah. He'll have you for company."

She started to correct him, and then decided it wasn't worth it. The waitress came and took their orders, saving Ross from that line of conversation. They ordered two fish sandwiches—"sammies," as her dad had called them—fries, and a milkshake for Petey.

Petey played with his straw. "Sorry about your dad, Ross. He sounds really cool. I don't have a mom. I mean, I used to. But I don't know her."

Christ...what was she supposed to say to that? *Channel Cole with Jemma...*

"Oh...well...I'm really sorry your mom isn't in your life, Petey." Ross struggled to begin, but then picked up steam as she hit a place of comfort. "I can tell you from firsthand experience that she's really missing out on an awesome son. But your dad is extra super, so I think he counts as a double parent."

Petey smiled at her, but his eyes were solemn. "My dad was sad sometimes before. But he's happy now. He smiles and laughs all the time. And sings. And I'm not even grossed out when he kisses you when you guys think I'm not looking."

Ross fought to close her gaping mouth. She realized she probably resembled old Moby hanging from the ceiling. "Uh, well—"

"Hey, Ross?"

"Yeah?" she responded weakly, not sure she was prepared for any more Petey comments. She was still reeling from the last ones.

"Are you going to marry my dad? I used to want him to marry Ms. Gaby, but he can't 'cause she's married to Mr. Ted. But I-I think you're nicer. And more fun. Don't tell Kingsley I said that. You...um"—he blushed, cheeks coloring a vibrant pink—"you could be my mom. I mean...if you wanted. Then you and my dad and I could be a family."

"Oh, Petey." Something deep in Ross's heart shifted. "I...well, I'm flattered. That's just about the most wonderful thing anyone's ever said to me."

Petey's face fell, his eyes filling with tears. "But you don't want me either."

Ross scooted out of the booth and came to his side, gathering him in her arms. She kissed the top of his head. "Far from it, Petey Grace. I am your friend, and that is special. I am in your life and I will always be your friend. And your dad's friend. You have no idea how much you mean to me."

Ross realized that the truth and vehemence in her words were born of something wholly unexpected—a bond with this child who had burrowed into her heart. This was unforeseen, but she could figure it out. Her relationship with him could be similar to hers with Jemma. Except in her heart, she knew there was one big, complicated, sexy-as-fuck difference. *Xander.*

Taking a shaky breath, she continued, choosing her words with care. "Your dad and I like each other a lot. We are having fun together, but that doesn't mean we're getting married. And I don't live in Virginia, Petey. I'm about to live in New York City."

"But you could live here."

"It's not that simple, Slugger."

Petey smiled at the use of the nickname. But his eyes were still sad. "So, you're not going to be my mom?"

"I'm going to be something cooler—your lifelong friend. And maybe you can come up with your dad to New York, or I'll see you when you visit my goddaughter, Jemma."

Petey's eyes lit up at the mention of Jemma. Soon, he was distracted by stories of things to do in Manhattan and Baltimore. *Crisis averted, I hope.*

Much later, Xander having returned to the cottage and Petey sound asleep, they quietly made good on their earlier promises, arching into each other and collapsing into shared ecstasy.

"God we're good at that together." He kissed Ross's forehead, pushing a sweaty tendril aside, then sighed. "Would you hate me if I worked for about a half hour?"

"What's up?"

"I owe the dean some revisions to a syllabus, and I want to get it done before your party. I should have done it ages ago, but someone—" he tapped her cheek "—has been a bit of a distraction."

Ross smiled. "I am not feeling very guilty about this," she responded with flirty nonchalance.

Xander's dimples emerged. "Good. You shouldn't. I'm a big boy. I know what I'm doing." He climbed out of bed in all his naked gloriousness to grab his laptop.

"Yes, you are, and yes, you do," Ross purred, casting a meaningful look at the splendid member between his legs.

Laughing, Xander sat against the headboard. Ross cataloged him with appreciative eyes. The wire rim glasses he wore only for computer work perched on his nose. Bare chested with a sexy smattering of chest hair. Sheet covering those powerful thighs.

An ache of desire pulsed between her legs, even though she was still sated and pleasantly sore from their recently completed activities.

He looked up with a wry grin. "This syllabus. Rick's a solid guy and an incredible mentor...but his plans are circa 1995 in so many ways. I feel like what's here doesn't reflect what he did in the classroom, and I can't replicate that. So, I need to redesign. And it's just overwhelming. I know what I want to do. And the dean believes in me. But this just feels like a lot."

Ross reached up and brushed the soft blond hair on his forehead, her heart bursting with tenderness for this man. "You're a talented architect. And I know you're an amazing teacher. You'll inspire the next generation. That's your superpower."

Xan paused, mouth opening and closing in surprise. He shifted, moving his laptop to the nightstand, then wrapping his long fingers around Ross's wrist and tugging her toward him. "How do you do that?"

"Do what?"

"Make me feel so able when I'm feeling—" he motioned to the laptop "—very not able."

"I have skilllllz," she drew out playfully.

"That you do, woman." He eased her on top of him, and Ross groaned in appreciation as his hard-again cock nudged toward her entrance.

"Hey, horndog, I thought you had work to do?"

"It'll keep for a minute," he murmured, sighing as he slid into her, bottoming out deep inside.

They had eschewed condoms after their poolside chat, and Ross savored the decadent warmth of him bare inside her.

"God, you feel good." *Apparently Xan savored the latex-less sensation too.*

"It'll keep for a *minute*?" Ross rolled her hips, taking him even deeper.

"Ok...definitely longer..."

And over their hushed moans as she rose inexorably toward completion with this incredible man, all Ross could hear was the echo of his son.

My dad was sad sometimes before. But he's happy now... You could be my mom. I mean...if you wanted. Then you and my dad and I could be a family.

She fisted her hand against her heart, holding in the love she could feel building for Alexander Grace and his son. And she was powerless to stop it. Honestly...she didn't want to. And that scared her more than anything.

CHAPTER THIRTY-SIX

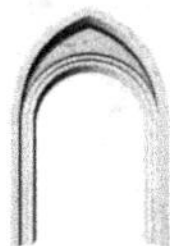

Ross

For several days leading up to the party, Ross had been forbidden by Xan from going to one specific part of the property. And it was killing her. The old barn at the edge of Hon's property, diagonal from both her grandmother's and her sister's homes, had been one of her favorite places to play growing up.

She tempered her raging curiosity by focusing on how special it felt to be with Tiercy at the farmhouse, reminiscing about happy times, adroitly avoiding unhappy memories, and generally catching up on life. Even though Ross had only been in the Shenandoah Valley for a few weeks, it felt much longer since she was used to seeing Tiercy at least a couple times a week.

With a few hours to go before the party, the afternoon sunlight slanted through the windows of Ross's bedroom as they took their time getting ready. Tiercy was curled up in Ross's bed, her auburn hair in hot rollers, happily devouring cheese straws. Ross, sitting at her vanity, closed her eyes and released a small sigh of happiness. She wanted to commit this perfect moment to memory.

Tamping down a wave of sadness that this was likely one of the last times, among hundreds, she and Tiercy would spend in the room, Ross turned to her best friend with raised eyebrows and teased, "Enjoying your snack?"

Tiercy licked her fingers with theatrical exaggeration. "I always forget how much I love Hon's cheese straws. I love them more than I love Cole right now."

"Don't get crumbs in my bed, you harlot, or we're switching rooms and Cole can get cheese straws in his crack," Ross snickered.

"Lovely image."

"You can lick them out."

"Also a lovely image."

"Hey, don't diss the butt stuff. I highly recommend it. Five stars out of five."

"Word," Tiercy breathed and they burst out laughing.

Ross turned and faced her best friend. "I cannot tell you how chuffed I am that you're here."

"Chuffed? Interesting SAT word. A British SAT word. Where'd you pick that up?"

"Editing a British actress's memoir. Honor Wheatley. I feel like I get extra bonus points for using it on my birthday."

"We'll take it under advisement. Wait—Honor Wheatley is writing a memoir? And you scored it?"

"Yes. It was my final project at my old job. It's all about her childhood health issues and growing up as English showbiz royalty. She's awesome. Surprisingly down to earth. And so freaking glamorous. I have a total girl crush on her. Shame her boyfriend is a twat."

"That is so cool that you get to work with her. Now, show me what you're wearing tonight."

"I have two options. But I can't decide. The first is this seafoam green chiffony-ish strapless maxi dress." Ross slid it over her head and it swirled around her. She felt like a goddess.

"Wowza. I sort of want to jump you. That's going to be a tough act to follow. What's the second one?"

Ross reached into her closet and pulled out a simple fitted knit dress with a halter strap. "The second is this navy dress."

"Try it on."

Ross shimmied out of the maxi and into the navy dress. Falling mid-thigh, it hugged her slim curves, and scooped so deep it was essentially backless. The navy color made her green eyes pop and gave her skin a sun-kissed glow.

Just then, Cole walked in from the Jack and Jill bathroom and stopped. "Tiercy, do you know where my—"

"Hey! Knock first!" Ross admonished, wagging a finger.

"Hey! Lock it then," Cole bantered and then his eyes widened in admiration. "Look at you, birthday girl." He turned to Tiercy, wiping a fake tear. "Mama, our baby's all grown up."

Cole was like the big brother Ross always wanted but never had. At six-foot-four, with dark hair and a muscular build, he'd swept Tiercy, a grieving widow, clear off her feet. Ross, ever-protective, wasn't sure at first. But anyone with eyes could see the deep and abiding love Cole had for Tiercy. It was powerful.

And like an honorary little sister, Ross walked over and swatted him. "Shut up, Colburn. You like it?"

"I think my friend Alexander Grace is going to have you out of that in about thirty seconds flat."

"Cole!" Tiercy yelped, laughing.

"The man's an animal. Better make sure you wear a chastity belt under that or something." He scanned her and frowned. "Can you even wear underwear with that?" He pointed to Tiercy emphatically. "Jemma's going to be a nun."

"Get out, you brat!" Ross snorted. "Hey, wait," she yelled after him, "did you tell Xander?"

Cole paused in the doorway to the bathroom. Ross, Tiercy, and he had agreed earlier that Cole would break the news about Gideon. Ross, recalling Xander's reaction the last time they discussed Gid, was feeling squeamish about telling him. The last thing she wanted to do was hurt him, and she didn't trust herself at this point to say the right thing. So she'd deputized Cole to the task, to which he'd agreed, with reluctance—and only when Tiercy threatened to withhold all conjugal interaction.

"Not yet, but I will, Princess Overshare. Pinky promise." Cole held out a pinkie to her, his unique blue-gray eyes shining in mirth.

"I'm holding you to it," Ross warned with a smile, connecting her pinkie and his. "Don't let me down."

"Nevah," Cole announced. "Now, I'm leaving you ladies to... whatever it is you were doing that I probably don't want to hear or know about. I'll forge ahead and find my phone charger all by my brave self, which is why I came in." He leaned over, dropped a sweet kiss on Tiercy's head, and then strode through the bathroom door back to his room with one last endearing gaze at his wife.

"It's in the side pocket of your weekend bag," Tiercy called after him, positively glowing from just a few moments in her husband's presence.

Once again, Ross had the thought...if she could cry, tears of happiness for Tiercy would be the thing to trigger them. She looked over at her best friend, snuggled in the bed they'd shared during so many summers. Ross was blessed.

"Alrighty then...blue dress it is. And watch the crumbs, because apparently I'm getting laid tonight."

Ross caught an odd look on her friend's face. "What's that look for? There's no way *that* could have offended your delicate sensibilities after thirty years of friendship with me, especially considering our butt stuff conversation earlier."

"Hardly," Tiercy rolled her eyes. "I have met you, you know." Tiercy patted the bed. "Get over here. I need to tell you something."

"You're freaking me out."

"Sit. It's a good thing." Tiercy took a deep breath. "I wanted to tell you in person. I'm pregnant."

Ross shrieked, throwing her arms around her friend. "You're what? Tierce! That's awesome!! How far along are you?"

"I'm about nine weeks along—"

"*Nine* weeks? Does Cole know?"

Tiercy laughed. "Of course he knows."

Ross cocked her head. "You've known for nine weeks and you *haven't told me*?"

"I only found out the day you left for Virginia. That said...it wasn't totally unexpected. We were sort of trying but not trying—"

"Wait! You pulled the goalie and you didn't tell me that either?" Ross hollered, laughing.

But a touch of hurt stabbed beneath the joy dancing in her heart. One more thing she hadn't been told. Was she not trustworthy? Even to her best friend? She camouflaged that zing of pain and pulled Tiercy into a bear hug.

"Ross, I'm sorry." Tiercy's voice was muffled against her shoulder. Of course, Tiercy saw through her. Saw the sad. "I know it stings a bit that I didn't tell you about pulling the goalie. I—we just decided to keep this special little secret between Cole and me...just for a bit." Tiercy hurried on, "And of course you are the first person we told."

"Stings schmings. I totally get it, Tierce. Honest." She held up the Girl Scout finger sign, even though Ross had quit that group as soon as she'd learned she didn't get to do the cool things her friends in the Boy Scouts were doing. "I'm your bestie. But he's your husband. That's between you two, and I'm cool with it."

And she was. Tiercy would always be her best friend, and nothing could replace that. But Tiercy also had a husband now. And things were changing. For Tiercy, that meant bringing a new life into the world.

"A baby!" She squealed and clapped, leaning in to examine her friend's nonexistent baby bulge. "Hellloooo in there! I can't see any sign of you yet, but I'm your Auntie Ross. I'm going to spoil you and drive your dad and mom bonkers!"

Tiercy rested her hand on her flat belly, rolling her eyes in shared mirth with her friend. "Just like Jemma. And as for the no visible sign of this baby, take a gander at my awesome ever-growing pregnancy knockers in the dress I'm wearing tonight. You're gonna be jealous." She waggled her eyebrows at Ross. "I've been bursting to tell you, Ross. But I had to tell you in person. Last time, with Jemma, the circumstances were so sad. And I just really wanted to see your face when I told you."

"This face?" Ross made her eyes huge and put a massive, cheese-eating grin on her face, throwing her arms around her friend again, squeezing her.

Tiercy burst out laughing. "Gah...that's a creepy face. But something close to that." She laughed again. "But, Ross, when you were driving to Virginia, I almost blurted it out. I'd just found out. I peed on the stick that morning, and there it was…two lines…"

"Two lines," Ross whispered and then clapped. "What an awesome birthday present for me! I'm going to be an aunt again! Aaaand…I knew something was up on that damn drive. My Spidey-senses were tingling all over the place."

"I'm sorry I didn't tell you right away."

"Stop apologizing! It's so much better to learn in person. You were right, as usual, which is a really annoying thing about you." She held out her arms and Tiercy leaned in. "This is going to be one lucky baby. I love you, Tierce."

"Love you, too. But, Ross?"

"Yeah?"

"You're crushing my cheese straws."

CHAPTER THIRTY-SEVEN

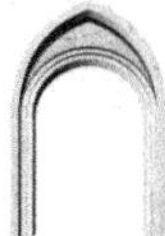

XANDER

Ross had confided in Xander that when she, Gaby, and Tiercy were growing up, the barn was the soundstage of their imaginations. It was a movie set. A theater. A dance studio. A stage on which they performed before tens of thousands of adoring fans. He found the notion charming and vowed to create something memorable there for her on this birthday.

It was in good condition—not dilapidated as many of its ilk. The Waldheims used it to store lawn and pool maintenance equipment, snow removal supplies, and other sundries. Xander had spent days reconfiguring the barn. And by midday Saturday, July fourth—thanks to a lot of helpers Xander had conscripted and a ton of his own sweat— it had been completely transformed into a red, white, and blue birthday wonderland for Ross. He knew she loved having a July fourth birthday, and went with that as a theme. But not kitschy. Nope, only class for Ross.

White flowers and ivy—a nod to her mother—adorned the rafters. Fairy lights twinkled from the ceiling, along with red, white, and blue Chinese lanterns. Caterers had brought in large round tables and high cocktail rounds. White toppers covered shimmering red and blue tablecloths. Small red and blue votives lit the tables. A riser for a live band was set up at one end of the barn. Along the other, long trestle tables groaned with catered food, including Ross's favorite barbecue. And a birthday cake designed to look like a stack of books rested on a round table in the corner.

As the appointed hour grew closer, Xander was as antsy and excited as a small child on Christmas morning. He checked the space over and over to be sure everything was perfect.

Twice Cole had started to tell him something, but Xander brushed him away with an impatient, "Later." He needed to make everything special for Ross.

All week she'd been free and cavalier. But he knew that deep down, she was rattled by the altercation with Ted and the revelations about her sister, as well as the memory of her last birthday in Virginia years ago— her last with her parents.

When it was close to go-time, he emerged from his shower and got dressed. New slacks and a pale pink button-down shirt, because Ross once told him she liked him in that color. Sport jacket. And his black cowboy boots. A bit of cologne—the scent she liked—but not too much. God...was he nervous?

"Petey, you almost ready? The sitter is coming by in five minutes to get you and then the mini-Monroes."

"Yes, sir." Petey came out of his room with a backpack and sleeping bag. The nanny who cared for Petey after school was going to watch him, the three Monroes, and Laverne overnight at her house. Bless her.

Fifteen minutes later, Xander had to pick his jaw off the ground.

Tiercy had stood at the bottom of the steps and called up to her friend in a singsong voice, "Oh, Ross. You have a gentleman caller for a date."

Then Ross emerged, coming down the stairs in a sinful, simple navy dress, high beige heels that made her legs go on forever, and long dark waves cascading down what he could see was her bare back. Xander was speechless.

Someone thumped his back. "This is when you say, 'Happy

birthday, Ross. You look amazing,' you dolt," Cole hissed from behind him, laughter in his voice.

Xander took two steps forward and held out both hands. Ross placed her hands in his and smiled shyly. Xan licked his lips and swallowed. "Happy birthday, Ross. You really do look amazing."

"Very original," came the sotto-voiced snicker behind him.

"Shut it, Colburn," murmured Xander out of the side of his mouth. "I mean it, Ross. You are exquisite, Principessa. I've never seen anyone lovelier. Happy birthday."

"Much better."

"And now I harm you." Xan turned and glowered at Cole, who aimed an angelic smile back at his friend.

"Come on, Gracie. Let's go show your girl her birthday barn."

Your girl. Xan blinked at the phrase. First Ted called him on it. Now Cole. Had she become his girl? Holy fuck.

She had.

He was falling in love with Ross Beaufort.

Her wit, her huge heart, her brilliant mind. Even her sharp edges, that protected what he knew was a tender, wounded heart. He was one thousand percent in love with her. Aaaand...this was not the time to have that revelation.

Xan recovered himself and rolled his eyes at Cole. "Who invited this guy? Ross, may I escort you into your party? Your guests await you." He released one hand and held out his arm. As Ross slid her hand around the crook of his elbow, Xander inhaled a shaky breath at how perfectly she fit against his body—and in his life.

"Shall we?"

CHAPTER THIRTY-EIGHT

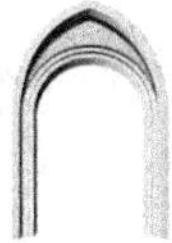

Ross

The pathway to the barn was adorned with LED candles in luminaria bags. Ross, Xander, Tiercy, and Cole chatted and laughed as Cole pretended to "fix" the bags, and then Xan fake-punched his friend. The evening fireflies had emerged, and the softest of summer breezes tickled Ross's hair against her shoulders.

Ross gently squeezed Xander's arm where her hand had remained since he offered it at the house. *Best freaking forearm porn of my life.* She smiled up at Xander, completely owning that she was a total smitten kitten. Unexpected and satisfying contentment suffused through her. Everything about this moment along the path was so...right. Even the mock praise currently being tossed her way by Cole.

"Ross, I'm impressed with your restraint at not sneaking a peek this week," he teased, earning another fake punch from Xan and an amused eye roll from Tiercy.

"Enough shenanigans," Tiercy commanded with a grin.

"Oooooh. Now we're in trouble," Cole sing-songed. "She brought out her teacher voice." Turning to his wife, he whispered, loud enough for Ross and Xander to hear, "And I'm kind of turned on by it."

All four devolved into laughter.

"Tiercy, I feel sorry for you." Xander aimed a dimpled smile her way. "Now, Ross's guests await her. Come along, Principessa. It's time to celebrate you."

They were steps from the barn entrance and Ross could hear the animated chatter of said guests and the low thrum of music.

Xander eased her hand from his arm, turning her to face him. *Damnation, he was a Hottie McHot Pants on steroids.*

"Close those beautiful green eyes, Principessa. I'll guide you in and tell you when to open them."

Nodding, Ross complied and allowed herself to be led through the doorway. Senses heightened with her lack of vision, she detected the hush that fell over the room, punctuated by excited whispers.

Xander's soft lips touched the edge of her ear, sending a riot of chills down her arms. "You can open your eyes now, Principessa," he commanded, his deep, soft voice causing a parallel shiver through her body.

She took her time, savoring the moment, and slowly opened her eyes.

"Xander," Ross gasped. "This is magical." Stunned, she clapped a hand over her mouth. The barn, her special childhood sanctuary, was completely transformed. Spinning around, she threw her arms around Xander's neck, breathing in his intoxicating scent. "It's...wonderful. I don't even have words. Thank you!"

More than fifty people were there, and as Ross reluctantly released her hold on Xan and turned back to her guests, the band began playing a rousing version of Happy Birthday. Everyone sang along, ending with applause.

She turned to Hon, who had moved to her other side as the guests sang. "You did all this?"

"Well, I *helped*. But most of the credit goes to Alexander, along with Ted, Gaby, Petey, Nick, Kingsley, Cole, Tiercy, and the caterers. And some other muscle Alexander and Ted brought in."

"It's beyond fabulous. All this for a thirty-fifth birthday? I can't believe all these people came." Ross paused, taking in the range of guests. Friends from Baltimore, her Aunt Francesca, cousins and their spouses, a few long-ago friends from Virginia summers, one of her good friends from New York and his husband. Even hunky Brinder Desai, the best friend of Tiercy's late husband—with whom Ross had also become close friends over the years—was there. "I'm overwhelmed. Thank you." She leaned in and kissed the soft, lined cheek she loved so much.

Before she could say any more, Ross was swept into the tide of the party. Hon beamed at her, dabbing tears as she watched Ross greet her guests. Even Gaby, who sat in a chair with her feet up, her hair a wheat blonde sheet in a high ponytail, gave her an unguarded, shining smile.

Ross made her way over to her sister. "How are you feeling? How's the wee one?"

"I'm good. No more spotting. Just a bit tired. The bleeding was normal, the doctor says, even if it looked scary. And the heartbeat is strong. This little nugget is doing great."

"I'm so glad." She leaned in and hugged her sister for the first time in...decades.

Gaby's eyes watered. "Happy birthday, Ross. You look spectacular tonight. That dress is incredible."

"Thanks, Gaby. You look beautiful too." For a moment, the sisters locked eyes in telegraphed remembrance of the last birthday at the farmhouse. Ross's sweet sixteen.

Gaby's voice was quiet. She reached out and gently squeezed Ross's hand. "At least that party wasn't here, Ross. That would really suck. You get to make a new memory here in the barn."

Ross nodded, unable to find words.

"I have a present for you." Gaby bit back a smile, her eyes shining. "I wanted to give it directly to you instead of leaving it on the table that is positively groaning with the weight of your gifts." She winked and handed Ross a wrapped box.

Ross, never one to wait on a present, tore the paper and lifted the lid. Inside was a Tommy Hilfiger sweater.

"No way! You didn't? This is just like the one—"

"That you ruined years ago. Yep!"

Ross squealed, causing several guests to look over and smile. "Where did you find this?"

"The wonders of eBay, my sweater-decimating sister."

"Hey, that was not my fault. Shirley was trying to get the bone I'd hidden in my sleeve."

"Sure, that's what happened," Gaby jokingly rolled her eyes. "It definitely didn't happen when you climbed out the window and caught it on the lattice."

"My story and I'm sticking to it. Seriously, though, Gaby. I love it! That is so clever. Thank you."

Almost shyly, Gaby reached for Ross, who squeezed her tight. Both sisters held on, overwhelmed by the moment.

Ross recovered first, taking a sip of the water she'd grabbed.

"Speaking of bones, things seem to be going well with Xan."

"Gaby—" Ross simultaneously choked out a laugh and on her water. "Oh my God. Warn a bitch, will you? I almost just choked to death on my birthday!"

"I may be a boring pregnant lady, but I still got it." Gaby winked and then scanned the room. "Well, go on and skedaddle, as Pop would say. You have people to greet. And I have to pee. Shocker. Walk me to the door?"

The sisters, arms linked, walked to the door, passing next to Tiercy and Cole. Gaby stopped in her tracks, fanning her face. "*Damnation*! Who is that?"

Ross tracked her admiring glance and her stomach plummeted to her knees. "Oh, fuckety fuck."

Tiercy nudged Cole hard in the ribs. "Gideon's here."

Cole's gaze flew to Ross's and then the door, where her friend—a strapping man in his late forties with dark hair—strode in with athletic grace, eyes seeking and finding Ross. As Gideon made his way through the crowd toward her, confident purpose in his step and a smile on his face, Ross rounded on Cole. "Number one, where is Xan? And number two, please tell me you told him Gideon is coming."

Cole rubbed his hand down the front of his face. "Um...I tried?"

"Cole! What the ever-loving—I counted on you! We pinky-promised," Ross screeched, forgetting about her barn full of guests. Her palms began to sweat. This was going to be awkward.

Chagrined, he put his drink down. "I'll go look for Xan." He glanced at the newly arrived guest. "Would it be bad if I asked him for his autograph?"

"Husband!" His wife's exasperated growl followed him.

Fuck. Ross closed her eyes in silent supplication to God, Buddha, Salvatore Ferragamo, Chris Evans, and any other deity she could think of. *Please don't let Xan be upset. I'm not sure I can bear it.*

Chapter Thirty-Nine

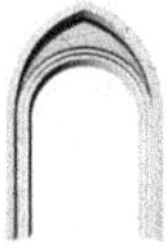

Leaving the bar with two whiskey sours, Xander turned just in time to see a familiar-looking man slide his arm around Ross and bestow upon her a much-more-than-friends kiss. Xander's breath caught, and serrated jealousy sliced through his chest. He squeezed the glasses, watching this man who was clearly quite physically familiar with his girl.

Dammit. She *was* his girl. She just didn't know it yet.

Xander was, as Ross would say, absofuckinglutely in love with her. And this douche was kissing *his girl*.

"Easy there, Gracie. Let me take those from you." Cole slid in next to him and eased the glasses from his hand. "A little tighter and those might have exploded in your hand, brother."

"Better them than me," Xander replied through clenched teeth, eyes still affixed to the scene unfolding before him.

To his relief, Ross quickly broke the kiss and backed away a bit. Still, Xander couldn't help but notice the becoming flush on her cheeks. The man slipped his arm around Ross, grinning at her and talking animatedly. Ross was listening and laughing, the mossy green sparkle of her eyes evident even from across the room.

Despite the muscled arm slung casually around her waist, she'd managed to put some distance between them. But Xander's gaze was locked on Ross clearly engaged in the conversation, amused at whatever he was saying.

He rubbed the knot of jealousy in his gut. Then it hit him. "Gideon *O'Grady*?!" The name came out of Xander's mouth in a purl of shock.

"Yeah." Cole confirmed.

"Gideon O'Grady is here. At Ross's party. *He's* Ross's Gideon?"

"Apparently. I take it you didn't know who he is?"

"I know of a *Gideon*. He's someone Ross used to—would sometimes—*see* when she went to New York." Xander struggled to find the words to describe Ross's relationship—even if she would never use that term—with the gentleman whose hand was now caressing her back.

"I see." Cole looked between Xan and the man across the room. "'Would' sounds like past tense. I'm not sure *he* knows that." Cole frowned in the direction of Gideon's hand.

Xander's blood pressure went up another few or dozen digits, not even lowering when Ross stepped to the side toward Tiercy and another guest, which caused the guy's hand to shift off her back.

"Tiercy told me she invited him before Ross ever even came to Virginia this summer. Gideon was doing humanitarian work in Africa and only replied earlier this week that he was coming."

"She didn't tell me Gideon was *that* Gideon." Xander's head whipped around. "Wait—did Ross know he was coming?"

"Ah, shit. Yes. And I was supposed to tell you today. Earlier. I tried. But you kept saying 'later.'" Cole's tone was apologetic, but also reflected his wariness of the human tinderbox next to him.

"*Fuck*, brother. That's the kind of thing you don't allow a friend to brush aside. You're supposed to say, 'Hey, Gracie. You know this Gideon dude that Ross has talked about? It's Gideon O'Grady, the former Gold-freaking-Glove third baseman for two different major league teams.' And didn't he just win a social justice award for his work with inner city kids? My parents went to the gala for it and my mom couldn't stop gushing about him. This dude is a legend." He raked his hand through his hair as he watched a small swell of recognition go through the guests.

Gideon, arm around Ross's waist again, began greeting people, even signing autographs. Xander choked on shock that battled with jealousy. "But why wouldn't she tell me? Unless she wanted to see him? Man, I can't compete with that," he whispered, almost winded by shock.

"Gracie, I don't want to have to do any relationship counseling while holding whiskey—What? It feels unprofessional," Cole defended, after catching a glimpse of Xander's incredulous face.

"Dude. You are a contractor not a counselor."

"And, yet, here's me telling you this truth. Looking at her while she looks at you, and then looking at her while she looks at him, I'd say there's no contest. You're welcome. Bill's in the mail."

Wanting to believe what his dork of an amazing friend had pronounced, Xander turned back toward Ross in time to see her gracefully dodge an incoming kiss from Gideon on the smooth guise of turning him to pass a paper to be autographed. As she did that, she caught Xander's penetrating gaze.

She looked...guilty.

She pivoted away and, in one deft move, passed Gideon a drink from the cocktail waiter Hon had hired for the evening. Gideon brushed a quick kiss on her cheek and lifted his glass in a toast to her.

Just then, Xander remembered the drinks he was getting for both him and Ross. Watching the byplay, Cole handed the tumblers back to his friend. "Go get your girl. And promise you aren't going to crush them this time? Terrible waste of alcohol." Cole's words were joking, but the laughter didn't reach his gray eyes, which were filled with concern for his closest friend.

Xander nodded, trying to relax his jaw, and resumed his trajectory toward Ross, hoping he'd figure out some non-asshat way to handle what seemed like the worst plot twist in his painstakingly planned evening. "Saints save me," he muttered to himself, using his mother's preferred sanitized expletive.

As it turned out, Hon did the saving. She climbed up on the stage, her pearly bob shining under the lights. Tapping a microphone, she called Ross onto the stage with her, allowing the birthday girl to gently extricate herself from the embrace of her erstwhile New York lover.

"Good evening. I am Leah Waldheim, and I'm Ross Ellen's proud grandmother. I have the pleasure of welcoming you this evening. I am so happy to have the beautiful birthday girl with us here at the farmhouse to celebrate her thirty-fifth trip around the sun!" Catcalls and wolf-whistles accompanied her pronouncement, and Ross shook her head, laughing. "Ross, I love you so much. And when I see you, I see echoes of your mother, Ivy. She and your father would also be so proud. You are an amazing woman."

More cheers erupted from the crowd, including competing loud ones from Xander and Gideon, who turned his head to see what other lion in the pride might be interested in this lioness. Xander met his gaze head on, not breaking eye contact until Gideon looked away. *Ha, point for me.*

"And now, it's my pleasure to turn the microphone over to another amazing woman, Ross's best friend from the time they were knee high to a grasshopper, Tiercy Colburn."

Tiercy, in a pale yellow scoop neck sundress that set off her auburn hair, stepped onto the stage, hugging first Hon and then Ross. Xander's eyes were trained on Ross as she stood with her best friend, their arms locked around each other's waists.

He tried to pay attention to Tiercy's speech, but all he could think of was his shock at Ross's failure to let him know Gideon was coming to the party. Did she not trust him enough to tell him herself about the snafu with Gideon's invitation? Or, much worse, perhaps it was that she didn't reciprocate the revelation he'd experienced as he watched her descend the stairs of the farmhouse earlier in the evening. From the moment he'd recognized his true feelings, Xander had a sense deep inside that Ross shared those feelings.

Hazarding a glance at the retired athlete-now-humanitarian, he fought a wave of dizziness. They'd all warned him not to fall. But...he couldn't help it.

Xander closed his eyes and prayed he was overreacting. To be fair, he hadn't even spoken with her about the mix-up, and he had promised to always go to her first. Steeling himself with a deep breath, he focused on the toast.

"Ross, from the moment we met over a swing set and a bouncy red ball, you've been my bestie. You're gorgeous—sometimes disconcertingly so. But you have this...earthiness that's endearing. You cuss like it's a second language," Tiercy declared with emphasis, invoking hearty laughter from Xander and the crowd. "Growing up you dated like a sailor on leave, with a string of broken hearts in your wake—"

Listening to this part and recalling Gideon standing so close to Ross, who would be leaving for Manhattan in just a few weeks, Xander's ears started to buzz again. He'd be in her wake too. She'd been honest about it all along. *Fuck.* He had to fight for her. Observing her glowing like fireworks in the space he'd designed for her, he knew. He just knew. Ross was his. And he was hers.

"—and you laugh like a drunken hyena. I think that's to make you more like your mere mortal friends...even if you do look like a goddess. It's a bewitching combination—I mean, if I were a guy, I'd tap that..."

Tiercy smacked her friend on the bottom and grinned, and Ross snort-laughed. The friends leaned against each other, laughing, heads touching, as Xan winked at Leah, huge smiles across their faces at the hijinks of the sister-friends.

Tiercy composed herself. "But the most amazing thing is that under all that gorgeousness is a heart of pure gold. When I couldn't even scrape myself off the ground, you helped put me back together, atom by atom. You helped make me whole again when I couldn't do it myself. Nobody makes me laugh harder than you. If I'm having a bad day, I pick up the phone and call you because I know I'm going to hear, 'What's up, Hooker Hips?' and I'll just crack up. You have the deepest, truest heart of any human being I've ever met. Happy birthday to the best bestie ever. I know this is going to be an amazing year for you. Cheers!"

The friends embraced to loud applause from the crowd. Behind them, the band struck up The Beatles' "You Say It's Your Birthday," as Ross and Tiercy exited the stage and melted into the crowd.

"Game on," Xander muttered and downed both drinks, ignoring

the raised eyebrows of his best friend standing by his side. He was contemplating heading to the bar for a third when he heard a wry voice.

"I thought maybe one of those was for me. Guess I was wrong." Ross was standing behind him, her teasing smile not quite matching the questioning look in her eyes.

"Yeah, well, I got thirsty. And you got waylaid by—"

"Where did you disappear to?" Gideon eased in next to Ross, bearing a vodka gimlet. "If I recall, this is your drink of choice."

Ross opened her mouth to speak, only to be cut off by Xander. "Actually, it's a whiskey sour these days. People move on."

Gideon shifted closer to Ross, a slight frown on the face that had graced dozens of sports and celebrity magazines. "Of course. Variety is the spice of life," he replied, not unkindly. He held out a well-manicured hand. "I don't believe we've been introduced. Gideon O'Grady. I'm a good friend of Ross's from Manhattan."

Xander squared up. "Of course. I've followed your career. Alexander Grace." Dolt. Why'd he use his full name? He never did that.

Cole uttered a small snort-cough, and Xander gave him a side eye. So much for the moral support from his friend.

"Sorry. Wrong pipe. Just a touch of gastritis-ignitis. Nothing serious. Alcohol flares it up." Cole motioned to his drink as Ross's eyes flared in surprise at the fake malady and Tiercy covered a smile with a swallow of her own water. Clearly Ross told Tiercy the Genevieve story. And, of course, Tiercy told Cole. Xander sighed. "John Colburn. You can call me Cole. Friend of *Alexander*," he emphasized the name, "and Ross is best friends with my wife, Tiercy."

"Nice to meet you both. I've heard Ross talk about Tiercy many times. Alexander, how do you know Ross?"

We have a summer deal. We're fucking each other's brains out until we can't see straight. But I'm in love with her. And she loves me. I just need to help her realize it. She's my girl.

Xander tried to telegraph what he wanted to say in a heavy-lidded glance at Ross, who looked away, swallowing a smile and a blush. He'd never intentionally tried to smolder before, but it was clear his efforts worked. "I'm a family friend. I live in a cottage on the property here, but Ross and I first met at Cole and Tiercy's wedding." *Memorably, asshat.*

Gideon grinned. "So, wait. You're friends with Cole, and Ross and Tiercy are best friends?"

Ross, Cole, and Xander all nodded, sharing smiles.

"That is spectacular." Gideon lifted his glass. "Cheers to friendship." He turned to Xander. "That's great for Ross that you're here. I know she was dreading this trip."

His insides thudded. Ross said she didn't have a relationship with Gideon, but he knew enough about her to have that particular insight.

"Gideon," Xan heard Cole chime in with what he recognized as a plain effort to change the subject. "Tell us about the legendary World Series game in 2008—"

Clearly, Gideon was down with that topic and started in on his reminiscence. Ross, an impish glimmer in her eyes, excused herself with a fake yawn. "I have only heard people ask you to tell this story sixty-five times. How you hit for the cycle. And the Brooks Robinson-style catch that's still on all the highlight reels."

"Considering that's the story you asked me to tell you when you picked me up at that bar..."

"I didn't pick you up. I asked for your autograph for my boss. Which is one hundred percent accurate."

"Not how I remember it, Ross." Gideon was laughing.

"We'll agree to disagree, Gid," she winked. "Now, I have a party to enjoy and guests to schmooze. I'll leave you gents to talk."

"That is quite a woman," Gideon marveled as he watched Ross walk away. "I look forward to having her in my city."

Xander hoped for the sake of this man's unbroken neck that his statement wasn't a double entendre. Gideon wouldn't be *having* Ross anywhere if Xander could help it. Observing Gideon's admiring eyes travel the length of Ross as she was spun in a smooth dance move by her and Tiercy's friend Brinder Desai, he finally understood the phrase "blood boil." He was sure if you put him under a microscope right now, you'd see little bubbles roiling in his veins and capillaries.

He couldn't prevent the acid in his voice as he responded, "Oh, it's your city? How much of Gotham do you own?"

If he heard the sarcasm, Gideon didn't let it show. He was still watching Ross. "Not much. Just a euphemism. I know it's not her favorite place, but I'm looking forward to helping Ross become an official Manhattanite. She's only dipped her toe in our fair metropolis. And I hope to be her dedicated ambassador."

"I thought Ross said you traveled a lot." Xander wondered if the pulse throbbing in his neck was visible.

"I make my own schedule." Gideon shrugged. "She's worth hanging around for."

Xander assessed him. He was taller than Xander, with dark brown eyes. Graying at the temples, but it didn't age him. Muscular. Definitely kept himself in shape. Good looks that Xan suspected had gotten him pretty much any woman he wanted. Xander saw green again, and it wasn't Ross's stunning eyes.

"Ross doesn't do relationships." Xander could have bitten off his own tongue. Even Cole turned to him with incredulous eyes, wordlessly begging him to STFU. But Xander couldn't stop. "Besides, since she's been here at the farmhouse, I think Ross has found her true love. The farmhouse, I mean. Virginia. The Shenandoah Valley. She's not a city girl."

"I don't know about that, Alexander," Gideon chuckled. "It is quaint here. Charming. Nice for a visit and a breather. But once she's settled into that amazing apartment on the Upper West Side, Ross will hit the ground running with her new role. She'll explore all the amazing things Manhattan and the boroughs have to offer." Another confident shoulder shrug. "As they say, 'How are you going to keep 'em down on the farm when they've seen Paree?'"

He hummed a bit. "Her friend texted me earlier this week that we wouldn't have time for a proper visit, but seeing her tonight...I regret that." Gideon smiled, not in a leering way, but simply in the way of a man appreciating a stunning woman.

For the third time that evening, Xander heard buzzing in his ears. Everything Gideon said was true. Unable to speak, Xander simply nodded, picturing all the things Gideon had conjured for them. Cole, sensing the disquiet, filled the conversational gap, engaging Gideon with more baseball talk.

Ten minutes later, Cole cleared his throat. Xander had stood there, largely silent but offering an occasional comment, and the sound startled him.

"Gideon, a pleasure talking with you." Cole shook his hand.

"You, too, Cole. And Alexander. Take care of Ross down here." He grasped Xander's hand and gave it a friendly pump.

Xander returned the shake, possibly grasping a little harder and a little longer than necessary.

CHAPTER FORTY

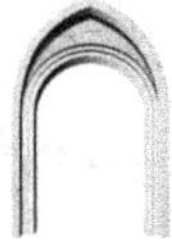

As the evening progressed Xander saw Ross start to head toward him a few times, always with a tentative smile and conciliatory eyes. He'd quickly turn away, pretending to be absorbed in conversation.

But his sonar was tuned to her. She sent off pulses in waves that connected to his core, and Xander always knew exactly where Ross was. Knew when she joined her Baltimore friends on the dance floor. Knew when she did a sexy dance with her (thankfully) gay friend from Brooklyn, as he watched her sinuous curves in that amazing dress. Knew when Gideon pulled her to him for a slow dance.

That one almost made him leave the party—or ram his fist down the guy's throat. Which was ridiculous, he knew. She owned his heart, although she might not realize it. But he wasn't sure he'd earned hers.

Not yet.

And then he saw it. Ross's subtle step backward at the beginning of her dance with Gideon. It was infinitesimal. But it was there. She didn't press herself into Gideon. She looked up at him with those amazing green eyes, laughed and possibly even flirted, but she wasn't molded to him. Not the way she did when they slow-danced in his kitchen after Petey went to sleep.

It was that tiny step back that propelled him to follow Ross as she left the barn a short while later. Heart pounding like a nerdy high-schooler about to face the prom queen, he headed outside.

Minutes later, he watched her exit the mobile event-style restroom Leah had rented, but she didn't head right back into the barn. Instead, she turned in the opposite direction, toward a large oak tree fifty yards away. She'd slipped off her heels and walked quietly in the night, the sandals dangling off her fingers.

Xander waited a bit and then followed her, stopping a few paces away near another tree. Accompanied only by the sounds of crickets, muted party music, distant laughter, and the feel of his thrumming pulse, he observed her.

God, he was so in love with her.

Now that he'd realized it, his heart was full with the knowledge of it. He wanted to tell her, but he knew now wasn't the time. Instead, he contented himself with the joy of watching her beauty in the summer night. In the partial moonlight, she was illuminated like an ethereal being.

She reached a graceful hand out to the oak, looking up. He knew there was a treehouse above her, one she'd convinced her father and grandfather to build thirty years ago. She turned and leaned back against the tree. He could see her taking deep breaths. Then her head dropped. She held it there for a moment and then thrust it back, hitting it solidly and intentionally against the tree trunk. "Fuck!" she hissed.

Startled, Xander rushed toward her, frightening Ross. "Jesus—Xan! What the ever—"

"Loving fuck am I doing here?" he finished, somewhat breathless but cocking a smile at their exchange from several weeks ago.

"You scared the shit out of me. What are you doing—were you following me?"

"Sort of. I—uh—wanted to talk to you alone, and when I saw you go outside, I thought that would be a good opportunity." He gave a weak shrug of his shoulders. High school nerd.

"It's about damn time," Ross murmured, hand on her heart, slowly recovering herself. "You've been avoiding me all night."

"Hard to get a word in. What with *Gideon O'Grady* glued to you. Thought it might be awkward." Xander hated how petulant and whiny he sounded.

Ross turned a bit, moonlight and oak leaves creating a chiaroscuro on her profile. "I deserve that. I know Cole didn't warn you."

"No." Xander's voice was low. Nerd boy was gone, replaced by a man who didn't understand her reticence to tell him. More than that, Xander was frustrated by his own ire at the situation. "Why wouldn't you tell me yourself—first that he was coming, and second that Gideon is fucking Gideon O'Grady?"

She turned back toward him, a wry smile on her face. "I've been asking myself those same questions. And the only answer I can come up with is...because I'm a chickenshit fuckstick." Now it was her turn to shrug her shoulders. "I suck."

Xander laughed despite himself. "Tiercy's right. You really do curse like a second language. But this does beg the question. Why were you 'a chickenshit fuckstick,' as you so artfully phrased it?"

"I don't know. That's the problem. Gideon and I are friends. So are you and I. And we aren't in a relationship. It shouldn't be a big deal to tell you. I've been really clear with that. It's just—"

"A summer deal. I know," Xan finished for her, biting down on the urge to confess his feelings. Not now, he reminded himself. Timing would be everything. He needed to keep earning her trust, and her love. "Then why not tell me?"

"Because I didn't want you to be mad. Because I didn't want you to be jealous. Because—because I'm not sure I really want him here. He doesn't *belong,* but on the other hand, he's my friend, and I enjoy his company, so why shouldn't he be here? God, I hate drama. It's ridiculous!" Ross pressed her head back hard against the tree.

"Hey now." Xan stepped forward and placed his hand between her head and the bark, feeling the decadent warmth of her against his palm. "Stop that. I'm sort of fond of that head. Treat it with care."

He leaned in close to her, heart throbbing, matching the cadence of the throbbing in his body. "You're right. I was mad, but only that you didn't trust me—as a friend, if nothing else."

He swallowed his lie. *Patience, Gracie.*

Ross started to talk, but he silenced her with his mouth on hers. Not a kiss. Just gentle pressure. "Sssh," he breathed against her mouth, his body pressed against her. "I need to say this. Tonight, when I saw him kiss you, I didn't like it, Ross. I had a special night planned. But more than that, the mouth on you should have been my mouth." Xan kissed her, showing her with his mouth and tongue the longing coursing through his heart and body. "And his hands on your back should have been my hands." He lifted his free hand and trailed it down her back.

"Xander—I—"

"Please, Ross? I need to try to finish what I'm saying here." He framed her face, staring into her moonlit eyes.

"Saying or doing?" Ross whispered, moving his hands back down her back with a sexy smile.

"Both." He ran his fingers along the cleft of her ass, feeling the answering clench of her globes against the fabric.

"Go on then." Her voice was breathless with want.

He reached down and trailed his fingers along her legs, lifting the hem of her dress. Hooking a finger around her thong, he tugged down the thin lace, following its descent until he was kneeling, and then nuzzling at the vee of her legs. "Hold your dress up, Principessa."

The vibration of Ross's quiet moan went straight to his aching cock. Xander took his time, working his tongue over and through her soft, wet folds with patience that was wavering under the pressure of his need.

Ross rocked her hips against his lips, seeking more friction. "More," she whispered. He ignored her and circled his tongue on the bundle of nerves, consumed with the scent and lure of her arousal. "Xander... more," she pleaded, pulling at his shoulders.

With that, he stood and welcomed a touch of cool air on his heated body. Then his finger was back, tantalizingly close to that nub of her pleasure. He pressed his forehead to hers, kissing her gently, exploring, promising with his mouth what the rest of him would soon give.

"I know time is running out for us in our summer deal, Principessa, but I've got you right now. You're *mine* now." Ross inhaled quickly, panting as he slid two fingers inside her. "So wet...so tight." Xander sighed against her mouth. "Ross," he whispered, as he prepared to enter her, "I know we don't do relationships." *Yet.* "But you're *my* summer deal. And a deal's a deal. So fuck Gideon." *You're mine.*

"No. Fuck *me*."

"Such language," Xander said, as he obliged. "Get on your knees, Principessa."

"By the tree? Not comfortable. And what if someone sees us?" Her voice was soft and ragged with need as she continued to work herself against his fingers, which he slid from her body to the sounds of her protesting whimper.

"We're far enough away from the action. And no one is going to come this direction." He shrugged off his sport jacket and tossed it on the soft grass away from the roots. They'd be in shadow. "Knees *now*, Ross," he commanded, his fingers back and tracing her wet heat, gliding through the decadent slickness that had flooded between her legs.

She stepped away with a heated look and went down on her knees on his jacket, easing her dress over her delectable ass until it was bunched around her waist. Xander unzipped his slacks, fisting the base of his cock to calm it the fuck down. Then he got on his knees behind her and powered inside her, balls deep, in one hard thrust.

"Yes, Xander," she gasped.

"What do you want, sweetheart?"

"You," she managed. "Harder."

He grabbed her hips and pounded into her. Over and over, he buried himself inside of her, sounds of the slapping of skin and their wet arousal heightening the pressure behind his balls. He was going to come soon. The need to release was just too intense. He licked his finger and then eased it inside her tight ring, working it in and out until she gripped him even tighter, her muscles spasming.

"Yes, oh fuck. Oh, Xan!"

Xander's own release exploded and he poured himself inside of her, pumping his hips as he chanted her name. "*Ross. Ross. My Ross.*" It was an incantation. A plea. A surrender.

Their summer deal might be coming to a close, but this wasn't over yet. They had barely begun.

Chapter Forty-One

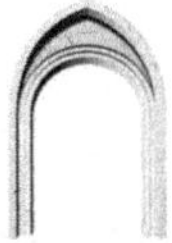

Ross

Her best friend's eyebrows rose as Ross returned to the festivities. While she and Xander had cleaned up and composed themselves during a hasty toilette-adjusting trip to the washroom trailer, her body was still humming and she knew her face and chest were flushed with what she and Tiercy called "sex blush."

She cast a glance at Xander, who didn't look even slightly disheveled. Other than a cocky grin nestled between those dimples, with his sport jacket folded up under his arm, it appeared as if he'd just been outside for some fresh air.

"Where did you go?" Tiercy asked. "Hon was looking for you. Cole and I were just heading out to check the washroom trailer." Tiercy paused, examining her best friend more closely. "You just boinked, didn't you!" she accused in a whisper-yell, her eyes wide, pointing between the two of them and dramatically mouthing "sex blush!"

Ross squirmed a bit under the appraising glance of her best friend and avoided eye contact with Xander. However, she sensed his smile almost as tangibly as she felt the evidence of their encounter in the residual ache between her thighs.

Cole burst out laughing. "One, yes, I believe they did. It's exactly how they looked on the day of our wedding. And, two, you really have to stop picking up euphemisms for sex at school." Cole cleared his throat, a gleam in his eye. "You weren't outside very long, Xan. That didn't take long at all."

"Twice as long as you ever could, brother."

Ross rolled her eyes as Xander fake punched Cole. She brushed a blade of grass from the knee of Xan's pants, catching Tiercy's amused glance at the less-than-surreptitious move.

Cole turned to the women. "Now, if you lovely ladies would please excuse us, Xan and I have to chat."

Xan looked back over his shoulder, eyes comically wide to convey "*save me,*" while Cole propelled him toward the band's sound board.

Ross laughed. He was so freaking sexy and adorable. "What was that about?" she asked Tiercy.

"Mum's the word. I know they have something planned, but that's all I'm going to say." She zipped her lips, wedding rings sparkling in the soft barn lighting.

"Seriously?"

"As serious as coffee in the morning, which I miss more than I could ever express these days."

Ross did a double take and busted out laughing. "Ohhhkaay. So clearly you aren't telling me."

"Nope. Just trust me." Tiercy caught her husband's eye and grinned. "Any minute now."

Brief squeaking feedback from the microphone drew their attention to the stage. The lead singer began saying something about a special guest performance and Tiercy pulled her front and center stage. The lights dimmed as the band performed the opening strains of The Cure's "Just Like Heaven."

Ross shrieked and clapped. She loved this song. She'd played it over and over for Xan, to the point that he jokingly threatened to uninstall her Spotify if she didn't stop. Then the singer stepped aside, revealing Xander on main vocals, a la Robert Smith, and Cole on the keyboards.

Tiercy screamed in joy and hooted, doing the Arsenio Hall arm pump in the air.

Stunned, Ross stood frozen. Her mouth hung open, a smile forming. "What the ever-loving fuck?" she whispered to herself. Xander's eyes locked on hers and a slow smile spread across his face as he sang.

Xander had peeled off his button down, revealing a black T-shirt. With the black pants, he looked incredibly sexy. Xander's deep voice filled the room, singing her favorite lyrics from the song.

The dam burst and Ross exploded into applause, whistling loudly. Tiercy grabbed her hand and they screamed like they did years ago at the concerts of their youth. Xander was sex appeal and charisma personified, the mic cradled in his large, sensual hands. Ross hoped fervently the lead singer would get laid by the fan in the front row later tonight.

As he continued singing, the rest of the crowd melted away, and she sang with him, her eyes fused with his. And when he got to the part of the song when the woman expresses that he won't ever know she's in love with him, Ross gasped for the second time that evening, pressing a shaking hand to her neck, pulse racing against her hand.

There it was—art turning the key to unlock hidden truths.

Her heart thudded in an unfamiliar cadence of emotion. And while her body had recognized and acknowledged it first, her pathetic, broken soul had finally caught up. Alexander Grace was hers. She was in love with him. She just wasn't sure what to do about it and what it meant for her life.

Later. She'd think about this later. For now...she just focused on the gorgeous man serenading her.

At the conclusion of the song, the crowd screamed for another— Ross and Tiercy hollering the loudest, laughter surrounding them. Unfortunately, it seemed Xander and Cole hadn't prepared one.

Instead, in a classic concert maneuver, Xander reached down and grabbed Ross's hand, hauling her onto the stage. In a Smith-esque English accent, he wished her "Happy Birthday" and then dipped her into a toe-curling kiss. The guests howled and clapped.

Xander righted her, and then kissed the tip of her nose. "Happy birthday, Principessa."

Movement at the back of the barn caught Ross's eye. She saw Gideon ease toward the door, casting a wistful smile. He dipped his chin in subtle understanding and slipped out.

CHAPTER FORTY-TWO

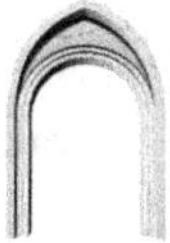

Ross

At 2 a.m., Ross climbed into bed, her ears ringing from the party, a smile plastered to her face.

Hon had said her goodnights much earlier. She and Aunt Francesca were leaving the next day for their annual summer vacation to Cumberland Island.

Ted and Gaby lasted until midnight, when Gaby drifted off to sleep at the table. Ross watched as Ted gently lifted her, honeymoon-style, and carried her out the door. Damnation. She was growing to like that big lug.

Guests had slowly peeled away, back to homes and hotels, and at 1 a.m., the band wrapped up.

For the next hour, she, Xander, Tiercy, and Cole stayed up talking as the caterers cleaned up the party.

At Cole's insistence, they eventually moved over to Xander's cottage, where Cole shared the news of Tiercy's pregnancy with Xander, who was elated for his friends. They talked in the desultory fashion of the weary but wired until Tiercy, too, succumbed to the exhaustion of early pregnancy.

"We are heading back to the farmhouse. My bride needs her rest."

"No boinking for you tonight," Ross teased. "Just snuggles with a tired preggie."

Cole gazed with fondness and love at his sleepy wife. It was clear he was fine with that. "What about you kids?"

Xander looked at Ross, both a question and a promise of more in his brown eyes. "You want to stay here, Principessa?"

Ross smiled. "I'd love to." *And so would my lady parts.* "But I want to be at the farmhouse when Hon wakes. She leaves at noon. I'd like to make her breakfast and spend as much time with her as I can before her vacation. I'm running out of time with her."

"I get it. Go get some rest, Birthday Girl."

"Not my birthday anymore. Now I'm thirty-five and a day."

"Hmm...I like a cougar."

Ross laughed as Xander leaned in for a goodnight kiss.

The friends said their farewells and three-quarters of the group headed back to the farmhouse.

Ross had just drifted off when she heard a rustle against her bedroom window. Sitting up, she saw a flash of light, and then the window slid open. One long leg came through, followed by an arm. Then a low *thwuck* as something hit the edge of the window, and a man's voice. "Shi—ow!"

Ross pulled her covers up to her chin and giggled.

Her nocturnal visitor finished his entry and turned to face her, angling the light of his iPhone away to illuminate the room but not blind her. He knew she was awake and he was grinning like mad.

"Buonasera, Principessa." He checked his phone. "Or should I say, Buongiorno." He walked over to her.

"I can't believe you climbed up the trellis and sneaked in!" Ross was trying hard to stifle her laughter.

"I was missing you." He moved closer, removing his shirt. "And it seemed the thing to do."

Just then, the door between the bedroom and the Jack-and-Jill bathroom opened, revealing Cole and Tiercy backlit against the bathroom nightlight.

"How many times do I have to tell you to knock?" Ross whisper-laughed into her hand, fighting hysterical laughter. She was still tipsy from the party and quite turned on by the shirtless man next to her bed.

"How many times do I have to tell you to lock it?" Cole bantered, also whispering and trying just as hard not to laugh. Turning to Xander, he cast an appraising glance at his bare chest. "Jesus. It's just like our college apartment senior year. Dude. The missus and I are trying to sleep. We have a long drive back tomorrow and she's incubating new life. Try to keep it down. We don't need to hear you two rutting."

The wide smile never leaving his face, Xander walked over, closed the door in Cole's face, locked it, and stage-whispered through the door, "Wear ear plugs. I'm getting laid and you're not. Just like college."

Ross woke early and snuggled into the hollow of Xander's shoulder. They'd only had sex once because they were both exhausted. It had been quiet, slow, and unexpectedly tender. When he'd surprised her in her room, she'd anticipated one of their more...athletic...encounters. Maybe it was a desire to respect the echoes of the mostly empty house, with Cole and Tiercy a stone's throw away and Hon a floor below them. But even with that, Xander and she came together in an entirely new and powerful connection. His eyes had never left hers. And when they met their peak, together, she swore she saw the beginnings of tears glisten in the rims of his eyes before he blinked and kissed her deeply. Then they both fell into a sound sleep.

That hadn't been sex; they'd made love.

She knew the tenets of their deal—no falling in love—and inexplicably, unexpectedly, she had broken it. She knew Xander had feelings for her, but he was still in love with his ex-wife, despite how deeply she'd hurt him, and had sworn off any more serious commitments. Further, she was leaving soon. Even if she could figure that part out—the whole distance thing—she wasn't sure it was wise.

Because, if she were being totally honest with herself, he scared her. This was the type of love that could break her. She didn't think she'd survive showing him her heart, only to hear he couldn't reciprocate the way she needed. And then she'd be alone again, just like she always had been.

Only this time it would be worse. Because this time, her heart would know what it was missing.

She had to walk away at the end of their six-week deal. It was the only way.

She noticed his breathing change and looked up at his beautiful, wonderful face. Her heart stabbed with longing and anticipated pain. Soon he wouldn't be hers anymore. But they were here together now, and she resolved to take advantage of every moment.

"Good morning." His deep voice rumbled with morning huskiness. "You were deep in thought, Principessa. Penny for it?"

She smiled and shook her head. "Just thinking about how amazing the party was, and that performance." She grinned at him. "And just the whole thing. Thank you. You made it really special." They fused in a kiss, morning breath be damned.

"Anything for you, Principessa." He glanced at the clock, raising his eyebrows. "Should I sneak out the way I came in?"

Ross turned to him and dropped a chaste kiss on the base of his throat, pausing a moment to feel the soft pulse against her lips. "Nope. Join us for breakfast. Twenty dollars says Hon knows you're here anyway. Nothing escapes her."

They chuckled together in the early morning light. In the quiet, they heard the rhythmic squeak of bedsprings in the other room. Their eyes met and they shared a smile.

"Looks like John-Cole-feel-the-burn is getting some overdue loving this morning. Good lad."

"From this house, no secrets are hid." Ross shook her head ruefully. "God, I love it here."

Xander's eyes were curious. "Are you sad that Hon is selling it?"

Ross sighed and settled against him, draping a leg over him, loving the feel of his legs against her own. "I don't know. Yes. I mean, I don't think I was at first. But now I am. How can I not be, after this time here? It's a special place. I just hope a great family buys it. One that will appreciate it and love it the way—the way we all did."

Xander examined her carefully. "We'll make sure of it." A small frown appeared between his brows.

Ross reached over and rubbed it with her finger. "I know this frown. It's the one that appears when you're thinking something you don't want to think, and you want to say something but you don't."

Xander raised his eyebrows, amused. "Really?"

"Yep." Ross nodded, leaning up on her elbow.

"No one's ever told me that before."

"Maybe you're getting old and it's a new frown and that's why I'm the first to notice."

"Hey!" Xander flipped on top of her and tickled her, wedging himself between her legs.

She giggled, offering only a half-hearted fight. "Frowny line is still there. You can't distract me with your hot body, Alexander Grace. Spit it out."

They might be teasing, but Ross knew something was up. She could read the vibe off him and the look in his eyes made her uncomfortable.

He paused. "You sure? I don't want you to be upset."

"Now you have to say it." She had the distinct sense she wasn't going to like this conversation.

"I have a question about Gideon."

Yep. Not liking it. Ross shifted under him to move away, but her head was nestled between his elbows. He pinned his hips against her and her traitorous hips instinctively rose to meet him, despite the topic at hand. She knew she'd have to pay the piper. There was no way Xander wouldn't want to discuss Gideon and Manhattan after seeing him last night. She'd only wondered how long it would take him to bring him up.

"When we do this"—he nudged against her and her legs opened further, her body signaling she was very, *very* ready for more—"you are so...free, so *mine*. Was it like that with him?" He examined her with vulnerable eyes, that small frown bisecting his sandy brows.

Ross snaked one arm up and gently rubbed the frown line, and then cupped his face. "No," she whispered. "Never. I've never had this before."

His small exhalation—of relief?—ghosted against her lips. But the frown line remained.

"I have another question. And here's where I don't want you to get mad. Please?"

Ross nodded. "Just ask me, Xan."

"You told me that you're monogamous in a relationship—or when you're 'hanging out' or whatever it is you want to call it."

"That's right." Ross cocked her head.

"We don't use protection. I get to feel you bare. No barriers between us. And it's amazing." Xander struggled to get out the words. "When you were with Gideon," he almost spat out the name, "did you use something?"

Ross sat up, pushing away from him, her heart thudding fast. "I told you very early on that I am careful and I'm monogamous. I don't understand why you'd ask me this? Don't you trust me?"

"Please come back here." He reached for her hand, stroking his thumb on the underside of her wrist, easing her back toward him so she rested with her back against his chest. "That's not what I'm saying, and I think you know it. I'm asking if he made the same commitment to you. If you had this same type of—deal—that we have." Xander motioned between the two of them. "So that you two didn't have to use protection. So he could feel you the way I have." His voice was barely a whisper, and she could hear the anxiety in it.

Ross closed her eyes, filling her lungs and exhaling. She knew he needed reassurance from her. After her revelation last night, she wasn't sure what this was between her and Xan. She needed time to think, to process. But she was in love with him, and it was clear her past with Gideon bothered him. She could give Xander the peace he needed about this.

"It wasn't like that. Gideon has two grown children. He and his ex-wife decided on a vasectomy years ago. He knew I'm on birth control, although he doesn't know about my inability to get pregnant. Despite that, not using a condom never even came up. We just always did."

Ross shrugged her shoulders and then added, "Xan, Gideon and I don't have the same type of—well—*this* that you and I have. No one's ever been...bare...with me before you. Ever. This is a first for me in so many ways." There. That was as close as she could come to saying what was in her heart without saying it.

"You were close enough to know about his children and a vasectomy. He knows that you were not looking forward to this trip. That you don't like New York. And that sure was a long way for him to travel just for a birthday party. Ross...the way he touched you..."

Ross kept her voice lowered to a whisper in pained awareness of the echoes in the room. "Xander. We are *friends*. We hang out when I'm in New York. We go to dinner."

"Yes, you 'hang out.' I know."

Ross played with his fingers, slowly interlacing them with hers. "I am so sorry I used that euphemism of 'hanging out' with you." Ross struggled with an uncomfortable burn of defensiveness and a tug of resentment formed low in her belly. They both had pasts. Why was this such a big deal to him?

"Gideon and I are friends. And more often than not, as I said, we just went to dinner. Plus, he's also good for awesome seats to baseball games."

Ross smiled and then sighed. "Xan, historically, I haven't exactly had a lot of free time when I went to New York. The trips are business-focused. And, quite frankly, I'm...not sure that I'll continue seeing him after I move to New York." Ross squeezed his hands. "But, I have to tell you, I feel a little slut-shamed here. I don't think you meant it that way. But, Xander, I've been with a lot of men. I enjoy sex. You know this about me. Despite that, I've never allowed anyone to be inside my body without protection."

Xander eased her around to face him, framing her face in his strong, but gentle hands. "Jesus. I'm so sorry, Ross. You are not—that word. Far from it. I never meant to imply that or make you feel that way. It's not about sex, Ross. I don't care how many partners you've had. I mean, I'd prefer not to think about it." He rubbed a hand down his face. "Christ. I feel like an ass right now and I just don't know the right words to explain and apologize.

"I just...I've never been so fucking jealous in my life as I was last night when I saw him kiss you, and put his hands on your back. He wants more from you than 'hanging out,' Ross. I'd bet my life on it.

Then, after we made love last night, I kept wondering if you'd ever been with him like that. I'm not...I'm not accustomed to being eaten up with jealousy like that.

"I know...we said we aren't each other's forever. That's not our deal." She saw his Adam's apple bob as he swallowed hard, and she gulped past the rock in her own throat as he repeated the words of their deal. "But right now...you're mine. Please forgive me? I never want to hurt you." Then he whispered. "I knew I shouldn't have asked."

"Then why'd you do it?"

"Well...you did nudge me. Frowny line and everything." Xander motioned to his forehead, cajoling.

"Xander..." Her response came low and warning.

"Jesus, Ross." Xander ran an exasperated hand through his hair, dropping back on the downy white pillow behind him. "Why do I do anything where you're concerned? Damned if I know. You are incredibly vexing. I've never been a jealous person. But for some reason, when it comes to Mr. Golden Glove laying his golden gloves on you—" he smirked as Ross laughed at his pathetic joke "—I find myself battling the green-eyed monster. And I know I don't have any right. Besides. It sucks. I wanted him to be a FIGJAM, and he's not."

Ross quirked a brow at him. "Gonna need a translation."

Xander pulled Ross toward him. "Fuck I'm Good. Just Ask Me." He punctuated each component of the acronym with a kiss on Ross's face and neck, causing her to squirm against him. "It's an acronym for guys who have an exceedingly high opinion of themselves."

"FIGJAM. Classic. But he is a really good guy—shockingly down to earth. And I feel terrible that he left without saying goodbye. I'll call him later and explain. Ugh!" she groaned, suppressing her volume in the echoey house as best she could. "See? Drama. And I'm not even in a relationship with him."

Ross sighed and shifted back onto her side and propped on her elbow, brushing a lock of dark blond hair out of Xander's eye. "You don't need to be jealous. And I do forgive you. I don't think you were being malicious. Or that you feel I'm a slut. *Whew.* I need coffee. Soon."

Ross paused, feeling the knot of resentment untangle, and then broke into a relaxed smile that she hoped made Xan's worried heart relax in equal measure. "That said, Alexander Grace, it makes me feel so relieved to know that you have something *fucking wrong* with you. You're hot, you sing, you're an awesome dad, you're amazing to my grandmother, and you are the best lay ever. Finally, I have found your fatal flaw. Muahaha!" Ross rubbed her hands diabolically.

Her bedmate arched his eyebrow. "Am I really your best lay ever?"

"Mmhmmm..." Ross purred, stretching in bed, her nipples hardening in anticipation. Xander's cock reciprocated, standing at attention between them.

"What time do you think Hon will be up?"

Ross rolled to look at the clock. "Not for at least another hour."

Xander narrowed his eyes and flipped her the rest of the way over onto her belly, leaning in to begin his ministrations. His tongue teased between her ass cheeks, pausing at her pucker and making her squirm.

She gasped as he slid a finger inside of her wet warmth, working her with his tongue and first one finger, then two. "Just like college...only way better..."

Chapter Forty-Three

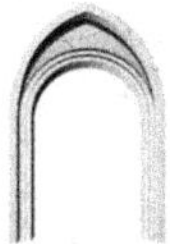

Ross

Ross, Xander, Hon, Cole, and Tiercy enjoyed a huge breakfast of eggs, pancakes, and bacon in the farmhouse. Hon had merely raised an eyebrow as she walked into the kitchen to find Xan in the clothes he'd been wearing the night before.

"You know, Alexander," she admonished, "trying those window hijinks at your age could lead to a broken bone. I thought you knew where I hide the key?"

Ross buried her blushing face in her Orioles mug as Tiercy cracked up. "Gosh, I love this place. So many amazing memories. I could sit in this kitchen all day, Hon."

Hon swept around and enveloped Tiercy in a hug. "As the granddaughter of my heart, you are always welcome."

"Until the new owners are here. I'm not sure they'd appreciate us having breakfast in their kitchen," Ross said, with a small frown.

Tiercy swept in with a joke. "Can you imagine? Them waking to find us all here?"

"Sounds amazing, actually," added Xander, and winked at Hon. "Just have to find the right owner."

"Sure. The right people who would let previous owners crash in their kitchen. Xander, you need more coffee, and a reality check." Ross rolled her eyes.

Xander shrugged his shoulders, clearly unoffended by her jest.

Too soon, Hon excused herself for final trip packing, giving Tiercy a kiss on the cheek and gently patting her stomach, having heard the good news herself. Then she went up on tiptoes to kiss Cole on his cheek. "Such lovely manners, standing for a lady. Take care of my girl, Cole."

"Yes, ma'am."

Tiercy and Cole had their overnight bags ready in the car. Ross enveloped her best friend in a fierce hug. "I'm so glad you could make it, Hooker Hips. I can't believe soon I'm not going to live ten minutes from you." Ross squeezed her again.

"Careful. You'll hurt my baby." Cole laughed.

"Which one?" Xander asked, smiling.

"Either one. Both."

"I don't care. I'm not letting go," Ross announced, arms still wrapped around her friend, face buried against her neck. "I can't stand that I won't be with you for this pregnancy. I may not even be there when little Ross Jr comes into the world."

"Whoa—wait. Ross Jr?" Tiercy burst out laughing.

"No? I thought maybe an honorific for the greatest friend of all time." Ross beamed a mischievous smile at her bestie.

"Have your own and name it that," Cole said.

"Not gonna happen," Ross sing-songed, not allowing the smile on her face to falter, despite the hurt in her heart for the babies she'd never carry inside her. "The only buns I bake are in a proper kitchen."

Tiercy gave Ross a soft, knowing kiss on the cheek. "You'll visit with me in a couple weeks. And you can come stay with us on weekends whenever you want. And this winter, if I even *think* I'm going into labor, I'll call you. You can catch the Acela train and be at the hospital in a couple hours."

"Promise?"

"Promise."

"Pinky swear?" Ross held out her pinky.

Tiercy did the same. They coiled fingers and squeezed.

"OK. Go. Jemma misses her mom and dad."

Cole gave her a bear hug. "Be good to Xan. And be good to yourself," he said in her ear so only she could hear. "See you in a couple weeks," he added for all to hear.

"Take care of my bestie."

Cole and Xan leaned in for a classic man hug, right hands clasped, left arms around their backs. Then they released their hands and embraced in a full hug. Both laughed at something that Cole whispered into Xander's ear.

"See you brother," Xan slapped him on the back. "No turkey taps this time." They cracked up.

In moments, they were off down the long road, Ross watching until they were out of sight. She turned to see Xander's searching brown eyes.

"For a moment there, Principessa, I thought you might cry. I was wondering what I might use for a tissue and decided my T-shirt is as good as anything."

Ross frowned a bit through her smile. "Here's the weird thing, Xan. I don't cry."

Xander tilted his head. Pulling her by the hand, they moved to the porch swing. Ross settled into its faded floral cushions, curling her feet under her.

"You don't cry? What does that mean?"

She paused, weighing whether to go there. "It means what it means. It also means that I barely got any sleep last night and I really don't want to talk about it. Don't you have to get Petey?"

Xander checked his watch. "I need to leave in an hour. Ross, you promised if I had a question about you, I could ask you. This has me intrigued. Indulge me."

For the second time in the morning, Ross rolled her eyes at him. "Whatever. Briefly. We will discuss this *ever so briefly*."

"Thank you." He dropped a kiss on her cheek. "Now, say more about this. Everyone cries. You just mean that you aren't a crier, I get it. But everyone cries a little when the occasion calls."

Ross shook her head and stared straight ahead.

"Hell, I cry like a baby."

Ross sighed. Xander was like a dog with a bone. He wasn't letting go of this one. She just had to decide how much she was going to share. "Like when?"

"When Petey was born, of course. I just sobbed. He was so beautiful. And when Aubrey left, but you probably figured that out. And when the divorce papers were delivered." Xander turned and grinned at her. "And at movies."

"I'll bite. What movies have made you cry?" *Good*, Ross thought. *Keep him talking about himself.*

"*Life is Beautiful*. The dad. The son. It just got me. And that was before Petey. *Up*, because I had always wanted a marriage like that. *Dead Poets Society*. More recently, *Rise of Skywalker*. Oh, and *Avengers: Endgame*. That one really wrecked me. You should have seen Cole and me, trying to look in opposite directions as we subtly wiped away our manly tears."

Smiling at the image, Ross leaned in and kissed him on the cheek. "You're a mush."

"I don't deny it."

His dimples flared and she kissed him again. He reached over and traced a finger down her cheek. "You really don't ever cry?"

"I can't."

"How about when Tiercy's husband died? Or when Jemma was born?"

"Probably the closest I've come. But I didn't. I just...don't. I was devastated when Luke died. And I was overjoyed when Jemma was born. But I didn't cry sad tears or bittersweet tears or tears of joy. Can we be finished with this line of questioning, please? I feel like a freakshow."

But Xan seemed fascinated. "What about if you're physically hurt?" He examined her closely. "I mean, I can clearly see tear ducts in those stunning green orbs. You look physically able."

Ross sighed again. "Guess we're not finished with this. It's a good thing you are the ultimate giver of orgasms." She wagged her finger at him. "I mean, once I sprained my ankle hiking. It hurt like hell and I think some reflexive tears happened. My eyes filled up. But it wasn't really crying. It was just a physiological response to physical pain."

She paused a beat, and stared off in the direction her parents were buried.

"It's hard to explain, but the best I can do is an analogy. I had this friend, Ann, in college. She couldn't burp. Just couldn't. Maybe she burped as a baby, but in her entire memory, she had never burped. One night, we made her chug a 2-liter of Diet Coke. How can anyone not belch after that? She drank it, and then proceeded to make these fake burp sounds—which were hilarious by the way—but just couldn't do it for real. I guess that's...how I am. Even if I want to, I just can't."

"When was the last time you remember crying? Surely you did as a child?"

Ross shifted abruptly, causing the swing to rock harder. Xander steadied it with his feet.

"I will tell you exactly the last time I cried. And then this conversation is finished and I never want to have it again, understand?"

She interlaced her fingers to stop the shaking, but nothing could stop the tapping of her foot. "The last time I cried was the morning after my parents died, when Hon came in to tell me. I have this memory of saying to her 'Are you sure? Are you sure?' and then I buried my head in her lap and I sobbed while Tiercy held my hand. Until," she continued, ice in her veins and her voice, "from the other room came the sounds of Gaby wailing. Hon had to leave me and run in there. There was such a commotion going on. I went through the bathroom. She and Pop were giving her medicine. Hon curled around her until she finally stopped crying and slept. And I just stood there watching. Forgotten. The end." She could see the white of her knuckle bones from clamping her hands together.

"I'm so sorry, Ross," he soothed. "That must have been awful."

"It was. And then at the funeral I didn't cry because Gaby wailed and carried on at the graveside like one of those women you see on the news throwing themselves on a casket." Ross's expression hardened. "There was no room for anyone else's grief. So there you have it. I'm a hardened freakshow."

Xander eased toward her, cradling his cool palm against her face. She was shocked at the heat coming off her skin. It was July in Virginia and the 10 a.m. humidity was rapidly rising, but Ross's furnace was firing with a burning intensity that came from something much deeper than summer heat.

"Ross." When she didn't react, he lifted her chin with one finger. "Ross, sweetheart. You aren't a freakshow. Far from it. I know you feel things deeply. I can see that this has you upset. For the second time today, I am so sorry I pushed. We don't need to talk about this ever again. It's OK, Ross."

He pulled her into his arms. At first, she was as wooden as the posts that stabilized the porch on which they sat. He stroked her back until she relaxed and became pliant in the succor of his arms.

"I've...tried to make myself cry, believe me."

Xander was silent, simply holding her and giving her space to continue. Eventually she started again with a self-deprecating laugh. "One weekend, I watched all sorts of sad movies. Nothing. Not even *Beaches* could seal the deal. I've read sad books. I get sad. I feel sad. But I don't cry. Sometimes...I think it would feel so much better if I could just let it out. Just once. But—" her voice lowered to a shaky whisper against his chest "—other times I worry if I ever get to where those tears are, that hidden place, I'm afraid if I start, I won't be able to stop."

They swung in silence for a few minutes, accompanied by the squeak of the rusting chain.

For a long time, he held her. At first, all Ross could hear was the ferocious beat of her own heart. Eventually, as she relaxed her head on Xan's chest, she tuned into the steady rhythm of his own heartbeat. At some point, her own heart must have synced cadence until she couldn't distinguish his from hers. And she experienced something she hadn't in a long time.

A sensation of deep, abiding peace.

Chapter Forty-Four

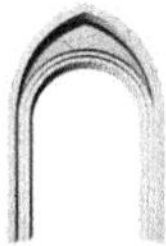

Ross

Two hours later, having said her farewells to the Monroe clan, fussing over Gaby and ensuring Ted would take good care of her, Hon returned to the farmhouse. She was in her bedroom packing the last of her suitcase. Francesca would be by shortly with a hired car to take the two septuagenarians to the airport for their annual trip to Cumberland Island, Georgia. Ross sat cross-legged on her grandmother's bed.

Hon filled a travel medication organizer, double checking the contents. Ross's eyes widened. "Have some pills, Hon."

Hon looked askance at Ross. "That's what happens when you are almost eighty, Ross Ellen. Pills for this, pills for that. Sometimes I feel like a pharmacy." She winked. "Still, it's not as many as some of my friends."

"Do you need all that?" Ross reached for a couple of the bottles and Hon batted her hand away.

"I wouldn't take them if I didn't, lovie. Now MYOB and hand me my purple bathing suit and my cover-up."

Ross passed her the items. "I remember watching you and Pop packing for this very same trip."

Hon paused, pushing a strand from her bob behind her ear, a reminiscent smile on her face. "Yes, Frederick and I, and Francesca and Paul, always loved this vacation. It was our special time together. Just the four of us. First as young marrieds. And, later, away from the kids. Now Frannie and I continue the tradition as old widowed ladies." Hon smiled sadly at Ross. "I just wish...." She shook her head and turned away, putting a brush in her bag.

Ross frowned. "You just wish what, Hon?"

Hon walked over to the bed. "Scoot over." With surprising agility for a woman about to celebrate her eightieth birthday in a month, Hon used the wooden step stool and climbed into the California king four-poster bed. She took Ross by the hand and laced her gnarled, arthritic fingers with her granddaughter's. Then she brought Ross's hand to her mouth and kissed it.

Ross waited. Long experience had taught her it was best not to rush Dr. Leah Waldheim.

"I wish you and Gaby had what Frannie and I have had. It's been one of the greatest gifts of my life."

"Hon, listen, that ship has—"

"Let me finish, Ross." Hon's voice was firm, but warm. "I have failed you. I have failed Gaby. I failed Ivy." Her voice cracked. "The worst thing a parent can do is bury her own child. And when I did that, I knew I'd touched the torments of hell. The idea that I'd never see her face or—or hear her voice, that laugh, that glorious laugh." Hon wiped her eyes. "I understood why people go into deep depressions after a loss. But I had you both to care for."

Hon turned to Ross. "And here is where I failed you and my daughter. I let this hatred fester between you and Gaby for two decades. Two decades, Ross! That is...unconscionable. When I leave this world and face my daughter—"

"No time soon," Ross interjected, her voice teasing but her eyes serious.

"—I must own the fact that I let you both wallow in this anger for a very long time. And I did nothing to stop it."

"Hon, we're grown women."

"You were girls. Children! I should have said something then. I should have. And Frederick wanted me to. But Gaby was so frail for so long, and you were so—so full of grief and anger. And I was so sad.

"And then time passed. I thought you both might get there on your own. I wanted you to do it yourselves. Then you built your own lives. And grew apart. It seemed to get worse, not better. I didn't know what to do. The void grew so much, I didn't know how to broach it. And it's not my story to tell." Hon sobbed into her hand.

Ross, at a loss, hopped up and grabbed a tissue from the box on Hon's side of the bed. She eased next to her grandmother, waiting while Hon composed herself.

Eventually, Hon blew her nose and wiped her eyes, made greener and rheumier by her tears. "Ross, hate corrodes the vessel that holds it. I know you resent Gaby for so many things that happened after your parents died. But there is so much you don't understand. You must speak to her. And then you must let go of all this anger you carry."

"It's not that easy."

"I never said it would be. But, Ross, you must do this. I won't be here forever. And all that will be left of my daughter and Adam is you and your sister. I need to be at peace knowing that you both can love each other again."

Hon picked up an old picture of Ross and Gaby from her nightstand and handed it to her. She had refused thus far to pack it, insisting it would be one of the last things to be boxed prior to the move.

"The gift of a sister is a treasure. She's a piece of your blood. Your shared self. Together, you are your parents. You are their legacy. Whether you realize it or not, there is an invisible thread that connects sisters. It can fray, almost to nothingness. You might think all hope is gone. But it can be knitted back into strength. You just have to try! Please, Ross Ellen, please try. For me." Hon gathered Ross into her arms and held her.

Ross tucked her head against her, picture in one hand, other arm wrapped against the soft, warm body of her mother's mother, feeling her 'angel's wings' in the thin summer cardigan. Ross inhaled, savoring the unique powdery scent of Hon.

"I love you, Hon. I'll do my best. I will."

"Do better than your best, Ross. I expect it." Hon's eyes bored into her.

"I'll talk to her. We're doing better. We're having a bit of a détente anyway, so maybe thirty-five is my age of reason." Ross winked in self-deprecation and smiled at Hon. "And I'll go through my boxes in the basement. Double promise on that one. Then, when you get back, we'll make one last lovely batch of brownies in the kitchen. Sound good?"

"Oh, speaking of that, I believe I may have a private offer on the house. A buyer came directly to Genevieve and me."

"You're just dropping that on me *now*?"

"We've been busy, Ross Ellen. Besides, I figured you'd hear about it from Xander."

"Xander?" Ross frowned. "Why would I hear about it from him?"

Hon smiled. "He's working on the negotiations with Genevieve. More to come. But, speaking of Alexander…"

"Hon, don't start," Ross warned. "We're just hanging out while I'm here."

Lies, lies. But Ross wasn't in a space to fully process this yet, even with Hon.

"Oh my girl. You can't lie to me. Tell me the truth. When did you fall in love with him?"

Ross hopped off the bed. "Fall in love? With Xander? Hon—have you been hitting the sauce?"

"You can't deflect with me, Ross Ellen. I've known you since you gulped your first breath of oxygen and then let out the mightiest wail I'd ever heard. You don't do anything in half-measures. And that includes when you finally give your heart to someone."

The two women faced off for a moment, the older set of green eyes twinkling in what Ross recognized as Hon's resolute acknowledgement of triumph.

"Fuck," Ross sighed.

"Yes, charmingly phrased. But, *fuck*, you've gone and fallen in love. Does it take you by surprise to hear me say it aloud?"

Ross collapsed into the sole chair remaining in the bedroom, closing her eyes in defeat. "This was just supposed to be a fun fling, Hon. I don't know when it happened, how it happened…or more accurately, how I let it happen, but that man chipped away at me and now it's all… *different*."

"And that makes you uncomfortable."

"We had *rules*, Hon!"

"Life's about sometimes breaking the rules that no longer make sense, precious."

Ross shook her head. "I love him, Hon. What the hell am I going to do?"

Hon walked over to her daughter's daughter, leaning over the chair to cradle Ross in a way she hadn't in years. "Frederick always used to say, 'If God leads you to it, God will lead you through it.' I think Xander was meant to be in your path and a part of your journey, Ross Ellen. There is something incredibly special about that man, and his son. And I know you know it. You are a very smart woman. What the hell are you going to do? You're going to figure it out. Because you're my beautiful girl, and that's what you do."

She stood up, all business, and brushed her hands together briskly. "Now, look at the time. Francesca will be here soon and I'm still not finished. Are you just going to sit there or are you going to help?" Hon cocked her head and grinned at her granddaughter.

Ross returned the smile, an echo of her grandmother's. "I love you so much, Hon. Thank you for being the very best grandmother ever, and for everything you've done for me. I am so glad I came home this summer."

Hon's eyes filled up again. "Oh, now. Don't go getting me crying again. I like to look glamorous when I travel."

She waved a hand and half-laughed. "Come here." She held her arms open to her granddaughter. "I am so glad you came this summer too. Thank you for being such an amazing granddaughter. I am so very, very proud of you. And I always have been. You are such a joy. I love you, Ross Ellen Beaufort. And remember this, no matter where you go and what you do and where you live, your home isn't a place. It's the people who are in your heart. As long as they are with you, in any way, even in memory, you're home."

CHAPTER FORTY-FIVE

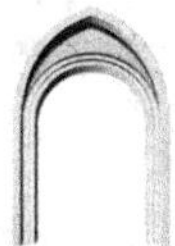

Ross

For two days, Ross practiced the fine art of procrastination. She lazed by the pool. She read. She, Xander, and Petey went for hikes and bike rides—her early awkwardness with the latter long-evaporated. He was as easy to love as his father.

Of course, she hadn't worked up the courage to say anything to Xander because, as of yet, she hadn't figured out a solution to the very real fact that in a short time, she would be based out of Manhattan. The more she thought about all of it, the more it freaked her out. Plus, she couldn't be sure Xander reciprocated the depth of her feelings.

Instead, she needed to focus on packing Hon's farmhouse. And even that proved to be harder than expected. She had a block about finishing and couldn't motivate herself on those final steps. At least she'd gone as far as having Xander bring the six boxes to Hon's office, where she'd walk past, look in, and then continue on. *Later*, she'd think. *I have time.*

With five days remaining on Hon's trip and the clock ticking on both the box excavation and her grandmother's expected tête-à-tête with her sister, Ross's frustration grew. In his inimitable way, Xander worked double time to lighten her mood. It was scary how well he knew her. Today, he had promised her a unique culinary experience.

That evening, after Ross had gone for a long run and then showered, she walked with resolve toward the cottage. Tonight. Tonight, after Petey was asleep, she would reveal her heart. And, hopefully, he would respond in parallel. Beyond that...well, they'd just figure it out.

Ross's musings were interrupted by the sound of a fire alarm from the direction of the cottage. She quickened her pace, hand poised on her phone to call 9-1-1. Then she heard laughter, the deep, resonant laugh of the man who had stolen her heart and the higher laugh of the boy who'd carved his own place in it, too.

Quietly, feeling a bit like a creeper, but unwilling to interrupt the tableau, she crept toward the window and listened.

CHAPTER FORTY-SIX

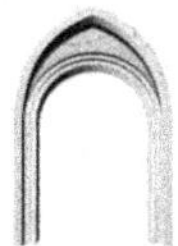

The smoke from the oven billowed toward the open window. Xander waved a hastily grabbed baking pan toward the smoke detector. His phone chimed with a call alert.

"Grab that, Petey, will you?"

Petey looked at the screen and tapped on it. "Hey, Mr. Ted."

Xander huffed a resigned laugh, knowing that his firefighter friend had heard the detector's shrill alarm and was checking in. So much for the homemade pizza. They'd have to call and order it instead. As he waved the pan, dissipating the smoke, he listened to Petey's half of the conversation.

"Yes, sir. We're fine. Dad and I burned the pizza."

"Yes, sir, we made it ourselves."

"No, sir. We aren't burning down the cottage." He smiled at Petey's giggle.

"Yes, sir, I'll tell him takeout is always safest. And what was the other word you said? Ok, Mr. Ted. I'll tell him he's a menace and he hasta bring you good scotch to make up for the heart—what was it?—heart 'tack he gave you. And what else?" Petey listened intently and then broke into a wide grin.

"OK. I'll tell him that too." Another giggle. "Goodbye, Mr. Ted." Petey turned to Xander, who had finally managed to shut off the blaring alarm. "That was—"

"Mr. Ted. I could tell." He winked at Petey. "It's nice to have neighbors who care, even if we did give him a heart attack, eh?"

Petey grinned back at him and motioned to the charred remains of his attempt at homemade pizza. "Mr. Ted said burning pizza and setting the cottage on fire isn't the way to Ross's heart." He broke into a fit of giggles in the way only a six-year-old can.

Xander's eyes widened and then he joined in with his son, wiping his hand over his face in chagrin. He should have known not to trust that oven...or himself. "No, that is definitely not the way to woo a lady, my son." Xander quickly used an app to order from the local pizza joint.

As he finished placing their order, Petey cocked an inquiring head at him. Uh oh. Xander knew that face well.

"What's woo, Dad?"

Xander tugged him close and ruffled his hair. "It's when you like a person and you do special things to show them."

"And then maybe they do special things to show you back? They woo, too?" Petey crinkled his nose at the rhyming phrase and broke again into peals of laughter. "Woo, too! Woo, too! Woo, too"

"God bless you," Xander joked.

"Daddy," Petey cackled. "You know I didn't sneeze!"

"You sure, Slugger? I was sure I heard 'achoo' at least three times. Maybe you're getting sick." He pretended to feel Petey's head with his wrist, the way Hon taught him. Before, he always used his hand. Apparently that wasn't the correct technique. Who knew?

"Daddy," Petey rolled his eyes. "I'm not sick. You're silly, Daddy."

Xander's heart caught at the endearment, as it had so many times. He knew the days of being called 'Daddy' by Petey were coming to an end, and he cherished every utterance. "It must be all the smoke. Must have gotten to you."

"Daaaaddy," Petey drawled, snorting as he helped Xander clean up the mess.

Snort-laughing, just like Ross, Xander mused, feeling dopey in love. Tonight. Tonight he'd tell her he'd fallen in love with her.

"Daddy?" Petey had his nose scrunched adorably, always the precursor to a barrage of questions.

"Yes, Sneezy?"

"Are you doing what Mr. Ted said? Do you want to...woo," he giggled again, "Ross?"

For as much as he wanted to yell, "Yes!" to the rooftops, and probably give Moose another heart attack from his bellow, he knew he had to move gently with Petey. This was about getting Petey's permission to bring Ross officially into their lives. He hadn't planned to do this yet, wanting to confirm Ross shared his feelings first. Maybe woo her a bit, as he smiled at the thought. But the opportunity was here, so what the hell. He went for it.

"Would you like that, Petey? If I wooed Ross?" They shared a smile at the word, which apparently was evermore going to be funny for them.

"I like her, Daddy." Petey frowned. "But—but she won't live here. She doesn't want to."

"What do you mean, buddy?" Xander mirrored his son's frown. This wasn't the way he expected this conversation to start.

Petey's downcast eyes filled with tears. "I asked her. At that restaurant where she took me. I asked if she was gonna marry you and if she'd be my mother. And she said she couldn't." A single tear slipped down Petey's cheek, and Xander's heart cracked open along a barely healed fault line.

Oh God. What had they talked about? And why hadn't Ross told him about this conversation? He sunk into a kitchen chair. Hand shaking, he pulled Petey into his lap.

"Tell me what she said, buddy."

How pathetic was he, pressing his small son for information?

"She said she couldn't be my mother. That she was moving to New York. But she'd always be your friend and my friend. And that was better than a mother. But, Daddy? That isn't how my heart feels. I think a mother is bigger than a friend."

Xander closed his eyes, unable to form words at the moment. The truth of the situation hit him like a hard punch to the gut. It was happening all over again.

Ross didn't want what he wanted. She wasn't in love with him.

Yes, she liked him. Yes, they had amazing chemistry. For sure, she enjoyed their *bedsport*. He knew he made her body hum. And, yes, they were indeed friends, as she shared with Petey. But, that was the extent of it for her, or she'd have answered in a different way. Maybe not just said it outright, but she might have phrased it differently.

And she definitely never shared that conversation with him. Probably because she didn't want to have to explain to him what she'd already more than articulated. As Ross had insisted from the beginning, she wasn't interested in a relationship and she didn't want to spend her life with them. And she flat out told Petey, albeit kindly.

He inhaled a shaking breath. It was Aubrey, all over again. He wanted something—deeply, passionately. But, like Aubrey, Ross didn't. At least to the same degree. Or even at all. Plus ça change, plus c'est la même chose. The more things change, the more they stayed the same.

Xander dropped his head, rubbing his chin on Petey's soft hair. One thing was certain, things had changed in one key way. He had Petey now, and he'd never let his son be hurt again. He had to downplay his feelings so Petey didn't get even more attached than he was now. It was clear that Ross didn't share his feelings, and she'd tried to let Petey down gently. He would never put her in the position of having to do the same to him. And he certainly wouldn't try to persuade her to embrace his dream of them as a family. That didn't work six years ago, and it wouldn't work now.

Xander cleared his throat and eased Petey off his lap. He summoned a smile so fake he hoped it wouldn't be obvious to his boy. "Well, Mr. Woo-too," he joked—lamely, "I like Ross, too. But I'm not going to woo h-her." Petey frowned, and Xander wondered if Petey heard his voice catch on the last word. "Just like Ross said, we are friends. And we will always be friends."

"But not my mommy?" Petey whispered.

"No, buddy. Not your mommy." Xander was sure his heart was ripping apart inside his body as he said the words. "You have a mommy, and she loves you enough to let me take care of you when she can't herself. Ross is our friend, that's all."

That's all. Xander swallowed a sob of finality. He knew, once Ross was safely in New York, he would grieve the loss of her as the love of his life. But tonight? Tonight he'd fake it 'til he made it, as Ross would say. And then, when Petey was in bed, he'd honor her wishes and end things.

In the span of one conversation, everything had changed.

CHAPTER FORTY-SEVEN

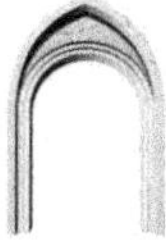

Ross

Ross held her hand to the back of her mouth, choking back a sob. That's what she got for eavesdropping on what started as a humorous moment between Xander—the man who held her heart—and the boy who stole hers. When Petey asked if Xander planned to woo her, Ross's heart skipped at least three beats. She'd held her breath, listening for him to say what she'd hoped with every atom of her being to hear. If he had, she would have burst into the cottage and thrown herself in his arms.

She pinched her nose against the wave of hurt. Instead, she heard Xander tell Petey that he wasn't going to woo her. That she wasn't Petey's mommy, and would never be. He went on to put her firmly in the friend zone. And the pain that lanced through her heart was far beyond any she'd endured...since her parents died. Since several doctors told her it was highly unlikely she'd ever be a mother.

Christ. She almost went in there tonight and bared her heart. How hideously embarrassing would that have been? Here she thought Xander reciprocated her fragile, beautiful new feelings. Instead, it was exactly as he'd insisted from the beginning. He didn't want a relationship. He didn't want to be a family with her and Petey. His heart clearly still belonged to Aubrey.

Ross sunk to the ground, head resting on her knees in defeat. Why had she even come to Virginia? She hated it here, and now there was just one—really two—more reasons to hurt when thinking about this cursed place. She dug her fingers into her damn dry eyes. If ever she needed a good cry, now was it.

Instead, her eyes remained just as barren as she'd make her heart. She would go to Manhattan and throw herself into her career. She'd sleep with Gideon—Ross's body shivered in denial at that traitorous thought. No, she wouldn't ever have sex with Gideon again. But also never again would she allow her heart to be pulverized. Twice in one lifetime—three if you count news of her infertility—well, it was just too much to ever allow to happen again.

Her leg shook as her foot bounced against the soft grass. Ross wondered how long she could sit out there before Xander would wonder where she was and call her. She quickly turned her phone on silent, so it wouldn't out her hiding place. Eventually she'd have to get up, and when she did, she'd summon her inner Swift and fake it 'til she made it. Xander would never know how he broke her heart one summer evening under his oak tree. Instead, once Petey went to bed, she'd tell him it was time to end their summer deal.

Watching Xander's and Petey's shapes across the window in the kitchen, Ross had the distinct feeling of watching a dream tableau dissipate in front of her eyes.

In the span of one conversation, everything had changed.

Chapter Forty-Eight

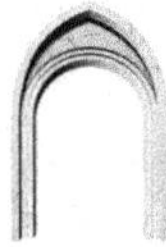

Ross

It was a pizza delivery man pulling into the driveway that eventually uprooted Ross from her spot beneath the tree. Standing on shaky legs, she put on a false smile—fake it, baby— and collected the pizzas. When she offered money, he assured her that Xander had already paid and tipped him via an app.

Ross startled as Xander opened the door to the cottage at dinnertime with a grand flourish. He and Petey had created a mini Italian café in the cottage, with candles in Chianti bottles and checkered tablecloths. Petey even had a fake mustache drawn on.

"Buongiorno, Principessa!" Xander declared, bowing extravagantly. Was it her, or did his smile not reach his eyes?

Petey giggled, doing the same, adding, "Welcome-a to-a our house-a," in a terrible Italian accent, sounding more like the Count from *Sesame Street*. Despite her aching heart, Ross struggled to contain her laughter.

"Thank you, gentlemen." Passing the pizza boxes over to Xander, she raised a quizzical brow at him. He couldn't know she overheard the smoke detector and the news of the charred pizza. He responded with a sheepish grin.

"We tried to make homemade pizza. Harder than it seems. Small oven fire. All good. Ted even called when he heard the alarm. Handy to have a firefighter nearby..."

Ross, struggling to behave like normal—whatever that was—went down on one knee to face Petey. "Perhaps your Dad should stick to grilling?"

Petey grinned and smiled up at his dad. Ross was relieved not to see any of the sadness she'd overheard from him. Kids were resilient. He'd forget her in no time, she lied to herself.

"Indeed." Xander waggled his eyebrows at her and Petey did the same. "Slice of pizza pie and some vino, Ross?"

Ross looked back and forth between the two, shook her head and held out her hand. "Peas in a pod."

Xander and Petey pulled out her chair, and she hoped like hell neither could see her inner turmoil. This whole evening was starting to feel like a horrible farewell—a taste of a life she could never have before leaving for a life she no longer wanted.

After demolishing his slices, Petey went outside to play with Nick, Kingsley, and Laverne, with strict orders to be back by dark.

The adults stayed at the table, still picking at the pizza.

Xander seemed to be working up the courage to say something.

"You have that frown again." Ross both loved and now hated that she had this insight into him.

"Busted."

"Probably gonna have to Botox that shit," she attempted to tease.

"Nah. I have Ross-tox. She makes me spill my guts and the line disappears." He frowned again, and then took her hand and kissed it. Then he turned it over and kissed the other side. Her heart frayed even more.

"Well," she belted, probably too heartily, because Xander actually startled at the volume of her voice. "That's the benefit of non-relationship hanging out. When you get in a relationship, you can't tell the truth like that. Kid gloves and all. Drama. Nooo thank you."

Jesus. What fresh hell was this?

Xander sat up straighter. His eyes dimmed, the sparkle and warmth that had been there moments before were gone. "Non-relationship hanging out," he echoed, the frown still there.

"So what were you thinking about?" she urged, hoping he'd just ignore her bizarre, lying, word vomit.

He kissed her hand again, closing his eyes. But there was something different—something *off*—about this kiss. Frowning, she realized he looked sad. This mercurial shift in his mood had her stomach plummeting. This was it. He was going to end things before she could. Her leg bounced under the table.

"I know we said...would you...what if I wanted—"

"Good lord, Grace. How much of this have you had? You're perseverating." Ross picked up the almost-empty bottle of wine and squinted into it, trying to joke her way into calm.

"Nice SAT word," he retorted, but the mood was tense. "What I need to say is..." He looked at her with those brown-sugar eyes, and now his leg bounced. He scanned her face, and then something shut off in his eyes. "Ross, I don't think I can do this anymore. I think we need to end our summer deal early."

Ross stared at him, stunned into speechlessness, even though she had come into the cottage prepared to announce the same to him. She knew her mouth was wide open and she snapped it closed.

What the ever-loving fuck was she going to do?

Xander sat across from her, looking more miserable with every passing second. They sat in silence, the last pizza slice forgotten and cold in the box between them. Ross could hear her heart thrumming in her ears.

"I didn't mean for it to come out like that, Ross. But as I kissed your hand, I realized I'm not doing either of us any favors. You and I both agreed to some ground rules, and...well...." He reached for the new bottle of wine and poured himself a glass, then took a long swallow. "I didn't want to have a relationship either, Ross. We have that in common. You're leaving Virginia soon, moving to Manhattan and starting a job there. My life is here—one that I finally feel good about. This"—he motioned between the two of them—"has been incredible.

You are incredible. But we both know this needs to end here, before we —before we catch feelings that we can't have. Right?"

Despite the warmth of the summer air around them, Ross felt chilled to the bone. She couldn't summon words. Coming here tonight, she'd planned to bare her heart to him. To tell him she'd fallen in love. She'd been building up the courage all evening at the farmhouse. Until she heard him speak his truth to Petey.

And yet, for a moment, even though she'd heard him tell Petey that they were only friends, and that he didn't want to woo her, she thought he was working up the nerve to tell her that he loved her. And now...she sucked in a sharp breath. Christ, this hurt like fucking fuck.

"Ross..." His voice was hoarse. "Principessa...if I don't do this now..." he trailed off. "Say something."

Ross dissociated, as if she were outside her own body. She observed her left ring finger tapping lightly on the table. She saw the detritus of their meal. She watched the candlelight illuminate a crescent of unshed tears in Xander's eyes. Was this what dying felt like?

Finally, Ross found her voice. "I think you're right," she croaked.

Chapter Forty-Nine

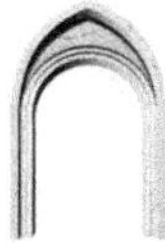

XANDER

"You do?" He had almost revealed that he loved her. Despite everything he knew to be true, every fear in his heart, he almost told her anyway. He'd prepared this entire tableau to finally tell her. Deep down, he had been sure she loved him, too. He knew he was the one who set that silly rule, but rules sometimes had to be broken.

All he knew was, once he acknowledged his own heart, it was clear he'd never truly loved Aubrey—not the way you love someone to whom you commit your life. That, he knew, was the way he loved Ross. And with that recognition also came the realization that he wanted to spend the rest of his life with her.

He'd spent the last weeks wondering how he could make a long-distance relationship work alongside the demands of parenting and his job. For at least the next year, he was committed to UVA, and he didn't want to uproot Petey. And, yet, there had to be a way. Love finds a way.

But when she casually referenced their non-relationship, the last shimmer of hope was extinguished inside him. She didn't want more. She was leaving. Xander's stomach churned.

Ross wouldn't make eye contact with him. She stared at the

tablecloth, tracing an unseen pattern. "This got a little too intense too fast. We've had fun with our summer deal, Xander Grace. I have a couple weeks left here. Let me focus on Hon and getting her settled, and then I'll head to New York." Ross stood and, with brusque movements, began clearing the table.

Xander was gut-punched. Even as he blurted out his lie, he'd hoped she'd call him on his bullshit and confess her own feelings. But she didn't. Another complex woman breaking his heart. Except said organ ached unspeakably worse this time.

Some primal survival mechanism kicked in, allowing him to breathe past his desolation and try to function.

"You don't need to do that. I'll take care of it." Xander reached over and took the plate from her hand.

Then some sadistic element inside had him tugging her gently toward him with his other hand. He scanned her face. It was like stone. She had flipped the inevitable switch and was gone from him in every way he truly needed.

He grasped the evaporating remains of their relationship, desperate at this point for any vestige of what they had. And, yes, it *had* been a relationship, whether she wanted to admit it or not. "The end of the summer deal doesn't prevent us from remaining friends, does it? Can I —can we still...talk?"

"I don't think that's a good idea. Maybe it's best if you just leave me alone."

Ross pulled away from him and walked out of the cottage without looking back.

And his heart shattered.

Chapter Fifty

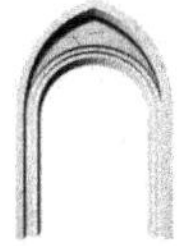

Ross

er heart shattered.

Chapter Fifty-One

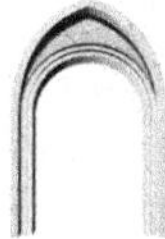

Ross

Ross held tight to the Orioles mug—a talisman, perhaps, against the pain of the morning's work. It had been a fitful night's sleep, her mind whirling with the surreal turn of events. Even though they'd ended things, even though she'd expressly told him to leave her alone, she'd kept expecting Xander to climb through the window. Or at least text her.

But the only texts she received were from Hon telling her how much fun she and Aunt Francesca were having, describing their meals, and showing pictures from the beach. They'd even attempted a selfie, which resulted in most of their faces cut off, but you could see how hard the sisters were laughing. Ross loved it.

But nothing from Xander. And so Ross didn't sleep. What was the line from *Turandot*? Nessun dorma. No one sleeps. Well, not Ross. That was for sure.

"This sucks," she said aloud in Hon's kitchen, half expecting her to come into the room and chastise her for her word choice. "Why didn't you just fess up, you fool? Why didn't you just tell him how you feel?" she muttered, as she stared at the pile of boxes that seemed to gloat at her. "Why? Because, as has been established, I'm chickenshit." She hit the table.

"Because I can't do this. I fucked up the one thing I've truly wanted. But it doesn't matter, because he doesn't want me—a cold, barren, emotionally remote woman with a geographically undesirable job in Manhattan who has no fucking clue how to be in a relationship and how to be a mother. And now what do I do?" Ross's voice dropped to an agonized whisper. She rested her head on her hands, bumping into her coffee.

Ross inhaled deeply, shaking herself from her pathetic musings. This was not her style. "OK. Almost had a coffee calamity there. That would've sucked. That'll snap a woman out of it. No more wallowing in Xanderville, Ross Ellen. First, you need to stop talking to yourself in the kitchen like an ever-loving fool. Second, get to work. These boxes won't sort themselves. 'Once more unto the breach.' Isn't that right, Henry the Fifth? Let's get this shit done."

She gulped a fortifying swallow of coffee, turned up the Alexa to the highest volume, and set her mind on the task ahead.

Ross dragged the boxes into the kitchen, one by one. For some reason, she didn't want to do what she was calling Beaufort Memory Excavation in the office. It seemed to make more sense in the kitchen, the hub of so many family memories. By midmorning, fortified by half a pot of coffee, her arms aching from the exercise of box-lugging, she dug into the first one.

It was from her room at the farmhouse, which Hon had packed up years ago, and included whatever Ross had deemed important enough to bring with her but not important enough to take back to Baltimore when she left temporarily at the end of each summer, or permanently when—well, *when*.

Ross spent thirty minutes entertained by the flotsam of her younger self. Old photo booth picture strips of her and Tiercy. *Those are keepers.* Bathing suits, some even with just the barest hints of chlorine amidst the musty scent of age. *Why the hell did Hon keep those?* She came across her posters, gleefully unrolling the one of Justin Timberlake.

Even though she knew she was alone, she looked around to be sure, and then kissed him once again on the mouth. "For old time's sake, JT.

And, just so you know, you get even hotter and more successful." She bid the poster adieu and tossed it in her refuse pile, with only a small tug of nostalgic regret.

The second box was filled with books from many ages of her life. Her pool books. Sweet Valley High! She had loved those books as a preteen, much to Hon's chagrin. Ross flipped through one of the books, dog-eared and pool-water-warped—she could practically smell the Coppertone. Her adult self cringed at the desecration of the pages even as she smiled at the memory of her, Tiercy, and Gaby gleefully sharing the novels.

The third and fourth boxes were items of her parents that Hon had specifically earmarked for Ross. Gaby had already received hers years ago, but Ross had refused to take possession of hers. Her parents' jewelry had already been dispersed. Ivy hadn't worn much. Gaby had Adam's wedding ring. In fact, Ted now wore it. Ross would one day have Ivy's engagement ring, if she wanted it, which Hon said was in a safe, along with other jewelry.

There was furniture too, including antique pieces in this very farmhouse, that would be Ross's one day. They had been at the house in Baltimore. Hon couldn't take it to the condo, so Ross was arranging for storage. Would she ever want it?

She was moving into a furnished apartment. In fact, Ross had never owned a place. She had the money to buy one, but, as an avowed commitment-phobe, owning a home conveyed too much permanence for her, so she just rented places over the years. Her place in the Baltimore suburbs, which was ten minutes from Tiercy's, could have been a corporate apartment, such was the generic nature of the furnishings. Ross's intention was to donate that furniture to a local charity that would see it dispersed to a family that needed it more than she did.

Her kitchen was the exception. It featured organized cabinets of high-end bakeware. That would go with her to Manhattan. In fact, it was already lovingly packed and ready for the move.

There it was again. That sinking feeling in the pit of her stomach.

"Ignore it," Ross directed herself aloud. "Adventure. New

opportunity. Loser still talking to herself in the kitchen. Alexa, play The Cure."

Thankfully, Alexa listened well and filled the room with music. Then she heard the opening strains of the song Xander sang to her just the other day.

"Alexa, turn that shit off."

"*I'm sorry. I didn't quite get that,*" the small round device replied.

"Fucking-a!" Ross lunged for the device and viciously unplugged it. "Ha. Teach you not to listen, girl." She brushed off her hands dramatically. "Back to work, Beaufort."

She turned to the next pile. These boxes had other, more sentimental items. Ross girded herself. The Orioles mug would be hers, that she knew, and she was taking it to New York. She took a fortifying breath and opened the first. Her mother's china. Lovingly wrapped. Gaby got the crystal. Ross the china. What she'd do with it, she didn't know.

Ross moved to the next box. Her mom's baby book for her. It went all the way up to Ross's fifteenth birthday. Ross flipped through all the pictures—some she'd never seen. The last time she'd looked at the book she'd been in middle school. After that, it had seemed immature to look at a baby book. But it was clear her mother had continued to document Ross's growth and milestones.

There was a picture of her with her mom in Baltimore, standing at their house, arms around each other, laughing. Who had taken it? Why were they laughing? Ross vaguely remembered the moment. Could almost hear her mother laughing.

As she looked, Ross realized that in this picture, her mother would have been not that much older than she was now. The resemblance to herself was...striking. Hon had said it, many times. But Ross had always dismissed it. She always knew she resembled Hon, but not her mother. Not like this.

She flashed to the time before smartphones, when you'd run to get film developed, and then wait—impatiently—for your pictures, to have treasures like this revealed. Ross teased the picture loose and held it close to her chest. Then she brought it to her lips, and kissed her mom. She was framing this one and taking it to New York.

She had no idea her mother kept up the album that long. Her throat ached with unshed tears, and, once again, Ross wished she could cry.

"Last box. Get it over with." Ross grabbed the scissors and sliced it open.

From the first look, it was clear the box had been mislabeled. This was Gaby's box, again largely from her farmhouse bedroom. On the top was Gaby's pink leather diary.

In a breath, time evaporated. Seized by some long-dormant impulse, Ross was tempted to be a bratty little sister again. She couldn't help herself. Gaby had been obsessive about that diary. She wrote in it daily from her sixteenth birthday on (it had been a present from another cheerleader), and Ross and Tiercy used to pretend to sneak in and read it, making up passages to "quote" aloud, to Gaby's mortification. They were never true, and often Ross got in trouble. But she was always curious what Gaby did write in there.

Exhibiting tremendous self-control, Ross kept it closed. Instead, she brushed off her pants and eased out of the chair. The box was too heavy to carry, but she decided to walk over to Gaby's, return the diary, and maybe Moose would be around to grab the box.

Several cars were in the driveway when she got there and she heard male voices and laughter. One of those was definitely Xander's. Ross's stomach clenched and her heart thudded. She stood on the steps, frozen with indecision. The front door popped open, startling her.

"Whoa!" a gorgeous Black man said. "You scared me!"

"Oh, sorry. Hey. Hi. I'm Ross. Gaby's sister." Ross held out her hand, recovering her faculties.

"Sorry for screeching like a wuss, Ross-Gaby's-sister. My voice hasn't been that high since before puberty. I didn't expect to find anyone out here." He took her hand, a quizzical smile on his face. "Carl. Nice to meet you. I work at the station with Ted. So, Ross, are you in the habit of just standing on the Monroes' porch in the dark?"

Ross dropped her head in embarrassment, laughing. "No. I was debating about whether to interrupt what is clearly Ted's poker night. I'm packing up the farmhouse and I have a box for Gaby that's too heavy for me. But I'll come back tomorrow."

"Carl—what're you doing? You getting your phone charger from the car or running out to cry on the porch 'cause we're taking all your money? We're waiting on you for the next hand." Ted came out to the porch. "Oh, hey, Ross. What are you doing here?"

"Hey, Moose. Listen, sorry to interrupt poker night. I didn't realize. I'll come back tomorrow."

"What did you need? Everything ok at the house?"

"Yes, I was just going through my boxes and realized I had one of Gaby's. It's no biggie. I would've brought it over myself, but it's too heavy."

"No worries, Ross. I can swing by in the morning before my shift and grab it."

"Thanks, Moose. Oh, and tell Gaby it had her diary in it," Ross sing-songed with a wink, waving it in the air. "So far I've exercised extreme restraint, but if I'm feeling bratty, I can't promise that will continue. I always wanted to read that thing."

Ross watched as all the color drained from Ted's face.

"Ted, Carl...you guys get lost in the dark? Did you need a losers' cuddle out here?" Xander came laughing out the door, and then broke off, seeing the blanched face of his friend. Then his eyes swung to Ross.

Her breathing hitched. Seeing him was a gut-punch she didn't need. Ross's heart was beating fast, both from Ted's strange reaction and the arrival of Xander, who was destroying her by his very presence.

"What's going on out here?" he asked, clearly doing better than she was.

He seemed calm, although concerned about Ted. No evidence of post-deal aftereffects.

Unlike Ross. She hadn't been able to manage anything other than breathing since she heard his voice—and even that was labored. Her hands shook. Her leg bounced. She fought to regain her equilibrium. He clearly wasn't as gutted by the end of them as she was.

"I'm actually not sure. I just came by to tell Ted I found a box of Gaby's. I teased him about finding Gaby's diary and then he looked like he was going to barf."

Xander and Ted exchanged wordless looks.

Carl politely excused himself, clearly uncomfortable with, and probably confused by, the scene unfolding on the porch.

"Does someone want to tell me why the discovery of Gaby's teenage diary seems to be such a big deal?" Ross looked between the men, who remained silent as statues on the porch. "Hello?" She snapped her fingers.

Ted raked his hands through his hair. "So you didn't read any of it?"

"No. But if I didn't want to before, I definitely do now."

Ted folded his massive arms across his chest.

"Ross..." Xander began.

"I'm not sure what this has to do with you, Xander, since that diary long predates you in our lives. But clearly there is something in there she doesn't want me to read. Hon said there are things I don't know about the night my parents died. Is there something about that in this diary? Am I right?" She turned to Ted, who stood in silence, not moving except the rapid blinking of his eyes.

That was all the confirmation Ross needed. "Tell my sister I didn't touch her diary. Here." She thrust it at Ted. "Take it. But do me a favor. Tell her to come see me. I am so tired of being in the dark about things. Of being the odd woman out."

Ted nodded his head, resigned. "I'll send her over. But, please, be gentle with her. It was a bad night."

"What was a bad night?" Once again, she was met with silence, but the men exchanged wary glances.

"She'll tell you."

"Ross, please..." Xander reached for her, but she spun away from him. Everything was churning in her head, and tangling together in a way she couldn't process. The death of her parents. Her estrangement with Gaby. Xander. The move to New York. Pain sliced across the top of her head and her heart raced as she fought for control.

"I am so sick of all this drama...and of being treated like an outsider in my own family. Jesus. I can't leave here soon enough." Ross turned on her heel and sprinted back to the farmhouse.

CHAPTER FIFTY-TWO

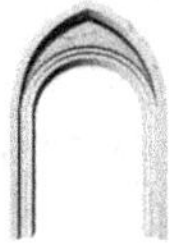

XANDER

For long moments, Xander and Ted stood on the porch in a scene reminiscent of their thwarted game night weeks before. The chatter of field crickets and cicadas around them punctuated their stunned silence. Eventually, Xander broke his gaze from the treeline leading to Leah's, where Ross had run. Ted was leaning forward on the railing, both hands grasping the wood.

"Ted," he began. "Fuck, man. You need to call Gaby."

"No shit," he gritted. "I'm just psyching myself up for it. Xan, she's going to be gutted. I told her Hon wanted everything out in the open, but I know she was prepared for it to happen after Leah's return. I'm so worried about her. And the baby. What if...what if Ross blows up at her and she loses it from the stress?"

Xander put a steadying hand on his friend's shoulder. "That's not going to happen. The baby is healthy, and Gaby is strong. And I know you don't want to hear this," he added, "but we need to trust in Ross to handle this as best she can. She knows her sister is pregnant, and she knows about the possible bed rest. She might be angry. She might be hurt. But she would never want any harm to come to the baby, or her sister for that matter."

Ted exhaled strongly through his nose. "I hope you're right."

Xander looked back to the trees. "I know I am. I know her."

Ted turned to him. "You're in love with her."

It was pointless to deny it. "I am. But she's not in love with me. So let's just leave it there."

"I'm not so sure you're right about that."

"I know that I am. Listen, you have bigger fish to fry. Go call Gaby. I'll tell the guys poker night is over. I won most of your money already anyway."

CHAPTER FIFTY-THREE

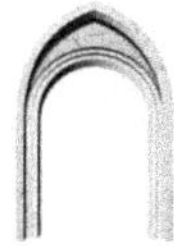

Ross

The door to the kitchen slapped open and Gaby arrived breathless, eyes a bit wild, the pink diary clutched to her chest.

"What the ever-loving fuck is in that diary, Gaby?" Ross asked in astonishment from the opposite doorway, where she'd entered as soon as she'd heard Gaby's arrival. "What could possibly be so bad to have Moose summon you, and send you scurrying over here? I thought he was going to rip that diary out of my hands when he saw it."

"I killed them."

Chapter Fifty-Four

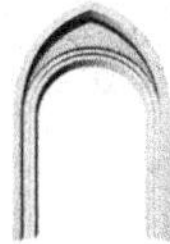

Ross

"What the ever-loving—?"

"Mom and Dad. I killed them. That's what the diary says. That and a bunch of other things about that night... and the months after." Gaby was breathing in staccato bursts, weaving on her feet.

Alarmed, Ross reached for her. "Gaby, sit before you pass out. And then tell me what the ever-loving fuck you're talking about."

She eased the diary from Gaby's white-knuckled grip and put it on the table. Ross sat across from her sister, her legs numb from the shock of the evening. "Tell me what happened," she whispered. "Please."

Gaby couldn't seem to speak. It was obvious she was trying to find the words, her mouth opening and then closing again. Ross felt like a parent waiting for a wayward, past-curfew child to come home. She bounced her foot and then forced it to stop. Unable to sit still, she stood and drank a glass of water, pouring one for Gaby as well. She placed it in front of her sister, where it remained, unseen.

Ross sat again and watched her sister and the clock.

After what seemed like hours, but was really only a few minutes, her sister finally spoke.

Gaby motioned to her own body. "I had to break out the mom-wear. With the fourth baby, your body just goes pffft." Gaby made a gesture of a body expanding. "But maybe I should have worn my Kevlar." She offered a small smile.

Ross didn't return it. "I don't feel like joking." She motioned to the diary on the table. "What do you mean you killed Mom and Dad, Gaby?" Her words echoed in the mostly empty kitchen.

Gaby carefully reached for her water, avoiding the diary like it was radioactive, a faraway look in her eyes. She swallowed a tiny sip, and then let out a massive exhalation, her cheeks puffing. She closed her eyes. "Let me just tell it, OK, Ross? Don't interrupt me. No matter how much you want to. Can you do that?"

"Yes. I can do that."

The room was still. Suddenly, Moose's concerned face flashed in Ross's mind, along with the ultrasound picture on Gaby's fridge.

"Gaby, do you want to move to a more comfortable room?"

"No. Just let me do this." Keeping her eyes closed, she began. "You remember how it was that summer. I was going into my senior year. I resented being at the farmhouse. All my friends were back home. There was this girl who lived nearby. Lola. She was a freshman at UVA. I saw her at the movies a couple times and in town. We struck up a friendship. I could bike over there. But more often, she'd come pick me up."

Ross remembered Lola. Remembered her hanging out at their grandparents' pool, and also vaguely recalled Lola at the funeral and how solicitous both she and her parents had been of Gaby. Ross shook away the cobwebs and tuned back in to what Gaby was saying.

"We'd been invited to a party. It was a bunch of UVA people she knew. Mom and Dad thought I was just going to her place and spending the night. But we were going to the party."

Gaby took a shuddering breath and Ross rose and moved to the chair next to her sister. Her fingers twitched at the desire to hold her hand. Giving in, she did, and was shocked at how cold her sister's fingers were. She stroked Gaby's hand between her own as her sister continued.

"There was a lot of drinking. And weed. I was feeling...I don't know. Rebellious. Mature. Pissed off because I was seventeen and I felt like I was being suffocated by Mom and Dad. I had gotten in a huge fight with Mom right before. I told her I ha-hated her. I didn't mean it. Lo and I drank and got a little high. And there was this really cute guy there. We started making out. But he told me that it wasn't gentlemanly to make out with a lady in front of people. So, he took me into a b-bedroom."

A knot of dread built in Ross's stomach. Her intuition told her what had happened next. Despite that, she still found herself gripping her sister's hand a bit harder and thinking, *Don't go with him, Gabs. Don't go!* And where the hell was Lola when all this was going on?

"I thought it was just harmless fooling around. We were just messing around. Until we weren't. He-he started lifting up my skirt. I had on an adorable denim skirt I'd borrowed from Lo. I told him no." Tears streaked down her face. "I told him no! I pushed his hand away. He said I was just being a-a d-dick tease but that I really wanted it. I tried to get out from under him. The music was so loud, Ross. I called out, but he put his hand on my mouth. It happened so fast. He had my skirt up and then my underwear off, and then he—he—" Gaby put her face in her hands and sobbed.

Ross grabbed the water and put it in her sister's hand. "Drink this," she commanded. Her sister, lost in horror, obeyed mechanically.

The undertow of the memory strong, Gaby resumed speaking—her voice the barest whisper. "I tried to fight him. I did. I know I bloodied his nose. I found blood on my shirt later. He hurt me. It hurt so much. And when he finished, he rolled over and passed out.

"I grabbed my underwear and ran out and found Lo outside. She held my hair while I threw up by a tree. We'd taken her car there, but we couldn't drive home. Remember that speech that Mom and Dad gave about calling them if we needed a ride? I couldn't go back in that house —not with him there—so we walked to a store and we called the farmhouse. This was before any of us had cellphones. Mom and Dad didn't ask any questions. They said they'd be there in fifteen minutes. Max.

"We waited. I think I was in shock. After thirty minutes, no sign of

Mom and Dad. We called back and Hon picked up. She was concerned, but her car was in the shop and she couldn't find Pop's keys. So, we called Lo's dad. He came within ten minutes."

Gaby looked at Ross for the first time since she came in. "Oh, God, Ross. I'm so sorry. I'm so sorry. I did it. It's my fault. I killed them. I'm sorry." She began to weep, the deep mournful cries of the bereaved. Her shoulders bowed in sorrow.

Ross watched her sister, frozen. Struggling, she found her voice. "No, you didn't, Gaby," she whispered.

"I did!" she sobbed. "Dr. Foster picked us up and he tried to drive me back to the farmhouse. But the main road was bl-blocked, with an acc-accident. Before the detour, though, I could see. I *could see it*." Gaby's wail was deep and guttural. "It was Mom and Dad's car. They were coming to get me and some drunken kid coming from that same party hit them head-on and killed them. I saw their car. It was so crumpled. I knew—I knew they were gone. Nobody survives that. Oh God, Ross. I killed them."

Gaby dropped down to the floor, and curled into a ball, crying. Ross slid to the floor and wrapped herself around her sister. Two commas, curled against the pain.

Ross let her sister cry it out, kissing and smoothing the back of her hair, as a mother would console a child. *Oh, Mom*, Ross thought. *Tell me what to do.*

The only response Ross could think of, the response of parents from time immemorial, was to hold her until she calmed. Ross flashed to the memory of Hon tucking herself around Gaby that morning so long ago and she finally understood.

Eventually, Gaby sniffled and lifted her head. Ross raised herself up, and then held out a hand for her sister. "Come on. Let's get your water and go somewhere more comfortable."

Once ensconced on the couch, Gaby turned puffy eyes to Ross. "I need to tell you what happened next."

"I always knew it was a college student leaving drunk from a party. But I wish I'd known the rest. Gaby, this has been a lot." Ross glanced at Gaby's belly and said a quick prayer for her unborn niece or nephew.

She hoped the strain of this wasn't hurting the baby. "Please, you don't have to tell me anything else right now. Let's just sit here."

"No. I owe you the whole story, Ross." Gaby heaved a shuddering sigh. "Dr. Foster got me home. Being an ER doc, he was able to get me a sedative. But I made Lola swear not to tell anyone about the rape."

"Why, Gaby? That asshole should've been held accountable. My God. You were *raped*."

"I had just seen the crushed car of our parents! It was all I could do to process that. I think, in my reptile brain, it was a survival thing."

Gaby rubbed her forehead, composing herself. "We arrived at the house with Dr. Foster, and the police were already there, telling Hon and Pop about the accident. Not only did they have to face the deaths of their daughter and son-in-law, they had to deal with their wreck of a granddaughter. As I know you will recall, I was pretty much a mess. Hence your moniker for me: Drama Gaby."

"Oh, Gaby..." Ross breathed, feeling lower than dirt. "All this time —all this fucking time. I've been so mad at you for being self-centered. And it was based on my own ignorance."

"You couldn't know. No one told you. They pretty much kept me tranquilized because when I came out of it, I got hysterical. Hon and Pop decided not to say anything to you because you were just so...angry."

"I was angry because the whole world turned upside overnight. I went to bed and everything was normal. I woke up and Mom and Dad were gone and you were—you were... Oh Gaby, I don't even have words. Everything changed in a blink. I was so mad at the world."

"You just shut down. You wouldn't even stand next to anyone at the funeral except Tiercy. You just stared at the ground. And then you decided to live with her family."

Ross turned and faced Gaby, filled with hurt and confusion "Why, Gaby?"

"Why what?" Gaby leaned toward her, gripping Ross's hand.

"Why didn't you tell me any of this when it happened? We used to be so close. I could have...helped you."

"I wish I had a good answer for you. We weren't as close that summer. We'd pulled apart—"

"You'd been raped! And you saw our parents' crushed car! Jesus, Gaby—what the ever-loving *fuck*. That isn't pulling apart...that's just fucked as hell up!"

"Ross...I'm sorry I didn't tell you. I really am—"

"I maybe understand why you didn't tell me right away. But how could you keep this massive secret from me for almost two decades? A secret that explains why everything was so screwed up for so long—"

Ross stopped, cutting herself off as the realization hit her. "And Hon!" Ross shot to her feet. "Hon," she whispered. "She knew this the whole time and she didn't trust me to tell me."

Ross wrapped her arms around her own waist against the hurt of Hon's part in all this. She was reeling from all of it, and just couldn't wrap her brain around any of it.

"Even if you couldn't tell me, she should have...I'm your sister. And I loved you!"

"No! Ross, I swear. It wasn't that way. She wanted to tell you right away but she was worried—" Gaby stopped.

"Go on. What was she worried about?"

"She was worried you would blame me for going to the party. At that point, I was having really...dark...thoughts. I found out later in therapy that she was worried I would harm myself. And, honestly, I came pretty close to self-harm a few times. That therapist saved my life. That's how bad things were."

Ross walked toward the window, staring out. "I was sixteen. Almost a legal adult. Not a child. I could have handled it. I could have been there for you, Gaby. Hon didn't trust me. Didn't think enough of me—of my character—to trust I'd do the right thing."

"It's not that. She wasn't thinking straight. She was grieving. Pop wanted to tell you. They argued about it."

"And *you* know all this. Because they trusted you enough to tell you. But Ross, the cold, unfeeling one didn't get the benefit of the doubt."

"It wasn't like that, Ross. Please come sit down and let me explain," Gaby begged, holding out her hand.

When Ross ignored her, Gaby continued, tentatively. "After I got better, she pleaded with me to tell you or to let her tell. But I—I wouldn't let her. I was ashamed. I knew you hated me. And part of me hated you too. Your life got to continue in Baltimore, at our high school, all happy and fun, with Tiercy taking my place as your sister. And I was here, broken and fucked up."

"My God, Gaby," Ross said, incredulous. "My life was not happy and fun. My parents died, too, you know. And I had to live next to the house where we grew up. Watch another family move in. And have Hon and Pop miss my special occasions because you were too 'fragile' to be left alone."

Gaby stared miserably at her hands. "This is why I didn't want to tell you."

"Because you knew I'd be angry?"

"No! Because I knew you would be hurt! Because I knew you'd hate me when you found out! I was afraid. I know you were mad at me for... for how weak I was. But I couldn't bear to tell you the truth."

Gaby launched herself toward her sister, blue eyes blazing. She grabbed Ross by the wrist. "I lost so much that day. I lost my innocence. I lost my parents. And because I couldn't face the hurt, I lost my sister."

Ross wrenched her arm free. "And I lost *my* parents, too. My childhood." Ross stared at her feet, swallowing past a lump of decades-old hurt. Her voice dropped to a shredded whisper. "But no one could take care of me because they were too focused on you."

Ross shook her head. "I would have understood. I would have. I do understand. What I don't understand is why no one thought I would. It fucking hurts, Gaby. It *hurts*. I have felt on the outside of this family for so long, and I was. But not even for the reason I thought."

She took a shuddering breath. "Look. I'm not sure we should continue this conversation right now. I don't want to say anything I'll regret later. And you need to take care of you and the baby. I am so horribly sorry for what happened to you, Gaby. I-I don't even have words to convey it. But the entire narrative of the most painful time of my life has just been turned upside down, and I need to process it. Alone. Please leave, Gaby. Please," she pleaded.

Tears in her eyes, Gaby nodded and walked back toward the kitchen door.

"And...uh, Gaby, text me when you get home. Just so, you know, I know you and the little nugget are OK."

"OK," Gaby whispered, head down.

Ross reached for her, stared at her hand hovering in the air, and then shook her head. "I'm sorry, Gabs. I just—I need some time." She turned on her heel and strode toward the staircase, taking the stairs two at a time.

CHAPTER FIFTY-FIVE

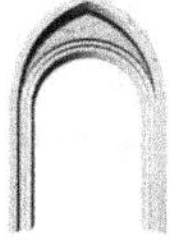

Ross

"I'm so glad you're there."

Thankfully, Tiercy picked up on the first ring. "No, 'What's up, Hooker Hips?' This must be bad."

"It's really bad."

Ross proceeded to tell Tiercy everything, blow by painful blow. In time-honored best friend fashion, Tiercy listened patiently, only interrupting to offer exclamations of shock and support.

"Santa on a cracker. I had no idea…"

"You promise, Tierce? You really didn't know?"

"Ross, why would I? Of course I didn't know. I would have told you."

Ross shook her head. "I don't even know anymore. My whole damn family has been keeping a massive secret—really two secrets from me—for twenty years. It's one thing for it to be Gaby. But Hon? Why wouldn't Hon have ever said something?"

"I wish I knew, Ross. You could call her."

"No. I'm not doing that and spoiling her vacation. I'll talk to her when she gets back. It just—it just hurts so much, you know?"

"I know."

Ross was silent for a bit, gnawing on her cuticle. Her pulse was skittering and she took several deep breaths to try to calm it.

"Hey, Ross? We've always been straight with each other, even when the other didn't always want to hear it." Tiercy paused, and Ross knew from a fuck-ton of experience her bestie would be dropping a hammer. "And in that spirit, as your best friend, I need to say something here."

"Don't hold back, Jack." The words were joking but her tone was wary.

"You need to get over yourself."

Ross recoiled. "What's that supposed to mean?"

"It means that you learned something really horrible that happened to your sister—two horrible things, in one God-awful night. Your sister was *raped*, Ross—"

"I *know* she was fucking raped—"

"—and then immediately after that, she saw your parents' crushed car—the car they were in on the way to come get her. Either of those alone is appalling. But together? That would screw the strongest person up for a long time. And, no, it should never have been kept from you for as long as it has. You have every right to be upset by that. Angry even. But, Ross, damnit, your sister has been through hell. If you can't see that, you aren't the person I know you to be. Jesus, Ross, have some grace here. She has walked around believing on a certain level that she is responsible for the deaths of your parents. And despite all her counseling, and all her surface healing, I think somewhere inside of her is a seventeen-year-old girl who needs her sister to tell her that's not the case."

"Damnation," Ross whispered and then was silent for a long time. She pictured her teenage sister the morning she'd found out about her parents. Gaby curled in a fetal position, tucked up against the hurt of brutal physical violation and the horror of witnessing something so awful Ross couldn't even imagine. Ross tasted bile in her throat. "I need to go over there, Tierce. I told her she wasn't to blame, but I don't think she even heard me."

"Yes, you do, Ross Ellen. You need to free your sister from this burden she's been carrying." Quietly, Tiercy added, "It's what Ivy would expect of her daughter, and you should expect it of yourself."

"I need just a bit of time. My head is spinning. I don't want to fuck this up any more than it already is."

"Take the time you need. And then go free yourself while you free Gaby. It's time to let go."

oss spent the remainder of the evening processing the swirl of emotions in her head and her heart, trying to sort them into something manageable. She needed a fortifying drink and wished she could call Xander for one of his whiskey sours. Unsure of the right mix, she grabbed the Maker's Mark and gave herself a generous pour. Then she crawled into bed, cradling the whiskey.

Movement at the window startled her.

Xander.

He eased through the window and sat on the edge of her bed. Ross wanted to be angry at the unfairness of losing him too. But somehow all she could feel was battered inside.

"I was going to come in through the door, since I know where Hon hides the spare. But I didn't want to scare you. I figured the window was our thing."

"You did scare me. And we don't have a thing anymore, Xander."

Xander smiled sadly. "I guess we don't. I'm really sorry I startled you. The window...it, uh, seemed like a good idea at the time." He puffed out a deep exhalation. "I know I'm supposed to leave you alone, but I just wanted to check on you. I heard you had a rough night."

"News travels fast on the Waldheim Compound."

Ross's voice was wry, but inside her heart was twisting in agony. The last time they were in her bed together they had been making passionate love.

"Where's Petey?"

"Birthday party at a bounce house. Then spending the night."

"Ah." She nodded. "I bet he's loving that. Kid has quite the budding social life." She smiled, but her heart was so sad. "Tell me something. I've been replaying our conversation with Ted on the porch and one thing in this bizarre evening is crystal clear to me—you knew about my sister."

Xander closed his eyes and then nodded.

"Damnit, Xander," she cried. "How could you keep that from me? You've been Team Gaby all along. You were supposed to be *mine*." To her horror, her voice broke on the last word. She swallowed a sip to cover it, the burn of alcohol welcome on her throat.

"It wasn't for me to share. Jesus, Ross. You can't be mad at me for that. Be mad at me for other...things. But Gaby told me that before you and I ever had our summer deal. And it wasn't my place to reveal any of that to you. That would have been a violation of my friendship with her, regardless of anything between us. And I am, and will always be, Team Ross. You have to know that."

"How long have you known about what happened to Gaby?" she asked, aching with hurt that Gaby would tell a new friend what she couldn't tell her sister.

"It wasn't long after I moved into the cottage. I had Gaby and Ted over for a thank-you meal. All the kids were at Hon's. We were drinking and laughing, but I could tell that Ted was just...off. Anyway, it turns out there had been a fire that day. It was at the house where Gaby was... you know. Ted was one of the firefighters on scene. I think he wasn't going to talk about it, but then he just...started crying. He was wrecked. I didn't know what the hell was going on. He loves her so much, and being at that house, where someone violated the woman he loves...it just opened some deep vein of hurt. He sobbed in her arms.

"I knew it was something big, so I just left the cottage and gave them space. Sat outside and watched the stars. Later, Gaby came out and asked to talk with me. That's when she told me everything."

"Jesus. Poor Ted. I've spent a long time not liking him—mostly because he didn't like me." Ross shook her head. "I am such a tool."

Xander shook his head, a tender smile playing on his lips. "Principessa, you are far from that. It was a horrible confluence of events—"

"Great SAT word," Ross interjected, her body and words weighted in misery.

"—and everyone did what they thought was best in the moment. No one meant to hurt anyone in your family. Not Hon. Not Gaby. Not you. You're all amazing people. And I love each of you."

Ross's eyes flicked to him at that word.

He loved her? Or he loved her as a friend but wasn't in love with her? Or maybe just not enough.

Ross closed her eyes. She didn't have the emotional bandwidth to examine his words. Not when everything else about her world was caving in around her.

"Ross, I can see you're overwhelmed. And at the risk of overstepping one more time, I need to tell you that your sister has struggled with not sharing this with you. She does love you, Ross. It's been a burden on her heart. And she's blamed herself for everything— the death of your parents, her rape, the rift between you both which led to the strain on your family. She's carried all of that for a long time. It was wrong of her and your family to keep this from you, but this has been a secret that festered and grew out of control. I suspect the more time that passed, and the more your relationship frayed to nonexistence, the harder it became for her to tell you."

"It's all so fucked up, Xan." It was barely a whisper. "Just so surreal. There's this part of me that keeps wanting to clear my head and think this was all a bad dream. *None* of that was her fault. I know you're trying to make me feel better, but I think you possibly made me feel worse. I've carried so much anger for so long, and...now...I don't know what to feel."

"Of course you don't. You've had a lot thrown at you all at once. I know you're shocked and hurt by these secrets, and that's entirely fair. But I know this about you, Ross Beaufort. You are a beautiful, compassionate woman. You can find a way through it and make something extraordinary and special out of all this pain. Ross...you have the opportunity to give your sister a gift—an absolution and a healing that can only come from you. She needs it, Ross....and I think you do, too."

She swallowed past the hard lump in her throat. "You've—" Her voice croaked and she cleared it and began again. "You've given me a lot to think about, Xander. Thank you."

"Ross, I know this has been excruciating for you. It wasn't my intention to say all this. I actually came over to see if maybe you'd like me to just...hold you. Comfort you."

She stared into those beautiful brown eyes, her resolve wavering. If she leaned into him, the way she ached to down to her very marrow, she'd fall further. And if she fell, she'd be destroyed. Her heart couldn't take saying goodbye to Xander Grace again. He made it clear there wasn't a relationship in the cards for them, and she was leaving soon anyway. If she had any hope of moving forward, she couldn't even let herself have a moment with Xander. Because one moment would never be enough. Not when she knew what she really wanted was a lifetime with him.

"No. But...thank you...for all of this. You are a good man." She needed him to leave. She was suffocating under a tidal wave of emotion, and if he so much as touched her, she'd drown. "Go home, Xander."

CHAPTER FIFTY-SIX

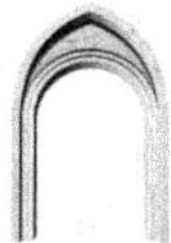

XANDER

Moonlight poured into the homey cottage. Xander nursed his drink, reflecting on the day. Without acknowledging its purpose, Ted had organized a poker night to distract him from his broken heart.

Xander had been moping around for days, not brave enough to face Ross and admit his true feelings but also not strong enough to fully stay away. He'd sit outside on his patio, laptop abandoned, listening for any sounds of Ross across the vast property. Xan knew it was pointless, but he yearned for just the tiniest signs of her presence. And yet he was denied even that small consolation. He missed the sound of her chatter with Petey, her snort-laugh, the feel of her warmth around his cock, the gasp of her release, the way she'd melt into him when he came up behind her and wrapped his arms around her.

He was a fucking coward. He'd spent countless hours chastising himself for that day in the cottage. The day he'd fully lied to her and to himself.

He could still see her face. The flash of hurt in her eyes. And shock.

He'd denied it to himself in the moment. Fuck. He didn't have a clue what she wanted, but he didn't know how to ask her either.

Aubrey had screwed with his head so much, he didn't know how to do this. He'd messed up one relationship by driving hard on what *he'd* wanted, completely missing what his partner had needed—to the detriment of her own mental health. And, yes, that had resulted in Petey, so it was hard for him to regret anything.

And, yet, he couldn't trust himself in a relationship. He didn't trust himself to know how to distinguish his wants and needs from Ross's. And he'd be damned if he steamrolled her. If she wasn't feeling what he was feeling—damn it—then he had to let her go. No matter how much that fucking shredded him.

He hadn't shared what went down with Gaby or Ted, and to the best of his knowledge Ross hadn't either. But his friends seemed to sense something was off. Thus the ill-fated poker night.

Despite his distraction, Xan had been winning round after round. He'd—almost—managed to not think of Ross every twenty seconds. He could go nearly a full minute before his mind wandered to her.

And then she showed up at the house. She looked tired, with circles under her eyes. A small part of him hoped she'd been missing him as much as he ached for her.

But then she waved that damn diary. The oxygen seemed to evaporate in the air around them, and he was torn between running to comfort Ross, helping Ted, or supporting Gaby. It was a shitshow. But the look on Ross's face—her dismissal of him, her anger—it clawed a hole in his hurting heart. He knew he'd thrown away the chance to be the person who held her, who took on her suffering, who loved her most of all.

And, yet, he couldn't stay away.

He'd seen the light in her bedroom window in the darkened farmhouse, and before he knew it, he'd scaled the lattice and climbed into her room. What he saw eviscerated his heart. It was clear she was shaken, wounded, stunned...and so fucking alone. He wanted to gather her in his arms, kiss her soft hair, ease her pain.

Instead, she sent him away.

He was good and fucked. His girl wasn't his girl anymore—if she even ever had been—and she'd be leaving soon for Manhattan. He downed the rest of his whiskey in one gulp, trying and failing to banish the unsettling thoughts of Ross landing in Gideon's waiting arms. He wanted her back, but he knew it was pointless. Once again, he was left alone with a heart broken by a complicated woman who didn't want him the way he wanted her. And he wanted a lifetime with her.

CHAPTER FIFTY-SEVEN

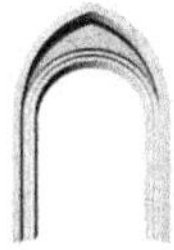

Ross

After a restless, sleepless night, Ross summoned the resolve to face Gaby. She could hear Hon, Tiercy, and Xander in her head all night.

What the hell are you going to do? You're going to figure it out. Because you're my beautiful girl, and that's what you do.

Free your sister from this burden...Free yourself...

You can find a way through it and to make something extraordinary and special out of all this pain. You have the opportunity to give your sister a gift—an absolution and a healing that can only come from you. She needs it....and I think you do, too.

Quietly, she trod across the grass, grateful for the one hundred yards despite the sultry heat so she could organize her jumble of thoughts. When she reached the Monroes' property, she could hear all three children laughing in the yard, and yipping puppy barks. The kids were playing in the pool, Gaby and Ted on lounge chairs, watching.

The smile on Gaby's face fell as she saw her sister, and Ted moved a touch closer to his wife, draping an arm around her shoulder.

"I come in peace," Ross joked, immediately regretting it. The children were oblivious, but the strain among the three adults was palpable. "Is there somewhere we can talk privately?" she asked her sister.

Ted pinned Ross with a glare. But now she saw him with new eyes. He was protecting the woman he loved. In that moment, Ross saw just how good of a team Gaby and Ted were, and her heart longed for the same thing with Xander—a team they'd never get to be.

She stepped toward them, hands out in supplication. "I promise not to upset your wife. I came to clear the air."

"It's OK, Ted." Gaby stood, one hand going to her growing belly. "We can go on the side porch."

When they were seated, Ross on a rocking chair, Gaby on the couch where Ross had found her sleeping so early in the visit—it seemed like months ago—Ross found that she didn't know where to begin. It was a minute or so before she found the words.

"I should start with an apology, for how I acted yesterday. I was guilty of what I've always accused you of—being self-centered. I hope you and the baby are OK." Ross swallowed. What she wouldn't give for a glass of whiskey right now. "I really am sorry, Gaby."

"The baby is doing fine." Ross noticed Gaby hadn't verified that she herself was fine. Understandable. "I accept your apology. And I should start with a thank you." Ross appreciated the olive branch from her sister. "Thank you for holding me while I cried. It meant a lot to me."

The sisters sat in silence, watching each other.

"Do you hate me? For killing them?" It was the smallest of whispers.

"Oh, Gabs. You *didn't* kill them." Propelled by instinct, she got up and knelt before her sister, forcing Gaby to look her in the eyes. "Do you hear me? You *did not* kill them. The drunk driver did. You did exactly what they told us to do. You called them when you needed them. That's what they wanted you to do. That other part of it was—it was an accident. Merest chance."

"I never should have lied to them and been at that party."

"Gaby..." Ross's voice was dry. "We spent all summer sneaking out. Come on. Let's be real. The fault in that accident is with the drunk college student who made a bad decision and got behind the wheel."

"I don't know if I'll ever forgive myself."

Ross got up and nudged her sister over so they sat side-by-side on the couch. "You know what Hon told me before she left? She said that hate corrodes the vessel that holds it. You need to stop hating yourself for something you didn't do."

"She said that?"

Ross nodded, smiling.

"God, I love her. And, Ross? It's really important that you understand this. Hon has wanted you to know essentially from the beginning, once I got strong enough to tell you myself. But ultimately, she has always respected it had to be me who told you. And she's hounded me about it for years."

As Ross took in Gaby's sad but conciliatory smile, a ripped piece of her heart knitted together. She fidgeted with the edge of her shorts. "Can I ask you something else?"

"What's that?"

"I understand why you wouldn't tell me. But did you ever tell Hon...about the rape?"

"Yes, I told Hon. I sort of had to. Ross, I was going to tell you this earlier, but you asked me to leave, OK?" At Ross's nod, Gaby continued. "About two months after the funeral, I had a positive pregnancy test."

"And the hits just keep coming," Ross said, emitting a low whistle. "Did you—well, you must have—terminated it?"

"By that time I had moved to Virginia, doing my senior year down here. I realized I was late. At that point, I was such a wreck, I was seeing a therapist. I told her first. She convinced me to tell Hon, who bought me a pregnancy test. Two lines," she confirmed. "We talked to Pop about it. We didn't have a lot of time. I was nine weeks by then. I thought about an abortion. Considered it strongly. But I decided I was going to keep it and give the baby up for adoption. Hon wasn't happy about it, but I wanted some good to come out of the whole damn thing. Give another family a chance to have a child. One week later, I started bleeding, and I lost the pregnancy." Gaby stroked her belly and then smiled.

"What is it?"

"Little butterfly flutters. In the beginning, when you start to feel movement, that's what it feels like—these little flutters. The baby just wanted me to know she's OK."

"*She's* OK? You think it's a girl?" Ross smiled.

Gaby bit her lip. "Promise not to tell Ted?" When Ross nodded, she continued. "When I had the bad spotting, at my ultrasound, the tech slipped. Called the baby a 'she.' Ted had left the room for a minute. It's a girl," Gaby whispered, glowing.

"Well, I'll be," murmured Ross. She leaned in, her hand hovering over her sister's gently raised abdomen. "May I?"

"Of course."

"Hey there, little one. I'm your Aunt Ross. I'm super cool. I know Daddy has a sister, but I'm your favorite aunt, all right? I'm going to spoil you like crazy."

Gaby laughed. "Nice. Way to indoctrinate them early."

"What happened to the bad guy, Gabs?"

"He's dead."

Ross's eyebrows flew up.

"Cancer. Non-Hodgkin's lymphoma. About eight years ago. He left behind a wife and a child."

"How do you know this?"

"I made it my business to know. I didn't report the rape, but I didn't say I wasn't haunted by it. I never saw him again, but I used to have nightmares. He was a student at UVA, and was a senior there when Ted and I were freshman. Ted once found him and waited for him outside a party with a couple friends. They held him while Ted, well, *Moose,* beat the shit out of him."

"You're *kidding.*" Ross's eyes widened.

"I kid you not."

"He told him that was just a taste of payback for raping an innocent girl and that if he so much as breathed uninvited near a young lady—or a young man for that matter—Ted would personally rip his dumb stick off."

"Fucking-A," marveled Ross. "I always liked Moose."

Now it was Gaby's turn to widen her eyes.

"Ok. Total lie. But remind me to fist-bump him next time I see him.

And buy him the most expensive bottle of scotch I can find." She frowned. "So the rapist is dead."

"Shortly after having Nick, I started having nightmares again. Having a child makes you feel vulnerable in startling ways. The world is suddenly a scary place and you want it to be safe for your child. Ted hired a private investigator. That's when we learned he'd died."

"Do you ever want to contact his widow and tell her that her husband was a date rapist?"

"No. I don't." Gaby was resolute. "He's dead, and with him the horrible thing he did to me. I don't need to ruin someone else's life, or his kid's life, because of what he did. And now that I've told you...I feel like I have even more peace." Gaby sighed. "Look, Ross. I'm not naïve enough to think that we can just...pretend we don't have all that water under the bridge... But I'd like to try to be sisters again."

Ross shook her head. "I'm the one who's been living an alternate reality. For twenty years, I've been acting like the sole wounded party here. Stewing on my resentment. God, I've been such an ass. No wonder you all hate me."

"We don't hate you. Well, Ted maybe a little." Gaby grinned.

"I'm sorry you couldn't trust me to tell me."

"I'm sorry I didn't tell you. I know that hurts you, deeply. I can see now that you've had almost twenty years of feeling like an outsider in this family, and it's my fault you were left in the dark about the biggest thing to happen in our lives." She grabbed Ross's hand. "But I need you to know... it wasn't about trust, Ross. I really wasn't in my right mind for a long time. And then when I was, I was too stubborn to tell you. Or let anyone else. And too hurt. And too jealous of you and Tiercy. And, ultimately, I was scared you'd blame me and you'd never forgive me for killing our parents."

"You didn't kill them, Gaby. And none of this was your fault. Not Mom and Dad's accident. Not your rape. The miscarriage. Not our rift —well, not all of it anyway. I think we can share blame on that one. It was all just—" Ross remembered Xander's words "—it was all just a horrible confluence of events, and you were a victim in the maelstrom. God...I wish I could go back in time and do it differently."

Gaby broke down, weeping into her sister's shirt with wrenching, cleansing tears almost two decades in the making. Ross just rocked her, kissing the top of her head, and let her sister finally be filled with the comfort she had missed for so many long years.

When Gaby's tears subsided, she wiped her eyes and offered a tremulous smile to her sister. "Drama Gaby, eh?

"No, absofuckinglutely not. *Brave* Gaby. You are so strong, and I'm just blown away at the life you've made for yourself in spite of so much pain. Drama Gaby was my misperception of the terrible reality you experienced. But Brave Gaby is very real and sitting in front of me...and I love her."

Gaby hiccupped a sob and threw her arms around Ross. "I love you, too, Ross. Thank you...for saying everything you just did. It...means more than I can ever share." She pulled back and offered a shaky smile. "And now I can be out of the doghouse with Hon. She'll be at peace now that I've finally told you."

"I won't be around much, what with my new job, but I'd like to try and build something new, Gaby. Based on what's real. I still cannot believe you went through all that and I didn't know. I could have helped you, and instead, I was oblivious. I abandoned you. I mocked you. Please forgive me for being such a horrible bitch. I hate myself right now."

"Don't. It'll corrode the vessel. And Hon wouldn't like that." Gaby smiled. "How about we forgive ourselves, forgive each other, and accept that things are not always as they appear. It's possible that you can spend a lifetime believing a reality that isn't true. Give yourself some grace, Ross. And I'll do the same."

"Grace...that's a great name for a baby girl."

Gaby tilted her head and then smirked. "I think you're right. But I also think you're a bit biased about the name 'Grace.'" She caught a glimpse of Ross's watch. "I need to get the kids dried off and then head to the store. You going to be OK? It's a lot to process."

"Yeah. Yeah, I'm good."

"You want to come over for a drink after they're in bed? Or, speaking of giving yourself grace, maybe you have plans with Xander?"

With mention of his last and first names in under a minute, Ross struggled to keep her face neutral. But it was hard. Thoughts of Xander were a constant accompaniment to everything whirling in her mind. Ross had hoped he'd check back in with her today, and her heart crumbled more with every passing hour. They had truly closed the door.

"Everything all right with you and Xan? You seem off, and he does too."

"Yep, fine. I think I'm just going to go back to the farmhouse, scroll through Instagram, and finish some packing." She gave her sister a tentative smile. "Would it be weird if we hugged again?"

"I think it would be weirder if we didn't."

CHAPTER FIFTY-EIGHT

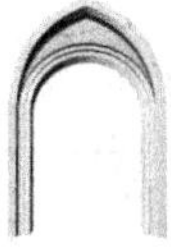

Ross

"Ding dong! It's me!" came the singsong voice.

"What fresh hell is this," Ross muttered into her brimming coffee cup. "And why is she coming through the back porch door?"

Gaby stifled a laugh as she rose and shifted Tara off her lap. "Sshh. Lower your voice," she whispered. "I texted her to come in this way."

"I thought it was because the bride of Satan doesn't need manners." Ross burped into her Orioles mug. "Ugh. Just the idea of her nauseates me."

"Careful," Gaby warned Ross, nodding toward her daughter as she choked on another laugh.

"Sorry. I'm not at my best at 8 a.m. when I haven't slept. Again."

"Come in, Genevieve." Gaby greeted the real estate agent, who glided in through the back screened porch wearing a Lily Pulitzer dress, Barbara Bush-style oversized pearls, and the largest diamond studs Ross had ever seen. "Nice to see you."

"Lovely to see you!" Genevieve air-kissed with Gaby. "And look at how positively *glowing* you are!" She turned to Tara. "And precious Tara —hellooo, little kitten! And good morning, Ross. How are you?" she trilled.

Ross mumbled something unintelligible into her mug of coffee. Other than their one visit in her bedroom, Xander continued to honor her directive to leave her alone and had remained incommunicado. Ross had tossed and turned all night, wondering if she should just go to the cottage and talk to him. But to what end? It wasn't going to change things. She was going to Manhattan. As the saying went, resistance was futile.

When the phone rang at seven thirty a.m., with Genevieve warbling that she had *an amazing offer* on the farmhouse and she *simply had to share it* with Gaby and Ross as Mrs. Waldheim's proxies while she was away, Ross grumbled her assent and called her sister. Gaby, as a mother of young children, was already awake, and made it into the kitchen, with Tara in tow, ahead of Ross. In fact, she had coffee brewing before Ross could fully open her eyes.

With the deepest, undying gratitude of the caffeine-needy, Ross had accepted the mug, mumbling "I'm liking this détente."

And now Genevieve, who apparently woke perky and stunning, was sitting at the table yammering breathless babble at them. Ross's ears were still full of morning cotton but perked at one word. "What about Xander?"

"Yes," Genevieve breathed, also seizing on the name. "As I was saying, normally he'd be here too, since Mrs. Waldheim made it clear she wanted him involved in any offers presented, as she values his eye as an artisan and his opinion as a businessman."

There it was—the artisan adoration again. Ross and Gaby avoided eye contact. Ross wasn't sure she could pull off the hiccup excuse again. She stuffed her face into the mug, taking a long sip, praying her sister wouldn't start up.

"However, being that this offer *directly* involves him, *ethically* I couldn't have him at the table here." Genevieve waved her French-manicured hands in dramatic supplication.

Both sisters sat a little straighter. Ross put down her mug. "Pardon?"

Tara, playing with a set of wooden spoons on the floor, parroted her aunt. "Pardon?"

"Yes," Genevieve breathed again. "Alexander has put in an offer on the farmhouse, including all the property, except of course what you own, Mrs. Monroe."

"He did what?" Ross blurted, aware she was gripping her mug entirely too tightly.

"He did what?" chimed Tara.

Gaby shushed Tara as the sisters' eyes met over the table.

"And don't say 'yes' again," Ross growled.

Startled, Genevieve opened her mouth to begin, and then seemed stuck.

Smoothly, Gaby stepped in. "Sorry. She's not a morning person." Gaby made wide, motherly warning eyes at Ross, who, chastened, took a repentant sip of coffee.

Somewhat recovered, Genevieve tried again. "Alexander is very taken with this property, and particularly the farmhouse. He received an offer for a full-time professorship at the University of Virginia—Go, Cavaliers!—and has been looking for a place to buy." Genevieve tittered. "He told me that when we did the walkthrough, he realized that he'd found what he's been looking for. Isn't that just magical?"

"Magical," intoned Ross, sarcasm dancing on her tongue. "Go on."

"Yes," Genevieve began, and then clearly realizing she'd said it again, hastily continued, without looking at Ross. "He mentioned something to Mrs. Waldheim, who was most receptive. But she wanted me to work out the specifics with Alexander and then present them to you both without her if she was still away. If you are amenable, then I am to let her know."

"Sweet merciful mother of Elvis," Gaby breathed.

"Pardon?" Genevieve looked confused.

"Pardon?" Tara parroted.

Gaby's awkward laugh at Tara's interjection did nothing to break the rising tension in the kitchen, or in Ross's stomach. "Sorry," her sister offered with a small shrug. "Trying not to curse in front of..." She pointed to Tara. "For obvious reasons."

Gaby darted a worry-infused glance at Ross, and probably rightfully so. If Ross's eyes could shoot lasers, Bougie Barbie would be blasted.

Ross smirked at the visual.

"Yes." Genevieve nodded and then blushed, again avoiding looking at Ross, thus missing her dramatic eye roll.

Jesus. Did this woman get paid by the 'yes'?

"I have the details of the offer here. It's most generous. In fact, I'd say far beyond what Mrs. Waldheim would get on the open market."

"How nice for you," snapped Ross. "Fatty commission."

"Well, ah, yes," Genevieve gulped past *the word*, "but this was Alexander's doing, really. Would you like to see the offer?" She slid the paperwork forward.

Ross sat with her arms folded across her chest, a scowl creeping across her face.

Once again, it was Gaby who smoothed things. "Genevieve, thank you so much for your hard work on this and for bringing the paperwork by this morning. It's quite...exciting. I'm sure you can understand that my sister and I will need some time to review this alone and discuss it."

"As your agent, I can help you understand and evaluate—"

"And we really appreciate that generous offer of your expertise and talent. We know where to find you and we will call you if we need you. But right now, we just need some time to think this through. After all, this is our childhood home in so many ways. It's quite emotional. Would you mind excusing us to evaluate this privately? And then, of course, we'll contact you."

Gaby wrapped the awkward meeting as she ushered Genevieve out the door, complete with farewells, another air kiss, and then an audible click of the screen door closing firmly.

Ross looked at her sister in admiration. "Girl...you are gooood."

"Thank you."

"Now what the fu—" Ross remembered Tara and caught herself. "What was he thinking? And, more to the point, why the fu—this not cursing is *hard*—why wouldn't he say anything to me?"

"Hanging out with you is like riding a bike. You never forget the sharp edge of that tongue—even censored for little pitchers with big ears. I take it you're not pleased with the idea of the offer."

"Has he said anything to you about this?"

Gaby held up her hands in innocence. "Not a word."

"Chickenshit gobshite asshat."

"Ross!" Gaby quickly put her hands over Tara's ears.

"Sorry!" Ross winced.

Tara didn't seem to have noticed. She was reabsorbed in the spoons and seemed to have abandoned her earlier parroting.

"Hmm. All that?"

"And more. It's just all I could come up with on one cup of coffee."

"You want another cup of coffee and then we'll review this?" Gaby waved the papers.

"No. I want to chug another cup, and then I'm going to march over there and chew him a new...you-know-what-hole."

The front door of the cottage was open. As Ross peered through the screen, a vision of breathy Genevieve crossed her mind—*Ding dong!*—and her blood heated with fresh anger that had only just slightly cooled on the walk over. Ross strode into the room, the screen door slamming behind her.

Xander startled, half standing up at the table where clearly he'd been settling in to work on his laptop. "Jesus, Ross. You scared the shit out of me."

Xander flopped back in the chair and ran a hand through damp hair. Ross tried not to notice his shirtless chest. It looked as though he was fresh from the shower. He was wearing athletic shorts, a pair of reading glasses...and nothing much else. His long legs were stretched under the table, the hair on them bleached blond from the summer sun. She could smell his spicy body wash.

He quickly went from startled to on alert. "What brings you charging into my place this morning?"

Ross swallowed past her dry mouth and beating heart. She

endeavored to look away from his bare chest, eyes fixing on a T-shirt draped over the chair where she usually sat.

He followed her gaze, flushing a bit. Grabbing it, he pulled it over his head. "I was just out of the shower and got caught up in doing class prep. Guess I got distracted and forgot to get dressed the rest of the way."

Ross looked around. "Where's Petey?"

"Over at the Monroes' house. He and Kingsley and Nick were walking Laverne. Ted's at work. Gaby has a sitter over for a while because she told me she has an interior decorating client to meet up with later this morning. Wait—I thought Gaby and Tara were coming over to see you this morning?"

Ross fastened a skeptical glare on Xander. "Indeed they were. Now we're finished. And do you know why Gaby needed to come over?"

Xander looked wary. "Should I?"

"Let's just say we had a visitor come to see us. One Genevieve St. James." Ross let it hang for a beat, holding him with her eyes. "Why wouldn't you tell me yourself about your offer on the farmhouse, Xander?"

He stood and poured himself a cup of coffee. "Care for one?"

Ross gave a small shake of her head.

Xander took a long sip, watching her over the rim of the "Best Dad" mug featuring a picture of a much-younger Petey.

Ross had reached the end of her fuse and her temper was about to blow. She let out a long, frustrated exhalation through her nose. "You know what? Never mind. I don't need to know. I don't know why I wasted my time coming over here. Gobshite chickenshit," she muttered and turned on her heel, reaching for the handle. "Oh...and congrats on the full professorship."

"Ross."

It was the tenor of his voice that stopped her in her tracks. Not angry. Not pleading. Just...a subterranean note of regret.

"For the record, I was going to tell you—about the job and about the offer on the farmhouse—the last time we were together over here. But when we ended things how we did, it just struck me as bad timing to talk about my professorship. And I thought, given everything, maybe it would be better to treat the offer like a business transaction. Through Genevieve. I thought you'd prefer that, given...um, how things are. With us. I didn't know that was happening this morning. I thought she was going to wait until tomorrow. At least, that was the plan." He looked at his phone. "Oh."

"Oh?" Ross raised an eyebrow.

"I missed a couple calls and texts from Gen. She went out of town for a couple days. I guess she got back early and wanted to get a hop on moving the offer along. I haven't really looked at my messages in a bit. I've sort of been avoiding my phone."

Ross, who had spent most of her adult life holding onto anger like it was an art form, wavered and fought against it. "I'm not buying that, Xander. You know what I think of *Gen*," Ross breathed her name in mocking imitation. "Why would I prefer to hear about the possible sale of my grandmother's home to my friend from that ridiculous woman?"

"Don't you mean to your *former summer deal*? I thought we couldn't be friends."

"You see this...this right here...is exactly why I don't do relationships. Too damn much drama. I relaxed things with you and— boom—now we've got ourselves a little drama-fest going on. And then I end up with friggin' Lily Pulitzer in my kitchen this morning."

"You told me to leave you alone!" Xan was incredulous. "I was honoring that. I know you don't care for Genevieve, but she is the listing agent and I thought this was the more professional way to go." He shook his head and then looked down.

Ross frowned at him. "And now you can't even be present with me. What's on your phone that's so damn important?"

"I also just missed two calls from your sister. And one from Ted."

The blood drained from her head and Ross swayed, lightheaded. "Oh my God. Petey? The baby? Call her. I left my phone at the house."

Xan had already tapped on Gaby's number. "Hers goes to voicemail. I'm calling him."

Ross stood frozen, her hand on the door handle, unsure whether to run to the farmhouse or the Monroes'. She watched Xander, and could hear her brother-in-law pick up, but couldn't make out the words. Then Xander's face drained of color.

"OK. Where is she now?...Oh no...oh my God...We'll be at the farmhouse in two minutes."

Ross was going to throw up. Every hair on her body stood at attention. "Tell me," she whispered urgently. "Is it Petey or the baby?"

"Neither. It's Hon. We need to get to the farmhouse. Now."

Chapter Fifty-Nine

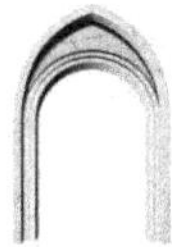

Ross

"Gaby? Gaby!" Ross barreled through the front door. "Where are you?"

"In here."

Ross and Xander followed the sound to Hon's bedroom, where they found Gaby sitting on the overstuffed reading chair by the French doors. Gaby was holding a picture of a young Hon, sobbing. Ross knelt in front of her. "Tell me."

"Aunt Francesca called, just a couple minutes after you left. Hon—Hon passed away last night. When she didn't get up for breakfast, Francesca went in to check on her. She—it was a heart attack. They said it was peaceful. In her sleep. Oh, Ross. She's gone. Hon's gone."

Ross struggled to pull air into her lungs.

"I don't understand," she wheezed. "She seemed so healthy."

"Aunt Fr-rancesca said she had some shortness of breath early in the trip and some pain in her shoulder and neck, but she thought it was from sleeping funny in a different b-bed." Gaby closed her eyes and wept. "We should have seen it, Ross. *I* should have seen it."

Ross leaned in and gathered her sister into her arms. Tears that refused to form stung the back of her eyes. "It's OK, Gaby. We didn't know. It's OK."

Chapter Sixty

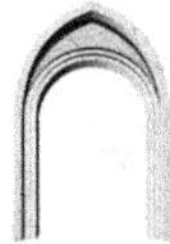

Ross

The service was beautiful. They held it on July fourteenth, two days before the anniversary of Ivy and Adam's deaths. The symmetry of the occasion was wrenching, but both sisters were in firm agreement the funeral could not be on July sixteenth.

At the gravesite—the first time Ross had been there since the interment of Ivy and Adam—Tiercy sat next to Ross and gripped her hand. Gaby sat on the other side, squeezing just as hard. Ross found herself marveling at the surrealism of the entire day—two decades since her parents' funerals. Around her she could see people crying. Her great-aunt. Her sister. Tiercy. Even Ted. Yet, she was numb.

Across from her, Xander watched, that small frown between his brows. He looked handsome in a dark suit. Petey was next to him, also bedecked in a suit, sniffling back tears. That alone should have sent a bolt to her withered heart.

And yet, Ross just sat there, shellshocked. She desperately wanted to weep. Unlike those many years ago, there was nothing to hold her back. Nothing but her own defective self. What was wrong with her that she couldn't perform this simple, universal act of grief?

She heard the Episcopal priest say "Amen" and then invite her, Francesca, and Gaby to each put a rose on the coffin. Gaby emitted a small sob as she lay hers, resting a hand next to it, and choking out, "I love you."

Ross, too, placed her hand on the coffin, startled by the incongruous warmth from the summer sun. "I love you, Hon," she whispered.

The funeral reception was at the Monroes' house. Ross insisted that it not be held at the farmhouse. She could barely process that Hon was gone. She kept expecting her to walk around the corner, her signature powdery scent announcing her presence before her footfall and voice.

"No way. I'm not allowing the teeming hordes to traipse through here," she'd declared. Ross couldn't stomach the thought of the hushed, sorrowful goodbyes in her grandmother's house of love. It was unfathomable.

The sisters made it through the day. When it was over, Gaby and Tiercy collapsed on the overstuffed couch in the living room, kicking off their shoes. Ross perched on the edge of it in solidarity.

"Oh sweet William Shatner," groaned Gaby in relief. "Blessed shoeless relief."

"Listen, Shoeless Joe, your feet stink. Move them the other way." Ross squirmed away as Gaby waggled her sweaty feet at her sister. "By the way...*sweet William Shatner*?"

"You know I've really had to watch my mouth around Tara. It just came out."

"Yes!" hollered Tiercy. "Same here with Jemma. She repeats everything." The women clinked their water glasses in motherly solidarity.

Gaby smiled over at Ross. Both sisters had matching dark circles under their eyes that no concealer could cover. "Ross, we've barely had a minute to talk. When are you heading home?"

Home. Where the hell was that?

With a dramatic grimace, Ross grabbed her sister's foot and began to knead it—a skill she learned when Tiercy was pregnant with Jemma and needed the relief after standing all day teaching. Gaby groaned in ecstasy.

"Seeing as how the paperwork is underway for the sale of the farmhouse, there really isn't a need for me to stay much longer. I thought I'd finish the last bit of sorting of Hon's stuff and leave in a couple days. I'll head to Baltimore, spend some time with Tierce and pack up the last of my things at my place, then head to Manhattan."

"I know you have to go. And I'm happy for you. But I feel like I just got you back and now I have to say goodbye." Gaby's eyes watered.

Ross gave one of her toes a gentle tug. "You're not losing me. We have things to settle with the estate. I'll be back. I promise I won't be a stranger. It won't be like...before."

Tiercy sighed, a small smile on her face. "Our little trio is back together. I love you both so much. But, Ross, I'm going to love you a lot less if you don't start rubbing my feet. I'm pregnant too, you know."

"Pregnant women. High maintenance," Ross joked as she switched pairs of feet to rub, ignoring her sister's fake pout.

CHAPTER SIXTY-ONE

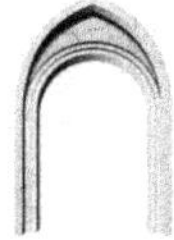

Ross

Three days later, Ross was placing the last of her things in her suitcase. Leaning into it, she tried the zipper, but it wouldn't close.

"Fuck. Too full. Too much crap. Ha. Too much baggage," Ross muttered, as she looked around the room. Had it really only been five-and-a-half weeks?

"Onward, Beaufort," she commanded, unpacking her suitcase to rearrange it, this time pulling out a few things from the bottom that had been in there since her arrival—a couple pairs of jeans and a very old, tattered but still serviceable, University of Maryland sweatshirt that she'd brought in case of cooler evenings.

A white piece of paper caught her eye. The edge of something was sticking out from under the nylon lining of the suitcase. Curious, she pulled it free and saw Hon's distinct Catholic school penmanship, slightly shaky with age but still classically beautiful.

"What the ever-loving fuck?"

Ross held the envelope with trembling hands. She couldn't open it here. In fact, she could barely breathe. The room suddenly felt suffocating. She turned and fled, running downstairs, out the door, and sprinted across the property, heading toward the barn. Seeing the tree, with its aging treehouse that she'd loved so much as a little girl, she stopped, panting, and slid down against it, feeling the scratch of bark against her back.

She lifted the envelope to her nose and sniffed, desperately seeking a trace of Hon's powdery fragrance. Ross's heart ached with fresh loss. The note smelled only of her luggage.

Carefully, she opened the seal.

Ross Ellen,

Surprise! Remember when you, Gaby, and Tiercy went to summer camp and your mom and I wrote you all those notes and hid them?

I thought I'd write a surprise note for you to find as you unpack at your new place. I tried to hide it well. If you don't find it, I'll have to fess up at some point and give you a clue! LOL, as the kids write these days.

I know you are feeling troubled by your move to Manhattan. You haven't said anything about it specifically, but your countenance reveals so much to me. In that way, like so many, you are so much like my beloved Ivy.

Thank you for coming to the farmhouse. It was hard on you, but I think you also had some good times. As I write this, I am preparing to leave for my trip with Frannie, and I mean to have a word with you about your sister when I return. Before then, I just want to say this: Talk to her and really listen. Then forgive her. Forgive yourself. And love her. A sister is a beautiful thing. You must treasure her.

I'm already running out of space on this notecard, but I also want to say something about Alexander. You know your own heart, Ross Ellen. And I would never presume to tell an adult what to do. But the way you and Alexander are together reminds me so much of Frederick and me. I see how he looks at you, and I watch you with him. There's something there, Ross Ellen—something special and unique.

You have some very deep wounds in your heart and you are afraid to let yourself love because you are afraid to lose the people you love. But I promise you, love is worth it. It's always worth it. And that kind of love lives in your heart forever. You just need to be brave enough to let it in.

I love you, Ross Ellen. More than I have words to convey. Your grandfather was the writer. He'd do this much better. Just know that you are my precious baby granddaughter. Now wrap your arms around yourself and give a great big squeeze. That's a hug from me until I see you again.

Hon

Chapter Sixty-Two

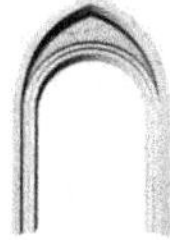

XANDER

He heard it as he was heading toward the barn. What was that sound? He paused and listened intently, and then heard it again. Shock froze him to the marrow and then catalyzed him. He knew that sound...and the person making it.

He took off toward the barn.

That's where he found her, sitting under her special tree, arms doubled around herself, her mouth open in a rictus of grief. He rushed to her side and gathered her into his arms as sobs wracked her body. She was crying so hard, she couldn't form words. He didn't try to speak or comfort her with words of his own. He knew there was nothing he could say at this moment. Instead, he held her until the worst of her tears were spent.

CHAPTER SIXTY-THREE

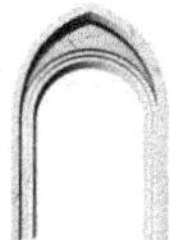

Ross

Slowly, ever so slowly, her torrent of sobs subsided to a steady downpour, Hon's words and her tears lancing an emotional wound that had festered inside her for years. Xander shifted and knelt before her, wiping her face with the edge of his shirt. He emitted a small whimper of sympathy as he touched her swollen eyelids.

"Ross, sweetheart, please stop crying. You're going to make yourself sick."

She sniffled and aimed for humor, still raw from her shocking crying jag. "I told you once I started, I wouldn't stop. Now your shirt is soaked."

"And I don't mind at all." Xander sat back and shifted her against him with a tenderness that made her shattered heart ache harder. "Oh, Ross. My Principessa."

"It was her time, Xan. I just wish I had a chance to say g-goodbye." She choked and sobbed, tasting the foreign tang of tear-salt on her lips. "I was fine. And then I found this note from her." She motioned to the paper in her hands. "I'd let you read it, but it's...private."

Xan nodded, maple eyes shining with sympathy and unshed tears.

"How did you know I was here?"

"I didn't. I've been looking for you everywhere. I didn't want you to leave without saying goodbye. I came this way on a hunch...and that's when I heard you."

Ross shifted away, avoiding his gaze. They hadn't talked at all in the three days since the funeral. Part of Ross was still angry about how she learned of his farmhouse offer, but the bigger reason was she knew she had to find the strength to drive away and start anew—even though that meant no Xander, no Petey.

"I went to the farmhouse first. I actually climbed up the trellis and went in through your window again. I thought it would be—" Xan shrugged, trying for a smile, but Ross could see the disquiet in his eyes.

"You have the frownie line." Ross fought the desire to press her lips there.

He smiled, the dimples appearing. "I need to say something to you and if I don't now..." He pinched his thumb and forefinger on the bridge of his nose. When he finally spoke, his voice was strained, but soft. "Ross, I spent many years grieving the loss of my marriage. But it wasn't until recently that I truly realized what I didn't have with Aubrey. Do you have any idea what that is? I told you the other night you had a gift to give Gaby and yourself. But you've also given me a gift. You've shown me how love should be. It's all the things that have come so easily and so naturally with you, from that first night we were together last August, after the rehearsal dinner." He ran his thumb in circles over the palm of her hand.

"I know our summer deal is over, Ross, but I'm officially breaking one of the rules anyway. I'm so deeply, wildly, completely in love with you. I wanted to tell you that night in the cottage, but I was a coward. My original plan had been to tell you I needed to end the summer deal early. Not because our time was up, but because I had broken one of our rules and fallen in love with you. I *love you*, Ross." He leaned in and kissed her, softly, and then deeper.

Ross swayed and held onto him. No man had ever said those words to her.

As the kiss ended, he tipped her chin so their eyes met. "What's more, I believe you're in love with me too."

Ross watched him, transfixed. He was a conjure man—casting a spell with his eyes, his deep voice, with everything about him that upended the things about herself that Ross had always thought to be true. She had heard of people's entire lives flashing before their eyes in the nanoseconds before a major accident. Had even wondered in very dark moments if it had happened to her own parents. It turned out it could also happen in the nanoseconds following revelations that shake you to the core.

She leaned back, shaking her head a tiny fraction, trying to clear it and needing the physical distance from Xander's powerful gravitational pull.

"I-I can't do this," she whispered, fully aware that Hon was probably frowning down on her from her perch in heaven for ignoring her words about Xan in the letter.

But too much had changed. She'd changed. Everything she thought was true had been turned upside down. She couldn't trust herself to think straight where Xander was concerned. Not right now.

"I have a life I need to get back to. For all that Virginia feels like home, I-I can't be here. I need to make a new life for myself. In New York. Xan, I know this—what we have—feels amazing now. But, I promise you, I have no idea how to be in a relationship, especially a long-distance one. We'd crack under the pressure, and you'd just end up hating me. It would hurt Petey. And I don't think I could bear that." She reached a conciliatory hand out at him, and then let it drop.

"Ross, please. I'm shredded here. I know we can figure this out." Xander pleaded with both words and those beautiful brown eyes.

"No, Xander. I just...can't."

In that moment, Ross experienced a very new and unwanted kind of pain—hurting someone so deeply you knew you'd never get another chance to fix it.

"Hey," she finally whispered. "I'll be back in the area periodically to visit Gaby. I'll come see you and Petey."

"Please...don't."

And without a glance back at her, he stood and walked away.

CHAPTER SIXTY-FOUR

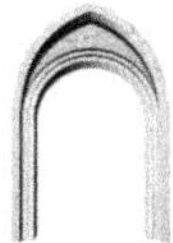

Ross

Ted closed the trunk with a thud. "Woman, I don't know what you have in that suitcase, but I'm pretty sure I need hernia surgery now."

Ross laughed. "Thanks for the assist, Moo-*Ted*." She gave him a hug and a kiss on the cheek.

Now that matters of the past were aired, things had thawed with her brother-in-law to a point of affection. He'd apologized for things he'd said to her over the years, especially this summer. And she did as well. There was healing to be done, and trust to be built, but they'd extended tenuous olive branches during her time in Virginia, and that was progress.

Gaby pulled her in close. "I love you...Skipper."

Ross chuckled in her sister's ear. "I haven't heard that one in ages... Barbie. Perhaps we should relegate that one to the memory banks."

"Are you going to go over to say goodbye to Xander and Petey?"

"I saw Petey yesterday with Kingsley and said my goodbyes to him then. I'm gonna miss him so much." Ross closed her eyes against a wave of sadness and loss. "He's a special one. Ten dollars says he grows up to marry her."

"Not if Jemma has anything to say about it," Gaby laughed.

"Oohh, love triangle!"

"But no Xander?" Gaby's eyes softened.

"No. We—uh—we already said goodbye."

"There's more to that story."

Ross nodded, digging her nails into her hands against the unrelenting sadness. "There is, but I can't talk about it right now. What I *can* say is how much I love you."

"I love you, too." The sisters wrapped their arms around each other and held tight. "I think Hon would be happy and proud of us."

"Me too." Ross wiped small tears from the corners of her eyes.

"Now, go take Manhattan by storm!"

Ross saluted as she climbed in the car. Driving down the lane, she watched her sister in the rearview mirror, the farmhouse becoming smaller and smaller. So much like that other summer. But this time, she knew she'd be back.

Chapter Sixty-Five

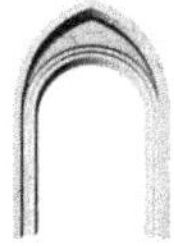

XANDER

As Ross turned onto the main road, Xander moved toward Gaby from the hidden spot where he'd been watching her departure.

"I never took you for a coward, Alexander Grace."

"I never took me for one either. But this isn't cowardice. This is fool me once, shame on you. Fool me twice, shame on me."

At Gaby's perplexed look, he continued, "I won't make the same mistake twice. I persuaded Aubrey to be something she wasn't, to make a life she didn't really want. In the end, she was miserable, and I was miserable. I won't do that again. Not to Petey. Not to Ross. Not to me."

"Maybe." Gaby pinned her blue eyes on Xander. "But Ross isn't Aubrey. And I think you're both just being chickenshit. Lick your wounds. And then fight for her. Or maybe I'll yell at her and tell her to fight for you. Either way, you're both lying to yourselves right now, and if we've learned anything these past couple weeks, it's the value of telling the truth."

Gaby went up on tiptoes and kissed him on the cheek. "Love you, Xander. Come over for dinner tonight."

CHAPTER SIXTY-SIX

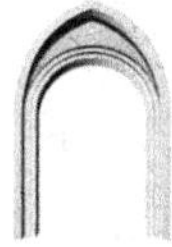

XANDER

Xander stood in the quiet of the farmhouse kitchen. The calendar read October, but it was the gold and red trees that truly reflected the date.

As he looked out the window, he was captivated by the autumnal hues. It was Friday, and he didn't have to teach. Petey was in school, and Xander should have been spending the day grading. But Gaby had messaged him earlier in the week that Ross was coming into Virginia from New York—her first visit since July—to settle the estate. She'd stay at the farmhouse one last time. Then, Xander would finally close on the farmhouse and he and Petey could move in. And that would allow him to initiate his plan to win Ross back.

He texted Gaby from his iPhone.

XANDER

> All set here. I've prepped the owner's suite and made sure there's coffee and cream. I have everything ready for when Ross arrives later today.

His fingers had stalled briefly before he typed Ross' name.

Gaby's words to him from the summer echoed in his mind. *I never took you for a coward, Alexander Grace.*

And yet he had been. He'd allowed Ross to drive away. He had to for the sake of his heart and Petey's.

In tacit agreement, neither he nor Ross had contacted each other. The start of the academic year was busy for both Xan and Petey, and he was grateful for the redeployment of his son's nanny to ease some of the burden of single fatherhood, especially with Leah gone.

Xan pressed a hand to his chest against the grief. In so many ways, it was as if he'd lost a member of his own family.

And yet, most often, his grief centered on the loss of another green-eyed woman. He'd catch himself thinking of Ross dozens of times a day. Those emerald eyes. That laugh. The feel of her tears as he wiped them on that last morning.

Gaby had hounded him to go to New York and fight for her. Every time he wavered, he imagined her with Gideon O'Grady, laughing over dinner at a Manhattan restaurant, and then him taking her to bed. And if that visceral image weren't enough to shake him and tear him up, the easily accessed memory of Aubrey abandoning him and Petey was sufficient. He wouldn't make the same mistake twice.

Still, in the quiet hours, when he was most honest with himself, he knew his own heart. And one early September day, with the prescience of youth, Petey spurred him to action. They were eating dinner in the cottage, reviewing the latest construction designs for the farmhouse on Xander's laptop.

"Daddy," Petey had said. "I've been thinking."

"About what, Slugger?"

Petey beamed at the use of his preferred nickname. "I like all this a lot. And it would be cool to live here. But it's just a house. I think we should move to New York and be with Ross. Then you won't be sad anymore. And we can be a family."

Xander's jaw had dropped. He had never been so utterly poleaxed. "But...Petey—it's not that simple. My job. Your school. Friends. And I don't think that's what Ross wants, buddy."

"Daddy, you can get a new job. I can go to a new school. But there's only one Ross. And we love her. And she loves us."

A huge smile spread across Xander's face as a leaden weight lifted off his chest. His son had distilled it perfectly. There is only one Ross. And they loved her.

And with that, he set about fighting for his woman.

Standing in the kitchen, with Ross finally on her way to Virginia, he remembered his favorite morning from July. Softly, he began singing. "*Nessun dorma, nessun dorma. Tu pure, o Principessa...*" The hairs on the back of his neck stood up.

Slowly, he turned. There, wearing a pair of jeans, a long-sleeve T-shirt, a North Face nylon vest, and a cautious smile, was Ross.

"What the—?"

"Ever-loving fuck am I doing here?" Ross finished softly.

Xander, heart racing at both her earlier-than-expected arrival and the force of her beauty, laughed despite himself at the symmetry of her joke.

"I get that a lot," she added, continuing their dialogue from the beginning of the summer.

"Well played." Slowly he scanned her. She was gorgeous. New York clearly agreed with her. Her face glowed. Her eyes seemed greener. Her hair had a luster to it that made him want to reach out and rub it between his fingers, as he'd done many times in bed with her. "You're early."

"Aren't you going to say anything else? Welcome back? Good to see you?" Ross's voice was soft, unsure. She waited, like a deer alerted in caution before potential danger. He watched the small, graceful movement of her neck as she swallowed. "How about if I start, by apologizing for how I left. I was a confused ball of emotions—what with the revelations about Gaby and the night my parents died, Hon's death, and then you breaking the summer deal rules. And like a coward,

I just...ran away from it. I am so sorry, Xander. I know I hurt you. And you deserved so much more from me."

Ross gently wrung her hands. As she shifted her weight between legs, Xander wondered if she realized she was consciously stopping her leg from bouncing. His heart, already healing at the site of her, knitted together a bit more at her nervous tell.

Nerves are good. If she's nervous, it's because she cares.

Ross let out a breath that puffed her cheeks, motioning to him. "Now you go."

Now it was his turn to sigh. "I don't know what to say." He gave a low chuckle, shaking his head. He didn't know how it was possible to feel so many things at once, each one vying for dominance. Talk about a confused ball of emotions. "I mean, I know what I *want* to say. Christ, I've been rehearsing it for weeks. Petey's been helping. And now I'm all discombobulated." He laughed ruefully again, noting the confusion in those moss green eyes he'd dreamed about for weeks.

He exhaled, rubbing his hand down his face. "I'm royally screwing this up. Can you leave and walk back in so I get a do-over?" Xander squeezed the back of his neck, offering a sheepish—and he hoped conciliatory—grin.

"Have you been sniffing paint fumes?"

Xander hung his head and laughed. "No. It's just, you're a couple hours early, and I thought I'd have time to prepare myself. I have so much I want to say to you."

"Me too. Xander, I—"

"No, me first. *Please.* Ross, Petey said something to me back in September. And it took a six-year-old to make a grown man realize his priorities. He told me I could get a new job in New York, and he could find a new school, but there is only one you. And we love you. I love you, Ross."

She stood frozen.

"Ross?" he prompted at her continued silence. "We used to be better at this conversation thing."

"You—you can't move to New York."

Xander's heart crashed into his stomach. *No. No, no, no. This isn't how this is supposed to go down.*

Ross halted his catastrophizing, reaching out a shaking hand to him. "You can't move to New York because I'm *leaving* New York."

Xander startled. "Where are you going?"

"Here," she said.

"Here?" He blinked several times, as if that would clear his obviously malfunctioning ears.

She hurriedly continued, "I quit my new job. I'm back with my old company. I left New York."

"Really?" Xander's heart tried to resume a normal cadence.

She nodded. "It—it wasn't for me. I knew it almost right away. I walked into that cold Upper West Side apartment, and I—I felt hollow. Within the month, I began negotiating with my new company to allow me to work from somewhere else, but they needed a New York-based editor. And that's not me.

"As it turns out, my former company wanted me back. Honor Wheatley's memoir isn't quite finished, and she asked specifically for me to help. A bridge you don't burn is a bridge you can cross again, and I'd stayed in close contact. I negotiated a raise and I can work from home, with only the occasional trip to Manhattan, which is how I did it before. I'm not managing my own division, but it's a good trade-off. The senior editor over that division is retiring in a couple years, and then it will be mine."

"I'm happy for you, Ross. Congratulations."

Xander tried to process what he was hearing, and not fixate that she hadn't told him she loved him too. Perhaps she truly had closed the door and he'd missed his opportunity with this glorious woman.

"Xan," she continued. "Th-there's more. I know you've been waiting for Gaby and me to settle the estate so you can purchase the farmhouse. I—uh—I wanted you to know that you aren't going to be able to buy it."

"What?" Xan's jaw dropped. It was like the room tilted a little under his feet. "Why, Ross? Is it because we—because I—"

"You aren't going to be able to buy it because I'm buying out Gaby's share and I'm going to live here."

Xander frowned. "I don't understand."

She offered him a tentative smile. "There's a reason. One truly excellent reason. If you just let me explain." She took a shaky breath. "This is my home. You were the one who helped me realize it. But... there's more. I have something else to tell you. I'm pregnant." The last part came out barely more than a whisper. "We're pregnant, Xander."

He goggled at her. "You're preg—? But I thought you couldn't—" Xander dropped to the chair in shock. "How? When?"

"Every GYN I've ever had has told me it is next to impossible for me to get pregnant." When Xander couldn't manage to form words, she continued, "About a month or so before I came to Virginia, I had a procedure, a laparoscopy, for fibroids. It comes with my 'feminine condition.' I guess they roto-rootered me pretty well. And they gave me some antibiotics after the procedure to prevent infection. I had a period about a week before I arrived. I kept taking my pills. All was normal. And you and I did our thing. A lot."

Ross cocked an ironic eyebrow. *Yes, they certainly had done their thing...a lot.*

"And then I left. It wasn't until about three weeks ago when I realized I hadn't had my period since the beginning of June. It must have happened early on in—in our summer deal. I'm almost four months pregnant."

He stood, stunned. "You just found out three weeks ago and you're almost four months along? How? I mean, you really didn't know?"

"Not a clue. I had some mild symptoms, but I thought it was grief, and...well...homesickness. I was caught up in my new job and my personal misery, trying to reconcile the loss of Hon...and of you and Petey. And I've never been regular, so it's not unusual to miss a couple months." Ross threw her hands in the air. "Jesus, Xan, it's not like I've been pregnant before! And I sure as hell didn't even remotely consider it a possibility."

She took a deep drink from her water thermos, then shook her head and laughed. "Coincidentally, the same thing happened to Tiercy with Jemma. I just didn't suspect. And then when I did, I went to the doctor. I didn't believe him. I kept making him repeat it."

"Does she know? Tiercy?"

"No. I haven't told anyone."

He scanned her belly, which looked flat in her jeans. Ross put a hand there. "The baby's there. I promise." She reached into her purse and pulled out a filmy piece of paper. "I have a picture. Do you want to see her?"

"*Her*? It's a girl?"

"It's a girl."

Wordlessly, Xan reached for the scan film and examined it. He traced the picture with his finger, wonderment on his face. A tear fell down his cheek, which he brushed away. Then, without touching Ross, he handed the picture back to her.

She shook her head, a soft smile on her beautiful face. "No. You keep it. That one's for you. I have another."

"What do you want, Ross?" Xander's voice was strained and the ultrasound picture shook in his hand.

"I need to sit. My legs are shaking."

Xander reached over and pulled out the chair for her, holding it steady as she sank into it with a shaky sigh. His own legs still wobbly, he plopped in the chair diagonal to hers, shifting so he could scan the beautiful face of the woman who had etched herself into his tattered heart. And he waited, hope pulsing in his veins.

"What I wouldn't kill for a drink. I miss it. And coffee. God, I miss coffee. It's only been three weeks. How do women do this?"

"You're stalling."

"I know. I even practiced the whole drive down. This is fucking *hard*. Oops. Need to watch my mouth. She has teeny-tiny little ears now."

Ross puffed out her cheeks. "OK. Here goes. When the doctor told me I was pregnant, there was a part of me that just couldn't believe him. He even came around and sat with me. He thought I was going to faint. I thought I was, too." Ross smiled at the memory. "You know what he told me? He said this baby is a rarity. He's been in practice for thirty years, and he's seen this maybe a half-dozen times max. She's a tiny, rare little miracle, who fought her way into my bumpy, awful uterus against the odds.

"I left the appointment in a daze and went to a nearby park. It was the strangest sensation to realize—to realize that...I'm not alone. I sat there for hours, and I kept coming back, again and again, to the notion that this little baby was a gift from my parents and Hon to let me know I don't have to be alone anymore. And I'm not just talking about the baby. I'm talking about *you*." Ross wailed the last word, putting her face in her hands and sobbing.

Xander reached over and stroked her shoulder, stunned to the core. He waited for her to compose herself. Eventually, she wiped her eyes, sniffled a bit and began again.

"Ever since my parents died, I walled myself off emotionally to everyone except Tiercy and Hon. They were the only people strong enough to bust through my defenses. I've been scared, utterly petrified of losing the people I love. And then when Tiercy lost Luke, it just reinforced it for me. Relationships scare the hell out of me. I blamed it on my hatred of drama, which is partly true. Relationship drama is exhausting. And part of me has enjoyed an unencumbered lifestyle. But it was Hon who made me face my real fear—to let myself love deeply and then lose that love.

"Sh-she wrote me the most beautiful note, and hid it in my suitcase before she l-left. I swear, Xander, I think she knew. The doctor said it was just a massive heart attack and these things happen. She was almost eighty. But I think she knew it was coming."

Ross took a deep swallow of her water. With shaking hands she placed the thermos on the table, almost tipping it over when she caught the edge of the coaster. They each grabbed for it, hands colliding.

Xander's eyes fastened on their hands as a bolt of chemistry sizzled between them. He started to pull back but she held fast to him.

"Xander," she whispered, squeezing his hand.

He slowly lifted his gaze, finding shining green eyes and a tremulous smile.

Ross blew out a long breath.

"I have spent my entire adult life living a lie—the lies I told myself and the things I believed to be true about my sister. I told myself I didn't love the farmhouse, because I couldn't face the pain of it. I told myself I didn't love my sister, because I wasn't brave enough to face her and my own faults that came with it. I convinced myself I d-didn't want kids when I was told I couldn't have any and didn't want to face that hurt. But most of all, I know what my heart felt like when my parents died. I was so empty and alone. My heart was shattered. I told myself I'd never love anyone new. Then, I wouldn't be hurt like that again. I didn't think I could take it.

"Then I told myself I didn't love you. But I did. I do. Xander, I love you so much. More than I even have the proper words to convey. The words don't exist to describe h-how," Ross hiccuped a sob and then continued, her tears making the grassy green of her eyes even more pronounced, "how much much I love you. And I was stupid and cowardly enough to walk away. Run away. But now I'm back, and I love you so much, and I'm scared as fuck! Sorry, baby!"

Ross dropped her head on her arms, weeping.

"Oh my beautiful Principessa." Xander shifted his chair closer, running a soothing hand over her hair and wrapping his other arm around her. It was the closest they'd come to a hug in months. Xan breathed in deeply, inhaling her unique scent. God, he'd missed her.

Ross continued to sob quietly, and Xander's heart ached...and soared at the same time.

She loves me.

Needing to be closer, Xan reached over and eased her onto his lap, rocking her, gently brushing his hand down the back of her hair. This woman—this strong, ballsy, hilarious, glorious woman—had catapulted into his life with steamy, decadent, filthy, mind-blowing sex. And then proceeded to blast her way, albeit unwillingly on both their parts, into his scabbed-over, very cautious heart. The woman who couldn't cry, but who also angrily rejected being called 'cold and unfeeling' by her sister, was now nestled in his lap, soaking his shirt with her tears.

Xander recognized the moment for what it was for Ross—cathartic, releasing, lightening—and held his own swirling emotions and questions at bay, contenting himself with the soothing rightness of having Ross back in his arms.

Eventually, she gathered herself to continue. "While I never said the words, aloud or to myself, I thought it would be emotionally safest for me to live my life as I'd designed it—without the complications of a relationship and without the danger of being hurt again. And then you came along with your frownie line and your dimples and your delicious summer deal, and I realized deep down that maybe I could want all that.

I *did* want it. You were strong enough to bust through all my walls. You weren't afraid of my jagged edges. But it didn't matter, because just when I was figuring that out, you told me you didn't want it."

"Ross, my God. I didn't mean it." He cupped her face, wiping a stray tear with his thumb. "I was scared. You scared me because of all these huge feelings I have for you, and I didn't want to be hurt again. You made it clear you didn't want to commit, and I didn't want another Aubrey situation, forcing you to be something you're not. But in my heart..." he trailed off.

"I'm not Aubrey!"

"I know that. I know," he soothed. "And that's why I bared my heart by the tree that day. And when you turned me down, I knew I would never force you into something you don't want."

"But I did want it. I *do* want it," Ross whispered. "In the park that day, the baby and I made a pact. I told her we were going home. I already had the wheels in motion, but her itty-bitty presence just confirmed the rightness of it." Ross lifted a knowing eyebrow. "I also told her I'd be removing the trellis from outside the upstairs bedroom and I'd have none of her shenanigans as I'd invented them all and she's not getting anything past me. The deal was I'd do all this, but she had to hang in with me and not—not leave me. And she has. She's strong, like her great-grandmother, her grandmother, and her aunt. God," she whispered, "me...a *mother*. Can you imagine?"

"She is strong. Like her mother." The smile that broke across his face reached all the way into his healing heart. *She*. A daughter. His and Ross's daughter.

Ross returned his smile with a teary, wobbly one of her own. "I just kept coming back to one truth—this baby deserves her home. And I deserve mine. I love that Tiercy, Gaby, and I are all going to have children close in age. It's a tiny piece of redemption for the lost time we should have had together, in the form of the next generation. It was so special here growing up, and I want that for her." Ross rested his hand gently on her stomach.

Xander fought to breathe amidst a whirling tide of emotions. Relief at seeing Ross—he finally understood the phrase 'sight for sore eyes.' Shock and amazement at her announcement. *Shit—and holy wow—Ross is pregnant with my baby! I'm going to be a dad again!* And utter, unrestrained joy. *She loved him.*

And then a pulse of fear. "And she's really OK? Are you OK?"

Like a magnet, Xander returned a shaking hand to her flat tummy, tenderly cupping it. His eyes fastened to where his hand rested above their child. God, now that he had her back, a baby growing inside the woman who owned every ounce of him, he couldn't bear the thought of anything happening to either of them.

Xander's overloaded heart thumped. "You're both healthy?"

Ross laughed. "We're both awesome. No troubles whatsoever. Other than"—Ross cringed—"apparently, I'm of 'advanced maternal age.' I told Dr. DeSimone if he ever used that phrase with me again, I'd rip his larynx out of his throat."

Xander buried his face in her hair, chuckling. "I can only imagine." He shifted her to face him and tipped her chin up, looking at the green eyes that captivated him from the first time he met her. "I'll ask you again, Ross Ellen. What do you want?"

Ross traced the small indentations in his cheeks, the vestiges of his dimples. "You. I didn't just break that rule, I annihilated that fucker. Oops. Sorry, baby." They laughed as she clapped a hand over her mouth. Then Ross lifted somber eyes to him. "I'm committing. I'm in this. I'm buying the farmhouse, and I'm having our baby. You and Petey are my home. And I want to make a home—here—with the four of us. I want you, Alexander Grace. All the strings and all the clings. Any relationship drama you want to throw my way. A lifetime deal. If you'll have me."

Xander drew in a long, deep breath, feeling like he was fully breathing for the first time in, well, in his life. "Ross Beaufort, you entranced me from the beginning. But you had my heart from that morning we sat in this kitchen, just like this, after I sang opera to you. I was so in love with you, and too afraid to admit it, to myself most of all."

Taking her face in his hands, Xander trailed soft kisses across her cheeks to her beautiful lips, tasting salt. "You're crying again." He thumbed the tears away, pressing tender kisses under her eyes.

"I know. It's these damn pregnancy hormones. Now that I've started this boo-hoo business, I can't stop. I predicted that shit, by the way. Ooops...sorry again, little one." She held her hands over her belly, as if to muffle the sound.

Xander laughed and kissed the fresh tracks, moving down to her lips, paying special attention to her fuller top lip that he couldn't seem to get off his mind in the dark hours when his body craved hers. Grateful to have her back in his arms—in his life, for good—he pressed his lips to hers and kissed her, gently but thoroughly, infusing it with his unspoken vow:

Mine, Principessa. And I'm yours.

With a small whimper, Ross sank into the embrace and held on tight. He was never letting her go.

Chapter Sixty-Seven

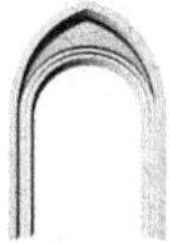

Ross

"Did you really plan to move to New York?" Ross snuggled in deeper against Xander's chest. It felt so very, very right to be there.

"I already had the plans in motion."

"Can you unplan them?" She pulled back and grinned at him.

"Absofuckinglutely."

She covered her belly with her hands again, laughing with a freeness she'd never imagined she'd feel. "Language, dear!" Leaning back, she beseeched him with earnest eyes. "Xander, I do have one request."

"Name it."

"I want to name our baby Leah."

"I wouldn't have it any other way."

Suddenly he leaned back, eyes gleaming. "Hang on. We need to do something. Can you wait here for a minute? I have something I need to get. I'll be just a little bit. Stay there. No. Wait. Can you meet me at your treehouse?"

Several minutes later, surrounded by fall foliage, Ross inhaled the crisp Virginia autumn air as Xander came running toward her, breathless.

"Slow down!" she laughed. "What's the hurry?"

"It's just that I've been fantasizing about doing this. And I would have had it ready, but you were early..." Xander panted, hands on his knees. "God, I need to do more cardio. And now you're here. I really get to do this. In Virginia, where you belong, by your special treehouse."

He went down on one knee, holding up a ring, a diamond in an antique setting that had been her mother's, and her paternal grandmother's before that. Ross put a shaking hand to her mouth.

"Ross Ellen Beaufort, I love you, with all my heart and all my soul. Do you remember when I told you about the beauty of the arch? How two weaknesses become a strength? There is nothing stronger than when two people lean toward each other and join, allowing their weakness to become a source of strength. I'm stronger when I'm with you. Would you do me the honor of leaning on me for the rest of your life, and allowing me to lean on you?"

The sight of Xander, kneeling there in the sun, smiling up at her with such love, holding her mother's ring, tapped a new emotion for Ross—tears of joy. She cradled her hand over her belly and sobbed, and sobbed, and then sobbed some more.

Standing and lifting the edge of his shirt, as he'd done that summer, Xander dried her face. Smiling at her, he remarked dryly, "I never expected that reaction. I had hoped for a yes—"

"Yes!" laughed Ross through her tears of joy. "Yes, I'll marry you! I love you, Alexander Grace.... Gosh, now I'm Drama Ross."

"*Vincero!*" Xander sang, and Ross's heart danced with such happiness she was afraid it would burst out of her chest.

"Beautifully played, Calaf." She hiccupped a tear-filled laugh of joy. Suddenly she stopped, her eyes widening in wonderment. "Oh! Oh..."

"What is it?" Xan froze, alarm blanching his face.

A slow smile spread across Ross's face. "Little butterfly wings."

"Pardon?"

"Our daughter. I think I just felt Leah move."

Xander pulled her close. "I feel like my heart is going to burst with joy." He slid the ring on her finger.

"When did you get this?"

"In September. Gaby had it in the safe in her basement with the rest of your mom's jewelry. She's only mentioned it 4,752 times in the last three months."

"Oh. Subtle," laughed Ross again. "There is one thing that I thought about. I don't want to be Ross Grace. It sounds terrible."

"You thought about that this fast?"

"No, I've thought about it a bit before. Maybe 4,752 times in the last three months," she admitted sheepishly.

"Ross Beaufort-Grace has a nice sound to it."

"That it does." Ross wiped another tear that had fallen down her cheek.

"Crying pregnant lady," Xander teased.

"So cliché." Ross raised her eyebrows in invitation.

"We're quite talented at cliché-ing."

"You know, pregnant women, particularly those in the second trimester, are very horny."

Xander's eyes darkened. One moment she was standing apart from him and in a blink, he'd pulled her into another kiss, twining his tongue around hers, his cock hard against her belly, her arousal growing at an astronomical rate.

"We can go to the cottage. Petey's at school." He skimmed his fingers under her vest and shirt, stopping briefly at her belly, a soft smile on his face. Then he eased his fingers further up and under her bra, seeking and finding the hardened pebbles of her nipples. She gasped and then sighed out a groan as he rubbed and gently tugged the nubs.

"Jesus, Xander..." she panted, pressing against him and drawing him into a carnal kiss of lips and tongues and need. "Don't...stop. They are so sensitive now. Put your mouth on me."

"We need to get to the cottage..." He rubbed his length between her legs, and she pressed back hard, desperate for friction and the heat coming off him as he kissed her and teased her nipples.

"Fuck the cottage." Ross pushed away, ripped her zipper down and threw her vest to the side, then yanked her long-sleeve tee over her head. "I need you now."

"God, you are so fucking beautiful." Xander's hair was tousled from her hands running through it in ecstasy, a sexy flush all over his skin. He pushed her back against the tree, and tugged down the straps of her satiny bra. "Jesus...your nipples..." He sucked one in his mouth, nibbling softly. Then he pulled it deeply and sucked hard, rolling the other nub between his fingers.

"Yes! Xan!" Ross ground against him, reaching for his zipper. "I'm going to fucking come—need you."

"That's it, sweetheart. Take my cock out," he ground out as Ross moaned and writhed against him, working his freed cock from root to tip.

He reached for her jeans and smiled against her lips when his fingers brushed across the soft maternity panel.

"No comments...on the mom wear," Ross reprimanded breathlessly, her head arcing against the tree as Xander continued his assault on her tender nipples. She could feel the tension growing between her legs, the gorgeous buildup of ache and need. She needed him to fill her.

Ross put her hands over his and wrenched her jeans and underwear off, offering a fleeting thank you to the pregnancy gods that she could still comfortably wear her thongs. "Xander...inside me...now..."

"Wrap your arms around me."

When she complied, Xander reached behind her knees and pulled her legs around his hips, groaning when his dick nestled toward her soft core. Anchoring one hand under her and the other cradled around to protect her back against the tree, Xander entered her to the hilt in one fierce, deep thrust. *Home.*

"Christ, Ross. Your pussy is so tight and hot." He rested his forehead to hers.

Xander filled her perfectly and Ross rocked her hips impatiently.

"What do you need, Principessa?"

"I need you to fuck me. Hard."

His warm brown eyes dark with lust and need, Xander eased out and then plunged into her again, still supporting her with one hand while the other pressed against the tree for leverage. She could feel the tightening of her impending orgasm around his cock. He thrust again, hard. And again.

"Yes...yes, Xander! Oh, God..." He kept thrusting as she detonated and came apart in his arms. Xander tilted her hips and drove deep, over and over, until his own release exploded out of him as he shouted her name.

He eased her shaking legs gently to the ground and sought her nipples again with his mouth. "Another, Ross," he murmured, reaching between her legs and circling the bundle of nerves as he filled her with his fingers. "I want you to come again."

"I—can't. Too sensitive." She was breathless, boneless...and yet she could feel the pressure build again as Xander worked her clit. He was gentle yet merciless.

"You can. One more."

Ross worked her hips against the onslaught. "Don't stop." His fingers were filling her, stretching her, his thumb pressing her clit. Then Xander leaned down and gave a hard suck to her nipple, and Ross screamed her release.

Pivoting to lean against the tree, he tucked her against him. She smiled and dropped a kiss on his heaving chest. "I can feel your heart racing."

He nuzzled her hair. "Out of practice." He chuckled against her hair. "But I can't wait to get back into the habit."

Ross stretched lazily against him, sated. "God...we really are good at cliché-ing together." She shivered.

"You cold, baby?"

"Mmmm...no. Well, maybe a little, but I don't want to move yet." She nestled into him. "I'm just—happy. And it wasn't that long ago when I didn't think anything like this would ever be possible."

Xander shifted so he could stroke the slightly rounded plane of her lower body. "I love you so much. Both of you." He twined their fingers together and kissed her tenderly.

"I love you, too, Xander. So very much."

"Want to know another cliché I want to do with you, Ross?"

"Hmmm?" she hummed lazily, cuddling closer to him.

"Happily ever after."

EPILOGUE

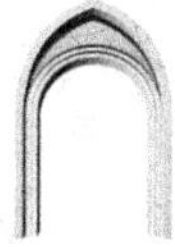

Ross

The snow had been steadily falling since dinner the night before, shrouding the Shenandoah valley in a blanket of white. It wasn't quite a blizzard, but they had about a foot of snow on the ground, with more on the way. Before they went to sleep, the area around the farmhouse had transformed into a winter wonderland. As pretty as it was, Ross prayed it was the last snow of the season. It wasn't unheard of to get a mid-March snow, but at this point, she was ready for spring. And for this baby to get. out. of. her. belly!

Ross eased out of the king bed she shared with Xander, careful not to wake him. The clock read 5 a.m. She twisted to her side to ease the dull ache in her back that had been a constant, but growing, annoyance.

Her husband slept peacefully on his side, the blankets rumpled around him.

Husband. She still thrilled at the word. They married in an intimate ceremony in the barn at Thanksgiving. Gaby and Tiercy had been her matrons of honor. Cole and Petey were Xander's best men. Ted had received a license online to officiate. Ross walked herself down the aisle to her future husband and gave herself to him in a ceremony that was short, tender, and filled with joy.

And now here she was, just a week or so until baby Leah should be making her appearance.

Ross reached for her robe and slippers, and shuffled upstairs to the nursery. Xander had been busy. All the plans he'd described during that initial walkthrough with Hon and Breathy Genevieve had come to fruition. He'd bumped out and redesigned the kitchen and expanded the upstairs bedrooms, which both now boasted small balconies. The bedroom that had been Ross's was now Leah's nursery. Petey had Gaby's former room. Xan had built a small home office for himself on the other side of the house. It was all stunning. And theirs.

Ross dropped into the glider rocker, groaning again at her back pain. "Ok, baby girl. Mommy loves you very much, but I'm ready to meet you. Not today, mind you. I think this snowstorm precludes that. Nice SAT word. But as soon as it melts, you can come out anytime. Deal?"

Ross watched the slow roll of her daughter across her belly, never ceasing to marvel at the miracle inside her. She knew every moment of this pregnancy defied the odds, and she embraced it.

"I'm ready to hold you in my arms, sweet love," she whispered. "Daddy and I, and your big brother Petey, are going to make such an incredible life for you, my miracle."

Ross rocked for a while. Then, restless, she decided to dress, eat a little breakfast, and do some work. It was still early—not even 7 a.m.— and the sun had just risen. She stepped into Xander's snow boots, her own not worth the struggle over her pregnant belly, and pulled on her coat, hat, and gloves. Xander had cleared a path to the cottage last night, but fresh accumulation added a couple inches. It was still lightly snowing, but the heavier snow wasn't predicted to fall again until later in the morning, closer to lunch.

"Here's the plan, Leah." Ross arched her aching back as she surveyed the terrain, hoping the walk would feel good, work out some of those kinks. "We'll work at the cottage for a couple hours and then come back for lunch and a nice nap before the snow gets bad. How's that sound?"

She made it to the cottage easily. During her pregnancy, Xander had turned it into Ross's office. The great room was still largely the same, with the addition of a Peloton for her and a new sectional couch with a long settee attached. The primary bedroom had been converted into a state-of-the-art office with a beautiful antique desk, double monitors, the world's most comfortable desk chair (Ross thought sometimes she loved that chair almost as much as she loved Xander), powerful Wi-Fi, and the silver candlesticks from Hon's office. He took the old bathroom and Petey's room and converted it into a huge bathroom for her in case she wanted to work out and then freshen up before a meeting. It was the perfect remote office for her.

Ross sat at her desk and opened her email. For the most part, she'd tidied all her work in anticipation of maternity leave, leaving just a few loose ends, including reviewing the galleys of Honor Wheatley's memoir.

"Oh!" Ross gasped. Pain sliced across her back and she doubled over, breathing heavily. "What the fuck. Oh—sorry, baby. Don't listen to Mommy, she has a potty mouth. But you should not emulate her, except her vocabulary. The good words, I mean." The pain passed, but Ross was shaken. That had been intense.

"Maybe we should head back and see Daddy? He's probably getting up any minute now and going to wonder where we went—Ow! Holy fucking shit! Sorry...Leah! Bad...Mommy." She bent over, resting her hands on her knees until she caught her breath.

"Now let's not get upset, Leah. But I think we should call Daddy." Ross lumbered to the desk and hit the button on favorites for "Hottie McHot Pants Hubby."

Xander immediately picked up. "Hey, sweetheart. I just woke up and was looking for you. Where'd you go, early riser?" His voice was craggy with sleep but filled with warmth and love.

Despite her shakiness, Ross smiled reflexively. God, she loved this man so much.

"Hey, baby. Listen, I'm at the cottage—"

"The cottage! What the hell are you doing there?"

"I woke early and decided to get some work done and then I—oh!

Fuuuck!" Ross groaned. The pain in her back was excruciating and coming in waves.

"Ross—sweetheart—what's wrong?" Xander sounded frantic. "I'm headed over. Shit—where are my boots?"

"I have them. I wore them over here. Xander, I think I need to go to the hospital. My back really hurts."

"I'm coming now."

"Hurry."

In under two minutes, Xander was sliding through the door, wearing only his pajama bottoms, a T-shirt, and his slippers. Ross was on the couch, fighting to remain calm despite the waves of pain.

"Xander..." She burst into tears.

"It's ok, Principessa. It's going to be ok." He gathered her into his arms. "Tell me what's going on."

"I have this intense back pain. You know I've been having it for a while, but this feels different. For the past couple days, it's been off and on. I had trouble sleeping with it last night. I woke this morning feeling restless, and then I came here thinking I could get some work done. Then, the pain got really bad and I called you." She started sobbing again. "I know it was stupid. What if I did something wrong? What if she's not ok? Ooooh...ow!"

"Hold my hand, Ross. Just breathe."

"Where's Petey?"

"He's on his way to Gaby's now. He took Squiggy over, too, so our puppy can play with his cousin, Laverne. Petey will be fine over there. He's a huge help with Grace, so I think Gaby will appreciate having him there for a bit."

The cottage door flew open and Ted hurried in, shaking off snow.

"You called Ted?"

"Ross, sweetheart, I had to."

"Why?"

"I think you're in labor." His voice was steady and calm, but Ross could see his hands trembling.

"No. No, I'm not. I can't be, Xander! It's not time. I'm not ready. I have emails!"

"Yes, Principessa." He pressed a soothing kiss to the top of her head. "I think our daughter wants to come meet us."

Ross's eyes were huge. "Get me to the hospital."

Xander and Ted exchanged looks.

"Why are you looking at each other like that?"

"Sweetheart, we can't get you to the hospital. It's why I called Ted. The road to the farmhouse isn't passable right now. We'll call your OB and 911, but the roads are bad, and they're calling for another foot today and an icy mix."

"Oh my God. This can't be happening...ugh...ooooh..." Ross panted through another wave, grasping Xander's hand.

"Ross." Ted took her hand. "I'm not here as your brother-in-law. I'm here as an EMT. I'm going to help you deliver little Leah." He spoke softly but with authority.

"Holy shit. You're going to have to look at my hoo-ha."

Xander stifled a laugh.

"It's not funny, Xander!" Ross wailed. "This is...untenable."

"Good SAT—"

"Not now, brother. Read the room," Ted smiled and turned back to her. "It'll be fine, Ross," Ted soothed. "Your body knows how to do this, and I'm trained to deliver a baby. I think Leah is as strong-willed as her mama, and she's not going to wait for this storm to be finished. I haven't examined you yet, but based on the frequency of what I'm sure are contractions, you're going to have your baby, possibly as soon as this morning. Now let's get you comfortable and I'm going to need to check things out and get everything ready."

Ross looked at Ted's feet and noticed he had brought a canvas medical bag with him.

"Shit just got real."

Ted winked at her. "What do you always say? Absofuckinglutely."

She put her hands over her tensing belly. "Language," she gasped out as another wave of pain rolled through her.

Within ten minutes, she was undressed from the waist down, covered in a sheet, and Ted had determined she was about five or six centimeters dilated as best he could tell. He went into the office to make a couple calls.

"Maybe she'll hold off?" Ross struggled up, Xander sitting behind her, rubbing her aching back. "Ooooh! Fuckety fuck! Shit—Xan. Ted!" she called. "I think I just peed myself!"

Ted hustled into the room, holding his cell, and examined the floor under her. "Ross, your water just broke. Leah is coming today. I've talked to your OB. She's stuck at her house, too. If the hospital can get an SUV to the main road leading to the farmhouse, we can work on plowing. But the snow is coming down hard. This baby will be here before we can get all that done. I think she's in a hurry, Ross. Let's work on getting Leah safely delivered and we'll figure out how to get you both to the hospital for evaluation. Deal?" He held out his hand.

She placed her trembling hand in his. "Ted Monroe, if someone had told me a year ago we'd be here, doing this today, I'd have called them one pancake short of a stack. But I have to tell you—" she gulped back a sob "—I am so glad my sister married you."

He leaned down and kissed her cheek. "Leah Grace has one amazing mom and dad. I'm honored to be here. Now let's do this."

XANDER

"I need you to push for me, Ross. We are so close." Xander keyed into Ted's voice. It was calm but authoritative, soothing Ross and him.

Xander knelt behind Ross, who'd moved to the floor by this point, holding up her shoulders. "Come on, Principessa. Let's meet our baby."

"You just shut up. You and your super sperm...uuunnnnnhhhhhh!"

"That's right, Ross. That was a good push," Ted encouraged, sweat dampening his shirt. They'd been at this for more than three hours, and Ross was close. He told Ross he'd suspected she'd been having back labor for a couple days, and active labor had moved quickly.

"This is all your fault, Xander Grace," she panted between contractions. "Your perfect sperm ignored my birth control and navigated the rocky terrain of my defective, bumpy uterus—uuuunnnnhhhhh!"

"Here we go, Ross. Big push. I can see her head!"

Ross let out a guttural groan from the deepest recesses of her body, one that went on and on—

"Head's out—another push for the shoulders. Come on, Ross!"

Xander leaned over his wife and kissed her sweaty head. "C'mon, baby. I've got you."

Ross closed her eyes and Xan marveled as she pushed with all her strength.

Then the most beautiful sound filled the cottage—lusty baby wails, commingled with the laughter of her mother, father, and uncle.

"She's here! Leah Ivy Grace has arrived. Time of birth—" Ted checked his iPhone "—is 11:11 a.m. Congratulations!" Ted placed the baby on Ross's chest.

Ross burst into tears as Xander gathered his wife and new daughter into his arms. "Hi, Leah. I'm your Mommy. I am so happy to finally meet you, my little miracle. And I forgive you for all this drama."

Wiping his eyes and laughing, Xander looked over at Ted, who was weeping and chuckling as well. "Happy birthday, Leah. You are as pulchritudinous as your mother."

"Nice SAT word, Husband."

"Thank you, Wife." Xander gazed at Ross holding his daughter and knew they'd proven the arch axiom true. He tenderly stroked Leah's soft cheek. "A dramatic snowstorm arrival with a magical birth hour. So cliché. Welcome to the family, baby girl."

THE END

Next up is Brinder and Honor's story, Stardust. Here's a sneak peek.

Stardust

CATHRYN LYONS

Prologue

"No. No no *no*. This *can't* be real."

Honor's eyes locked on the paused video, heart racing. "I'm going to close my eyes now," she whispered to the empty room, "and when I open them, this will all just be a bad dream. Please, *please* let this not be what I think it is."

A sharp paradox to her current mood, the morning sun beamed in through the windows of her sunroom, casting a pale glare on her laptop monitor. Normally her happy place, where she read, wrote, and generally grounded herself in things that were real—so necessary, given her background and career—today the glass-enclosed sanctuary was on the precipice of becoming the setting of a horror scene.

Honor dropped her head into her hand and breathed deeply, the other hand reflexively pressing to the long-ago-healed scar on her sternum. She closed her eyes. "This cannot be happening. *Please.*"

Easing her eyes open, she scanned the frozen screen as she mindlessly rubbed the faded scar visible over her sleep tank. The same scar that makeup artists could hide. At the moment, Honor fervently wished for a life artist to hide the poo-show that was unfolding before her eyes. "It has to be an AI deep fake," she willed aloud, voice shaking.

And, yet...she knew. It was real. The freaking video was real. And she remembered the exact night this had been filmed, without her consent.

How did she know?

She'd been on top.

Her bare back to the camera, the full globes of her bottom clearly visible, resting on those legs she knew so well. Head thrown back in ecstasy.

The camera had been cleverly placed so it showed mostly her back, but a bit of her side, the profile of her chest—and the D cup breasts that hurt her back—framed in the center of the tableau.

Honor slid into a thousand-yard stare, remembering that evening almost two months ago. She'd met with her agent in London to discuss her next possible role, which would conveniently be filmed there as well. Then, her editor, Ross, joined via Zoom. Despite her current shock, a small smile crossed her face as she remembered the joy of the amazing news they'd shared.

After the meeting, she'd met with Crispin and they'd gone to dinner to celebrate her memoir landing in the top ten on two different bestseller lists. Honor would have loved nothing more than a romantic meal at home, but Crispin loved a specific Michelin-starred restaurant in the heart of London. It was a celebrity magnet, and therefore a paparazzi favorite, so Honor preferred not to go. But he loved their steak and cilantro mashed potatoes and she truly did salivate over the curry halibut. So she'd conceded.

As she'd usually done with Crispin. Easier than arguing.

Later, they'd relaxed in her preferred room at the posh boutique hotel she loved in Kensington so they didn't have to travel five-plus hours to her waterfront Pembrokeshire County home.

She remembered the welcome flare of her arousal as Crispin kissed along her neck, slowly disrobing her and placing her on the edge of the king bed. And her surprise when he eased between her legs, whispering that bestselling authors deserved a treat. She'd even enjoyed the flush of a building orgasm, an experience ever-elusive for her in any circumstance.

She'd gently tugged him away, breathlessly begging him to be inside her—a practiced part of their encounters, not fully fake but also not fully real for her either. Then her happy shock as he cocked a grin and stretched out on his back, guiding her on top of him.

Their sex life had been decent...but, admittedly...drab. Occasional oral sex, but she was always self-conscious about her lack of blow job skills. And reluctant to add to Crispin's frustration when she couldn't come from his oral efforts. Then, missionary sex. Always.

Crispin would often get upset with her, blaming her neuroses over her childhood heart surgeries for her inability to truly let go. So, she would do what was necessary: apply her Oscar-winning acting skills to some epic faking.

He'd come. Loudly. And then they'd snuggle, him kissing the top of her head before falling into a snore-ridden sleep.

But this time? He was giving her what she'd shyly requested the week prior—some variety to their intimacy. She loved him, and he was effusively expressing his deep love of her. So when he initiated a change of position, she'd been thrilled.

Their lovemaking had ended the same way, of course. But her passion was a bit more real, the excitement of change zinging between her legs. When she threw her head back (the moment currently paused on her laptop screen), that had been real.

Ironic. How she could be so comfortable on screen. So at home. How the big screen had been her salvation and, once upon a time, her deepest joy. And now? Her unwitting title role was about to blow her world wide open. If it hadn't already.

She hit play again, hoping the shock would ebb. Other celebrity sex tapes she knew about were often grainy. But not hers. No. This was high-definition. Artfully lit. Black and white.

Dissociating from her personal humiliation, and applying her trained industry eye, Honor could admit it was actually beautifully framed. And exceedingly and increasingly nauseating. A private moment with her now ex-boyfriend splashed all over a tabloid site. And heaven knew where else.

As the video ended, the sensation of utter violation settled in her gut. Mortification flooded her veins as tears filled her eyes, blurring everything. She gulped a sob, reflexively running the tips of her fingers along her scar once more. Honor wasn't sure which was racing harder— her heart or her head.

The chiming alert of her cell startled her.

It was her agent, Benoite.

A she-devil bulldog, Benny was terrifyingly intimidating when you first met her, or when crossed. But, when you were "hers," she was the staunchest advocate. A mama bear. The most assertive, self-assured woman Honor had ever met. She had a girl-crush on the forty-eight-year-old industry titan. Tall, icy-blond hair, pale blue eyes, a slim build, Benny was a Swedish-American former runway model-turned-uber-agent. She was a force. And she was currently blowing up Honor's phone.

Honor picked it up as if it were radioactive. Eleven missed calls in fifteen minutes. And dozens of texts. Ross. Benny. Her parents. Her brother. *Oh, cripes. They'd seen it. Seen* her. Mortification, and its mean-girl friend nausea, rose in her belly again.

Sighing, she answered, putting it on speaker. Her hand was shaking too hard to hold the phone for any length of time.

"Honor," came Benny's in-charge voice, carrying with confidence over the room. Just that one word, and Honor felt a bit (a very teensy-tiny bit) of relief.

"Yes," Honor croaked, answering her agent's unasked question.

"It's viral."

The confirmation of what Honor had already suspected made her head light. She forced herself to take three deep breaths, filling her lungs and slowly exhaling.

"Do we know who—who filmed it? Who leaked it?"

"Early speculation would be a staffer at the hotel. Maybe a maid. They had a new one start not long before you stayed there, so she's being checked out. We've got a tech team working on tracking the video's origins. And the entire PR and legal departments are working on getting it pulled down and scrubbed from as many sites as humanly possible. We are on this for you, Honor. We will manage and mitigate this. I need you to breathe. This isn't good, but everything is being handled swiftly."

Benny paused and Honor could hear the faint sounds of cheering in the background. She was probably at her son's hockey game, likely tucked in a corner so no one would overhear. Her agent was discreet and dedicated to her, but also would not want to miss a moment of her son's game, even if the ice time was early in the morning. That dedication to her family was one reason Honor loved Benny so much.

"Crispin's already called. He's very angry and is hollering for a lawsuit." Her agent cleared her throat. "And he's asking to see you."

"I don't—" Honor swallowed past the lump in her throat. "I don't want to see him."

"I figured." Benny's voice softened, a sure sign of her worry. "Where are you?"

"My house. Sunroom," Honor managed.

"Are you alone?"

"Yes. I was planning to go see my parents later. But now..."

She trailed off, unease triggering the palpitations that always alarmed her, no matter how often her cardiac surgeon and family friend, Rahul Desai, told her she was healed and healthy.

Dr. Desai. Brinder's dad. Her heart skipped. *Fudge!* He and Lady Jane probably knew about it too. And Brinder, a ghost of the past, living his best life in the States. Had he seen it too? Was there no end to the horror?

"Honor, are you there?"

"I'm here," Honor heard herself respond. *Huh. So this was what an out-of-body experience felt like.*

"Honor, try to hang in with me here. Do *not* go to your parents. Do not leave your house. Stay put. In fact, make sure you are in a room with privacy windows. Your sunroom has those, right?"

"Ye-yes," Honor choked out. "Why?"

"You've got paps set up at your gate and on the water outside your property. I need you to lay low. I'm sending a car for you, disguised as a delivery truck, but I doubt the vultures will be fooled." Benny's assertive voice filled the room, leaving no room for argument.

"Where am I going?"

"Virginia."

Acknowledgments

Arches is a special story for me. I wrote the first draft in college—just playing around and reveling in the joy of my words pouring on the page. (In those days, I wrote on yellow lined legal pads! Yes, I'm "writing on paper" old.) Around 2018, I attended a writer's conference and was staying in a sunny loft apartment in Back Bay. I had finished *Heartstrings* and now Ross was talking to me. Nonstop. Ross, as you've figured out, is a force to be reckoned with, even in the nascent days of this story. (SAT word!) As I was prepping for a day of sessions, I realized I could connect one storyline from that early 1990s story from college to *Heartstrings* and then build off it. You can guess what happened: Instead of going to the sessions that day, Ross and Xander emerged (this time on a laptop!). As I wrote, Ross and Xander's story blossomed, as did Ross and Gaby's, as well as Ross and Hon's. Ross's story touched my heart. To feel broken, alone, and yet possess a strength and glimmer of inner hope that allows her to reimagine her life and embrace new, healing love—with Xan and with Gaby. I hope you've enjoyed reading *Arches* as much as I loved writing it.

To my parents, thank you for the selfless example of unconditional love. To quote Carly, nobody does it better.

To Rebecca, best bestie and my Chief Reader: thank you for all the reviews of chapters and versions of *Arches*. It is so much stronger because of you...as am I. Love you, Bestie.

Big thanks to the world's best seester Cyndi. Thank you for loving this story as much as I do, and for being my counterpart in the "Kirkwall Four." Thank you to Marlena, Rose Ellen, Nikki, and Heather, who each reviewed many drafts and offered excellent insights. To all my beta readers, thank you for spending your time helping my stories to improve. To Lara and Trish, thank you for helping shape my story over the years. Thank you, once again, to the late, incomparable John DeSimone, MD, for the medical insights. Big hugs to my friends who've offered endless moral support, including Alexis, Lin, Theresa, and my teammates.

To my readers...thank you for embracing me and my stories. I think of all the happiness so many authors have brought into my life through the gifts of their words. That I have an opportunity to do this...is mind-blowing.

To the Gorgeous Gurus who Make the Things Happen: Michelle Fewer, book doula extraordinaire, you are a mind-blowingly fabulous editor. But you are so much more. Trusted confidant. Romancelandia Sensei. Dear friend. To the indefatigable Rhon House...my partner in the Authory Stuff...thank you for sharing your special brand of book magic. It is compellingly accurate to say that I would not be here without you and your talents. Thank you also to the rockstar Julie Collier for sharing your expertise and making my books look so gorgeous. Cheers to Maria at Steamy Designs for another sexy cover and to Wander Aguiar for a stunning photo of Matheus R.

To Bob and Marion (in her eternal reward), I love being your daughter. You raised the most amazing son, and I'm fortunate beyond words to be his wife. And that great good fortune includes having you both in my life for the past two decades. Marion, I miss our talks about novels, our laughter, and hilarious conversations about grammar. Bob, you inspire me. You are one of the best and most honorable people I've ever known.

To Sutter...world's best and derpiest Golden...your mommy loves your sweet doggy face. Nose smooches and boops.

To Grant, Hays, and Owen: Publishing these novels is certainly exciting and joyous. But nothing has brought me more excitement and joy than being your mom. From the moment I knew about you, you were mine to love for eternity, and that is the greatest privilege of my life. I love you three so much. You are kind, thoughtful, funny, and supportive. True gentle-men. I am so damn proud of each of you and so honored to be your mom.

To my Roberto...I dedicated this novel to you. But I've also dedicated my life to you and our love. Best decision I ever made. Loving you is so easy, and you make the extraordinary in the ordinary magical. I have no idea how I got so lucky as to be the recipient of your love, but I'm not complaining! Thank you for making me laugh, for the world's best hugs, and for your unwavering support.

Also by Cathryn Lyons

Second Chance at Love Series

Heartstrings

What happens when you bury your heart with the love of your life—but someone gives its strings an unexpected tug?

Tiercy Somerville is quite sure you only get one love of your life. But just as she was building a life with hers, he was torn from her forever. Five years later, the popular high school English teacher and single mom has healed to a place of grief-tinged acceptance and peace, but her love of a lifetime still very much fills her heart, leaving no room for any other really big love. Or so she believes.

John Sims "Cole" Colburn is tired of playing the field. The construction firm CEO longs for the harmony, partnership, and deep abiding love his parents had. The problem is...his standards are probably impossibly high.

When their paths cross, the chemistry is instant, but neither is prepared for the intensity and passion of the journey ahead of them.

As their love deepens, Tiercy finds herself emotionally torn, questioning what she's always known. How can one person have two soulmates? And having found the love of his life, Cole must decide if he can bear not being the love of hers.

Arches

A sexy summer fling. A tangled past. A second chance at love.

Ross has a plan: pack up her grandmother's farmhouse, avoid old wounds, enjoy a little no-strings bedsport, and move on in Manhattan. She doesn't expect to rekindle the scorching chemistry with a hot, opera-singing single dad—or confront the shocking family secrets buried long ago.

Single dad Xander Grace has sworn off serious relationships—until Ross Beaufort, the unforgettable one-night stand who's haunted him for months, shows up at her grandmother's farmhouse...next to the property he's renting. She's only there for six weeks. A perfect summer fling.

As desire turns into something deeper, Ross must decide if she can let go of the past and fight for the future she never saw coming.

Stardust

A beloved silver screen star

A playboy doctor

Two scandals

One solution—fake date your long-lost first love

When two scandals unexpectedly reunite long-estranged first loves almost two decades after their painful breakup, can they put hurtful bygones aside to help each other? Will their surprising alliance lead to lost love found?

Honor Wheatley's world has just imploded. A decorated film actor, the beloved "nepo baby" and darling of the silver screen flees to the Shenandoah Valley to escape the fallout from a devastating scandal. When Honor's arranged lodging floods, she finds sanctuary in an unexpected place—the home of her first love and the man who shattered her surgically repaired heart years ago. And when Brinder agrees to be her personal guide on a sexual exploration journey as preparation for a film role—what could go wrong with that?

Dr. Brinder Desai has a well-earned reputation as a player, earning him the nickname Dr. Desiiigh. A fabricated scandal jeopardizes his dream job. Brinder needs to show stability or risk losing the position he loves. Having Honor Wheatley—the woman who broke Brinder's heart a lifetime ago and ruined him for relationships—in his home is a prescription for chaos he doesn't need. Except—fake dating the woman he lost could be the very thing he needs to keep his job.

Stardust is a steamy, emotional, and witty contemporary romance about lost love found, healing, redemption, and second chances.

About the Author

Cathryn Lyons loves novels. Seriously loves them. Especially romance. Reading (often devouring) them...and writing contemporary romance novels of her own. She has been writing since before she could even properly hold a pen.

She is married to her real-life Happily Ever After and they share three sons and the world's best and derpiest rescue Golden Retriever (from Turkey!). She is a lifelong Marylander, but wonders if her short stint in London counts as being cosmopolitan (the attribute, not the drink; although those are quite delicious).

Cathryn fills her creative bucket by writing stories she hopes bring as much joy, laughter, escapism...and sexy feelings...that she herself has experienced through the gift of others' words. She hopes you love her stories, and welcomes hearing from you. You can email her at cathrynlyonsromance@gmail.com, or follow her on Facebook, and Instagram.

Want to have a bit more unfiltered fun? (Sorry, Mom.) Join her Facebook reader group, Cathryn Lyons' Romance Den, and connect with other lionesses and lions who roar for joy at romance.